Praise for *The Eyre Affair* by Jasper Fforde

"Jasper Fforde's first novel, *The Eyre Affair*, is a spirited sendup of genre fiction—it's part hard-boiled mystery, part time-machine caper—that features a sassy well-read 'Special Operative in literary detection' named Thursday Next, who will put you more in mind of Bridget Jones than Miss Marple. Fforde delivers almost every sentence with a sly wink, and he's got an easy way with wordplay, trivia and inside jokes. . . . Fforde's verve is rarely less than infectious."
—*The New York Times Book Review*

"*The Eyre Affair* neatly delivers alternate history, Monty Python-esque comedy skits, Grand Guignol supervillains, thwarted lovers, po-mo intertexuality, political commentary, time travel, vampires, absent-minded inventors, a hard-boiled narrator, and lots, lots more. Need I say more? So, dear reader, suspend your disbelief, find a quiet corner and just surrender to the storytelling voice of the unstoppable, ever-resourceful Thursday Next."
—*The Washington Post*

"Delightfully clever . . . Filled with clever wordplay, literary allusion and bibliowit, *The Eyre Affair* combines elements of Monty Python, Harry Potter, Stephen Hawking and Buffy the Vampire Slayer. But its quirky charm is all its own."
—*The Wall Street Journal*

"Fforde's imaginative novel will satiate readers looking for a Harry Potter-esque tale. . . . *The Eyre Affair*'s literary wonderland recalls Douglas Adams' Hitchhiker series, the works of Lewis Carroll and Woody Allen's *The Kugelmass Episode*."
—*USA Today*

"Jasper Fforde's genre-busting, whoppingly imaginative first novel, *The Eyre Affair*, is packed with literary allusions. . . . Thanks to Fforde's terrific imagination, this definitely will not be the winter of our discontent."
—*The Miami Herald*

"For sheer inventiveness his book is hard to beat. *The Eyre Affair* is an exuberant melange of crime, comedy and alternative history."
—*Houston Chronicle*

"*The Eyre Affair* by Jasper Fforde could hardly be more delightful. . . . It takes a bold adventurer to play fast and loose with literature, and that's what we have in Thursday Next and Fforde."
—*Newsday*

"[Fforde] delivers multiple plot twists, rampant literary references and streams of wild metafictional invention in a novel that places literature at the center of the pop-cultural universe. . . . It all adds up to a brainy, cheerfully twisted adventure."
—*Time Out New York*

"[*The Eyre Affair*] is a blend of suspense and silliness, two parts fantasy (think *Alice in Wonderland* meets Superman), two parts absurdity (anything by Carl Hiaasen) and one part mystery (Agatha Christie meets Sue Grafton)."
—*St. Louis Post-Dispatch*

"Her name is Next. Thursday Next. And her story is as amusing and intriguing as the summary of her story told within the pages of *The Eyre Affair*. Next is a literary detective in a world so enamored with the written word that Shakespeare's *Richard III* is staged nightly as if it were *The Rocky Horror Picture Show*. . . . The novel's writing flows and the imaginative twists and turns in Next's world are handled smoothly."
—*Sun-Sentinel* (Fort Lauderdale)

PENGUIN BOOKS

THE EYRE AFFAIR

Jasper Fforde recently traded a varied career in the film industry for staring vacantly out of the window and arranging words on a page. *The Eyre Affair,* his first novel, was a recipient of a Young Adult Library Services Association (YALSA) 2003 Alex Award. He also is the author of the novel *Lost in a Good Book.* He lives and writes in Wales.

The Eyre Affair

A NOVEL

Jasper Fforde

PENGUIN BOOKS

For my father
John Standish Fforde
1920–2000

Who never knew I was to be published but
would have been most proud nonetheless
—and not a little surprised.

PENGUIN BOOKS
Published by the Penguin Group
Penguin Group (USA) Inc., 375 Hudson Street, New York, New York 10014, U.S.A.
Penguin Group (Canada), 90 Eglinton Avenue East, Suite 700, Toronto, Ontario,
Canada M4P 2Y3 (a division of Pearson Penguin Canada Inc.)
Penguin Books Ltd, 80 Strand, London WC2R 0RL, England
Penguin Ireland, 25 St Stephen's Green, Dublin 2, Ireland
(a division of Penguin Books Ltd)
Penguin Group (Australia), 250 Camberwell Road, Camberwell, Victoria 3124,
Australia (a division of Pearson Australia Group Pty Ltd)
Penguin Books India Pvt Ltd, 11 Community Centre, Panchsheel Park,
New Delhi – 110 017, India
Penguin Group (NZ), 67 Apollo Drive, Rosedale, North Shore 0632, New Zealand
(a division of Pearson New Zealand Ltd)
Penguin Books (South Africa) (Pty) Ltd, 24 Sturdee Avenue, Rosebank,
Johannesburg 2196, South Africa

Penguin Books Ltd, Registered Offices: 80 Strand, London WC2R 0RL, England

First published in the United States of America by Viking Penguin,
a member of Penguin Putnam Inc. 2002
Published in Penguin Books 2003

26 27 28 29 30

Copyright © Jasper Fforde, 2001
All rights reserved

ISBN 0-670-03064-3 (hc)
ISBN 978-0-14-200180-6 (pbk)
CIP data available

Printed in the United States of America
Set in Berkeley Medium
Designed by Francesca Belanger

Contents

1.

A Woman Named
Thursday Next

. . . The Special Operations Network was instigated to
handle policing duties considered either too unusual or
too specialized to be tackled by the regular force. There
were thirty departments in all, starting at the more mun-
dane Neighborly Disputes (SO-30) and going onto Literary Detectives (SO-27) and Art Crime (SO-24). Anything
below SO-20 was restricted information, although it was
common knowledge that the ChronoGuard was SO-12
and Antiterrorism SO-9. It is rumored that SO-1 was the
department that polices the SpecOps themselves. Quite
what the others do is anyone's guess. What *is* known is
that the individual operatives themselves are mostly ex-
military or ex-police and slightly unbalanced. "If you
want to be a SpecOp," the saying goes, "act kinda
weird . . ."

MILLON DE FLOSS
—*A Short History of the Special Operations Network*

MY FATHER had a face that could stop a clock. I don't mean
that he was ugly or anything; it was a phrase the ChronoGuard
used to describe someone who had the power to reduce time to
an ultraslow trickle. Dad had been a colonel in the Chrono-
Guard and kept his work very quiet. So quiet, in fact, that we
didn't know he had gone rogue at all until his timekeeping bud-
dies raided our house one morning clutching a Seize & Eradica-

tion order open-dated at both ends and demanding to know where and when he was. Dad had remained at liberty ever since; we learned from his subsequent visits that he regarded the whole service as "morally and historically corrupt" and was fighting a one-man war against the bureaucrats within the Office for Special Temporal Stability. I didn't know what he meant by that and still don't; I just hoped he knew what he was doing and didn't come to any harm doing it. His skills at stopping the clock were hard-earned and irreversible: He was now a lonely itinerant in time, belonging to not one age but to all of them and having no home other than the chronoclastic ether.

I wasn't a member of the ChronoGuard. I never wanted to be. By all accounts it's not a huge barrel of laughs, although the pay is good and the service boasts a retirement plan that is second to none: a one-way ticket to anywhere and anywhen you want. No, that wasn't for me. I was what we called an "operative grade I" for SO-27, the Literary Detective Division of the Special Operations Network based in London. It's *way* less flash than it sounds. Since 1980 the big criminal gangs had moved in on the lucrative literary market and we had much to do and few funds to do it with. I worked under Area Chief Boswell, a small, puffy man who looked like a bag of flour with arms and legs. He lived and breathed the job; words were his life and his love—he never seemed happier than when he was on the trail of a counterfeit Coleridge or a fake Fielding. It was under Boswell that we arrested the gang who were stealing and selling Samuel Johnson first editions; on another occasion we uncovered an attempt to authenticate a flagrantly unrealistic version of Shakespeare's lost work, *Cardenio*. Fun while it lasted, but only small islands of excitement among the ocean of day-to-day mundanities that is SO-27: We spent most of our time dealing with illegal traders, copyright infringements and fraud.

I had been with Boswell and SO-27 for eight years, living in a Maida Vale apartment with Pickwick, a regenerated pet dodo left over from the days when reverse extinction was all the rage and you could buy home cloning kits over the counter. I was keen—no, I was *desperate*—to get away from the LiteraTecs but transfers were unheard of and promotion a nonstarter. The only way I was going to make full inspector was if my immediate superior moved on or out. But it never happened; Inspector Turner's hope to marry a wealthy Mr. Right and leave the service stayed just that—a hope—as so often Mr. Right turned out to be either Mr. Liar, Mr. Drunk or Mr. Already Married.

As I said earlier, my father had a face that could stop a clock; and that's exactly what happened one spring morning as I was having a sandwich in a small café not far from work. The world flickered, shuddered and stopped. The proprietor of the café froze in midsentence and the picture on the television stopped dead. Outside, birds hung motionless in the sky. Cars and trams halted in the streets and a cyclist involved in an accident stopped in midair, the look of fear frozen on his face as he paused two feet from the hard asphalt. The sound halted too, replaced by a dull snapshot of a hum, the world's noise at that moment in time paused indefinitely at the same pitch and volume.

"How's my gorgeous daughter?"

I turned. My father was sitting at a table and rose to hug me affectionately.

"I'm good," I replied, returning his hug tightly. "How's my favorite father?"

"Can't complain. Time is a *fine* physician."

I stared at him for a moment.

"Y'know," I muttered, "I think you're looking younger every time I see you."

"I am. Any grandchildren in the offing?"

"The way I'm going? Not ever."

My father smiled and raised an eyebrow.

"I wouldn't say that *quite* yet."

He handed me a Woolworths bag.

"I was in '78 recently," he announced. "I brought you this."

He handed me a single by the Beatles. I didn't recognize the title.

"Didn't they split in '70?"

"Not always. How are things?"

"Same as ever. Authentications, copyright, theft—"

"—same old shit?"

"Yup." I nodded. "Same old shit. What brings you here?"

"I went to see your mother three weeks ahead your time," he answered, consulting the large chronograph on his wrist. "Just the usual—ahem—reason. She's going to paint the bedroom mauve in a week's time—will you have a word and dissuade her? It doesn't match the curtains."

"How is she?"

He sighed deeply.

"Radiant, as always. Mycroft and Polly would like to be remembered too."

They were my aunt and uncle; I loved them deeply, although both were mad as pants. I regretted not seeing Mycroft most of all. I hadn't returned to my hometown for many years and I didn't see my family as often as I should.

"Your mother and I think it might be a good idea for you to come home for a bit. She thinks you take work a little too seriously."

"That's a bit rich, Dad, coming from you."

"Ouch-that-hurt. How's your history?"

"Not bad."

"Do you know how the Duke of Wellington died?"

"Sure," I answered. "He was shot by a French sniper during the opening stages of the Battle of Waterloo. Why?"

"Oh, no reason," muttered my father with feigned innocence, scribbling in a small notebook. He paused for a moment.

"So Napoleon *won* at Waterloo, did he?" he asked slowly and with great intensity.

"Of course not," I replied. "Field Marshal Blücher's timely intervention saved the day."

I narrowed my eyes.

"This is all O-level history, Dad. What are you up to?"

"Well, it's a bit of a coincidence, wouldn't you say?"

"What is?"

"Nelson and Wellington, two great English national heroes *both* being shot early on during their most important and decisive battles."

"What are you suggesting?"

"That French revisionists might be involved."

"But it didn't affect the outcome of either battle," I asserted. "We still won on both occasions!"

"I never said they were good at it."

"That's ludicrous!" I scoffed. "I suppose you think the same revisionists had King Harold killed in 1066 to assist the Norman invasion!"

But Dad wasn't laughing. He replied with some surprise:

"Harold? Killed? How?"

"An arrow, Dad. In his eye."

"English or French?"

"History doesn't relate," I replied, annoyed at his bizarre line of questioning.

"In his eye, you say?— Time *is* out of joint," he muttered, scribbling another note.

"*What's* out of joint?" I asked, not quite hearing him.

"Nothing, nothing. Good job I was born to set it right—"

"*Hamlet?*" I asked, recognizing the quotation.

He ignored me, finished writing and snapped the notebook

shut, then placed his fingertips on his temples and rubbed them absently for a moment. The world joggled forward a second and refroze as he did so. He looked about nervously.

"They're onto me. Thanks for your help, Sweetpea. When you see your mother, tell her she makes the torches burn brighter—and don't forget to try and dissuade her from painting the bedroom."

"Any color but mauve, right?"

"Right."

He smiled at me and touched my face. I felt my eyes moisten; these visits were all too short. He sensed my sadness and smiled the sort of smile any child would want to receive from their father. Then he spoke:

"For I dipped into the past, far as SpecOps-12 could see—"

He paused and I finished the quote, part of an old Chrono-Guard song Dad used to sing to me when I was a child.

"—saw a vision of the world and all the options there could be!"

And then he was gone. The world rippled as the clock started again. The barman finished his sentence, the birds flew onto their nests, the television came back on with a nauseating ad for SmileyBurgers, and over the road the cyclist met the asphalt with a thud.

Everything carried on as normal. No one except myself had seen Dad come or go.

I ordered a crab sandwich and munched on it absently while sipping from a mocha that seemed to be taking an age to cool down. There weren't a lot of customers and Stanford, the owner, was busy washing up some cups. I put down my paper to watch the TV when the Toad News Network logo came up.

Toad News was the biggest news network in Europe. Run by the Goliath Corporation, it was a twenty-four-hour service with up-to-date reports that the national news services couldn't possibly hope to match. Goliath gave it finance and stability, but also a slightly suspicious air. No one liked the Corporation's pernicious hold on the nation, and the Toad News Network received more than its fair share of criticism, despite repeated denials that the parent company called the shots.

"This," boomed the announcer above the swirling music, "is the Toad News Network. The Toad, bringing you News Global, News Updates, News *NOW!*"

The lights came up on the anchorwoman, who smiled into the camera.

"This is the midday news on Monday, May 6, 1985, and this is Alexandria Belfridge reading it. The Crimean Peninsula," she announced, "has again come under scrutiny this week as the United Nations passed resolution PN17296, insisting that England and the Imperial Russian Government open negotiations concerning sovereignty. As the Crimean War enters its one hundred and thirty-first year, pressure groups both at home and abroad are pushing for a peaceful end to hostilities."

I closed my eyes and groaned quietly to myself. I had been out there doing my patriotic duty in '73 and had seen the truth of warfare beyond the pomp and glory for myself. The heat, the cold, the fear, the death. The announcer spoke on, her voice edged with jingoism.

"When the English forces ejected the Russians from their last toehold on the peninsula in 1975, it was seen as a major triumph against overwhelming odds. However, a state of deadlock has been maintained since those days and the country's mood was summed up last week by Sir Gordon Duff-Rolecks at an antiwar rally in Trafalgar Square."

The program cut to some footage of a large and mainly peaceful demonstration in central London. Duff-Rolecks was standing on a podium and giving a speech in front of a large and untidy nest of microphones.

"What began as an excuse to curb Russia's expansionism in

1854," intoned the MP, "has collapsed over the years into nothing more than an exercise to maintain the nation's pride . . ."

But I wasn't listening. I'd heard it all before a zillion times. I took another sip of coffee as sweat prickled my scalp. The TV showed stock footage of the peninsula as Duff-Rolecks spoke: Sebastopol, a heavily fortified English garrison town with little remaining of its architectural and historical heritage. Whenever I saw these pictures the smell of cordite and the crack of exploding shells filled my head. I instinctively stroked the only outward mark from the campaign I had—a small raised scar on my chin. Others had not been so lucky. Nothing had changed. The war had ground on.

"It's all bullshit, Thursday," said a gravelly voice close at hand.

It was Stanford, the café owner. Like me he was a veteran of the Crimea, but from an earlier campaign. Unlike me he had lost more than just his innocence and some good friends; he lumbered around on two tin legs and still had enough shrapnel in his body to make half a dozen baked bean tins.

"The Crimea has got sod all to do with the United Nations."

He liked to talk about the Crimea with me despite our opposing views. No one else really wanted to. Soldiers involved in the ongoing dispute with Wales had more kudos; Crimean personnel on leave usually left their uniforms in the wardrobe.

"I suppose not," I replied noncommittally, staring out of the window to where I could see a Crimean veteran begging at a street corner, reciting Longfellow from memory for a couple of pennies.

"Makes all those lives seem wasted if we give it back now," added Stanford gruffly. "We've been there since 1854. It belongs to *us*. You might as well say we should give the Isle of Wight back to the French."

"We *did* give the Isle of Wight back to the French," I replied patiently; Stanford's grasp of current affairs was generally confined to first division croquet and the love life of actress Lola Vavoom.

"Oh yes," he muttered, brow knitted. "We did, didn't we? Well, we shouldn't have. And who do the UN think they are?"

"I don't know but if the killing stops they've got my vote, Stan."

The barkeeper shook his head sadly as Duff-Rolecks concluded his speech:

". . . there can be little doubt that the Czar Romanov Alexei IV *does* have overwhelming rights to sovereignty of the peninsula and I for one look forward to the day when we can withdraw our troops from what can only be described as an incalculable waste of human life and resources."

The Toad News anchorwoman came back on and moved to another item—the government was to raise the duty on cheese to 83 percent, an unpopular move that would doubtless have the more militant citizens picketing cheese shops.

"The Ruskies could stop it tomorrow if they pulled out!" said Stanford belligerently.

It wasn't an argument and he and I both knew it. There was nothing left of the peninsula that would be worth owning whoever won. The only stretch of land that hadn't been churned to a pulp by artillery bombardment was heavily mined. Historically and morally the Crimea belonged to Imperial Russia; that was all there was to it.

The next news item was about a border skirmish with the People's Republic of Wales; no one hurt, just a few shots exchanged across the River Wye near Hay. Typically rambunctious, the youthful president-for-life Owain Glyndwr VII had blamed England's imperialist yearnings for a unified Britain; equally typically, Parliament had not so much as even made a statement about the incident. The news ground on, but I wasn't really paying attention. A new fusion plant had opened in Dungeness and the president had been there to open it. He grinned dutifully as the flashbulbs went off. I returned to my paper and read a story about a parliamentary bill to remove the dodo's protected species status after their staggering increase in numbers; but I couldn't concentrate. The Crimea had filled my mind with its unwelcome memories. It was lucky for me that my pager bleeped and brought with it a much-needed reality check. I tossed a few notes on the counter and sprinted out of the door as the Toad News anchorwoman somberly announced that a young surrealist had been killed—stabbed to death by a gang adhering to a radical school of French impressionists.

2.

Gad's Hill

> . . . There are two schools of thought about the resilience
> of time. The first is that time is highly volatile, with every
> small event altering the possible outcome of the earth's
> future. The other view is that time is rigid, and no matter
> how hard you try, it will always spring back toward a
> determined present. Myself, I do not worry about such
> trivialities. I simply sell ties to anyone who wants to buy
> one . . .
>
> Tie seller in Victoria, June 1983

MY PAGER had delivered a disconcerting message; the un-
stealable had just been stolen. It was not the first time the *Martin Chuzzlewit* manuscript had been purloined. Two years before
it had been removed from its case by a security man who wanted
nothing more than to read the book in its pure and unsullied
state. Unable to live with himself or decipher Dickens's handwriting past the third page, he eventually confessed and the
manuscript was recovered. He spent five years sweating over
lime kilns on the edge of Dartmoor.

Gad's Hill Palace was where Charles Dickens lived at the end
of his life, but not where he wrote *Chuzzlewit*. That was at De-
vonshire Terrace, when he still lived with his first wife, in 1843.
Gad's Hill is a large Victorian building near Rochester which had

fine views of the Medway when Dickens bought it. If you screw up your eyes and ignore the oil refinery, heavy water plant and the ExcoMat containment facility, it's not too hard to see what drew him to this part of England. Several thousand visitors pass through Gad's Hill every day, making it the third-most popular area of literary pilgrimage after Anne Hathaway's cottage and the Brontës' Haworth House. Such huge numbers of people had created enormous security problems; no one was taking any chances since a deranged individual had broken into Chawton, threatening to destroy all Jane Austen's letters unless his frankly dull and uneven Austen biography was published. On that occasion no damage had been done, but it was a grim portent of things to come. In Dublin the following year an organized gang attempted to hold Jonathan Swift's papers to ransom. A protracted siege developed that ended with two of the extortionists shot dead and the destruction of several original political pamphlets and an early draft of *Gulliver's Travels*. The inevitable had to happen. Literary relics were placed under bullet-proof glass and guarded by electronic surveillance and armed officers. It was not the way anyone wanted it, but it seemed the only answer. Since those days there had been few major problems, which made the theft of *Chuzzlewit* all the more remarkable.

I parked my car, clipped my SO-27 badge into my top pocket and pushed my way through the crowds of pressmen and gawkers. I saw Boswell from a distance and ducked under a police line to reach him.

"Good morning, sir," I muttered. "I came as soon as I heard."

He put a finger to his lips and whispered in my ear:

"Ground-floor window. Took less than ten minutes. Nothing else."

"What?"

Then I saw. Toad News Network's star reporter Lydia Startright was about to do an interview. The finely coiffured TV journalist finished her introduction and turned to us both. Boswell employed a neat sidestep, jabbed me playfully in the ribs and left me alone under the full glare of the news cameras.

"—of *Martin Chuzzlewit*, stolen from the Dickens Museum at Gad's Hill. I have with me Literary Detective Thursday Next. Tell me, Officer, how it was possible for thieves to break in and steal one of literature's greatest treasures?"

I murmured "bastard!" under my breath to Boswell, who slunk off shaking with mirth. I shifted my weight uneasily. With the enthusiasm for art and literature in the population undiminished, the LiteraTec's job was becoming increasingly difficult, made worse by a very limited budget.

"The thieves gained entrance through a window on the ground floor and went straight to the manuscript," I said in my best TV voice. "They were in and out within ten minutes."

"I understand the museum was monitored by closed-circuit television," continued Lydia. "Did you capture the thieves on video?"

"Our inquiries are proceeding," I replied. "You understand that some details must be kept secret for operational purposes."

Lydia lowered her microphone and cut the camera.

"Do you have *anything* to give me, Thursday?" she asked. "The parrot stuff I can get from anyone."

I smiled.

"I've only just got here, Lyds. Try me again in a week."

"Thursday, in a week this will be archive footage. Okay, roll VT."

The cameraman reshouldered his camera and Lydia resumed her report.

"Do you have any leads?"

"There are several avenues that we are pursuing. We are

confident that we can return the manuscript to the museum and arrest the individuals concerned."

I wished I could share my own optimism. I had spent a lot of time at Gad's Hill overseeing security arrangements, and I knew it was like the Bank of England. The people who did this were good. *Really* good. It also made it kind of personal. The interview ended and I ducked under a SpecOps DO NOT CROSS tape to where Boswell was waiting to meet me.

"This is one hell of a mess, Thursday. Turner, fill her in."

Boswell left us to it and went off to find something to eat.

"If you can see how they pulled this one off," murmured Paige who was a slightly older and female version of Boswell, "I'll eat my boots, buckles and all."

Both Turner and Boswell had been at the LiteraTec department when I turned up there, fresh from the military and a short career at the Swindon Police Department. Few people ever left the LiteraTec division; when you were in London you had pretty much reached the top of your profession. Promotion or death were the usual ways out; the saying was that a LiteraTec job wasn't for Christmas—it was for life.

"Boswell likes you, Thursday."

"In what sort of way?" I asked suspiciously.

"In the sort of way that he wants you in my shoes when I leave—I became engaged to a rather nice fellow from SO-3 at the weekend."

I should have been more enthusiastic, but Turner had been engaged so many times she could have filled every finger and toe—twice.

"SO-3?" I queried, somewhat inquisitively. Being in SpecOps was no guarantee you would know which departments did what—Joe Public were probably better informed. The only SpecOps divisions I knew about for sure below SO-12 were SO-9, who were Antiterrorist, and SO-1, who were Internal Affairs—the SpecOps police; the people who made sure we didn't step out of line.

"SO-3?" I repeated. "What do *they* do?"

"Weird Stuff."

"I thought SO-2 did Weird Stuff?"

"SO-2 do *Weirder* Stuff. I asked him but he never got around to answering—we were kind of busy. Look at this."

Turner had led me into the manuscript room. The glass case that had held the leather-bound manuscript was empty.

"Anything?" Paige asked one of the scene-of-crime officers.

"Nothing."

"Gloves?" I asked.

The SOCO stood up and stretched her back; she hadn't discovered a single print of any sort.

"No; and that's what's so bizarre. It doesn't look like they touched the box at all; not with gloves, not a cloth—nothing. According to me this box hasn't been opened and the manuscript is still inside!"

I looked at the glass case. It was still locked tight and none of the other exhibits had been touched. The keys were kept separately and were at this moment on their way from London.

"Hello, that's odd—" I muttered, leaning closer.

"What do you see?" asked Paige anxiously.

I pointed to an area of glass on one of the side panels that undulated slightly. The area was roughly the size of the manuscript.

"I noticed that," said Paige. "I thought it was a flaw in the glass."

"Toughened bullet-proof glass?" I asked her. "No chance. And it *wasn't* like this when I supervised the fitting, I can assure you of that."

"What, then?"

I stroked the hard glass and felt the shiny surface ripple beneath my fingertips. A shiver ran up my back and I felt a curious sense of uncomfortable familiarity, the feeling you might get when a long-forgotten school bully hails you as an old friend.

"The work feels familiar, Paige. When I find the perpetrator, it'll be someone I know."

"You've been a LiteraTec for seven years, Thursday."

I saw what she meant.

"Eight years, and you're right—you'll probably know them too. Could Lamber Thwalts have done this?"

"He *could* have, if he wasn't still in the hokey—four years still to go over that *Love's Labor's Won* scam."

"What about Keens? He could handle something as big as this."

"Milton's no longer with us. Caught analepsy in the library at Parkhurst. Stone-cold dead in a fortnight."

"Hmm."

I pointed at the two video cameras.

"Who did they see?"

"No one," replied Turner. "Not a dicky bird. I can play you the tapes but you'll be none the wiser."

She showed me what they had. The guard on duty was being interviewed back at the station. They were hoping it was an inside job but it didn't look like it; the guard had been as devastated as any of them.

Turner shuttled the video back and pressed the play button.

"Watch carefully. The recorder rotates the five cameras and films five seconds of each."

"So the longest gap between cameras is twenty seconds?"

"Got it. You watching? Okay, there's the manuscript—" She pointed at the book, clearly visible in the frame as the VCR flicked to the camera at the front door. There was no movement. Then the inside door through which any burglar would have to come; all the other entrances were barred. Then came the corridor; then the lobby; then the machine flicked back to the manuscript room. Turner punched the pause button and I leaned closer. The manuscript was gone.

"Twenty seconds to get in, open the box, take *Chuzzlewit* and then leg it? It's not possible."

"Believe you me, Thursday—it happened."

The last remark came from Boswell, who had been looking over my shoulder.

"I don't know how they did it, but they did. I've had a call from Supreme Commander Gale on this one and he's being leaned on by the prime minister. Questions have already been asked in the House and someone's head is going to roll. Not mine, I assure you."

He looked at us both rather pointedly, which made me feel especially ill at ease—I was the one who had advised the museum on its security arrangements.

"We'll be onto it straight away, sir," I replied, punching the pause button and letting the video run on. The views of the building changed rhythmically, revealing nothing. I pulled up a chair, rewound the tape and looked again.

"What are you hoping to find?" asked Paige.

"Anything."

I didn't find it.

3.

Back at My Desk

Funding for the Special Operations Network comes directly from the government. Most work is centralized, but all of the SpecOps divisions have local representatives to keep a watchful eye on any provincial problems. They are administered by local commanders, who liaise with the national offices for information exchange, guidance and policy decisions. Like any other big government department, it looks good on paper but is an utter shambles. Petty infighting and political agendas, arrogance and sheer bloody-mindedness almost *guarantees* that the left hand doesn't know what the right is doing.

MILLON DE FLOSS
—*A Short History of the Special Operations Network*

TWO DAYS of fruitless hunting for *Chuzzlewit* had passed without even the slightest clue as to where it might be. There had been whispers of reprimands, but only if we could figure out how the manuscript was taken. It would seem a bit ludicrous to be chastised for leaving a loophole in the security arrangements but not know what it was. Now slightly despondent, I was sitting at my desk back at the station. Recalling my conversation with Dad, I phoned my mother to ask her not to paint the bedroom mauve. The call backfired slightly as she thought this a *grand* idea and hung up before I could argue. I sighed and flipped through the telephone messages that had accumulated over the past two days. They were mostly from informers and concerned citizens who had been robbed or cheated and wanted to know if we had made any headway. It was all small beer compared to *Chuzzlewit*—there were a lot of gullible people out there buying first editions of Byronic verse at knockdown prices, then complaining bitterly when they found out they were fakes. Like most of the other operatives, I had a pretty good idea who was behind all of this, but we never caught the big fish—just the "utterers," the dealers who sold it all on. It smacked of corruption in high places but we never had any proof. Usually I read my messages with interest, but today none of it seemed terribly important. After all, the verses of Byron, Keats or Poe are real whether they are in bootleg form or not. You can still read them for the same effect.

I opened the drawer of my desk and pulled out a small mirror. A woman with somewhat ordinary features stared back at me. Her hair was a plain mousy color and of medium length, tied up rather hastily in a ponytail at the back. She had no cheekbones to speak of and her face, I noticed, had just started to show some rather obvious lines. I thought of my mother, who had looked as wrinkled as a walnut by the time she was forty-five. I shuddered, placed the mirror back in the drawer and took out a faded and slightly dog-eared photograph. It was a photo of myself with a group of friends taken in the Crimea when I had been simply Corporal T. E. Next, 33550336, Driver: APC, Light Armored Brigade. I had served my country diligently, been involved in a military disaster and then honorably discharged with a gong to prove it. They had expected me to give talks about recruitment and valor but I had disappointed them. I attended one regimental reunion but that was it; I had found myself looking for the faces that I knew weren't there.

In the photo Landen was standing on my left, his arm

around me and another soldier, my brother, his best mate. Landen lost a leg, but he came home. My brother was still out there.

"Who's that?" asked Paige, who had been looking over my shoulder.

"Whoa!" I yelped. "You just scared the crap out of me!"

"Sorry! Crimea?"

I handed her the photo and she looked at it intently.

"That must be your brother—you have the same nose."

"I know, we used to share it on a rota. I had it Mondays, Wednesd—"

"—then the other man must be Landen."

I frowned and turned to face her. I *never* mentioned Landen to anyone. It was *personal*. I felt kind of betrayed that she might have been prying behind my back.

"How do you know about Landen?"

She sensed the anger in my voice, smiled and raised an eyebrow.

"*You* told me about him."

"I did?"

"Sure. The speech was slurred and for the most part it was garbage, but he was certainly on your mind."

I winced.

"Last year's Christmas bash?"

"Or the year before. You weren't the only one talking garbage with slurred speech."

I looked at the photo again.

"We were engaged."

Paige suddenly looked uneasy. Crimean fiancés could be *seriously* bad conversation topics.

"Did he . . . ah . . . come back?"

"Most of him. He left a leg behind. We don't speak too much these days."

"What's his full name?" asked Paige, interested in finally getting something out of my past.

"It's Parke-Laine. Landen Parke-Laine." It was the first time I had said his name out loud for almost longer than I could remember.

"Parke-Laine the writer?"

I nodded.

"Good-looking bloke."

"Thank you," I replied, not quite knowing what I was thanking her for. I put the photograph back in my drawer and Paige clicked her fingers.

"Boswell wants to see you," she announced, finally remembering what she had come over to say.

Boswell was not alone. A man in his forties was waiting for me and rose as I entered. He didn't blink very much and had a large scar down one side of his face. Boswell hummed and hawed for a moment, coughed, looked at his watch and then said something about leaving us to it.

"Police?" I asked as soon as we were alone. "Has a relative died or something?"

The man closed the Venetian blinds to give us more privacy.

"Not that I heard about."

"SO-1?" I asked, expecting a possible reprimand.

"Me?" replied the man with genuine surprise. "No."

"LiteraTec?"

"Why don't you sit down?"

He offered me a seat and then sat down in Boswell's large oak swivel chair. He had a buff file with my name on the cover which he flopped on the desk in front of him. I was amazed by how thick the file was.

"Is that all about me?"

He ignored me. Instead of opening my file, he leaned forward and gazed at me with his unblinking eyes.

"How do you rate the *Chuzzlewit* case?"

I found myself staring at his scar. It ran from his forehead down to his chin and had all the size and subtlety of a shipbuilder's weld. It pulled his lip up, but apart from that his face was pleasant enough; without the scar he might have been handsome. I was being unsubtle. He instinctively brought up a hand to cover it.

"Finest Cossack," he murmured, making light of it.

"I'm sorry."

"Don't be. It's hard not to gawp."

He paused for a moment.

"I work for SpecOps-5," he announced slowly, showing me a shiny badge.

"SO-5?" I gasped, failing to hide the surprise in my voice. "What do you lot do?"

"That's restricted, Miss Next. I showed you the badge so you could talk to me without worrying about security clearances. I can okay that with Boswell if you'd prefer?—"

My heart was beating faster. Interviews with SpecOps operatives farther up the ladder sometimes led to transfers—

"So, Miss Next, what do you think about *Chuzzlewit*?"

"You want my opinion or the official version?"

"Your opinion. Official versions I get from Boswell."

"I think it's too early to tell. If ransom is the motive then we can assume the manuscript is still in one piece. If it's stolen to sell or barter we can also consider it in one piece. If terrorism is the game then we might have to be worried. In scenarios one and three the LiteraTecs have sod all to do with it. SO-9 get involved and we're kind of out of the picture."

The man looked at me intently and nodded his head.

"You don't like it here, do you?"

"I've had enough, put it that way," I responded, slightly less guardedly than I should. "Who are you, anyway?"

The man laughed.

"Sorry. Very bad manners; I didn't mean all the cloak-and-dagger stuff. The name's Tamworth, head field operative at SO-5. Actually," he added, "that doesn't mean so much. At present there are just me and two others."

I shook his outstretched hand.

"Three people in a SpecOps division?" I asked curiously. "Isn't that kind of mean?"

"I lost some guys yesterday."

"I'm sorry."

"Not that way. We just made a bit of headway and that's not always good news. Some people research well in SO-5 but don't like the fieldwork. They have kids. I don't. But I understand."

I nodded. I understood too.

"Why are you talking to me?" I asked almost casually. "I'm SO-27; as the SpecOps transfer board so kindly keeps telling me, my talents lie either in front of a LiteraTec desk or a kitchen stove."

Tamworth smiled. He patted the file in front of him.

"I know all about that. SpecOps Central Recruiting don't really have a good word for 'No,' they just fob. It's what they're best at. On the contrary, they are fully aware of your potential. I spoke to Boswell just now and he thinks he can just about let you go if you want to help us over at SO-5."

"If you're SO-5 he doesn't have much choice, does he?"

Tamworth laughed.

"That's true. But _you_ do. I'd never recruit anyone who didn't want to join me."

I looked at him. He meant it.

"Is this a transfer?"

"No," replied Tamworth, "it isn't. I just need you because

you have information that is of use to us. You'll be an observer; nothing more. Once you understand what we're up against you'll be very glad to be just that."

"So when this is over I just get thrown back here?"

He paused and looked at me for a moment, trying to give the best assurance that he could without lying. I liked him for it.

"I make no guarantees, Miss Next, but anyone who has been on an SO-5 assignment can be pretty confident that they won't be SO-27 forever."

"What is it you want me to do?"

Tamworth pulled a form from his case and pushed it across the table to me. It was a standard security clearance and, once signed, gave SpecOps the right to almost everything I possessed and a lot more besides if I so much as breathed a word to someone with a lesser clearance. I signed it dutifully and handed it back. In exchange he gave me a shiny SO-5 badge with my name already in place. Tamworth knew me better than I thought. This done, he lowered his voice and began:

"SO-5 is basically a Search & Containment facility. We are posted with a man to track until found and contained, then we get another. SO-4 is pretty much the same; they are just after a different thing. Person. You know. Anyway, I was down at Gad's Hill this morning, Thursday—can I call you Thursday?—and I had a good look at the crime scene at first hand. Whoever took the manuscript of *Chuzzlewit* left no fingerprints, no sign of entry and nothing on any of the cameras."

"Not a lot to go on, was there?"

"On the contrary. It was just the break I've been waiting for."

"Did you share this with Boswell?" I asked.

"Of course not. We're not interested in the manuscript; we're interested in the man who stole it."

"And who's that?"

"I can't tell you his name but I can write it."

He took out a felt tip and wrote "Acheron Hades" on a notepad and held it up for me to read.

"Look familiar?"

"*Very* familiar. There can't be many people who haven't heard about him."

"I know. But you've met him, haven't you?"

"Certainly," I replied. "He was one of the lecturers when I studied English at Swindon in '68. None of us were surprised when he switched to a career of crime. He was something of a lech. He made one of the students pregnant."

"Braeburn; yes, we know about her. What about you?"

"He never made me pregnant, but he had a good try."

"Did you sleep with him?"

"No; I didn't figure sleeping with lecturers was really where I wanted to be. The attention was flattering, I suppose, dinner and stuff. He was brilliant—but a moral vacuum. I remember once he was arrested for armed robbery while giving a spirited lecture on John Webster's *The White Devil*. He was released without charge on that occasion, but the Braeburn thing was enough to have him dismissed."

"He asked you to go with him yet you turned him down."

"Your information is good, Mr. Tamworth."

Tamworth scribbled a note on his pad. He looked up at me again.

"But the important thing is: You know what he looks like?"

"Of course," I replied, "but you're wasting your time. He died in Venezuela in '82."

"No; he just made us *think* he had. We exhumed the grave the following year. It wasn't him at all. He feigned death so well that he fooled the doctors; they buried a weighted coffin. He has powers that are slightly baffling. That's why we can't say his name. I call it Rule Number One."

"His name? Why not?"

"Because he can hear his own name—even whispered—over a thousand-yard radius, perhaps more. He uses it to sense our presence."

"And why do you suppose he stole *Chuzzlewit*?"

Tamworth reached into his case and pulled out a file. It was marked "Most Secret—SpecOps-5 clearance only." The slot in the front, usually reserved for a mugshot, was empty.

"We don't have a picture of him," said Tamworth as I opened the file. "He doesn't resolve on film or video and has never been in custody long enough to be sketched. Remember the cameras at Gad's Hill?"

"Yes?"

"They didn't pick anyone up. I went through the tapes very carefully. The camera angle changed every five seconds yet there would be *no way* anyone could dodge all of them during the time they were in the building. Do you see what I mean?"

I nodded slowly and flicked through the pages of Acheron's file. Tamworth continued:

"I've been after him for five years. He has seven outstanding warrants for murder in England, eighteen in America. Extortion, theft and kidnapping. He's cold, calculating and quite ruthless. Thirty-six of his forty-two known victims were either SpecOps or police officers."

"Hartlepool in '75?" I asked.

"Yes," replied Tamworth slowly. "You heard about it?"

I had. Most people had. Hades had been cornered in the basement of a multistory car park after a botched robbery. One of his associates lay dead in a bank nearby; Acheron had killed the wounded man to stop him talking. In the basement, he persuaded an officer into giving him his gun, killing six others as he walked out. The only officer who survived was the one whose gun he had used. That was Acheron's idea of a joke. The officer in question never gave a satisfactory explanation as to *why* he had given up his firearm. He had taken early retirement and gassed himself in his car six years later after a short history of alcoholism and petty theft. He came to be known as the seventh victim.

"I interviewed the Hartlepool survivor before he took his own life," Tamworth went on, "after I was instructed to find . . . *him* at any cost. My findings led us to formulate Rule Number Two: If you ever have the misfortune to face him in person, *believe nothing that he says or does*. He can lie in thought, deed, action and appearance. He has amazing persuasive powers over those of weak mind. Did I tell you that we have been authorized to use maximum force?"

"No, but I guessed."

"SO-5 has a shoot-to-kill policy concerning our friend—"

"Whoa, whoa, wait a sec. You have the power to eliminate *without* trial?"

"Welcome to SpecOps-5, Thursday—what did you think *containment* meant?"

He laughed a laugh that was slightly disturbing.

"As the saying goes: *If you want to get into SpecOps, act kinda weird*. We don't tend to pussyfoot around."

"Is it legal?"

"Not in the least. It's Blind Eye Grand Central below SpecOps-8. We have a saying: *Below the eight, above the law*. Ever hear it?"

"No."

"You'll hear it a lot. In any event we make it our Rule Number Three: Apprehension is of minimal importance. What gun do you carry?"

I told him and he scribbled a note.

"I'll get some fluted expansion slugs for you."

"There'll be hell to pay if we get caught with those."

"Self-defense only," explained Tamworth quickly. "*You* won't be dealing with this man; I just want you to ID him if he shows. But listen: If the shit hits the fan I don't want any of my people left with bows and arrows against the lightning. And anything less than an expanding slug is about as much good as using wet cardboard as a flak jacket. We know almost nothing about him. No birth certificate, not even a reliable age or even who his parents were. He just appeared on the scene in '54 as a petty criminal with a literary edge and has worked his way steadily upward to being number three on the planet's most-wanted list."

"Who're number one and two?"

"I don't know and I have been reliably informed that it's far better *not* to know."

"So where do we go from here?"

"I'll call you. Stay alert and keep your pager with you at all times. You're on leave as of now from SO-27, so just enjoy the time off. I'll be seeing you!"

He was gone in an instant, leaving me with the SO-5 badge and a thumping heart. Boswell returned, followed by a curious Paige. I showed them both the badge.

"Way to go!" said Paige, giving me a hug, but Boswell seemed less happy. After all, he did have his own department to think about.

"They can play very rough at SO-5, Next," said Boswell in a fatherly tone. "I want you to go back to your desk and have a long calm think about this. Have a cup of coffee and a bun. No, have *two* buns. Don't make any rash decisions, and just run through all the pros and cons of the argument. When you've done that I would be happy to adjudicate. Do you understand?"

I understood. In my hurry to leave the office I almost forgot the picture of Landen.

4.

Acheron Hades

. . . The best reason for committing loathsome and detestable acts—and let's face it, I am considered something of an expert in this field—is purely for their own sake. Monetary gain is all very well, but it dilutes the taste of wickedness to a lower level that is obtainable by anyone with an overdeveloped sense of avarice. True and baseless evil is as rare as the purest good—and we all know how rare *that* is . . .

ACHERON HADES
—*Degeneracy for Pleasure and Profit*

TAMWORTH DIDN'T call that week, nor the week after. I tried to call him at the beginning of the third week but was put through to a trained denialist who flatly refused to admit that Tamworth or SO-5 even *existed*. I used the time to get up-to-date with some reading, filing, mending the car and also—because of the new legislation—to register Pickwick as a pet rather than a wild dodo. I took him to the town hall where a veterinary inspector studied the once-extinct bird very carefully. Pickwick stared back forlornly, as he, in common with most pets, didn't fancy the vet much.

"*Plock-plock,*" said Pickwick nervously as the inspector expertly clipped the large brass ring around his ankle.

"No wings?" asked the official curiously, staring at Pickwick's slightly odd shape.

"He's a Version 1.2," I explained. "One of the first. They didn't get the sequence complete until 1.7."

"Must be pretty old."

"Twelve years this October."

"I had one of the early Thylacines," said the official glumly. "A Version 2.1. When we decanted him he had no ears. Stone deaf. No warranty or anything. Bloody liberty, I call it. Do you read *New Splicer*?"

I had to admit that I didn't.

"They sequenced a Steller's sea cow last week. How do I even get one of those through the door?"

"Grease its sides?" I suggested. "And show it a plate of kelp?"

But the official wasn't listening; he had turned his attention to the next dodo, a pinkish creature with a long neck. The owner caught my eye and smiled sheepishly.

"Redundant strands filled in with flamingo," he explained. "I should have used dove."

"Version 2.9?"

"2.9.1, actually. A bit of a hotchpotch but to us he's simply Chester. We wouldn't swap him for anything."

The inspector had been studying Chester's registration documents.

"I'm sorry," he said at last. "2.9.1s come under the new Chimera category."

"What do you mean?"

"Not enough dodo to be dodo. Room seven down the corridor. Follow the owner of the pukey, but be careful; I sent a quarkbeast down there this morning."

I left Chester's owner and the official arguing together and took Pickwick for a waddle in the park. I let him off the leash and he chased a few pigeons before fraternizing with some feral dodos who were cooling their feet in the pond. They splashed excitedly and made quiet *plock plock* noises to one another until it was time to go home.

Two days after that I had run out of ways to rearrange the furniture, so it was lucky that Tamworth called me. He told me he was on a stakeout and that I needed to join him. I hastily scribbled down the address and was in the East End in under forty minutes. The stakeout was in a shabby street of converted warehouses that had been due for demolition two decades before. I doused the lights and got out, hid anything of value and locked the car carefully. The battered Pontiac was old and grotty enough not to arouse suspicion in the grimy surroundings. I glanced around. The brickwork was crumbling and heavy smears of green algae streaked the walls where the down pipes had once been. The windows were cracked and dirty and the brick wall at ground level was stained alternately with graffiti or the sooty blackness of a recent fire. A rusty fire escape zigzagged up the dark building and cast a staccato shadow on the potholed road and several burned-out cars. I made my way to a side door according to Tamworth's instructions. Inside, large cracks had opened up in the walls and the damp and decay had mixed with the smell of Jeyes fluid and a curry shop on the ground floor. A neon light flashed on and off regularly, and I saw several women in tight skirts hovering in the dark doorways. The citizens who lived in the area were a curious mix; the lack of cheap housing in and around London attracted a cross section of people, from locals to down-and-outs to professionals. It wasn't great from a law-and-order point of view, but it did allow SpecOps agents to move around without raising suspicion.

I reached the seventh floor, where a couple of young Henry Fielding fanatics were busy swapping bubble-gum cards.

"I'll swap you one Sophia for an Amelia."

"Piss off!" replied his friend indignantly. "If you want Sophia you're going to have to give me an Allworthy plus a Tom Jones, *as well* as the Amelia!"

His friend, realizing the rarity of a Sophia, reluctantly agreed. The deal was done and they ran off downstairs to look for hubcaps. I compared a number with the address that Tamworth had given me and rapped on a door covered with peeling peach-colored paint. It was opened cautiously by a man somewhere in his eighties. He half-hid his face from me with a wrinkled hand, and I showed him my badge.

"You must be Next," he said in a voice that was really quite sprightly for his age. I ignored the old joke and went in. Tamworth was peering through some binoculars at a room in the building opposite and waved a greeting without looking up. I looked at the old man again and smiled.

"Call me Thursday."

He seemed gratified at this and shook my hand.

"The name's Snood; you can call me Junior."

"Snood?" I echoed. "Any relation to Filbert?"

The old man nodded.

"Filbert, ah yes!" he murmured. "A good lad and a fine son to his father!"

Filbert Snood was the only man who had even remotely interested me since I left Landen ten years ago. Snood had been in the ChronoGuard; he went away on assignment to Tewkesbury and never came back. I had a call from his commanding officer explaining that he had been unavoidably detained. I took that to mean another girl. It hurt at the time but I hadn't been in love with Filbert. I was certain of that because I *had* been in love with Landen. When you've been there you know it, like seeing a Turner or going for a walk on the west coast of Ireland.

"So you're his father?"

Snood walked through to the kitchen but I wasn't going to let it go.

"So how is he? Where's he living these days?"

The old man fumbled with the kettle.

"I find it hard to talk about Filbert," he announced at length, dabbing the corner of his mouth with a handkerchief. "It was *so* long ago!"

"He's dead?" I asked.

"Oh no," murmured the old man. "He's not dead; I think you were told he was unavoidably detained, yes?"

"Yes. I thought he had found someone else or something."

"We thought you would understand; your father was or is, I suppose, in the ChronoGuard and we use certain—let me see—*euphemisms*."

He looked at me intently with clear blue eyes staring through heavy lids. My heart thumped heavily.

"What are you saying?" I asked him.

The old man thought about saying something else but then lapsed into silence, paused for a moment and then shuffled back to the main room to mark up videotape labels. There was obviously more to it than just a girl in Tewkesbury, but time was on my side. I let the matter drop.

It gave me a chance to look around the room. A trestle table against one damp wall was stacked with surveillance equipment. A Revox spool-to-spool tape recorder slowly revolved next to a mixing box that placed all seven bugs in the room opposite and the phone line onto eight different tracks of the tape. Set back from the windows were two binoculars, a camera with a powerful telephoto lens, and next to this a video camera recording at slow speed onto a ten-hour tape.

Tamworth looked up from the binoculars.

"Welcome, Thursday. Come and have a look!"

I looked through the binoculars. In the flat opposite, not

thirty yards distant, I could see a well-dressed man aged perhaps fifty with a pinched face and a concerned expression. He seemed to be on the phone.

"That's not him."

Tamworth smiled.

"I know. This is his brother, Styx. We found out about him this morning. SO-14 were going to pick him up but *our* man is a much bigger fish; I called SO-1, who intervened on our behalf; Styx is our responsibility at the moment. Have a listen."

He handed me some earphones and I looked through the binoculars again. Hades' brother was sitting at a large walnut desk flicking through a copy of the *London and District Car Trader*. As I watched, he stopped, picked up the phone and dialed a number.

"Hello?" said Styx into the phone.

"Hello?" replied a middle-aged woman, the recipient of the call.

"Do you have a 1976 Chevrolet for sale?"

"Buying a car?" I asked Tamworth.

"Keep listening. Same time every week, apparently. Regular as clockwork."

"It's only got eighty-two thousand miles on the clock," continued the lady, "and runs really well. MOT and tax paid 'til year's end too."

"It sounds *perfect*," replied Styx. "I'll be willing to pay cash. Will you hold it for me? I'll be about an hour. You're in Clapham, yes?"

The woman agreed, and she read over an address that Styx didn't bother writing down. He reaffirmed his interest and then hung up, only to call a different number about another car in Hounslow. I took off the headphones and pulled out the headset jack so we could hear Styx's nasal rasp over the loudspeakers.

"How long does he do this for?"

"From SO-14 records, until he gets bored. Six hours, sometimes eight. He's not the only one either. Anyone who has ever sold a car gets someone like Styx on the phone at least once. Here, these are for you."

He handed me a box of ammunition with expanding slugs developed for maximum internal damage.

"What is he? A buffalo?"

But Tamworth wasn't amused.

"We're up against something *quite* different here, Thursday. Pray to the GSD you never have to use them, but if you do, don't hesitate. Our man doesn't give second chances."

I took the clip out of my automatic and reloaded it and the spare I carried with me, leaving a standard slug on top in case of an SO-1 spot check. Over in the flat, Styx had dialed another number in Ruislip.

"Hello?" replied the unfortunate car owner on the other end of the line.

"Yes, I saw your advert for a Ford Granada in today's *Trader*," continued Styx. "Is it still for sale?"

Styx got the address out of the car owner, promised to be around in ten minutes, put the phone down and then rubbed his hands with glee, laughing childishly. He put a line through the advert and then went onto the next.

"Doesn't even have a license," said Tamworth from the other side of the room. "He spends the rest of his time stealing ballpoints, causing electrical goods to fail *after* the guarantee has expired and scratching records in record shops."

"A bit childish, isn't it?"

"I'd say," replied Tamworth. "He's possessed of a certain amount of wickedness, but nothing like his brother."

"So what's the connection between Styx and the *Chuzzlewit* manuscript?"

"We suspect that he may have it. According to SO-14's surveillance records he brought in a package the evening of the break-in at Gad's Hill. I'm the first to admit that this is a long shot but it's the best evidence of *his* whereabouts these past three years. It's about time he broke cover."

"Has he demanded a ransom for the manuscript?" I asked.

"No, but it's early days. It might not be as simple as we think. Our man has an estimated IQ of one eighty, so simple extortion might be too easy for him."

Snood came in and sat down slightly shakily at the binoculars, put on the headphones and plugged in the jack. Tamworth picked up his keys and handed me a book.

"I have to meet up with my opposite number at SO-4. I'll be about an hour. If anything happens, just page me. My number is on redial one. Have a read of this if you get bored."

I looked at the small book he had given me. It was Charlotte Brontë's *Jane Eyre* bound in thick red leather.

"Who told you?" I asked sharply.

"Who told me what?" replied Tamworth, genuinely surprised.

"It's just . . . I've read this book a lot. When I was younger. I know it very well."

"And you like the ending?"

I thought for a moment. The rather flawed climax of the book was a cause of considerable bitterness within Brontë circles. It was generally agreed that if Jane had returned to Thornfield Hall and married Rochester, the book might have been a lot better than it was.

"No one likes the ending, Tamworth. But there's more than enough in it regardless of that."

"Then a reread will be especially instructive, won't it?"

There was a knock at the door. Tamworth answered it and a man who was all shoulders and no neck entered.

"Just in time!" said Tamworth, looking at his watch.

"Thursday Next, this is Buckett. He's temporary until I get a replacement."

He smiled and was gone.

Buckett and I shook hands. He smiled wanly as though this sort of job was not something he relished. He told me that he was pleased to meet me, then went to speak to Snood about the results of a horse race.

I tapped my fingertips on the copy of *Jane Eyre* that Tamworth had given me and placed it in my breast pocket. I rounded up the coffee cups and took them next door to the cracked enamel sink. Buckett appeared at the doorway.

"Tamworth said you were a LiteraTec."

"Tamworth was correct."

"I wanted to be a LiteraTec."

"You did?" I replied, seeing if there was anything in the fridge that wasn't a year past its sell-by date.

"Yeah. But they said you had to read a book or two."

"It helps."

There was a knock at the door and Buckett instinctively reached for his handgun. He was more on edge than I had thought.

"Easy, Buckett. I'll get it."

He joined me at the door and released the safety from his pistol. I looked at him and he nodded back in reply.

"Who's there?" I said without opening the door.

"Hello!" replied a voice. "My name's Edmund Capillary. Have you ever stopped to wonder whether it was *really* William Shakespeare who penned all those wonderful plays?"

We both breathed a sigh of relief and Buckett put the safety back on his automatic, muttering under his breath:

"Bloody Baconians!"

"Steady," I replied, "it's not illegal."

"More's the pity."

"Shh."

I opened the door on the security chain and found a small man in a lumpy corduroy suit. He was holding a dog-eared ID for me to see and politely raised his hat with a nervous smile. The Baconians were quite mad but for the most part harmless. Their purpose in life was to prove that Francis Bacon and not Will Shakespeare had penned the greatest plays in the English language. Bacon, they believed, had not been given the recognition that he rightfully deserved and they campaigned tirelessly to redress this supposed injustice.

"Hello!" said the Baconian brightly. "Can I take a moment of your time?"

I answered slowly:

"If you expect me to believe that a lawyer wrote *A Midsummer Night's Dream,* I must be dafter than I look."

The Baconian was not to be put off. He obviously liked fighting a poor argument; in real life he was most likely a personal accident barrister.

"Not as daft as supposing that a Warwickshire schoolboy with almost no education could write works that were not for an age but for all time."

"There is no evidence that he was without formal education," I returned evenly, suddenly enjoying myself. Buckett wanted me to get rid of him but I ignored his gesticulations.

"Agreed," continued the Baconian, "but I would argue that the Shakespeare in Stratford was *not* the same man as the Shakespeare in London."

It was an interesting approach. I paused and Edmund Capillary took the opportunity to pounce. He launched into his well-rehearsed patter almost automatically:

"The Shakespeare in Stratford was a wealthy grain trader and buying houses when the Shakespeare in London was being pursued by tax collectors for petty sums. The collectors traced him to Sussex on one occasion in 1600; yet why not take action against him in Stratford?"

"Search me."

He was on a roll now.

"No one is recorded in Stratford as having any idea of his literary success. He was never known to have bought a book, written a letter or indeed done anything apart from being a purveyor of bagged commodities, grain and malt and so forth."

The small man looked triumphant.

"So where does Bacon fit into all this?" I asked him.

"Francis Bacon was an Elizabethan writer who had been forced into becoming a lawyer and politician by his family. Since being associated with something like the theater would have been frowned upon, Bacon had to enlist the help of a poor actor named Shakespeare to act as his front man—history has mistakenly linked the two Shakespeares to give added validity to a story that otherwise has little substance."

"And the proof?"

"Hall and Marston—both Elizabethan satirists—were firmly of the belief that Bacon was the true author of *Venus and Adonis* and *The Rape of Lucrece*. I have a pamphlet here which goes into the matter further. More details are available at our monthly gatherings; we used to meet at the town hall but the radical wing of the New Marlovians fire-bombed us last week. I don't know where we will meet next. But if I can take your name and number, we can be in touch."

His face was earnest and smug; he thought he had me. I decided to play my trump card.

"What about the will?"

"The will?" he echoed, slightly nervously. He was obviously hoping I wasn't going to mention it.

"Yes," I continued. "If Shakespeare were *truly* two people, then why would the Shakespeare in Stratford mention the London Shakespeare's theater colleagues Condell, Heming and Burbage in his will?"

The Baconian's face fell.

"I was hoping you wouldn't ask." He sighed. "I'm wasting my time, aren't I?"

"I'm afraid you are."

He muttered something under his breath and moved on. As I threw the bolt I could hear the Baconian knocking at the next door to ours. Perhaps he'd have better luck down the corridor.

"What is a LiteraTec doing here anyway, Next?" asked Buckett as we returned to the kitchen.

"I'm here," I answered slowly, "because I know what *he* looks like; I'm not permanent in the least. As soon as I've fingered his man, Tamworth will transfer me back again."

I poured some yogurty milk down the sink and rinsed out the container.

"Might be a blessing."

"I don't see it that way. What about you? How did you get in with Tamworth?"

"I'm antiterrorist usually. SO-9. But Tamworth has trouble with recruitment. He took a cavalry saber for me. I owe him."

He dropped his eyes and fiddled with his tie for a moment. I peered cautiously into a cupboard for a dishcloth, discovered something nasty and then closed it quickly.

Buckett took out his wallet and showed me a picture of a dribbling infant that looked like every other dribbling infant I had ever seen.

"I'm married now so Tamworth knows I can't stay; one's needs change, you know."

"Good-looking kid."

"Thank you." He put the picture away. "You married?"

"Not for want of trying," I replied as I filled the kettle. Buckett nodded and brought out a copy of *Fast Horse*.

"Do you ever flutter on the gee-gees? I've had an unusual tip on Malabar."

"I don't. Sorry."

Buckett nodded. His conversation had pretty much dried up.

I brought in some coffee a few minutes later. Snood and Buckett were discussing the outcome of the Cheltenham Gold Stakes Handicap.

"So you know what he looks like, Miss Next?" asked the ancient Snood without looking up from the binoculars.

"He was a lecturer of mine when I was at college. He's tricky to describe, though."

"Average build?"

"When I last saw him."

"Tall?"

"At least six-six."

"Black hair worn swept back and graying at the temples?"

Buckett and I looked at one another.

"Yes?—"

"I think he's over there, Thursday."

I jerked the headphone jack out.

"—Acheron!!" came Styx's voice over the loudspeaker. "Dear brother, *what* a pleasant surprise!"

I looked through the binoculars and could see Acheron in the flat with Styx. He was dressed in a large gray duster jacket and was exactly how I remembered him from all those years ago. It didn't seem as though he had aged even one day. I shivered involuntarily.

"Shit," I muttered. Snood had already dialed the pager number to alert Tamworth.

"Mosquitoes have stung the blue goat," he muttered down the phone. "Thank you. Can you repeat that back and send it twice?"

My heart beat faster. Acheron might not stay long and I was in a position for advancement beyond the LiteraTecs for good. Capturing Hades would be something no one could ever ignore.

"I'm going over there," I said almost casually.

"*What?!*"

"You heard. Stay here and call SO-14 for armed backup, silent approach. Tell them we have gone in and to surround the building. Suspect will be armed and highly dangerous. Got it?"

Snood smiled in the manner that I had so liked in his son and reached for the telephone. I turned to Buckett.

"You with me?"

Buckett had turned a little pale.

"I'm . . . ah . . . with you," he replied slightly shakily.

I flew out of the door, down the stairs and into the lobby.

"Next!—"

It was Buckett. He had stopped and was visibly shaking.

"What is it?"

"I . . . I . . . can't do this," he announced, loosening his tie and rubbing the back of his neck. "I have the kid!—You don't know what *he* can do. I'm a betting man, Next. I *love* long odds. But we try and take him and we're both dead. I beg you, wait for SO-14!"

"He could be long gone by then. All we have to do is *detain* him."

Buckett bit his lip, but the man was terrified. He shook his head and beat a hasty retreat without another word. It was unnerving to say the least. I thought of shouting after him but remembered the picture of the dribbling kid. I pulled out my automatic, pushed open the door to the street and walked slowly across the road to the building opposite. As I did so Tamworth drew up in his car. He didn't look very happy.

"What the hell are you doing?"

"Pursuing the suspect."

"No you're not. Where's Buckett?"

"On his way home."

"I don't blame him. SO-14 on their way?"

I nodded. He paused, looked up at the dark building and then at me.

"*Shit.* Okay, stay behind and stay sharp. Shoot first, then question. Below the eight—"

"—above the law. I remember."

"Good."

Tamworth pulled out his gun and we stepped cautiously into the lobby of the converted warehouse. Styx's flat was on the seventh floor. Surprise, hopefully, would be on our side.

5.

Search for the Guilty,
Punish the Innocent

. . . Perhaps it was as well that she had been unconscious for four weeks. She had missed the aftermath, the SO-1 reports, the recriminations, Snood and Tamworth's funerals. She missed everything . . . except the blame. It was waiting for her when she awoke . . .

MILLON DE FLOSS
—*Thursday Next—A Biography*

I TRIED to focus on the striplight above me. I knew that *something* had happened but the night when Tamworth and I tackled Acheron Hades had, for the moment at least, been erased from my mind. I frowned, but only fractured images paraded themselves in my consciousness. I remembered shooting a little old lady three times and running down a fire escape. I had a dim recollection of blasting away at my own car and being shot in the arm. I looked at my arm and it was, indeed, tightly bound with a white bandage. Then I remembered being shot again—in the chest. I breathed in and out a couple of times and was relieved that no crackly rasp reached my ears. There was a nurse in the room who said a few words I couldn't decipher and smiled. I thought it odd and then lapsed once again into grateful slumber.

The next time I awoke it was evening and the room seemed colder. I was alone in a single hospital ward with seven empty beds. Just outside the door I could see an armed police officer on guard duty, while inside a vast quantity of flowers and cards vied for space. As I lay in bed the memories of the evening returned and tumbled out of my subconscious. I resisted them as long as I could but it was like holding back a flood. Everything that had happened that night came back in an instant. And as I remembered, I wept.

Within a week I was strong enough to get out of bed. Paige and Boswell had both dropped by, and even my mother had made the trip up from Swindon to see me. She told me she had painted the bedroom mauve, much to Dad's disappointment— and it was my fault for suggesting it. I didn't think I'd bother trying to explain. I was glad of any sympathy, of course, but my mind was elsewhere: there had been a monumental fiasco and someone was going to be responsible; and as the sole survivor of that disastrous evening, I was the strongest and only candidate. A small office was procured in the hospital and into it came Tamworth's old divisional commander, a man whom I had never met named Flanker, who seemed utterly devoid of humor and warmth. He brought with him a twin-cassette tape deck and several SO-1 senior operatives, who declined to give their names. I gave my testimony slowly and frankly, without emotion and as accurately as possible. Acheron's strange powers had been hinted at before, but even so Flanker was having trouble believing it.

"I've read Tamworth's file on Hades and it makes pretty weird reading, Miss Next," he said. "Tamworth was a bit of a loose cannon. SO-5 was his and his alone; Hades was more of an obsession than a job. From our initial inquiries it seems that he has been flaunting basic SpecOps guidelines. Contrary to popular belief, we *are* accountable to Parliament, albeit on a very discreet basis."

He paused for a moment and consulted his notes. He

looked at me and switched on the tape recorder. He identified the tape with the date, his name and mine, but only referred to the other operatives by numbers. That done, he drew up a chair and sat down.

"So what happened?"

I paused for a moment and then began, giving the story of my meeting with Tamworth right up until Buckett's hasty departure.

"I'm glad that someone seemed to have some sense," murmured one of the SO-1 agents. I ignored him.

"Tamworth and I entered the lobby of Styx's property," I told them. "We took the stairs and on the sixth floor we heard the shot. We stopped and listened but there was complete silence. Tamworth thought we had been rumbled."

"You *had* been rumbled," announced Flanker. "From the transcript of the tape we know that Snood spoke Hades' name out loud. Hades picked it up and reacted badly; he accused Styx of betraying him, retrieved the package and then killed his brother. Your surprise attack was no surprise. He *knew* you were both there."

I took a sip of water. If we had known, would we have retreated? I doubted it.

"Who was in front?"

"Tamworth. We edged slowly around the stairwell and looked onto the seventh-floor landing. It was empty apart from a little old lady who was facing the lift doors and muttering angrily to herself. Tamworth and I edged closer to Styx's open door and peered in. Styx was lying on the floor and we quickly searched the small apartment."

"We saw you on the surveillance video, Next," said one of the nameless operatives. "Your search was conducted well."

"Did you see Hades on the video?"

The same man coughed. They had been having trouble

coming to terms with Tamworth's report, but the video was un-equivocal. Hades' likeness had not shown up on it at all—just his voice.

"No," he said finally. "No, we did not."

"Tamworth cursed and walked back to the door," I continued. "It was then that I heard another shot."

I stopped for a moment, remembering the event carefully, yet not fully understanding what I had seen and felt. I remembered that my heart rate had dropped; everything had suddenly become crystal clear. I had felt no panic, just an overwhelming desire to see the job completed. I had seen Tamworth die but had felt no emotion; that was to come later.

"Miss Next?" asked Flanker, interrupting my thoughts.

"What? Sorry. Tamworth was hit. I walked over but a quick glance confirmed that the wound was incompatible with survival. I had to assume Hades was on the landing, so I took a deep breath and glanced out."

"What did you see?"

"I saw the little old lady, standing by the lift. I had heard no one run off downstairs, so assumed Hades was on the roof. I glanced out again. The old lady gave up waiting and walked past me on her way to the stairs, splashing through a puddle of water on the way. She *tut-tutted* as she passed Tamworth's body. I switched my attention back to the landing and to the stairwell that led to the roof. As I walked slowly toward the roof access, a doubt crept into my mind. I turned back to look at the little old lady, who had started off down the stairs and was grumbling about the infrequency of trams. Her footprints from the water caught my eye. Despite her small feet, the wet footprints were made by a man's-size shoe. I required no more proof. It was Rule Number Two: Acheron could lie in thought, deed, action and *appearance*. For the first time ever, I fired a gun in anger."

There was silence, so I continued.

"I saw at least three of the four shots hit the lumbering figure on the stairs. The old lady—or, at the very least, her image—tumbled out of sight and I walked cautiously up to the head of the stairwell. Her belongings were strewn all the way down the concrete steps with her shopping trolley on the landing below. Her groceries had spilled out and several cans of cat food were rolling slowly down the steps."

"So you hit her?"

"Definitely."

Flanker dug a small evidence bag out of his pocket and showed it to me. It contained three of my slugs, flattened as though they had been fired into the side of a tank.

When Flanker spoke again his voice was edged with disbelief.

"You say that Acheron disguised himself as an old lady?"

"Yes, sir," I replied, looking straight ahead.

"How did he do that?"

"I don't know, sir."

"How could a man over six foot six dress in a small woman's clothes?"

"I don't think he did it *physically;* I think he just projected what he *wanted* me to see."

"That sounds crazy."

"There's a lot we don't know about Hades."

"*That* I can agree with. The old lady's name was Mrs. Grimswold; we found her wedged up the chimney in Styx's apartment. It took three men to pull her out."

Flanker thought for a moment and let one of the other men ask a question.

"I'm interested to know why you were both armed with expanding ammunition," said one of the other officers, not looking at me but at the wall. He was short and dark and had an annoying twitch in his left eye. "Fluted hollow points and high-power loads. What were you planning to shoot? Buffalo?"

I took a deep breath.

"Hades was shot six times without any ill effects in '77, sir. Tamworth gave us expanded ammunition to use against him. He said he had SO-1 approval."

"Well, he didn't. If the papers get hold of this there will be hell to pay. SpecOps doesn't have a good relationship with the press, Miss Next. *The Mole* keeps on wanting access for one of its journalists. In this climate of accountability the politicians are leaning on us more and more. Expanding ammunition!—Shit, not even the Special Cavalry use those on Russians."

"That's what I said," I countered, "but having seen the state of these"—I shook the bag of flattened slugs—"I can see that Tamworth showed considerable restraint. We should have been carrying armor-piercing."

"Don't even think about it."

We had a break then. Flanker and the others vanished into the next room to argue while a nurse changed the dressing on my arm. I had been lucky; there had been no infection. I was thinking about Snood when they returned to resume the interview.

"As I walked carefully down the stairwell it was apparent that Acheron was now unarmed," I continued. "A nine-millimeter Beretta lay on the concrete steps next to a tin of custard powder. Of Acheron and the little old lady, there was no sign. On the landing I found a door to an apartment that had been pushed open with great force, shearing both hinge pins and the Chubb door bolt. I quickly questioned the occupants of the apartment but they were both insensible with laughter; it seemed Acheron had told them some sort of a joke about three anteaters in a pub, and I got no sense out of either of them."

One of the operatives was slowly shaking her head.

"What is it now?" I asked indignantly.

"Neither of the two people you describe remember you or Hades coming through their apartment. All they recall is the door bursting open for no apparent reason. How do you account for this?"

I thought for a moment.

"Obviously, I can't. Perhaps he has control over the weak-minded. We still only have a small idea of this man's powers."

"Hmm," replied the operative thoughtfully. "To tell the truth, the couple *did* try to tell us the joke about the anteaters. We wondered about that."

"It wasn't funny, was it?"

"Not at all. But they seemed to think it was."

I was beginning to feel angry and didn't like the way the interview was going. I collected my thoughts and continued, arguing to myself that the sooner this was over, the better.

"I looked slowly around the apartment and found an open window in the bedroom. It led out onto the fire escape, and as I peered out I could see Acheron's form running down the rusty steps four floors below. I knew I couldn't catch him, and it was then that I saw Snood. He stumbled out from behind a parked car and pointed his revolver at Hades as he dropped to the ground. At the time, I didn't understand what he was doing there."

"But you know now?"

My heart sank.

"He was there for *me*."

I felt tears well up and then fought them down. I was damned if I was going to start crying like a baby in front of this bunch, so I expertly turned the sniff into a cough.

"He was there because he knew what he had done," said

Flanker. "He knew that by speaking Hades' name out loud he had compromised you and Tamworth. We believe he was trying to make amends. At eighty-nine years of age, he was attempting to take on a man of superior strength, resolve and intellect. He was brave. He was stupid. Did you hear anything they said?"

"Not at first. I proceeded down the fire escape and heard Snood yell out 'Armed Police!' and 'On the ground!' By the time I reached the second floor, Hades had convinced Snood to give up his weapon and had shot him. I fired twice from where I was; Hades stumbled slightly but he soon recovered and sprinted for the nearest car. My car."

"What happened then?"

"I clambered down the ladder and dropped to the ground, landing badly on some trash and twisting my ankle. I looked up and saw Acheron punch in the window of my car and open the door. It didn't take him much more than a couple of seconds to tear off the steering lock and start the engine. The street was, I knew, a cul-de-sac. If Acheron wanted to escape it would have to be through me. I hobbled out into the middle of the road and waited. I started firing as soon as he pulled away from the curb. All my shots hit their mark. Two in the windscreen and one in the radiator grille. The car kept accelerating and I kept firing. A wing mirror and the other headlamp shattered. The car would hit me if it carried on as it was, but I didn't really care anymore. The operation was a mess. Acheron had killed Tamworth and Snood. He'd kill countless others if I didn't give it my all. With my last shot I hit his offside front tire and Acheron finally lost control. The car hit a parked Studebaker and turned over, bounced along on its roof and finally teetered to a stop barely three feet from where I stood. It rocked unsteadily for a moment and then was still, the water from the radiator mixing with the petrol that leaked onto the road."

I took another sip of water and looked at the assembled faces. They were following my every word, but the hardest part of it was yet to come.

"I reloaded, then pulled open the driver's door of the up-turned car. I had expected Acheron to tumble out in a heap, but Hades, not for the first time that night, had failed to live up to expectations. The car was empty."

"Did you see him escape?"

"No. I was just pondering this when I heard a familiar voice behind me. It was Buckett. He had returned.

" 'Where is he?' " Buckett yelled.

" 'I don't know,' I stammered in reply, checking the back of the car. 'He was here!—'

" 'Stay here!' shouted Buckett. 'I'm going to check around the front!'

"I was glad to be given orders and spared the burden of ini-tiative. But as Buckett turned to leave he shimmered slightly and I knew something was wrong. Without hesitating, I shot Buckett in the back three times. He collapsed in a heap—"

"You shot *another* operative?" said one of the SO-1 crowd with an incredulous tone. "In the *back*?" I ignored her.

"—only it wasn't Buckett, of course. The figure that picked itself up from the road to face me was Acheron. He rubbed his back where I had hit him and smiled benignly.

" 'That wasn't very sporting!' he said with a smile.

" 'I'm not here for the sport,' I assured him."

One of the SO-1 officers interrupted me.

"You seem to shoot a lot of people in the back, Next. Point-blank range with fluted slugs and he *survived*? I'm sorry, this is quite impossible!"

"It happened."

"She's lying!—" he said indignantly. "I've had just about enough of this!—"

But Flanker laid a hand on his arm to quieten him.

"Carry on, Miss Next."

I did.

" 'Hello, Thursday,' Hades said.

" 'Acheron,' I replied.

"He smiled.

" 'Tamworth's blood is getting cold on the concrete upstairs and it's all your fault. Just give me your gun and we can finish this all up and go home.'

"Hades reached out his hand and I felt a strong impulse to give him my weapon. But I had turned him down before when he was using more persuasive methods—when I was a student and he was a lecturer. Perhaps Tamworth knew I was strong enough to resist him; perhaps this was another reason he wanted me on his team. I don't know. Hades realized this and said instead in a genial manner:

" 'It's been a long time. Fifteen years, isn't it?'

" 'Summer of '69,' I replied grimly. I had little time for his games.

" 'Sixty-nine?' he asked, having thought about it for a moment. '*Sixteen* years, then. I seem to remember we were quite chummy.'

" 'You were a brilliant teacher, Acheron. I've not met an intellect to compare with yours. Why all this?'

" 'I could say the same about you,' returned Acheron with a smile. 'You were the only student of mine whom I could ever describe as *brilliant*, yet here you are, working as a glorified plod; a LiteraTec; a lackey for the Network. What brought you to SO-5?'

" 'Fate.'

"There was a pause. Acheron smiled.

" 'I always liked you, Thursday. You turned me down and, as we all know, there is nothing more seductive than resistance. I often wondered what I'd do if we met again. My star pupil, my protégée. We were nearly lovers.'

" 'I was *never* your protégée, Hades.'

"He smiled again.

" 'Have you ever wanted a new car?' he asked me quite suddenly.

"I did, of course, and said so.

" 'How about a large house? How about *two* large houses? In the country. With grounds. *And* a Rembrandt.'

"I saw what he was up to.

" 'If you want to buy my compliance, Acheron, you have to choose the right currency.'

"Acheron's face fell.

" 'You are strong, Thursday. Avarice works on most people.'

"I was angry now.

" 'What do you want with the *Chuzzlewit* manuscript, Acheron? To sell it?'

" 'Stealing and selling? How *common*,' he sneered. 'I'm sorry about your two friends. Hollow-points make quite a mess, don't they?'

"We stood there facing one another. It wouldn't be long before SO-14 were on the scene.

" 'On the ground,' I ordered him, 'or I swear I'll fire.'

"Hades was suddenly a blur of movement. There was a sharp crack and I felt something pluck at my upper arm. There was a sensation of warmth and I realized with a certain detached interest that I had been shot.

" 'Good try, Thursday. How about with the other arm?'

"Without knowing it, I had loosed off a shot in his direction. It was this that he was congratulating me on. I knew that I had thirty seconds at best before the loss of blood started to make me woozy. I transferred the automatic to my left hand and started to raise it again.

"Acheron smiled admiringly. He would have continued his brutal game for as long as he could but the distant wail of police sirens hastened him into action. He shot me once in the chest and left me for dead."

The SO-1 officials shuffled slightly as I concluded my story. They swapped looks, but I had no interest in whether they believed me or not. Hades had left me for dead but my time wasn't yet up. The copy of *Jane Eyre* that Tamworth had given me had saved my life. I had placed it in my breast pocket; Hades' slug had penetrated to the back cover but had not gone through. Broken ribs, a collapsed lung and a bruise to die for—but I had survived. It was luck, or fate, or whatever the hell you want to make of it.

"That's it?" asked Flanker.

I nodded.

"That's it."

It wasn't it, of course, there was a lot more, but none of it was relevant to them. I hadn't told them how Hades had used Filbert Snood's death to grind me down emotionally; that was how he managed to get the first shot in.

"That's about all we need to know, Miss Next. You can return to SO-27 as soon as you are able. I would remind you that you are bound by the confidentiality clause you signed. A misplaced word could have very poor consequences. Is there anything you would like to add yourself?"

I took a deep breath.

"I know a lot of this sounds far-fetched, but it is the truth. I am the first witness who has seen what Hades will do to survive. Whoever pursues him in the future must be fully aware of what he is capable of.'

Flanker leaned back in his chair. He looked at the man with the twitch, who nodded in return.

"Academic, Miss Next."

"What do you mean?"

"Hades is dead. SO-14 are not complete losers despite a certain trigger-happiness. They pursued him up the M4 that night until he crashed his car by junction twelve. It rolled down an embankment and burst into flames. We didn't want to tell you until we'd heard your evidence."

The news hit me squarely and hard. Revenge had been a prime emotion keeping me together over the past two weeks. Without a burning desire to see Hades punished, I might not even have made it at all. Without Acheron all my testimony would be left unproven. I hadn't expected it all to be believed, but at least I could look forward to being vindicated when others came across him.

"Sorry?" I asked suddenly.

"I said that Hades was dead."

"No he isn't," I said without thinking.

Flanker supposed that my reaction was the effect of traumatic shock.

"It might be difficult to come to terms with, but he is. Burned almost beyond recognition. We had to identify him by dental records. He still had Snood's pistol with him."

"The *Chuzzlewit* manuscript?"

"No sign—we think destroyed as well."

I looked down. The whole operation had been a fiasco.

"Miss Next," said Flanker, standing up and laying a hand on my shoulder, "you will be pleased to hear that none of this will be published below SO-8. You can return to your unit without a blemish on your record. There were errors, but none of us have any idea how anything might have turned out given a different set of circumstances. As for us, you won't be seeing us again.'

He turned off the cassette recorder, wished me good health

and walked out of the room. The other officers joined him, except for the man with the twitch. He waited until his colleagues were out of earshot then whispered to me:

"I think your testimony is bullshit, Miss Next. The service can ill afford to lose the likes of Fillip Tamworth."

"Thank you."

"What for?"

"For telling me his first name."

The man moved to say something, thought the better of it and then left.

I got up from the table in the impromptu interview room and stared out of the window. It was warm and sunny outside and the trees swayed gently in the breeze; the world looked as though it had little room for people like Hades. I allowed the thoughts of the night to come back again. The part I hadn't told them was about Snood. Acheron had talked some more that night. He had indicated the tired and worn body of Snood and said:

"Filbert asked me to say he was sorry."

"That's Filbert's father!—" I corrected him.

"No," he chuckled. "That was Filbert."

I looked at Snood again. He was lying on his back with his eyes open and the likeness was unmistakable, despite the sixty-year age gap.

"Oh my God, no! Filbert? Was that him?"

Acheron seemed to be enjoying himself.

" 'Unavoidably detained' is a ChronoGuard euphemism for a time aggregation, Thursday. I'm surprised you didn't know that. Caught outside the herenow. Sixty years piled onto him in less than a minute. It's little surprise he didn't want you to see him."

There hadn't been any girl in Tewkesbury after all. I had

heard about time dilations and temporal instabilities from my father. In the world of the Event, the Cone and the Horizon, Filbert Snood had been unavoidably detained. The tragedy of it was, he never felt he could tell me. It was then, as I hit my lowest, that Acheron had turned and fired. It was as he had planned it.

I walked slowly back to my room and sat on the bed feeling utterly dejected. Tears come easily to me when no one is about. I wept copiously for about five minutes and felt a great deal better, blew my nose noisily then switched on the television as a distraction. I rattled through the channels until I chanced across the Toad News Network. It was more about the Crimea, of course.

"Still on the subject of the Crimea," announced the anchorwoman, "the Goliath Corporation Special Weapons Division has unveiled the latest weapon in the struggle against the Russian aggressors. It is hoped that the new Ballistic Plasma Energy Rifle—code-named 'Stonk'—will be the decisive weapon to change the tide of the war. Our defense correspondent James Backbiter takes us through it."

The scene changed to a close-up of an exotic-looking weapon handled by a soldier in military SpecOps uniform.

"This is the new Stonk plasma rifle, unveiled today by the Goliath Special Weapons Division," announced Backbiter, standing next to the soldier on what was obviously a test range. "We can't tell you very much about it for obvious reasons, but we can show its effectiveness and report that it uses a bolt of concentrated energy to destroy armor and personnel up to a mile away."

I watched in horror as the soldier demonstrated the new weapon. Invisible bolts of energy tore into the target tank with the power of ten of our howitzers. It was like an artillery piece in the palm of your hand. The barrage ended and Backbiter asked a colonel a couple of obviously posed questions as soldiers paraded with the new weapon in the background.

"When do you suppose the frontline troops will be issued with Stonk?"

"The first weapons are being shipped now. The rest will be supplied just as soon as we can set up the necessary factories."

"And finally, its effect on the conflict?"

A small amount of emotion flickered on the colonel's face.

"I predict Stonk will have the Russians suing for peace within a month."

"Oh, *shit*," I murmured out loud. I'd heard this particular phrase many times during my time in the military. It had supplanted the hoary old "over by Christmas" for sheer fatuousness. It had always, without exception, been followed by an appalling loss of life.

Even before the first deployment of the new weapon, its mere existence had upset the balance of power in the Crimea. No longer keen on a withdrawal, the English government was trying to negotiate a surrender of all Russian troops. The Russians were having none of it. The UN had demanded that both sides return to the talks in Budapest, but it had all stalled; the Imperial Russian Army had dug themselves in against the expected onslaught. Earlier in the day the Goliath Special Weapons spokesman had been instructed to appear before Parliament to explain the delay of the new weapons, as they were now a month behind schedule.

A screech of tires roused me from my thoughts. I looked up. In the middle of the hospital room was a brightly painted sports car. I blinked twice but it didn't vanish. There was no earthly reason why it should be in the room or even any evidence as to how it got there, the door being only wide enough for a bed, but there it was. I could smell the exhaust and hear the engine ticking over, but for some reason I did not find it at all unusual. The occupants were staring at me. The driver was a woman in her midthirties who looked sort of familiar.

"Thursday!—" cried the driver with a sense of urgency in her voice.

I frowned. It all *looked* real and I was definitely sure I had seen the driver somewhere before. The passenger, a young man in a suit whom I didn't know, waved cheerily.

"He didn't die!" said the woman, as though she wouldn't have long to speak. "The car crash was a blind! Men like Acheron don't die that easily! Take the LiteraTec job in Swindon!"

"Swindon?—" I echoed. I thought I had escaped that town—it afforded me a few too many painful memories.

I opened my mouth to speak but there was another screech of rubber and the car departed, folding up rather than fading out until there was nothing left but the echo of the tires and the faint smell of exhaust. Pretty soon that had gone too, leaving no clue as to its strange appearance. I held my head in my hands. The driver had been *very* familiar. It had been me.

My arm was almost healed by the time the internal inquiry circulated its findings. I wasn't permitted to read it but I wasn't bothered. If I had known what was in it, I would probably only have been more dissatisfied and annoyed than I was already. Boswell had visited me again to tell me I had been awarded six months' sick leave before returning, but it didn't help. I didn't want to return to the LiteraTec's office; at least, not in London.

"What are you going to do?" asked Paige. She had turned up to help me pack before I was discharged from the hospital.

"Six months' leave can be a long time if you've got no hobbies or family or boyfriend," she went on. She could be very direct at times.

"I have lots of hobbies."

"Name *one*."

"Painting."

"Really?"

"Yes, really. I'm currently painting a seascape."

"How long has it taken you so far?"

"About seven years."

"It must be very good."

"It's a piece of crap."

"Seriously, though," said Turner, who had become closer to me in these past few weeks than during the entire time we had known each other, "what are you going to do?"

I handed her the SpecOps 27 gazette; it outlined postings around the country. Paige looked at the entry that I had circled in red ink.

"Swindon?"

"Why not? It's home."

"Home it might be," replied Turner, "but weird it *definitely* is." She tapped the job description. "It's only for an operative— you've been acting inspector for over three years!"

"Three and a half. It doesn't matter. I'm going."

I didn't tell Paige the real reason. It could have been a coincidence, of course, but the advice from the driver of the car had been most specific: *Take the LiteraTec job in Swindon!* Perhaps the vision had been real after all; the gazette with the job offer had arrived *after* the visitation by the car. If it had been right about the job in Swindon, it stood to reason that perhaps the news about Hades was also correct. Without any further thought, I had applied. I couldn't tell Paige about the car; if she had known, friendship notwithstanding, she would have reported me to Boswell. Boswell would have spoken to Flanker and all sorts of unpleasantness might have happened. I was getting quite good at concealing the truth, and I felt happier now than I had for months.

"We'll miss you in the department, Thursday."

"It'll pass."

"*I'll* miss you."

"Thanks, Paige, I appreciate it. I'll miss you too."

We hugged, she told me to keep in touch, and left the room, pager bleeping.

I finished packing and thanked the nursing staff, who gave me a brown paper parcel as I was about to leave.

"What's this?" I asked.

"It belonged to whoever saved your life that night."

"What do you mean?"

"A passerby attended to you before the medics arrived; the wound in your arm was plugged and they wrapped you in their coat to keep you warm. Without their intervention you might well have bled to death."

Intrigued, I opened the package. Firstly, there was a handkerchief that despite several washings still bore the stains of my own blood. There was an embroidered monogram in the corner that read EFR. Secondly the parcel contained a jacket, a sort of casual evening coat that might have been very popular in the middle of the last century. I searched the pockets and found a bill from a milliner. It was made out to one Edward Fairfax Rochester, Esq., and was dated 1833. I sat down heavily on the bed and stared at the two articles of clothing and the bill. Ordinarily I would not have believed that Rochester could have torn himself from the pages of *Jane Eyre* and come to my aid that night; such a thing is, of course, quite impossible. I might have dismissed the whole thing as a ludicrously complicated prank had it not been for one thing: Edward Rochester and I had met once before . . .

7.

The Goliath Corporation

. . . No one would argue that we owe a debt of gratitude
to the Goliath Corporation. They helped us to rebuild after the Second War and it should not be forgotten. Of
late, however, it seems as though the Goliath Corporation is falling far short of its promises of fairness and altruism. We are finding ourselves now in the unfortunate
position of continuing to pay back a debt that has long
since been paid—with interest . . .

Speech to Parliament by English Goliathsceptic
SAMUEL PRING

I was in the SpecOps Memorial Cemetery in Highgate looking at Snood's headstone. It read:

Filbert R. Snood
A fine operative who gave his
years in the line of duty.
Time waits for no man
SO-12 & SO-5
1953–1985

They say the job ages you—and it had aged Filbert a lot.
Perhaps it had been for the best when he didn't call after the accident. It couldn't have worked and the breakup when it

came—as it surely would—might have been too painful. I placed a small stone atop his headstone and bid him adieu.

"You were lucky," said a voice. I turned and saw a short man in an expensive suit sitting on the bench opposite.

"I'm sorry?" I asked, taken aback by the intrusion into my thoughts. The small man smiled and stared at me intently.

"I'd like to speak to you about Acheron, Miss Next."

"It's one of the rivers that flow to the underworld," I told him. "Try the local library under Greek mythology."

"I was referring to the person."

I stared at him for a moment, trying to figure out who he was. He wore a small porkpie hat balanced on top of a rounded head that had been crew cut like a tennis ball. His features were sharp, his lips thin, and he was not what you'd call an attractive-looking human being. He sported heavy gold jewelery and a diamond tiepin that twinkled like a star. His patent-leather brogues were covered in white spats and a gold watch chain dangled from his waistcoat pocket. He was not alone. A young man also in a dark suit with a bulge where a pistol should be was standing next to him. I had been so wrapped up in my own thoughts I hadn't noticed them approach. I figured they were SpecOps Internal Affairs or something; I guessed that Flanker and Co. weren't finished with me yet.

"Hades is dead," I replied simply, unwilling to get embroiled.

"You don't seem to think so."

"Yeah, well, I've been given six months off due to work-related stress. The shrink reckons I'm suffering from false memory syndrome and hallucinations. I shouldn't believe anything I say, if I were you—and that includes what I just told you."

The small man smiled again, displaying a large gold tooth.

"I don't believe you're suffering from stress at all, Miss Next. I think you're as sane as I am. If someone who survived the

Crimea, the police and then eight years of tricky LiteraTec work came to me and told me that Hades was still alive, I'd listen to them."

"And who might you be?"

He handed me a gold-edged card with the dark blue Goliath Corporation logo embossed on it.

"The name's Schitt," he replied. "Jack Schitt."

I shrugged. The card told me he was head of Goliath's internal security service, a shadowy organization that was well outside government; by constitutional decree they were answerable to no one. The Goliath Corporation had honorary members in both houses and financial advisers at the Treasury. The judiciary was well represented with Goliath people on the selection panel for High Court judges, and most major universities had a Goliath overseer living within the faculty. No one ever noticed how much they influenced the running of the country, which perhaps shows how good at it they were. Yet, for all Goliath's outward benevolence, there were murmurs of dissent over the Corporation's continued privilege. Their public servants were unelected by the people or the government and their activities enshrined in statute. It was a brave politician who dared to voice disquiet.

I sat next to him on the bench. He dismissed his henchman.

"So what's your interest in Hades, Mr. Schitt?"

"I want to know if he's alive or dead."

"You read the coroner's report, didn't you?"

"It only told me that a man of Hades' height, stature and teeth was incinerated in a car. Hades has got out of worse scrapes than that. I read *your* report; *much* more interesting. Quite why those clowns in SO-1 dismissed it out of hand I have no idea. With Tamworth dead you're the only operative who knows anything about him. I'm not really concerned about whose fault it was that night. What I want to know is this: What was Acheron going to do with the manuscript of *Martin Chuzzlewit*?"

"Extortion, perhaps?" I ventured.

"Possibly. Where is it now?"

"Wasn't it with him?"

"No," replied Schitt evenly. "In your testimony you said he took it with him in a leather case. No trace was found of it in the burned-out car. If he *did* survive, so did the manuscript."

I looked at him blankly, wondering where all this was going.

"He must have passed it to an accomplice, then."

"Possibly. The manuscript could be worth up to five million on the black market, Miss Next. A lot of money, don't you think?"

"What are you suggesting?" I asked sharply, my temper rising.

"Nothing at all; but your testimony and Acheron's corpse don't really add up, do they? You said that you shot him after he killed the young officer."

"His name was Snood," I said pointedly.

"Whoever. But the burned corpse had no gunshot wounds despite the many times you shot him when he was disguised as Buckett or the old woman."

"Her name was Mrs. Grimswold."

I stared at him. Schitt continued.

"I saw the flattened slugs. You would have got the same effect if you had fired them into a wall."

"If you have a point, why don't you get to it?"

Schitt unscrewed the cap of a Thermos flask and offered it to me. I refused; he poured himself a drink and continued:

"I think you know more than you say you do. We only have your word for the events of that night. Tell me, Miss Next, what was Hades planning to use the manuscript for?"

"I told you: I have no idea."

"Then why are you going to work as a LiteraTec in Swindon?"

"It was all I could get."

"That's not true. Your work has been consistently assessed above average and your record states that you haven't been back to Swindon in ten years despite your family living there. A note appended to your file speaks of 'romantic tensions'. Man trouble in Swindon?"

"None of your business."

"In my line of work I find there is very little that *isn't* my business. There are a host of other things a woman with your talents could do, but to go back to Swindon? Something tells me you have another motive."

"Does it really say all that in my file?"

"It does."

"What color are my eyes?"

Schitt ignored me and took a sip of coffee.

"Colombian. The best. You think Hades is alive, Next. I think you have an idea where he is and I'm willing to guess that he is in Swindon and that's why you're going there. Am I correct?"

I looked him straight in the eye.

"No. I'm just going home to sort myself out."

Jack Schitt remained unconvinced.

"I don't believe there is such a thing as stress, Next. Just weak people and strong people. Only strong people survive men like Hades. You're a strong person."

He paused.

"If you change your mind, you can call me. But be warned. I'll be keeping a close eye on you."

"Do as you will, Mr. Schitt, but I've got a question for you."

"Yes?"

"What's *your* interest in Hades?"

Jack Schitt smiled again.

"I'm afraid that's classified, Miss Next. Good-day."

He tipped his hat, rose and left. A black Ford with smoked-glass windows pulled up outside the cemetery and drove him quickly away.

I sat and thought. I had lied to the police psychiatrist in saying I was fit for work and lied to Jack Schitt in saying that I wasn't. If Goliath was interested in Hades and the *Chuzzlewit* manuscript, it could only be for financial gain. The Goliath Corporation was to altruism what Genghis Khan was to soft furnishings. Money came first to Goliath and nobody trusted them farther than they could throw them. They may have rebuilt England after the Second War, they may have reestablished the economy. But sooner or later the renewed nation had to stand on its own and Goliath was seen now as less of a benevolent uncle than a despotic stepfather.

8.

Airship to Swindon

. . . There is no point in expending good money on the pursuit of an engine that can power aircraft without propellers. What is wrong with airships anyway? They have borne mankind aloft for over a hundred relatively accident-free years and I see no reason to impugn their popularity . . .

Congresswoman Kelly, arguing against parliamentary funds for the development of a new form of propulsion, August 1972

I took a small twenty-seater airship to Swindon. It was only half-full and a brisk tailwind allowed us to make good time. The train would have been cheaper, but like many people I love to fly by gasbag. I had, when I was a little girl, been taken on an immense clipper-class airship to Africa by my parents. We had flown slowly across France, over the Eiffel Tower, past Lyon, stopped at Nice, then traveled across the sparkling Mediterranean, waving at fishermen and passengers in ocean liners who waved back. We had stopped at Cairo after circling the Pyramids with infinite grace, the captain expertly maneuvering the leviathan with the skillful use of the twelve fully orientable propellers. We had continued up the Nile three days later to Luxor, where we joined a cruise ship for the return to the coast. Here we boarded the *Ruritania* for the return to England, by way of the Straits of Gibraltar and the Bay of Biscay. Little wonder that I tried to return to the fond memories of my childhood as often as I could.

"Magazine, ma'am?" asked a steward.

I declined. In-flight airship magazines were always dull, and I was quite happy just to watch the English landscape slide past beneath me. It was a glorious sunny day, and the airship droned past the small puffy clouds that punctuated the sky like a flock of aerial sheep. The Chilterns had risen to meet us and then dropped away as we swept past Wallingford, Didcot and Wantage. The Uffington White Horse drifted below me, bringing back memories of picnics and courting. Landen and I had often been there.

"Corporal Next?—" inquired a familiar voice. I turned to find a middle-aged man standing in the aisle, a half-smile on his face. I knew instantly who it was, even though we had not met for twelve years.

"Major!—" I responded, stiffening slightly in the presence of someone who had once been my superior officer. His name was Phelps, and I had been under his command the day the Light Armored Brigade had advanced into the Russian guns in error as they sought to repulse an attack on Balaclava. I had been the driver of the armored personnel carrier under Phelps; it had not been a happy time.

The airship started the slow descent into Swindon.

"How have you been, Next?" he asked, our past association dictating the way in which we spoke to one another.

"I've been well, sir. Yourself?"

"Can't complain." He laughed. "Well, I could, but it wouldn't do any good. The damn fools made me a colonel, dontcha know it."

"Congratulations," I said, slightly uneasily.

The steward asked us to fasten our seat belts and Phelps sat down next to me and snapped on the buckle. He carried on talking in a slightly lower voice.

"I'm a bit concerned about the Crimea."

"Who isn't?" I countered, wondering if Phelps had changed his politics since the last time we had met.

"Quite. It's these UN johnnies poking their noses where they're not welcome. Makes all those lives seem wasted if we give it back now."

I sighed. His politics *hadn't* changed and I didn't want an argument. I had wanted the war finished almost as soon as I got out there. It didn't fit into my idea of what a *just* war should be. Pushing Nazis out of Europe had been *just*. The fight over the Crimean Peninsula was nothing but xenophobic pride and misguided patriotism.

"How's the hand?" I asked.

Phelps showed me a lifelike left hand. He rotated the wrist and then wiggled the fingers. I was impressed.

"Remarkable, isn't it?" he said. "They take the impulses from a sensor thingummy strapped to the muscles in the upper arm. If I'd lost the blasted thing above the elbow I'd have looked a proper Charlie."

He paused for a moment and returned to his first subject.

"I'm a bit concerned that public pressure might have the government pulling the plug before the offensive."

"Offensive?"

Colonel Phelps smiled.

"Of course. I have friends higher up who tell me it's only a matter of days before the first shipment of the new plasma rifles arrives. Do you think the Russians will be able to defend themselves against Stonk?"

"Frankly, no; that is unless they have their own version."

"Not a chance. Goliath is the most advanced weapons company in the world. Believe me, I'm hoping as much as the next man that we never have to use it, but Stonk is the high ground this conflict has been waiting for."

He rummaged in his briefcase and pulled out a leaflet.

"I'm touring England giving pro-Crimea talks. I'd like you to come along."

"I don't really think—" I began, taking the leaflet anyway.

"Nonsense!" replied Colonel Phelps. "As a healthy and successful veteran of the campaign it is your duty to give voice to those that made the ultimate sacrifice. If we give the peninsula back, every single one of those lives will have been lost in vain."

"I think, sir, that those lives have already been lost and no decision we can make in any direction can change that."

He pretended not to hear and I lapsed into silence. Colonel Phelps's rabid support of the conflict had been his way of dealing with the disaster. The order was given to charge against what we were told would be a "token resistance" but turned out to be massed Russian field artillery. Phelps had ridden the APC on the outside until the Russians opened up with everything they had; a shell-burst had taken his lower arm off and peppered his back with shrapnel. We had loaded him up with as many other soldiers as we could, driving back to the English lines with the carrier a mound of groaning humanity. I had gone back into the carnage against orders, driving among the shattered armor looking for survivors. Of the seventy-six APCs and light tanks that advanced into the Russian guns, only two vehicles returned. Out of the 534 soldiers involved, 51 survived, only 8 of them completely uninjured. One of the dead had been Anton Next, my brother. Disaster doesn't even *begin* to describe it.

Fortunately for me the airship docked soon after and I was able to avoid Colonel Phelps in the airfield lounge. I picked up my case from baggage retrieval and stayed locked in the ladies' until I thought he had gone. I tore his leaflet into tiny pieces and flushed them down the toilet. The airfield lounge was empty when I came out. It was bigger than was required for the amount of traffic that came to town; an off-white elephant that reflected the dashed hopes of Swindon's town planners. The concourse outside was similarly deserted except for two students holding an anti-Crimea war banner. They had heard of Phelps's arrival and hoped that they could turn him from his prowar campaigning. They had two chances: fat and slim.

They looked at me and I turned quickly away. If they knew who Phelps was, they might quite conceivably know who I was as well. I looked around the empty pickup point. I had spoken on the phone to Victor Analogy—the head of the Swindon LiteraTecs—and he had offered to send a car to pick me up. It hadn't arrived. It was hot, so I removed my jacket. A looped recording came over the Tannoy exhorting nonexistent drivers not to park in the deserted white zone, and a bored-looking worker came by and returned a few trolleys. I sat down next to a Will-Speak machine at the far end of the concourse. The last time I was in Swindon the airship park had been simply a grass field with a rusty mast. I guessed that much else had changed too.

I waited five minutes, then stood and paced impatiently up and down. The Will-Speak machine—officially known as a Shakespeare Soliloquy Vending Automaton—was of *Richard III*. It was a simple box, with the top half glazed and inside a realistic mannequin visible from the waist up in suitable attire. The machine would dispense a short snippet of Shakespeare for ten pence. They hadn't been manufactured since the thirties and were now something of a rarity; Baconic vandalism and a lack of trained maintenance were together hastening their demise.

I dug out a ten-pence piece and inserted it. There was a gentle whirring and clicking from within as the machine wound itself up to speed. There had been a *Hamlet* version on the corner of Commercial Road when I was small. My brother and I had pestered our mother for loose change and listened to the mannequin refer to things we couldn't really understand. It told us of "the undiscovered country." My brother, in his childish naïveté, had said he wanted to visit such a place, and he did, seventeen years later, in a mad dash sixteen hundred miles from home, the only sound the roar of engines and the *crump-crump-crump* of the Russian guns.

Was ever woman in this humor wooed? asked the mannequin, rolling its eyes crazily as it stuck one finger in the air and lurched from side to side.

Was ever woman in this humor won?

It paused for effect.

I'll have her, but I'll not keep her long . . .

"Excuse me?—"

I looked up. One of the students had walked up and touched me on the arm. He wore a peace button in his lapel and had a pair of pince-nez glasses perched precariously on his large nose.

"You're Next, aren't you?"

"Next for what?"

"Corporal Next, Light Armored Brigade."

I rubbed my brow.

"I'm not here with the colonel. It was a coincidence."

"I don't believe in coincidences."

"Neither do I. That's a coincidence, isn't it?"

The student looked at me oddly as his girlfriend joined him. He told her who I was.

"You were the one who *went back*," she marveled, as though I were a rare stuffed parakeet. "It was against a direct order. They were going to court-martial you."

6.

Jane Eyre: A Short Excursion into the Novel

Outside Styx's apartment was not the first time Rochester and I had met, nor would it be the last. We first encountered each other at Haworth House in Yorkshire when my mind was young and the barrier between reality and make-believe had not yet hardened into the shell that cocoons us in adult life. The barrier was soft, pliable and, for a moment, thanks to the kindness of a stranger and the power of a good storytelling voice, I made the short journey—and returned.

THURSDAY NEXT
—*A Life in SpecOps*

I T WAS 1958. My uncle and aunt—who even then seemed old—had taken me up to Haworth House, the old Brontë residence, for a visit. I had been learning about William Thackeray at school, and since the Brontës were contemporaries of his it seemed a good opportunity to further my interest in these matters. My Uncle Mycroft was giving a lecture at Bradford University on his remarkable mathematical work regarding game theory, the most practical side of which allowed one to win at Snakes and Ladders every time. Bradford was near to Haworth, so a combined visit seemed a good idea.

We were led around by the guide, a fluffy woman in her sixties with steel-rimmed spectacles and an angora cardigan who steered the tourists around the rooms with an abrupt manner, as though she felt that none of them could possibly know as much as she did, but would grudgingly assist to lift them from the depths of their own ignorance. Near the end of the tour, when thoughts had turned to picture postcards and ice cream, the prize exhibit in the form of the original manuscript of *Jane Eyre* greeted the tired museum-goers.

Although the pages had browned with age and the black ink faded to a light brown, the writing could still be read by the practiced eye, the fine spidery longhand flowing across the page in a steady stream of inventive prose. A page was turned every two days, allowing the more regular and fanatical Brontë followers to read the novel as originally drafted.

The day that I came to the Brontë museum the manuscript was open at the point where Jane and Rochester first meet; a chance encounter by a stile.

"—which makes it one of the greatest romantic novels ever written," continued the fluffy yet lofty guide in her oft-repeated monologue, ignoring several hands that had been raised to ask pertinent questions.

"The character of Jane Eyre, a tough and resilient heroine, drew her apart from the usual heroines of the time, and Rochester, a forbidding yet basically good man, also broke the mold with his flawed character's dour humor. *Jane Eyre* was written by Charlotte Brontë in 1847 under the pseudonym Currer Bell. Thackeray described it as 'the master work of a great genius.' We continue on now to the shop where you may purchase picture postcards, commemorative plates, small plastic imitation Heathcliffs and other mementos of your visit. Thank you for—"

One of the group had their hand up and was determined to have his say.

"Excuse me," began the young man in an American accent.

A muscle in the tour guide's cheek momentarily twitched as she forced herself to listen to someone else's opinion.

"Yes?" she inquired with icy politeness.

"Well," continued the young man, "I'm kinda new to this whole Brontë thing, but I had trouble with the end of *Jane Eyre*."

"Trouble?"

"Yeah. Like Jane leaves Thornfield Hall and hitches up with her cousins, the Riverses."

"I know who her cousins are, young man."

"Yeah, well, she agrees to go with this drippy St. John Rivers guy but not to marry him, they depart for India and that's the end of the book? Hello? What about a happy ending? What happens to Rochester and his nutty wife?"

The guide glowered.

"And what would you prefer? The forces of good and evil fighting to the death in the corridors of Thornfield Hall?"

"That's not what I meant," continued the young man, beginning to get slightly annoyed. "It's just that the book cries out for a strong resolution, to tie up the narrative and finish the tale. I get the feeling from what she wrote that she just kinda pooped out."

The guide stared at him for a moment through her steel-rimmed glasses and wondered why the visitors couldn't behave just that little bit more like sheep. Sadly, his point was a valid one; she herself had often pondered the diluted ending, wishing, like millions of others, that circumstances had allowed Jane and Rochester to marry after all.

"Some things will never be known," she replied noncommittally. Charlotte is no longer with us so the question is abstract. What we have to study and enjoy is what she has left us. The sheer exuberance of the writing easily outweighs any of its small shortcomings."

The young American nodded and the small crowd moved

on, my aunt and uncle among them. I hung back until only I
and a single Japanese tourist were left in the room; I then tried
to look at the original manuscript on tiptoe. It was tricky, as I
was small for my age.

"Would you like me to read it for you?" said a kindly voice
close at hand. It was the Japanese tourist. She smiled at me and
I thanked her for her trouble.

She checked that no one was around, unfolded her reading
glasses and started to speak. She spoke excellent English and
had a fine reading voice; the words peeled off the page into my
imagination as she spoke.

> . . . In those days I was young and all sorts of fancies bright
> and dark tenanted my mind; the memories of nursery sto-
> ries were there among other rubbish; and when they re-
> curred, maturing youth added to them a vigor and
> vividness beyond what childhood could give . . .

I closed my eyes and a thin chill suddenly filled the air
around me. The tourist's voice was clear now, as though speaking in the open air, and when I opened my eyes the museum
had gone. In its place was a country lane of another place entirely. It was a fine winter's evening and the sun was just dip-
ping below the horizon. The air was perfectly still, the color
washed from the scene. Apart from a few birds that stirred occasionally in the hedge, no movement punctuated the starkly
beautiful landscape. I shivered as I saw my own breath in the
crisp air, zipped up my jacket and regretted that I had left my
hat and mittens on the peg downstairs. As I looked about I
could see that I was not alone. Barely ten feet away a young
woman, dressed in a cloak and bonnet, was sitting on a stile
watching the moon that had just risen behind us. When she

turned I could see that her face was plain and outwardly unremarkable, yet possessed of a bearing that showed inner strength and resolve. I stared at her intently with a mixture of feelings. I had realized not long ago that I myself was no beauty, and even at the age of nine had seen how the more attractive children gained favor more easily. But here in that young woman I could see how those principles could be inverted. I felt myself stand more upright and clench my jaw in subconscious mimicry of her pose.

I was just thinking about asking her where the museum had gone when a sound in the lane made us both turn. It was an approaching horse, and the young woman seemed startled for a moment. The lane was narrow, and I stepped back to give the horse room to pass. As I waited, a large black-and-white dog rushed along the hedge, nosing the ground for anything of interest. The dog ignored the figure on the stile but stopped dead in his tracks when he saw me. His tail wagged enthusiastically and he bounded over, sniffing me inquisitively, his hot breath covering me in a warm cloak and his whiskers tickling my cheek. I giggled and the dog wagged his tail even harder. He had sniffed along this hedge during every single reading of the book for over 130 years, but had never come across anything that smelled so, well . . . *real*. He licked me several times with great affection. I giggled again and pushed him away, so he ran off to find a stick.

From subsequent readings of the book I was later to realize that the dog Pilot had never had the opportunity to fetch a stick, his appearances in the book being all too few, so he was obviously keen to take the opportunity when it presented itself. He must have known, almost instinctively, that the little girl who had momentarily appeared at the bottom of page eighty-one was unfettered by the rigidity of the narrative. He knew that he could stretch the boundaries of the story a small amount, sniffing along one side of the lane or the other since it wasn't specified; but if the text stated that he had to bark or run around or jump up, then he was obliged to comply. It was a long and repetitive existence, which made the rare appearances of people like me that much more enjoyable.

I looked up and noticed that the horse and rider had just passed the young woman. The rider was a tall man with distinguished features and a careworn face, bent into a frown by some musings that seemed to envelop him in thoughtful detachment. He had not seen my small form and the safe route down the lane led right through where I was standing; opposite me was a treacherous slab of ice. Within a few moments the horse was upon me, the heavy hooves thumping the hard ground, the hot breath from its velvety nose blowing on my face. Suddenly, the rider, perceiving the small girl in his path for the first time, uttered: "What the deuce—" and reined his horse rapidly to the left, away from me but onto the slippery ice. The horse lost its footing and went crashing to the ground. I took a step back, mortified at the accident I had caused. The horse struggled to gain a footing and the dog, hearing the commotion, returned to the scene, presented me with a stick and then barked at the fallen group excitedly, his deep growl echoing in the still evening. The young woman approached the fallen man with grave concern on her face. She was eager to be of assistance and spoke for the first time.

"Are you injured, sir?"

The rider muttered something incomprehensible and ignored her completely.

"Can I do anything?" she asked again.

"You must just stand on one side," answered the rider in a gruff tone as he rose shakily to his feet. The young woman

. . . Shine out, fair sun, till I have bought a glass, that I might see my shadow, as I pass.

There was a clicking and whirring and then the mannequin stopped abruptly, lifeless again until the next coin.

"Beautiful day," I commented once we were under way.

"Every day is a beautiful day, Miss Next. The name's Stoker—"

He pulled out onto the Stratton bypass.

"—SpecOps-17: Vampire and Werewolf Disposal Operations. Suckers and biters, they call us. My friends call me Spike. You," he added with a broad grin, "can call me Spike."

By way of explanation he tapped a mallet and stake that were clipped to the mesh partition.

"What do they call you, Miss Next?"

"Thursday."

"Pleased to meet you, Thursday."

He proffered a huge hand that I shook gratefully. I liked him immediately. He leaned against the door pillar to get the best out of the cooling breeze and tapped a beat out on the steering wheel. A recent scratch on his neck oozed a small amount of blood.

"You're bleeding," I observed.

Spike wiped it away with his hand.

"It's nothing. He gave me a bit of a struggle!—"

I looked in the back seat again. The wolf was sitting down, scratching its ear with a hind leg.

"—but I'm immunized against lycanthropy. Mr. Meakle just won't take his medication. Will you, Mr. Meakle?"

The wolf pricked up its ears as the last vestige of the human within him remembered his name. He started to pant in the heat. Spike went on:

"His neighbors called. All the cats in the neighborhood had gone missing; I found him rummaging in the bins behind Smiley-Burger. He'll be in for treatment, morph back and be on the streets again by Friday. He has rights, they tell me. What's your posting?"

"I'm . . . ah . . . joining SpecOps-27."

Spike laughed loudly again.

"A LiteraTec!? Always nice to meet someone as under-funded as I am. Some good faces in that office. Your chief is Victor Analogy. Don't be fooled by the gray hairs—he's as sharp as a knife. The others are all A-one Ops. A bit shiny-arsed and a mite too smart for me, but there you go. Where am I taking you?"

"The Finis Hotel."

"First time in Swindon?"

"Sadly, no," I replied. "It's my hometown. I was in the regular force here until '75. You?"

"Welsh Border guard for ten years. I got into some darkness at Oswestry in '79 and discovered I had a talent for this kind of shit. I trannied here from Oxford when the two depots merged. You're looking at the only Staker south of Leeds. I run my own office but it's mighty lonesome. If you know anyone handy with a mallet?—"

"I'm afraid I don't," I replied, wondering why anyone would consciously wish to fight the supreme powers of darkness for a basic SpecOps salary, "but if I come across anyone, I'll let you know. What happened to Chesney? He ran the department when I was here last."

A cloud crossed Spike's usually bright features and he sighed deeply.

"He was a good friend but he fell into shadows. Became a servant of the dark one. I had to hunt him down myself. The spike 'n' decap was the easy part. The tricky bit was having to tell his wife—she wasn't exactly overjoyed."

"I guess I'd be a bit pissed off too."

"Anyway," continued Spike, cheering up almost immediately, "you don't have to tell me shit, but what is a good-looking SpecOps doing joining the Swindon LiteraTecs?"

"I had a spot of bother in London."

"Ah," replied Spike knowingly.

"I'm also looking for someone."

"Who?"

I looked over at him and made an instant judgment call. If I could trust anyone, I could trust Spike.

"Hades."

"Acheron? Flatline, sister. The man's toast. Crashed and burned at J-twelve on the four."

"So we're led to believe. If you hear anything?—"

"No problem, Thursday."

"And we can keep this between ourselves?"

He smiled.

"After staking, secrets is what I do best."

"Hang on—"

I had caught sight of a brightly colored sports car in a second-hand car lot on the other side of the road. Spike slowed down.

"What's up?"

"I . . . er . . . need a car. Can you drop me over there?"

Spike executed an illegal U-turn, causing the following car to brake violently and slew across the road. The driver started to hurl abuse until he saw that it was a SpecOps black and white, then wisely kept quiet and drove on. I retrieved my bag.

"Thanks for the lift. I'll see you about."

"Not if I see you first!" said Spike. "I'll see what I can dig up on your missing friend."

"I'd appreciate it. Thanks."

"Good-bye."

"So long."

"Cheerio," said a timid-sounding voice from the back. We both turned and looked into the rear of the car. Mr. Meakle had changed back. A thin, rather pathetic-looking man was sitting in the back seat, completely naked and very muddy. His hands were clasped modestly over his genitals.

"Mr. Meakle! Welcome back!" said Spike, grinning broadly as he added in a scolding tone: "You didn't take your tablets, did you?"

Mr. Meakle shook his head miserably.

I thanked Spike again. As he drove off I could see Mr. Meakle waving to me a bit stupidly through the rear window. Spike did another U-turn, causing a second car to brake hard, and was gone.

I stared at the sports car on the front row of the lot under a banner marked BARGAIN. There could be no mistake. The car was definitely the one that had appeared before me in my hospital room. *And I had been driving it.* It was me who had told me to come to Swindon. It was me who had told me that Acheron wasn't dead. If I hadn't come to Swindon then I wouldn't have seen the car and wouldn't have been able to buy it. It didn't make a great deal of sense, but what little I did know was that I had to have it.

"Can I help you, madam?" asked an oily salesman who had appeared almost from nowhere, rubbing his hands nervously and sweating profusely in the heat.

"This car. How long have you had it?"

"The 356 Speedster? About six months."

"Has it ever been up to London in that time?"

"London?" repeated the salesman, slightly puzzled. "Not at all. Why?"

"No reason. I'll take it."

The salesman looked slightly shocked.

"Are you sure? Wouldn't you like something a little more practical? I have a good selection of Buicks which have just come in. Ex-Goliath but with low mileage, you know—"

"This one," I said firmly.

The salesman smiled uneasily. The car was obviously at a giveaway price and they didn't stand to make a bean on it. He muttered something feeble and hurried off to get the keys.

I sat inside. The interior was spartan in the extreme. I had never thought myself very interested in cars, but this one was different. It was outrageously conspicuous with curious paint-work in red, blue and green, but I liked it immediately. The salesman returned with the keys and it started on the second turn. He did the necessary paperwork and half an hour later I drove out of the lot into the road. The car accelerated rapidly with a rasping note from the tailpipe. Within a couple of hundred yards the two of us were inseparable.

9.

The Next Family

. . . I was born on a Thursday, hence the name. My brother was born on a Monday and they called him Anton—go figure. My mother was called Wednesday but was born on a Sunday—I don't know why—and my father had no name at all—his identity and existence had been scrubbed by the ChronoGuard after he went rogue. To all intents and purposes he didn't exist at all. It didn't matter. He was always Dad to me . . .

THURSDAY NEXT
—*A Life in SpecOps*

I TOOK my new car for a drive in the countryside with the top down; the rushing air was a cool respite from the summer heat. The familiar landscape had not changed much; it was still as beautiful as I remembered. Swindon, on the other hand, had changed a great deal. The town had spread outward and up. Light industry went outward, financial glassy towers in the center went up. The residential area had expanded accordingly; the countryside was just that much farther from the center of town.

It was evening when I pulled up in front of a plain semidetached house in a street that contained forty or fifty just like it. I flipped up the hood and locked the car. This was where I had grown up; my bedroom was the window above the front door.

The house had aged. The painted window frames had faded and the pebbledash facing seemed to be coming away from the wall in several areas. I pushed open the front gate with some difficulty as there was a good deal of resistance behind it, and then closed it again with a similar amount of heaving and sweating— a task made more difficult by the assortment of dodos who had gathered eagerly around to see who it was and then *plock*ed excitedly when they realized it was someone vaguely familiar.

"Hello, Mordacai!" I said to the oldest, who dipped and bobbed in greeting. They all wanted to be made a fuss of after that, so I stayed awhile and tickled them under their chins as they searched my pockets inquisitively for any sign of marshmallows, something that dodos find particularly irresistible.

My mother opened the door to see what the fuss was about and ran up the path to meet me. The dodos wisely scattered, as my mother can be dangerous at anything more than a fast walk. She gave me a long hug. I returned it gratefully.

"Thursday!—" she said, her eyes glistening. "Why didn't you tell us you were coming?"

"It was a surprise, Mum. I've got a posting in town."

She had visited me in hospital several times and bored me in a delightfully distracting manner with all the minutiae of Margot Vishler's hysterectomy and the Women's Federation gossip.

"How's the arm?"

"It can be a bit stiff sometimes and when I sleep on it, it goes completely numb. Garden's looking nice. Can I come in?"

My mother apologized and ushered me through the door, taking my jacket and hanging it up in the cloakroom. She looked awkwardly at the automatic in my shoulder holster so I stuffed it in my case. The house, I soon noticed, was *exactly* the same: the same mess, the same furniture, the same smell. I paused to look around, to take it all in and bathe in the security of fond memories. The last time I had been truly happy was in

Swindon, and this house had been the hub of my life for twenty years. A creeping doubt entered my mind about the wisdom of leaving the town in the first place.

We walked through to the lounge, still poorly decorated in browns and greens and looking like a museum of velour. The photo of my passing-out parade at the police training college was on the mantelpiece, along with another of Anton and myself in military fatigues smiling under the harsh sun of the Crimean summer. Sitting on the sofa were an aged couple who were busy watching TV.

"Polly!—Mycroft!—Look who it is!"

My aunt reacted favorably by rising to meet me, but Mycroft was more interested in watching *Name That Fruit!* on the television. He laughed a silly snorting laugh at a poor joke and waved a greeting in my direction without looking up.

"Hello, Thursday, *darling*," said my aunt. "Careful, I'm all made up."

We pointed cheeks at each other and made *mmuuah* noises. My aunt smelled strongly of lavender and had so much makeup on that even good Queen Bess would have been shocked.

"You well, Aunty?"

"Couldn't be better." She kicked her husband painfully on the ankle. "Mycroft, it's your niece."

"Hello, pet," he said without looking up, rubbing his foot. Polly lowered her voice.

"It's such a worry. All he does is watch TV and tinker in his workshop. Sometimes I think there's no one at home at all."

She glared hard at the back of his head before returning her attention to me.

"Staying for long?"

"She's been posted here," put in my mother.

"Have you lost weight?"

"I work out."

"Do you have a boyfriend?"

"No," I replied. They would ask me about Landen next.

"Have you called Landen?"

"No, I haven't. And I don't want you to either."

"*Such* a nice lad. *The Toad* did a fantastic review of his last book: *Once Were Scoundrels*. Have you read it?"

I ignored her.

"Any news from Father?—" I asked.

"He didn't like the mauve paint in the bedroom," said my mother. "I can't think why you suggested it!"

Aunt Polly beckoned me closer and hissed unsubtly and very loudly in my ear:

"You'll have to excuse your mother; she thinks your dad is mixed up with *another woman*!"

Mother excused herself on a lame pretext and hurriedly left the room.

I frowned.

"What kind of woman?"

"Someone he met at work—Lady Emma someone-or-other."

I remembered the last conversation with Dad; the stuff about Nelson and the French revisionists.

"Emma *Hamilton*?"

My mother popped her head around the door from the kitchen.

"You know her?" she asked in an aggrieved tone.

"Not personally. I think she died in the mid-nineteenth century."

My mother narrowed her eyes.

"That old ruse."

She steeled herself and managed a bright smile.

"Will you stay for supper?"

I agreed, and she went to find a chicken that she could boil all the taste out of, her anger at Dad for the moment forgotten. Mycroft, the gameshow ended, shuffled into the kitchen wearing a gray zip-up cardigan and holding a copy of *New Splicer* magazine.

"What's for dinner?" he asked, getting in the way. Aunt Polly looked at him as you might a spoiled child.

"Mycroft, instead of wandering around wasting your time, why don't you waste Thursday's and show her what you've been up to in your workshop?"

Mycroft looked at us both with a vacant expression. He shrugged and beckoned me toward the back door, changing his slippers for a pair of gumboots and his cardigan for a truly dreadful plaid jacket.

"C'mon then, m'girl," he muttered, shooing the dodos from around the back door where they had been mustering in hope of a snack, and strode toward his workshop.

"You might repair that garden gate, Uncle—it's worse than ever!"

"Not at all," he replied with a wink. "Every time someone goes in or out they generate enough power to run the telly for an hour. I haven't seen you about recently. Have you been away?"

"Well, yes; ten years."

He looked over his spectacles at me with some surprise.

"Really?"

"Yes. Is Owens still with you?"

Owens was Mycroft's assistant. He was an old boy who had been with Rutherford when he split the atom; Mycroft and he had been at school together.

"A bit tragic, Thursday. We were developing a machine that used egg white, heat and sugar to synthesize methanol when a power surge caused an implosion. Owens was meringued. By the time we chipped him out the poor chap had expired. Polly helps me now."

We had arrived at his workshop. A log with an ax stuck in it was all that was keeping the door shut. Mycroft fumbled for the switch and the striplights flickered on, filling the workshop with a harsh fluorescent glow. The laboratory looked similar to the last time I had seen it in terms of untidiness and the general bric-à-brac, but the contraptions were different. I had learned from my mother's many letters that Mycroft had invented a method for sending pizzas by fax and a 2B pencil with a built-in spell-checker, but what he was currently working on, I had no idea.

"Did the memory erasure device work, Uncle?"

"The what?"

"The memory erasure device. You were testing it when I last saw you."

"Don't know what you're talking about, dear girl. What do you make of this?"

A large white Rolls-Royce was sitting in the center of the room. I walked over to the vehicle as Mycroft tapped a fluorescent tube to stop it flickering.

"New car, Uncle?"

"No, no," said Mycroft hurriedly. "I don't drive. A friend of mine who hires these out was lamenting about the cost of keeping two, one black for funerals and the other white for weddings—so I came up with this."

He reached in and turned a large knob on the dashboard. There was a low hum and the car turned slowly off-white, gray, dark gray and then finally to black.

"That's very impressive, Uncle."

"Do you think so? It uses liquid crystal technology. But I took the idea one step farther. Watch."

95

He turned the dial several more notches to the right and the car changed to blue, then mauve, and finally green with yellow dots.

"One-color cars a thing of the past! But that's not all. If I switch on the car's Pigmentizer like *so*, the car should . . . yes, yes, look at that!"

I watched with growing astonishment as the car started to fade in front of my eyes; the liquid crystal coating was emulating the background grays and browns of Mycroft's workshop. Within a few seconds the car had blended itself perfectly into the background. I thought of the fun you could have with traffic wardens.

"I call it the ChameleoCar; quite fun, don't you think?"

"Very."

I put out my hand and touched the warm surface of the camouflaged Rolls-Royce. I was going to ask Mycroft if I could have the cloaking device fitted to my Speedster but I was too late; enthused by my interest he had trotted off to a large roll-top bureau and was beckoning me over excitedly.

"Translating carbon paper," he announced breathlessly, pointing to several piles of brightly colored metallic film. "I call it Rosettionery. Allow me to demonstrate. We'll start with a plain piece of paper, then put in a Spanish carbon, a second slip of paper—must get them the right way up!—then a Polish carbon, more paper, German and another sheet and finally French and the last sheet . . . *there.*"

He shuffled the bundle and laid it on the desk as I pulled up a chair.

"Write something on the first sheet. Anything you want."

"Anything?"

Mycroft nodded so I wrote: *Have you seen my dodo?*

"Now what?"

Mycroft looked triumphant.

"Have a look, dear girl."

I lifted off the top carbon and there, written in my own handwriting, were the words: ¿Ha visto mi dodo?

"But that's amazing!"

"Thank you," replied my Uncle. "Have a look at the next!"

I did. Beneath the Polish carbon was written: Gdzie jest moje dodo?

"I'm working on hieroglyphics and demotic," Mycroft explained as I peeled off the German translation to read: Haben Sie mein Dodo gesehen? "The Mayan Codex version was trickier but I can't manage Esperanto at all. Can't think why."

"This will have dozens of applications!" I exclaimed as I pulled off the last sheet to read, slightly disappointingly: Mon aardvark n'a pas de nez.

"Wait a moment, Uncle. My aardvark has no nose?"

Mycroft looked over my shoulder and grunted.

"You probably weren't pressing hard enough. You're police, aren't you?"

"SpecOps, really."

"Then this might interest you," he announced, leading me off past more wondrous gadgets, the use of which I could only guess at. "I'm demonstrating this particular machine to the police technical advancement committee on Wednesday."

He stopped next to a device that had a huge horn on it like an old gramophone. He cleared his throat.

"I call it my Olfactograph. It's very simple. Since any bloodhound worth its salt will tell you that each person's smell is unique like a thumbprint, then it follows that a machine that can recognize a felon's individual smell must be of use where other forms of identification fail. A thief may wear gloves and a mask, but he can't hide his scent."

He pointed at the horn.

"The odors are sucked up here and split into their individual parts using an Olfactroscope of my own invention. The component parts are then analyzed to give a 'pongprint' of the criminal. It can separate out ten different people's odors in a single room and isolate the newest or the oldest. It can detect burned toast up to six months after the event and differentiate between thirty different brands of cigar."

"Could be handy," I said, slightly doubtfully. "What's this over here?"

I was pointing to what looked like a trilby hat made from brass and covered in wires and lights.

"Oh yes," said my uncle, "*this* I think you will like."

He placed the brass hat on my head and flicked a large switch. There was a humming noise.

"Is something meant to happen?" I asked.

"Close your eyes and breathe deeply. Try to empty your mind of any thoughts."

I closed my eyes and waited patiently.

"Is it working?" asked Mycroft.

"No," I replied, then added: "Wait!" as a stickleback swam past. "I can see a fish. Here, in front of my eyes. Wait, there's another!"

And so there was. Pretty soon I was staring at a whole host of brightly colored fish all swimming in front of my closed eyes. They were on about a five-second loop; every now and then they jumped back to the starting place and repeated their action.

"Remarkable!"

"Stay relaxed or it will go," said Mycroft in a soothing voice. "Try this one."

There was a blur of movement and the scene shifted to an inky-black starfield; it seemed as though I were traveling through space.

"Or how about this?" asked Mycroft, changing the scene to

a parade of flying toasters. I opened my eyes and the image evaporated. Mycroft was looking at me earnestly.

"Any good?" he asked.

I nodded.

"I call it a Retinal Screen-Saver. Very useful for boring jobs; instead of gazing absently out of the window you can transform your surroundings to any number of soothing images. As soon as the phone goes or your boss walks in you blink and *bingo!*—you're back in the real world again."

I handed back the hat.

"Should sell well at SmileyBurger. When do you hope to market it?"

"It's not really ready yet; there are a few problems I haven't quite fixed."

"Such as what?" I asked, slightly suspiciously.

"Close your eyes and you'll see."

I did as he asked and a fish swam by. I blinked again and could see a toaster. Clearly, this needed some work.

"Don't worry," he assured me. "They will have gone in a few hours."

"I preferred the Olfactroscope."

"You haven't seen anything yet!" said Mycroft, skipping nimbly up to a large work desk covered by tools and bits of machinery. "This device is probably my most amazing discovery ever. It is the culmination of thirty years' work and incorporates biotechnology at the very cutting edge of science. When you find out what this is, I promise you, you'll flip!"

He pulled a tea towel off a goldfish bowl with a flourish and showed me what appeared to be a large quantity of fruitfly larvae.

"Maggots?"

Mycroft smiled.

"Not maggots, Thursday, *bookworms*!"

He said the word with such a bold and proud flourish that I thought I must have missed something.

"Is that good?"

"It's *very* good, Thursday. These worms might *look* like a tempting snack for Mr. Trout, but each one of these little fellows has enough new genetic sequencing to make the code embedded in your pet dodo look like a note to the milkman!"

"Hold on a sec, Uncle," I said. "Didn't you have your Splicense revoked after that incident with the prawns?"

"A small misunderstanding," he said with a dismissive wave of his hand. "Those fools at SpecOps-13 have no idea of the value of my work."

"Which is?—" I asked, ever curious.

"Ever smaller methods of storing information. I collected all the finest dictionaries, thesauri and lexicons, as well as grammatical, morphological and etymological studies of the English language, and encoded them all within the DNA of the worm's small body. I call them HyperBookworms. I think you'll agree that it's a remarkable achievement."

"I agree. But how would you access this information?"

Mycroft's face fell.

"As I said, a remarkable achievement with one small drawback. However, events ran ahead of themselves; some of my worms escaped and bred with others that had been encoded with a complete set of encyclopedic, historical and biographical reference manuals; the result was a new strain I named Hyper-BookwormDoublePlusGood. These chaps are the *real* stars of the show."

He pulled a sheet of paper from a drawer, tore off a corner and wrote the word "remarkable" on the small scrap.

"This is just to give you a *taste* of what these creatures can do."

So saying, he dropped the piece of paper into the goldfish bowl. The worms wasted no time and quickly surrounded the small scrap. But instead of eating it they merely conglomerated around it, squirmed excitedly and explored the interloper with apparent great interest.

"I had a wormery back in London, Uncle, and they didn't like paper either—"

"Shh!" murmured my uncle, and beckoned me closer to the worms.

Amazing!

"What is?" I asked, somewhat perplexed; but as soon as I looked at Mycroft's smiling face I realized it wasn't him speaking.

Astonishing! said the voice again in a low murmur. *Incredible! Astounding! Stunning!*

I frowned and looked at the worms, which had gathered themselves into a small ball around the scrap of paper and were pulsating gently.

Wonderful! mumbled the bookworms. *Extraordinary! Fantastic!*

"What do you think?" asked Mycroft.

"Thesaurean maggots—Uncle, you never cease to amaze me!"

But Mycroft was suddenly a lot more serious.

"It's more than just a bio-thesaurus, Thursday. These little chaps can do things that you will scarce believe."

He opened a cupboard and pulled out a large leather book with PP embossed on the spine in gold letters. The casing was richly decorated and featured heavy brass securing straps. On the front were several dials and knobs, valves and knife switches. It certainly *looked* impressive, but not all Mycroft's devices had a usefulness mutually compatible with their looks. In the early seventies he had developed an extraordinarily beautiful machine that did nothing more exciting than predict with staggering accuracy the number of pips in an unopened orange.

"What is it?" I asked.

"This," began Mycroft, smiling all over and puffing out his chest with pride, "is a—"

But he never got to finish. At that precise moment Polly announced "Supper!" from the door and Mycroft quickly ran out, muttering something about how he hoped it was snorkers and telling me to switch off the lights on my way out. I was left alone in his empty workshop. Truly, Mycroft had surpassed himself.

Dazzling! agreed the bookworms.

Supper was a friendly affair. We all had a lot of catching up to do, and my mother had a great deal to tell me about the Women's Federation.

"We raised almost seven thousand pounds last year for ChronoGuard orphans," she said.

"That's very good," I replied. "SpecOps is always grateful for the contributions, although to be fair there are other divisions worse off than the ChronoGuard."

"Well, I know," replied my mother, "but it's all *so* secret. What do all of them do?"

"Believe me, I have no more idea than you. Can you pass the fish?"

"There isn't any fish," observed my aunt. "You haven't been using your niece as a guinea pig have you, Crofty?"

My uncle pretended not to hear; I blinked and the fish vanished.

"The only other one I know under SO-20 is SO-6," added Polly. "That was National Security. We only know *that* because they all looked after Mycroft so well."

She nudged him in the ribs but he didn't notice; he was busy figuring out a recipe for unscrambled eggs on a napkin.

"I don't suppose a week went by in the sixties when he wasn't being kidnapped by one foreign power or another," she sighed wistfully, thinking of the exciting old days with a whiff of nostalgia.

"Some things have to be kept secret for operational purposes," I recited parrot fashion. "Secrecy is our biggest weapon."

"I read in *The Mole* that SpecOps is riddled with secret societies. The Wombats in particular," murmured Mycroft, placing his completed equation in his jacket pocket. "Is this true?"

I shrugged.

"No more than in any other walk of life, I suppose. I've not noticed it myself, but then as a woman I wouldn't be approached by the Wombats anyway."

"Seems a bit unfair to me," said Polly in a tut-tutting voice. "I'm fully in support of secret societies—the more the better—but I think they should be open to everyone, men *and* women."

"Men are welcome to it," I replied. "It means that at least half the population won't have to make complete idiots of themselves. It surprises me that you haven't been approached to join, Uncle."

Mycroft grunted.

"I used to be one at Oxford many years ago. Waste of time. It was all a bit silly; the pouch used to chafe something awful and all that gnawing played hell with my overbite."

There was a pause.

"Major Phelps is in town," I said, changing the subject. "I met him on the airship. He's a colonel now but is still blasting the same old line."

By an unwritten rule, no one ever spoke of the Crimea or Anton in the house. There was an icy hush.

"Really?" replied my mother with seemingly no emotion.

"Joffy has a parish up at Wanborough these days," announced Polly, hoping to change the subject. "He's opened the first GSD church in Wessex. I spoke to him last week; he says that it has been quite popular."

Joffy was my other brother. He had taken to the faith at an early age and tried all sorts of religions before settling for the GSD.

"GSD?" murmured Mycroft. "What in heaven's name is that?"

"Global Standard Deity," answered Polly. "It's a mixture of all the religions. I think it's meant to stop religious wars."

Mycroft grunted again.

"Religion isn't the cause of wars, it's the excuse. What's the melting point of beryllium?"

"180.57 degrees centigrade," murmured Polly without even thinking. "I think Joffy is doing a grand job. You should call him, Thursday."

"Maybe."

Joffy and I had never been close. He had called me Doofus and smacked me on the back of my head every day for fifteen years. I had to break his nose to make him stop.

"If you are calling people why don't you call—"

"Mother!"

"He's quite successful now, I understand, Thursday. It might be good for you to see him again."

"Landen and I are finished, Mum. Besides, I have a boyfriend."

This, to my mother, was *extremely* good news. It had been of considerable anguish to her that I wasn't spending more time with swollen ankles, hemorrhoids and a bad back, popping out grandchildren and naming them after obscure relatives. Joffy wasn't the sort of person who had children, which kind of left it up to me. In all honesty I wasn't against the idea of kids, it was just that I wasn't going to have them on my own. And Landen had been the last man to have remotely interested me as a possible life partner.

"A boyfriend? What's his name?"

I said the first name that popped into my head.

"Snood. *Filbert* Snood."

"Nice name." My mother smiled.

"Daft name," grumbled Mycroft. "Like Landen Parke-Laine, come to that. Can I get down? It's time for *Jack Spratt's Casebook*."

Polly and Mycroft both got up and left us. Landen's name didn't come up again and neither did Anton's. Mum offered me my old room back but I quickly declined. We had argued ferociously when I had lived at home. Besides, I was almost thirty-six. I finished my coffee and walked with my mother to the front door.

"Let me know if you change your mind, darling," she said. "Your room is the same as it always was."

If that were true the dreadful posters of my late teenage crushes would still be up on the wall. It was a thought too hideous to contemplate.

10.

The Finis Hotel, Swindon

Miltons were, on the whole, the most enthusiastic poet followers. A flick through the London telephone directory would yield about four thousand John Miltons, two thousand William Blakes, a thousand or so Samuel Coleridges, five hundred Percy Shelleys, the same of Wordsworth and Keats, and a handful of Drydens. Such mass name-changing could have problems in law enforcement. Following an incident in a pub where the assailant, victim, witness, landlord, arresting officer and judge had all been called Alfred Tennyson, a law had been passed compelling each namesake to carry a registration number tattooed behind the ear. It hadn't been well received—few really practical law-enforcement measures ever are.

MILLON DE FLOSS
—*A Short History of the Special Operations Network*

I PULLED into a parking place in front of the large floodlit building and locked the car. The hotel seemed to be quite busy, and as soon as I walked into the lobby I could see why. At least two dozen men and women were milling about dressed in large white baggy shirts and breeches. My heart sank. A large notice near reception welcomed all comers to the 112th Annual John Milton Convention. I took a deep breath and fought my way to the reception desk. A middle-aged receptionist with oversize earrings gave me her best welcoming smile.

"Good evening, madam, welcome to the Finis, the last word in comfort and style. We are a four-star hotel with many modern features and services. Our sincere wish is to make *your* stay a happy one!"

She recited it like a mantra. I could see her working at Smiley-Burger just as easily.

"The name's Next. I have a reservation."

The receptionist nodded and flicked through the reservation cards.

"Let's see. Milton, Milton, Milton, Milton, Milton, Next, Milton, Milton, Milton, Milton, Milton, Milton. No, sorry. It doesn't look like we have a booking for you."

"Could you check again?"

She looked again and found it.

"Here it is. Someone had put it with the Miltons by accident. I'll need an imprint of a major credit card. We take: Babbage, Goliath, Newton, Pascal, Breakfast Club and Jam Roly-Poly."

"Jam Roly-Poly?"

"Sorry," she said sheepishly, "wrong list. That's the choice of puddings tonight." She smiled again as I passed over my Babbage charge card.

"You're in room 8128," she said, handing me my key attached to a key ring so large I could barely lift it. "All our rooms are fully air-conditioned and are equipped with minibar and tea-making equipment. Did you park your car in our spacious three-hundred-place self-draining car park?"

I hid a smile.

"Thank you, I did. Do you have any pet facilities?"

"Of course. All Finis hotels have full kennel facilities. What sort of pet?"

"A dodo."

"How sweet! My cousin Arnold had a great auk once called Beany—he was Version 1.4 so didn't live long. I understand they're a lot better these days. I'll reserve your little friend a place. Enjoy your stay. I hope you have an interest in seventeenth-century lyrical poets."

"Only professionally."

"Lecturer?"

"LiteraTec."

"Ah."

The receptionist leaned closer and lowered her voice.

"To tell you the truth, Miss Next, I *hate* Milton. His early stuff is okay, I suppose, but he disappeared up his own arse after Charlie got his head lopped off. Goes to show what too much republicanism does for you."

"Quite."

"I almost forgot. These are for you."

She produced a bunch of flowers from under the desk as if in a conjuring trick.

"From a Mr. Landen Parke-Laine—"

Blast. Rumbled.

"—and there are two gentlemen waiting in the Cheshire Cat for you."

"The Cheshire Cat?"

"It's our fully stocked and lively bar. Tended to by professional and helpful bar staff, it is a warm and welcoming area in which to relax."

"Who are they?"

"The bar staff?"

"No, the two gentlemen."

"They didn't give any names."

"Thank you, Miss?—"

"Barrett-Browning," said the receptionist, "Liz Barrett-Browning."

"Well, Liz, keep the flowers. Make your boyfriend jealous. If Mr. Parke-Laine calls again, tell him I died of hemorrhagic fever or something."

I pushed my way through the throng of Miltons and onto the Cheshire Cat. It was easy to find. Above the door was a large red neon cat on a green neon tree. Every couple of minutes the red neon flickered and went out, leaving the cat's grin on its own in the tree. The sound of a jazz band reached my ears from the bar as I walked across the lobby, and a smile crossed my lips as I heard the unmistakable piano of Holroyd Wilson. He was a Swindon man, born and bred. He could have played any bar in Europe with one phone call, but he had chosen to remain in Swindon. The bar was busy but not packed, the clientele mostly Miltons, who were sitting around drinking and joking, lamenting the Restoration and referring to each other as John.

I went up to the bar. It was happy hour in the Cheshire Cat, any drink for 52.5 p.

"Good evening," said the barman. "Why is a raven like a writing desk?"

"Because Poe wrote on both?"

"Very good." He laughed. "What's it to be?"

"A half of Vorpal's special, please. The name's Next. Anyone waiting for me?"

The barman, who was dressed like a hatter, indicated a booth on the other side of the room in which two men were sitting, partially obscured by shadows. I took my drink and walked over. The room was too full for anyone to start any trouble. As I drew closer I could see the two men more clearly.

The elder of the two was a gray-haired gentleman in his mid-seventies. He had large mutton-chop sideburns and was dressed in a neat tweed suit with a silk bow tie. His hands were holding a pair of brown gloves on top of his walking stick and I could see a deerstalker hat on the seat next to him. His face had a ruddy appearance, and as I approached he threw back his head and laughed like a seal at something the younger man had said.

The man opposite him was aged about thirty. He sat on the front of his seat in a slightly nervous manner. He sipped at a tonic water and wore a pinstripe suit that was expensive but had seen better days. I knew I had seen him before somewhere but couldn't think where.

"You gentlemen looking for me?"

They both got up together. The elder of the two spoke first.

"Miss Next? Delighted to make your acquaintance. The name's Analogy. Victor Analogy. Head of Swindon LiteraTecs. We spoke on the phone."

He offered his hand and I shook it.

"Pleased to meet you, sir."

"This is Operative Bowden Cable. You'll be working to-gether."

"I am very pleased to make your acquaintance, madam," said Bowden quite grandly, slightly awkwardly and very stiffly.

"Have we met before?" I asked, shaking his outstretched hand.

"No," said Bowden firmly. "I would have remembered."

Victor offered me a seat next to Bowden, who shuffled up making polite noises. I took a sip of my drink. It tasted like old horse blankets soaked in urine. I coughed explosively. Bowden offered me his handkerchief.

"Vorpal's special?" said Victor, raising an eyebrow. "Brave girl."

"Th-thank you."

"Welcome to Swindon," continued Victor. "First of all I'd

like to say how sorry we were to hear about your little incident. By all accounts Hades was a monster. I'm not sorry he died. I hope you are quite recovered?"

"I am, but others were not so fortunate."

"I'm sorry to hear that, but you are very welcome here. No one of your caliber has ever bothered to join us in this backwater before."

I looked at Analogy and was slightly puzzled.

"I'm not sure I understand what you're driving at."

"What I mean—not to put too fine a point on it—is all of us in the office are more academics than typical SpecOp agents. Your post was held by Jim Crometty. He was shot dead in the old town during a bookbuy that went wrong. He was Bowden's partner. Jim was a very special friend to us all; he had a wife, three kids. I want . . . no, I want *very badly* the person who took Crometty from us."

I stared at their earnest faces with some confusion until the penny dropped. They thought I was a full and pukka SO-5 operative on a rest-and-recuperation assignment. It wasn't unusual. Back at SO-27 we used to get worn-out characters from SO-9 and SO-7 all the time. Without exception they had all been mad as pants.

"You've read my file?" I asked slowly.

"They wouldn't release it," replied Analogy. "It's not often we get an operative moving to our little band from the dizzy heights of SpecOps-5. We needed a replacement with good field experience but also someone who can . . . well, how shall I put it?—"

Analogy paused, apparently at a loss for words. Bowden answered for him.

"We need someone who isn't frightened to use *extreme force* if deemed necessary."

I looked at them both, wondering whether it would be better to come clean; after all, the only thing I had shot recently was my own car and a seemingly bullet-proof master criminal. I was officially SO-27, not SO-5. But with the strong possibility of Acheron still being around, and revenge still high on my agenda, perhaps it would be better to play along.

Analogy shuffled nervously.

"Crometty's murder is being looked after by Homicide, of course. Unofficially we can't do a great deal, but SpecOps has always prided itself on a certain *independence*. If we uncovered any evidence in the pursuit of other inquiries, it would not be frowned upon. Do you understand?"

"Sure. Do you have any idea who killed Crometty?"

"Someone said that they had something for him to see, to buy. A rare Dickens manuscript. He went to see it and . . . well, he wasn't armed, you know."

"Few LiteraTecs in Swindon even know how to use a firearm," added Bowden, "and training for many of them is out of the question. Literary detection and firearms don't really go hand in hand; pen mightier than the sword and so forth."

"Words are all very well," I replied coolly, suddenly enjoying the SO-5 woman-of-mystery stuff, "but a nine-millimeter really gets to the root of the problem."

They stared at me in silence for a second or two. Victor drew out a photograph from a buff envelope and placed it on the table in front of me.

"We'd like your opinion on this. It was taken yesterday."

I looked at the photo. I knew the face well enough.

"Jack Schitt."

"And what do you know about him?"

"Not much. He's head of Goliath's Internal Security Service. He wanted to know what Hades had planned to do with the *Chuzzlewit* manuscript."

"I'll let you into a secret. You're right that Schitt's Goliath but he's *not* Internal Security."

"What, then?"

"Advanced Weapons Division. Eight billion annual budget and it all goes through him."

"Eight billion?"

"*And* loose change. Rumor has it they even went over *that* budget to develop the plasma rifle. He's intelligent, ambitious and quite inflexible. He came here two weeks ago. He wouldn't be in Swindon at all unless there was something here that Goliath found of great interest; we think Crometty went to see the original manuscript of *Chuzzlewit* and if that is so—"

"—Schitt is here because I am," I announced suddenly. "He thought it suspicious that I should want an SO-27 job in Swindon of all places—no offense meant."

"None taken," replied Analogy. "But Schitt being here makes me think that Hades is still about—or at the very least Goliath *think* so."

"I know," I replied. "Worrying, isn't it?"

Analogy and Cable looked at one another. They had made the points they wanted to make: I was welcome here, they were keen to avenge Crometty's death and they didn't like Jack Schitt. They wished me a pleasant evening, donned their hats and coats and were gone.

The jazz number came to an end. I joined in the applause as Holroyd got shakily to his feet and waved at the crowd before leaving. The bar thinned out rapidly once the music had finished, leaving me almost alone. I looked to my right, where two Miltons were busy making eyes at one another, and then at the bar, where several suited business reps were drinking as much as they could on their overnight allowance. I walked over to the piano and sat down. I struck a few chords, testing my arm at first, then becoming more adventurous as I played the lower half of a duet I remembered. I looked at the barman to order another drink but he was busy drying a glass. As the intro for the top part of the duet came around for the third time, a man's hand reached in and played the first note of the upper part exactly on time. I closed my eyes; I knew who it was instantly, but I wasn't going to look up. I could smell his aftershave and noticed the scar on his left hand. The hair on the back of my neck bristled slightly and I felt a flush rise within me. I instinctively moved to the left and let him sit down. His fingers drifted across the keys with mine, the two of us playing together almost flawlessly. The barman looked on approvingly, and even the suited salesmen stopped talking and looked around to see who was playing. Still I did not look up. As my hands grew more accustomed to that long-unplayed tune I grew confident and played faster. My unwatched partner kept up the tempo to match me.

We played like this for perhaps ten minutes, but I couldn't bring myself to look at him. I knew that if I did I would smile and I didn't want to do that. I wanted him to know I was still pissed off. *Then* he could charm me. When the piece finally came to an end I continued to stare ahead. The man next to me didn't move.

"Hello, Landen," I said finally.

"Hello, Thursday."

I played a couple of notes absently but still didn't look up.

"It's been a long time," I said.

"A *lot* of water under the bridge," he replied. "Ten years' worth."

His voice sounded the same. The warmth and sensitivity I had once known so well were still there. I looked up at him, caught his gaze and looked away quickly. I had felt my eyes moisten. I was embarrassed by my feelings and scratched my nose nervously. He had gone slightly gray but he wore his hair in much the same manner. There were slight wrinkles around his eyes, but they might just as easily have been from laughing as from age. He was thirty when I walked out; I had been twenty-six. I wondered whether I had aged as well as he had. Was I too old to still hold a grudge? After all, getting into a strop with Landen wasn't going to bring Anton back. I felt an urge to ask him if it was too late to try again, but as I opened my mouth the world juddered to a halt. The D sharp I had just pressed kept on sounding and Landen stared at me, his eyes frozen in midblink. Dad's timing could not have been worse.

"Hello, Sweetpea!" he said, walking up to me out of the shadows. "Am I disturbing anything?"

"Most definitely—yes."

"I won't be long, then. What do you make of this?"

He handed me a yellow curved thing about the size of a large carrot.

"What is it?" I asked, smelling it cautiously.

"It's the fruit of a new plant designed completely from scratch seventy years from now. Look—"

He peeled the skin off and let me taste it.

"Good, eh? You can pick it well before ripe, transport it thousands of miles if necessary and it will keep fresh in its own hermetically sealed biodegradable packaging. Nutritious and tasty, too. It was sequenced by a brilliant engineer named Anna Bannon. We're a bit lost as to what to call it. Any ideas?"

"I'm sure you'll think of something. What are you going to do with it?"

"I thought I'd introduce it somewhere in the tenth millennium before the present one and see how it goes—food for mankind, that sort of thing. Well, time waits for no man, as we say. I'll let you get back to Landen."

The world flickered and started up again. Landen opened his eyes and stared at me.

"Banana," I said, suddenly realizing what it was that my father had shown me.

"Pardon?"

"Banana. They named it after the designer."

"Thursday, you're making no sense at all," said Landen with a bemused grin.

"My dad was just here."

"Ah. Is he still of all time?"

"Still the same. Listen, I'm sorry about what happened."

"Me too," replied Landen, then lapsed into silence. I wanted to touch his face but instead I said:

"I missed you."

It was the wrong thing to say and I cursed myself; too much, too soon. Landen shuffled uneasily.

"You should take aim more carefully. I missed you a lot too. The first year was the worst."

Landen paused for a moment. He played a few notes on the piano and then said:

"I have a life and I like it here. Sometimes I think that Thursday Next was just a character from one of my novels, someone I made up in the image of the woman I wanted to love. Now . . . well, I'm over it."

It wasn't *really* what I was hoping to hear, but after all that had happened I couldn't blame him.

"But you came to find me."

Landen smiled at me.

"You're in my town, Thurs. When a friend comes in from out of town, you look them up. Isn't that how it's supposed to work?"

"And you buy them flowers? Does Colonel Phelps get roses too?"

"No, he gets lilies. Old habits die hard."

"I see. You've been doing well for yourself."

"Thanks," he replied. "You never answered my letters."

"I never *read* your letters."

"Are you married?"

"I can't see that's any of your business."

"I'll take that as a no."

The conversation had taken a turn for the worse. It was time to bale out.

"Listen, I'm bushed, Landen. I have a very big day ahead of me."

I got up. Landen limped after me. He had lost a leg in the Crimea but he was well used to it by now. He caught up with me at the bar.

"Dinner one night?"

I turned to face him.

"Sure."

"Tuesday?"

"Why not?"

"Good," said Landen, rubbing his hands. "We could get the old unit back together—"

This wasn't what I had in mind.

"Hang on. Tuesday's not very good after all."

"Why not? It was fine three seconds ago. Has your dad been around again?"

"No, I just have a lot of things that I have to do and Pickwick needs kenneling and I have to pick him up at the station as airships make him nervous. You remember the time we took him up to Mull and he vomited all over the steward?"

I checked myself. I was starting to blabber like an idiot.

"And don't tell me," added Landen, "you have to wash your hair?"

"Very funny."

"What work are you doing in Swindon anyway?" asked Landen.

"I wash up at SmileyBurger."

"Sure you do. SpecOps?"

I nodded my head.

"I joined Swindon's LiteraTec unit."

"Permanently?" he asked. "I mean, you've come back to Swindon for good?"

"I don't know."

I placed my hand on his. I wanted to hug him and burst into tears and tell him I loved him and would *always* love him like some huge emotional dumb girlie, but time wasn't quite right, as my father would say. I decided to get on the question offensive instead so I asked:

"Are *you* married?"

"No."

"Never thought about it?"

"I thought about it a lot."

We both lapsed into silence. There was so much to say that neither of us could think of any way to start. Landen opened a second front:

"Want to see *Richard III*?"

"Is it still running?"

"Of course."

"I'm tempted but the fact remains I don't know when I will be free. Things are . . . volatile at present."

I could see he didn't believe me. I couldn't really tell him I was on the trail of a master criminal who could steal thoughts and project images at will; who was invisible on film and could murder and laugh as he did so. Landen sighed, dug out a calling card and placed it on the counter.

"Call me. Whenever you're free. Promise?"

"Promise."

He kissed me on the cheek, finished his drink, looked at me again and limped out of the bar. I was left looking at his calling card. I didn't pick it up. I didn't need to. The number was the one I remembered.

My room was exactly like all the other rooms in the hotel. The pictures were screwed to the walls and the drinks in the mini-bar had been opened, drunk, then resealed with water or cold tea by traveling reps too mean to pay for them. The room faced north; I could just see the airship field. A large forty-seater was moored on the mast, its silver flanks floodlit in the dark night. The small dirigible that had brought me in had continued onto Salisbury; I briefly thought about catching it again when it called on its return the day after tomorrow. I turned on the television just in time to catch *Today in Parliament*. The Crimean debate had been raging all day and wasn't over yet. I emptied my pockets of loose change, took my automatic out of its shoulder holster and opened the bedside drawer. It was full. Apart from the Gideon's Bible there were the teachings of Buddha, a GSD volume of prayer and a Wesleyian pamphlet, two amulets from the Society for Christian Awareness, the thoughts of St. Zvlkx and the now mandatory *Complete Works of William Shakespeare*. I removed all the books, stuffed them in the cupboard and placed my automatic in the drawer instead. I unzipped my case and started to organize my room. I hadn't rented out my apartment in London; I didn't know if I was staying here or not. Oddly, the town had started to feel very comfortable and I wasn't sure whether I liked that or not. I laid everything on my bed and then put it all carefully away. I placed a few books on the desk and the life-saving copy of *Jane Eyre* onto the bedside table. I picked up Landen's photo and walked over to the bureau, thought for a moment and then placed it upside down in my knicker drawer. With the real thing around I had no need for an image. The TV droned on:

". . . despite intervention by the French and a Russian guarantee of safe habitation for English settlers, it looks as though the English government will not be resuming its place around the table at Budapest. With England still adamant about an offensive using the new so-called Stonk plasma rifle, peace will *not* be descending on the Black Sea peninsula . . ."

The anchorman shuffled some papers.

"Home news now, and violence flared again in Chichester as a group of neosurrealists gathered to celebrate the fourth anniversary of the legalization of surrealism. On the spot for Toad News Network is Henry Grubb. Henry, how are things down there?"

A shaky live picture came onto the screen, and I stopped for a moment to watch. Behind Grubb was a car that had been overturned and set on fire, and several officers were in riot gear. Henry Grubb, who was in training for the job of Crimean correspondent and secretly hoped that the war wouldn't end until he had had a chance to get out there, wore a navy blue flak jacket and spoke with the urgent, halting speech of a correspondent in a war zone.

"Things are a bit hot down here, Brian. I'm a hundred yards from the riot zone and I can see several cars overturned and on fire. The police have been trying to keep the factions apart all day, but the sheer weight of numbers has been against them. This evening several hundred Raphaelites surrounded the *N'est pas une pipe* public house where a hundred neosurrealists have barricaded themselves in. The demonstrators outside chanted Italian Renaissance slogans and then stones and missiles were thrown. The neosurrealists responded by charging the lines protected by large soft watches and seemed to be winning until the police moved in. Wait, I can just see a man arrested by the police. I'll try and get an interview."

I shook my head sadly and put some shoes in the bottom of

the wardrobe. There was violence when surrealism was banned and there was violence as the same ban was lifted. Grubb continued his broadcast as he intercepted a policeman marching away a youth dressed in sixteenth-century garb with a faithful reproduction of the "Hand of God" from the Sistine chapel tattooed on his face.

"Excuse me, sir, how would you counter the criticism that you are an intolerant bunch with little respect for the value of change and experimentation in all aspects of art?"

The Renaissancite glanced at the camera with an angry scowl.

"People say we're just Renaissancites causing trouble, but I've seen Baroque kids, Raphaelites, Romantics and Mannerists here tonight. It's a massive show of classical artistic unity against these frivolous bastards who cower beneath the safety of the word 'progress.' It's not just—"

The police officer intervened and dragged him away. Grubb ducked a flying brick and then wound up his report.

"This is Henry Grubb, reporting for Toad News Network, live from Chichester."

I turned off the television with a remote that was chained to the bedside table. I sat on the bed and pulled out my hair tie, let my hair down and rubbed my scalp. I sniffed dubiously at my hair and decided against a shower. I had been harder than I intended with Landen. Even with our differences we still had more than enough in common to be good friends.

11.

Polly Flashes Upon
the Inward Eye

I think Wordsworth was as surprised to see me as I was
him. It can't be usual to go to your favorite memory only
to find someone already there, admiring the view ahead
of you.

POLLY NEXT
—interviewed exclusively for *The Owl on Sunday*

As I was dealing with Landen in my own clumsy way, my
uncle and aunt were hard at work in Mycroft's workshop. As I
was to learn later, things seemed to be going quite well. To begin
with, at any rate.

Mycroft was feeding his bookworms in the workshop when
Polly entered; she had just completed some mathematical cal-
culations of almost incomprehensible complexity for him.

"I have the answer you wanted, Crofty, my love," she said,
sucking the end of a well-worn pencil.

"And that is?" asked Mycroft, busily pouring prepositions
onto the bookworms, who devoured the abstract food greedily.

"Nine."

Mycroft mumbled something and jotted the figure down on
a pad. He opened the large brass-reinforced book that I had not
quite been introduced to the night before to reveal a cavity into
which he placed a large-print copy of Wordsworth's poem "I

Wandered Lonely as a Cloud." To this he added the book-worms, who busily got to work. They slithered over the text, their small bodies and unfathomable collective id unconsciously examining every sentence, word, vowel sound and syllable. They probed deeply into the historical, biographical and geographical allusions, then they explored the inner meanings hidden within the meter and rhythm and juggled ingeniously with subtext, content and inflection. After that they made up a few verses of their own and converted the result into binary.

Lakes! Daffodils! Solitude! Memory! whispered the worms excitedly as Mycroft carefully closed the book and locked it. He connected up the heavy mains feed to the back of the book and switched the power switch to "on"; he then started work on the myriad of knobs and dials that covered the front of the heavy volume. Despite the Prose Portal being essentially a bio-mechanism, there were still many delicate procedures that had to be set before the device would work; and since the portal was of an absurd complexity, Mycroft was forced to write up the precise sequence of start-up events and combinations in a small child's exercise book of which—ever wary of foreign spies—he held the only copy. He studied the small book for several moments before twisting dials, setting switches and gently increasing the power, all the while muttering to himself and Polly:

"Binametrics, spherics, numerics. I'm—"

"On?"

"Off!" replied Mycroft sadly. "No, wait . . . *There!*"

He smiled happily as the last of the warning lights extinguished. He took his wife's hand and squeezed it affectionately.

"Would you care to have the honor?" he asked. "The first human being to step inside a Wordsworth poem?"

Polly looked at him uneasily.

"Are you sure it's safe?"

"As safe as houses," he assured her. "I went into 'The Wreck of the *Hesperus*' an hour ago."

"Really? What was it like?"

"Wet—and I think I left my jacket behind."

"The one I gave you for Christmas?"

"No; the other one. The blue one with large checks."

"That's the one I *did* give you for Christmas," she scolded. "I wish you would be more careful. What was it you wanted me to do?"

"Just stand here. If all goes well, as soon as I press this large green button the worms will open a door to the daffodils that William Wordsworth knew and loved."

"And if all *doesn't* go well?" asked Polly slightly nervously. Owens' demise inside a giant meringue never failed to impinge on her thoughts whenever she guinea-pigged one of her husband's machines, but apart from some slight singeing while testing a one-man butane-powered pantomime horse, none of Mycroft's devices had ever harmed her at all.

"Hmm," said Mycroft thoughtfully, "it is *possible* although highly unlikely that I could start a chain reaction that will fuse matter and annihilate the known universe."

"Really?"

"No, not really at all. My little joke. Are you ready?"

Polly smiled.

"Ready."

Mycroft pressed the large green button and there was a low hum from the book. The streetlights flickered and dimmed outside as the machine drew a huge quantity of power to convert the bookworm's binametric information. As they both watched, a thin shaft of light appeared in the workshop, as though a door had been opened from a winter's day into summer. Dust glistened in the beam of light, which gradually grew broader until it was large enough to enter.

"All you have to do is step through!" yelled Mycroft above the noise of the machine. "To open the door requires a lot of power; you have to hurry!"

The high voltage was making the air heavy; metallic objects close by were starting to dance and crackle with static.

Polly stepped closer to the door and smiled nervously at her husband. The shimmering expanse of white light rippled as she put her hand up to touch it. She took a deep breath and stepped through the portal. There was a bright flash and a burst of heavy electrical discharge; two small balls of highly charged gas plasma formed spontaneously near the machine and barreled out in two directions; Mycroft had to duck as one sailed past him and burst harmlessly on the Rolls-Royce; the other exploded on the Olfactograph and started a small fire. Just as quickly the light and sound died away, the doorway closed and the streetlights outside flickered up to full brightness again.

Clouds! Jocund company! Sprightly dance! chattered the worms contentedly as the needles flicked and rocked on the cover of the book, the two-minute countdown to the reopening of the portal already in progress. Mycroft smiled happily and patted his pockets for his pipe until he realized with dismay that it too was inside *Hesperus,* so instead he sat down on the prototype of a sarcasm early-warning device and waited. Everything, so far, was working *extremely* well.

On the other side of the Prose Portal, Polly stood on the grassy bank of a large lake where the water gently lapped against the shore. The sun was shining brightly and small puffy clouds floated lazily across the azure sky. Along the edges of the bay she could see thousands upon thousands of vibrant yellow daffodils, all growing in the dappled shade of a birch grove. A breeze, carrying with it the fresh scent of spring, caused the flowers to flutter and dance. All about her a feeling of peace and tranquillity ruled. The world she stood in now was unsullied by man's evil or malice. Here, indeed, was paradise.

"It's beautiful!" she said at last, her thoughts finally giving birth to her words. "The flowers, the colors, the scent—it's like breathing champagne!"

"You like it, madam?"

A man aged about eighty was facing her. He was dressed in a black cloak and wore a half-smile upon his weathered features. He gazed across at the flowers.

"I often come here," he said. "Whenever the doldrums of depression fall heavy on my countenance."

"You're very lucky," said Polly. "We have to rely on *Name That Fruit!!*"

"*Name That Fruit?*"

"It's a quiz show. You know. On the telly."

"Telly?"

"Yes, it's like the movies but with commercials."

He frowned at her without comprehension and looked at the lake again.

"I often come here," he said again. "Whenever the doldrums of depression fall heavy on my countenance."

"You said that already."

The old man looked as though he were awakening from a deep sleep.

"What are you doing here?"

"My husband sent me. My name is Polly Next."

"I come here when in vacant or pensive mood, you know."

He waved a hand in the direction of the flowers.

"The daffodils, you understand."

Polly looked across at the bright yellow flowers, which rustled back at her in the warm breeze.

"I wish my memory was this good," she murmured.

The figure in black smiled at her.

"The inward eye is all I have left," he said wistfully, the smile leaving his stern features. "Everything that I once was is now here; my life is contained in my works. A life in volumes of words; it is poetic."

He sighed deeply and added:

"But solitude isn't always blissful, you know."

He stared into the middle distance, the sun sparkling on the waters of the lake.

"How long since I died?" he asked abruptly.

"Over a hundred and fifty years."

"Really? Tell me, how did the revolution in France turn out?"

"It's a little early to tell."

Wordsworth frowned as the sun went in.

"Hello," he muttered, "I don't remember writing that—"

Polly looked. A large and very dark rain cloud had blotted out the sun.

"What do you—?" she began, but when she looked around Wordsworth had gone. The sky grew darker and thunder rumbled ominously in the distance. A strong wind sprang up and the lake seemed to freeze over and lose all depth as the daffodils stopped moving and became a solid mass of yellow and green. She cried out in fear as the sky and the lake met; the daffodils, trees and clouds returning to their place in the poem, individual words, sounds, squiggles on paper with no meanings other than those with which our own imagination can clothe them. She let out one last terrified scream as the darkness swept on and the poem closed on top of her.

12.

SpecOps-27:
The Literary Detectives

> . . . This morning Thursday Next joined the LiteraTec office in place of Crometty. I cannot help thinking that she is particularly unsuited to this area of work and I have my doubts as to whether she is as sane as she thinks she is. She has many demons, old and new, and I wonder whether Swindon is quite the right place to try and exorcise them . . .
>
> From Bowden Cable's diary

THE SWINDON SpecOps headquarters were shared with the local police; the typically brusque and no-nonsense Germanic design had been built during the Occupation as a law court. It was big too, which was just as well. The way into the building was protected by metal detectors, and once I had shown my ID I walked into the large entrance hall. Officers and civilians with identity tags walked briskly amid the loud hubbub of the station. I was jostled once or twice in the throng and made a few greetings to old faces before fighting my way to the front desk. When I got there, I found a man in a white baggy shirt and breeches remonstrating with the sergeant. The officer just stared at him. He'd heard it all before.

"Name?" asked the desk sergeant wearily.

"John Milton."

"*Which* John Milton?"

John Milton sighed.

"Four hundred and ninety-six."

The sergeant made a note in his book.

"How much did they take?"

"Two hundred in cash and all my credit cards."

"Have you notified your bank?"

"Of course."

"And you think your assailant was a Percy Shelley?"

"Yes," replied the Milton. "He handed me this pamphlet on rejecting current religious dogma before he ran off."

"Hello, Ross," I said.

The sergeant looked at me, paused for a moment and then broke into a huge grin.

"Thursday! They told me you'd be coming back! Told me you made it all the way to SO-5 too."

I returned his smile. Ross had been the desk sergeant when I had first joined the Swindon police.

"What are you doing here?" he asked. "Starting up a regional office? SO-9 or something? Add a touch of spice to tired old Swindon?"

"Not exactly. I've transferred into the LiteraTec office."

A look of doubt crossed Ross's face but he quickly hid it.

"Great!" he enthused, slightly uneasily. "Drink later?"

I agreed happily, and after getting directions to the LiteraTec office, left Ross arguing with Milton 496.

I took the winding stair to the upper floor and then followed directions to the far end of the building. The entire west wing was filled with SpecOps or their regional departments. The Environmental SpecOps had an office here, as did Art Theft and the ChronoGuard. Even Spike had an office up here, although he was rarely seen in it; he preferred a dark and rather fetid lockup in the basement car park. The corridor was packed with bookcases and filing cabinets; the old carpet had almost worn through in the center. It was a far cry from the LiteraTec office in London, where we had enjoyed the most up-to-date information retrieval systems. At length I reached the correct door and knocked. I didn't receive an answer so I walked straight in.

The room was like a library from a country home somewhere. It was two stories high, with shelves crammed full of books covering every square inch of wall space. A spiral staircase led to a catwalk which ran around the wall, enabling access to the upper shelves. The middle of the room was open plan with desks laid out much like a library's reading room. Every possible surface and all the floor space were piled high with more books and papers, and I wondered how they managed to get anything done at all. About five officers were at work, but they didn't seem to notice me come in. A phone rang and a young man picked it up.

"LiteraTec office," he said in a polite voice. He winced as a tirade came down the phone line to him.

"I'm very sorry if you didn't like *Titus Andronicus*, madam," he said at last, "but I'm afraid it's got nothing to do with us— perhaps you should stick to the comedies in future."

I could see Victor Analogy looking through a file with another officer. I walked to where he could see me and waited for him to finish.

"Ah, Next! Welcome to the office. Give me a moment, will you?"

I nodded and Victor carried on.

". . . I think Keats would have used less flowery prose than this and the third stanza is slightly clumsy in its construction. My feeling is that it's a clever fake, but check it against the Verse Meter Analyzer."

The officer nodded and walked off. Victor smiled at me and shook my hand.

"That was Finisterre. He looks after poetry forgery of the nineteenth century. Let me show you around."

He waved a hand in the direction of the bookshelves.

"Words are like leaves, Thursday. Like people really, fond of their own society."

He smiled.

"We have over a billion words here. Reference mainly. A good collection of major works and some minor ones that you won't even find in the Bodleian. We've got a storage facility in the basement. That's full as well. We need new premises but the LiteraTecs are a bit underfunded, to say the least."

He led me around one of the desks to where Bowden was sitting bolt upright, his jacket carefully folded across the back of his chair and his desk so neat as to be positively obscene.

"Bowden you've met. Fine fellow. He's been with us for twelve years and concentrates on nineteenth-century prose. He'll be showing you the ropes. That's your desk over there."

He paused for a moment, staring at the cleared desk. I was not supernumerary. One of their number had died recently and I was replacing him. Filling a dead man's shoes, sitting in a dead man's chair. Beyond the desk sat another officer, who was looking at me curiously.

"That's Fisher. He'll help you out with anything you want to know about legal copyright and contemporary fiction."

Fisher was a stocky man with an odd squint who appeared to be wider than he was tall. He looked up at me and grinned, revealing something left over from breakfast stuck between his teeth.

Victor carried on walking to the next desk.

"Seventeenth- and eighteenth-century prose and poetry are looked after by Helmut Bight, kindly lent to us by our opposite number across the water. He came here to sort out a problem with some poorly translated Goethe and became embroiled with a neo-Nazi movement attempting to set Friedrich Nietzsche up as a fascist saint."

Herr Bight was about fifty and looked at me suspiciously. He wore a suit but had removed his tie in the heat.

"SO-5, eh?" asked Herr Bight, as though it were a form of venereal disease.

"I'm SO-27 just like you," I replied quite truthfully. "Eight years in the London office under Boswell."

Bight picked up an ancient-looking volume in a faded pigskin binding and passed it across to me.

"What do you make of this?"

I took the dusty tome in my hand and looked at the spine.

"The Vanity of Human Wishes," I read. "Written by Samuel Johnson and published in 1749, the first work to appear in his own name."

I opened the book and flicked through the yellowed pages. "First edition. It would be very valuable, if—"

"If?—" repeated Bight.

I sniffed the paper and ran a finger across the page and then tasted it. I looked along the spine and tapped the cover, finally dropping the heavy volume on the desk with a thump.

"—if it were real."

"I'm impressed, Miss Next," admitted Herr Bight. "You and I must discuss Johnson some time."

"It wasn't as difficult as it looked," I had to admit. "Back in London we've got two pallet-loads of forged Johnsonia like this with a street value of over three hundred thousand pounds."

"London *too?*" exclaimed Bight in surprise. "We've been after this gang for six months; we thought they were local."

"Call Boswell at the London office; he'll help in any way he can. Just mention my name."

Herr Bight picked up the phone and asked the operator for a number. Victor guided me over to one of the many frosted-glass doors leading off the main chamber into side offices. He opened the door a crack to reveal two officers in shirtsleeves who were interviewing a man dressed in tights and an embroidered jacket.

"Malin and Sole look after all crimes regarding Shakespeare."

He shut the door.

"They keep an eye on forgery, illegal dealing and overtly free thespian interpretations. The actor in with them was Graham Huxtable. He was putting on a felonious one-man performance of *Twelfth Night*. Persistent offender. He'll be fined and bound over. His Malvolio is *truly* frightful."

He opened the door to another side office. A pair of identical twins were operating a large computing engine. The room was uncomfortably hot from the thousands of valves, and the clicking of relays was almost deafening. This was the only piece of modern technology that I had seen so far in the office.

"These are the Forty brothers, Jeff and Geoff. The Fortys operate the Verse Meter Analyzer. It breaks down any prose or poem into its components—words, punctuation, grammar and so forth—then compares that literary signature with a specimen of the target writer in its own memory. Eighty-nine percent accuracy. Very useful for spotting forgeries. We had what purported to be a page of an early draft of *Antony and Cleopatra*. It was rejected on the grounds that it had too many verbs per unit paragraph."

He closed the door.

"That's all of us. The man in overall charge of Swindon SpecOps is Commander Braxton Hicks. He's answerable to the Regional Commander based in Salisbury. He leaves us alone most of the time, which is the way we like it. He also likes to see any new operatives the morning they arrive, so I suggest you go and have a word. He's in room twenty-eight down the corridor."

We retraced our steps back to my desk. Victor wished me well again and then disappeared to consult with Helmut about some pirate copies of *Doctor Faustus* that had appeared on the market with the endings rewritten to be happy.

I sat down in my chair and opened the desk drawer. There was nothing in it; not so much as a pencil shaving. Bowden was watching me.

"Victor emptied it the morning after Crometty's murder."

"James Crometty," I murmured. "Suppose you tell me about him?"

Bowden picked up a pencil and tried to balance it on its sharp end.

"Crometty worked mainly in nineteenth-century prose and poetry. He was an excellent officer but excitable. He had little time for procedure. He vanished one evening when he said he had a tip-off about a rare manuscript. We found him a week later in the abandoned Raven public house on Morgue Road. They had shot him six times in the face."

"I'm sorry to hear that."

"I've lost friends before," said Bowden, his voice never wavering from the measured pace of speech he used, "but he was a close friend and colleague and I would gladly have taken his place."

He rubbed his nose slightly; it was the only sign of outward emotion that he had shown.

"I consider myself a spiritual man, Miss Next, although I am not religious. By spiritual I merely mean that I feel I have good in my soul and am inclined to follow the correct course of action given a prescribed set of circumstances. Do you understand?"

I nodded.

"Having said that, I would still be *very* keen to end the life of the person who did this foul deed. I have been practicing on the range and now carry a pistol full time; look—"

"Show me later, Mr. Cable. Do you have any leads?"

"None. Nothing at all. We don't know who he was seeing or why. I have contacts over at Homicide; they have nothing either."

"Being shot six times in the face is the mark of a person with a gleeful passion for the undertaking of their duties," I told him. "Even if Crometty had been carrying a gun I don't think it would have made much difference."

"You could be right," sighed Bowden. "I can't think of a single time that a pistol has been drawn on a LiteraTec investigation."

I agreed. Ten years ago in London it had been the same. But big business and the huge amounts of cash in the sale and distribution of literary works had attracted a bigger criminal element. I knew of at least four London LiteraTecs who had died in the line of duty.

"It's becoming more violent out there. It's not like it is in the movies. Did you hear about the surrealist riot in Chichester last night?"

"I certainly did," he replied. "I can see Swindon involved in similar disturbances before too long. The art college nearly had a riot on its hands last year when the governors dismissed a lecturer who had been secretly encouraging students to embrace abstract expressionism. They wanted him charged under the Interpretation of the Visual Medium Act. He fled to Russia, I think."

I looked at my watch.

"I have to go and see the SpecOps commander."

Bowden allowed a rare smile to creep upon his serious features.

"I bid you good luck. If you would permit me to offer you some advice, keep your automatic out of sight. Despite James's untimely death, Commander Hicks doesn't want to see the LiteraTecs permanently armed. He believes that our place is firmly at a desk."

I thanked him, left my automatic in the desk drawer and walked down the corridor. I knocked twice and was invited into the outer office by a young clerk. I told him my name and he asked me to wait.

"The Commander won't be long. Fancy a cup of coffee?"

"No thanks."

The clerk looked at me curiously.

"They say you've come from London to avenge Jim Crometty's death. They say you killed two men. They say your father's face can stop a clock. Is this true?"

"It depends on how you look at it. Office rumors are pretty quick to get started, aren't they?"

Braxton Hicks opened the door to his office and beckoned me in. He was a tall, thin man with a large mustache and a gray complexion. He had bags under his eyes; it didn't look as though he slept much. The room was far more austere than any commander's office I had ever seen. Several golf bags were leaning against the wall, and I could see that a carpet putter had been hastily pushed to one side.

He smiled genially and offered me a seat before sitting himself.

"Cigarette?"

"I don't, thank you."

"Neither do I."

He stared at me for a moment and drummed his long fingers on the immaculately clear desk. He opened a folder in front of him and read in silence for a moment. He was reading my SO-5 file; obviously he and Analogy didn't get on well enough to swap information between clearances.

"Operative Thursday Next, eh?" His eyes flicked across the pertinent points of my career. "Quite a record. Police, Crimea, rejoined the police, then moved to London in '75. Why was that?"

"Advancement, sir."

Braxton Hicks grunted and continued reading.

"SpecOps for eight years, twice commended. Recently loaned to SO-5. Your stay with the latter has been heavily censored, yet it says here you were wounded in action."

He looked over his spectacles at me.

"Did you return fire?"

"No."

"Good."

"I fired first."

"*Not* so good."

Braxton stroked his mustache thoughtfully.

"You were operative grade one in the London office working on Shakespeare, no less. Very prestigious. Yet you swap that for a grade three operative assignment in a backwater like this. Why?"

"Times change and we change with them, sir."

Braxton grunted and closed the file.

"Here at SpecOps my responsibility is not only with the LiteraTecs, but also Art Theft, Vampirism & Lycanthropy, the ChronoGuard, Antiterrorism, Civil Order and the dog pound. Do you play golf?"

"No, sir."

"Shame, shame. Where was I? Oh yes. Out of all those departments, do you know which I fear most?"

"I've no idea, sir."

"I'll tell you. None of them. The thing I fear most is SpecOps regional budget meetings. Do you realize what that means, Next?"

"No, sir."

"It means that every time one of you puts in for extra overtime or a special request, I go over budget and it makes my head hurt right *here*."

He pointed to his left temple.

"And I don't like that. Do you understand?"

"Yes, sir."

He picked up my file again and waved it at me.

"I heard you had a spot of bother in the big city. Other operatives getting killed. It's a whole new different alternative kettle of fish here, y'know. We crunch data for a living. If you want to arrest someone then have uniform do it. No running about shooting up bad guys, no overtime and definitely no twenty-four-hour surveillance operations. Understand?"

"Yes, sir."

"Now, about Hades."

My heart leaped; I had thought *that* would have been censored, if anything.

"I understand you think he is still alive?"

I thought for a moment. My eyes flicked to the file Hicks was holding. He divined my thoughts.

"Oh, that's not in here, my dear girl. I may be a hick commander in the boonies, but I do have my sources. You think he is still alive?"

I knew I could trust Victor and Bowden, but about Hicks I was not so sure. I didn't think I would risk it.

"A symptom of stress, sir. Hades is dead."

He plonked my file in the out-tray, leaned back in his chair and stroked his mustache, something he obviously enjoyed.

"So you're not here to try and find him?"

"Why would Hades be in Swindon if he were alive, sir?"

Braxton looked uneasy for a moment.

"Quite, quite."

He smiled and stood up, indicating that the interview was at an end.

"Good, well, run along. One piece of advice. Learn to play golf; you'll find it a very rewarding and relaxing game. This is a copy of the department's budget account and this is a list of all the local golf courses. Study them well. Good luck."

I went out and closed the door after me.

The clerk looked up.

"Did he mention the budget?"

"I don't think he mentioned anything else. Do you have a waste bin?"

The clerk smiled and pushed it out with his foot. I dumped the heavy document in it unceremoniously.

"Bravo," he said.

As I was about to open the door to leave a short man in a blue suit came powering through without looking. He was reading a fax and knocked against me as he went straight through to Braxton's office without a word. The clerk was watching me for my reaction.

"Well, well," I murmured, "Jack Schitt."

"You know him?"

"Not socially."

"As much charm as an open grave," said the clerk, who had obviously warmed to me since I binned the budget. "Steer clear of him. Goliath, you know."

I looked at the closed door to Braxton's office.

"What's he here for?"

The secretary shrugged, gave me a conspiratorial wink and said very pointedly and slowly:

"I'll get that coffee you wanted and it was *two* sugars, wasn't it?"

"No thanks, not for me."

"No, no," he replied. "*Two* sugars, TWO sugars."

He was pointing at the intercom on his desk.

"Heavens above!" he exploded. "Do I have to spell it out?"

The penny dropped. The clerk gave a wan smile and scurried out of the door. I quickly sat down, flipped up the lever marked "two" on the intercom and leaned closer to listen.

"I don't like it when you don't knock, Mr. Schitt."

"I'm devastated, Braxton. Does she know anything about Hades?"

"She says not."

"She's lying. She's here for a purpose. If I find Hades first we can get rid of her."

"Less of the *we*, Jack," said Braxton testily. "Please remember that I have given Goliath my full cooperation, but you are working under my jurisdiction and have only the powers that I bestow upon you. Powers that I can revoke at any time. We do this my way or not at all. Do you understand?"

Schitt was unperturbed. He replied in a condescending manner:

"Of course, Braxton, as long as you understand that if this thing blows up in your face the Goliath Corporation will hold you personally responsible."

I sat down at my empty desk again. There seemed to be a lot going on in the office that I wasn't a part of. Bowden laid his hand on my shoulder and made me jump.

"I'm sorry, I didn't wish to startle you. Did you get the commander's budget speech?"

"And more. Jack Schitt went into his office as though he owned the place."

Bowden shrugged.

"Since he's Goliath, then the chances are he does."

Bowden picked his jacket up from the back of his chair and folded it neatly across his arm.

"Where are we going?" I asked.

"Lunch, then a lead in the *Chuzzlewit* theft. I'll explain on the way. Do you have a car?"

Bowden wasn't too impressed when he saw the multicolored Porsche.

"This is hardly what one might refer to as low profile."

"On the contrary," I replied, "who would have thought a LiteraTec would drive a car like this? Besides, I *have* to drive it."

He got in the passenger seat and looked around slightly disdainfully at the spartan interior.

"Is there a problem, Miss Next? You're staring."

Now that Bowden was in the passenger seat I had suddenly realized where I had seen him before. He had been the passenger when the car had appeared in front of me at the hospital. Events had indeed started to fall into place.

14.

Lunch with Bowden

Bowden Cable is the sort of honest and dependable operative that is the backbone of SpecOps. They never win commendations or medals and the public has no knowledge of them at all. They are all worth ten of people like me.

THURSDAY NEXT
—*A Life in SpecOps*

BOWDEN GUIDED me to a transport café on the old Oxford road. I thought it was an odd choice for lunch; the seats were hard orange plastic and the yellowing Formica-covered tabletops had started to lift at the edges. The windows were almost opaque with dirt and the nylon net curtains hung heavily with deposits of grease. Several flypapers dangled from the ceiling, their potency long worn off, the flies stuck to them long since desiccated to dust. Somebody had made an effort to make the interior slightly more cheery by sticking up a few pictures hastily cut from old calendars; a signed photo of the 1978 England soccer team was hung above a fireplace that had been filled in and then decorated with a vase full of plastic flowers.

"Are you sure?" I asked, sitting gingerly at a table near the window.

"The food's good," responded Bowden, as though that was all that mattered.

A gum-chewing waitress came up to the table and put some bent cutlery in front of us. She was about fifty and was wearing a uniform that might have been her mother's.

"Hello, Mr. Cable," she said in a flat tone with only a sliver of interest in her voice, "all well?"

"Very well, thank you. Lottie, I'd like you to meet my new partner, Thursday Next."

Lottie looked at me oddly.

"Any relation to Captain Next?"

"He was my brother," I said loudly, as if wanting Lottie to know that I wasn't ashamed of the connection, "and he didn't do what they said he did."

The waitress stared at me for a moment, as if wanting to say something but not daring.

"What will you lot have, then?" she asked instead with forced cheerfulness. She had lost someone in the charge; I could sense it.

"What's the special?" asked Bowden.

"*Soupe d'Auvergne au fromage*," replied Lottie, "followed by *rojoes cominho*."

"What's that?" I asked.

"It's braised pork with cumin, coriander and lemon," replied Bowden.

"Sounds great."

"Two specials please and a carafe of mineral water."

She nodded, scribbled a note and gave me a sad smile before departing.

Bowden looked at me with interest. He would have guessed eventually that I was ex-military. I wore it badly.

"Crimea veteran, eh? Did you know Colonel Phelps was in town?"

"I bumped into him on the airship yesterday. He wanted me to go to one of his rallies."

"Will you?"

"You must be kidding. His idea of the perfect end to the Crimean conflict is for us to fight and fight until there is no one left alive and the peninsula's a poisoned and mined land no good for anything. I'm hoping that the UN can bring both governments to their senses."

"I was called up in '78," said Bowden. "Even got past basic training. Fortunately it was the same year the czar died and the crown prince took over. There were more pressing demands on the young emperor's time, so the Russians withdrew. I was never needed."

"I was reading somewhere that since the war started, only seven years of the one hundred and thirty-one have actually been spent fighting."

"But when they do," added Bowden, "they certainly make up for it."

I looked at him. He had taken a sip of water after offering the carafe to me first.

"Married? Kids?"

"No," replied Bowden. "I haven't really had time to find myself a wife, although I am not against the idea in principle. It's just that SpecOps is not really a great place for meeting people and I'm not, I confess, a great socializer. I've been short-listed for a post opening the equivalent of a LiteraTec office in Ohio; it seems to me the perfect opportunity to take a wife."

"The money's good over there and the facilities are excellent. I'd consider it myself given the opportunity," I replied. I meant it too.

"Would you? Would you really?" asked Bowden with a flush of excitement that was curiously at odds with his slightly cold demeanor.

"Sure. Change of scenery," I stammered, wanting to change the subject in case Bowden got the wrong idea. "Have you . . . ah . . . been a LiteraTec long?"

Bowden thought for a moment.

"Ten years. I came from Cambridge with a degree in nineteenth-century literature and joined the LiteraTecs straight away. Jim Crometty looked after me from the moment I started."

He stared out of the window wistfully.

"Perhaps if I'd been there—"

"—then you'd both be dead. Anyone who shoots a man six times in the face doesn't go to Sunday school. He'd have killed you and not even thought about it. There's little to be gained in what ifs; believe me, I know. I lost two fellow officers to Hades. I've been over it all a hundred times, yet it would probably happen exactly the same way if I had another chance."

Lottie placed the soup in front of us with a basket of freshly baked bread.

"Enjoy," said Lottie, "it's on the house."

"But!—" I began. Lottie silenced me.

"Save your breath," she said impassively. "After the charge. After the shit hit the fan. After the first wave of death—you went back to do what you could. *You went back*. I value that." She turned and left.

The soup was good; the *rojoes cominho* even better.

"Victor told me you worked on Shakespeare up in London," said Bowden.

It was the most prestigious area in which to work in the LiteraTec office. Lake poetry was a close second and Restoration comedy after that. Even in the most egalitarian of offices, a pecking order always established itself.

"There was very little room for promotion in the London office so after a couple of years I was given the Shakespeare work," I replied, tearing at a piece of bread. "We get a lot of trouble from Baconians in London."

Bowden looked up.

"How do you rate the Baconian theory?"

"Not much. Like many people I'm pretty sure there is more to Shakespeare than just Shakespeare. But Sir Francis Bacon using a little-known actor as a front? I just don't buy it."

"He was a trained lawyer," asserted Bowden. "Many of the plays have legal parlance to them."

"It means nothing," I replied, "Greene, Nashe and especially Ben Jonson use legal phraseology; none of them had legal training. And don't even get me started on the so-called codes."

"No need to worry about *that*," replied Bowden. "I won't. I'm no Baconian either. He didn't write them."

"And what would make you so sure?"

"If you read his *De Augmentis Scientarium* you'll find Bacon actually criticizing popular drama. Furthermore, when the troupe Shakespeare belonged to applied to the king to form a theater, they were referred to the commissioner for suits. Guess who was on that panel and most vociferously opposed the application?"

"Francis Bacon?" I asked.

"Exactly. Whoever wrote the plays, it wasn't Bacon. I've formulated a few theories of my own over the years. Have you ever heard of Edward De Vere, the seventeenth Earl of Oxford?"

"Vaguely."

"There is some proof that, unlike Bacon, he could actually write and write quite well—hang on."

Lottie had brought a phone to the table. It was for Bowden. He wiped his mouth with a napkin.

"Yes?"

He looked up at me.

"Yes, she is. We'll be right over. Thanks."

"Problems?"

"It's your aunt and uncle. I don't know how to say this but . . . they've been kidnapped!"

There were several police and SpecOps cars clustered around the entrance to my mother's house when we pulled up. A small crowd had assembled and was peering over the fence. The dodos had gathered on the other side and were staring back, wondering what the fuss was all about. I showed my badge to the officer on duty.

"LiteraTec?" he said scornfully. "Can't let you in, ma'am. Police and SpecOps-9 only."

"He's my uncle!—" I said angrily, and the officer reluctantly let me through. Swindon was the same as London: A LiteraTec's badge held about as much authority as a bus pass. I found my mother in the living room surrounded by damp Kleenex. I sat beside her and asked her what had happened.

She blew her nose noisily.

"I called them in for dinner at one. It was snorkers, Mycroft's favorite. There was no answer so I went down to his workshop. They were both gone and the double doors wide open. Mycroft wouldn't have gone out without saying anything."

This was true. Mycroft never left the house unless it was absolutely necessary; since Owens had been meringued Polly did all his running around.

"Anything stolen?" I asked a SpecOps-9 operative who stared at me coldly. He didn't relish being asked questions by a LiteraTec.

"Who knows?" he replied with little emotion. "I understand you'd been in his workshop recently?"

"Yesterday evening."

"Then perhaps you can have a look around and tell *us* if there is anything missing?"

I was escorted to Mycroft's workshop. The rear doors had been forced and I looked around carefully. The table where Mycroft had kept all his bookworms had been cleared; all I could see was the massive two-pronged power lead that would have slotted into the back of the Prose Portal.

"There was something right here. Several goldfish bowls full up with small worms and a large book a bit like a medieval church Bible—"

"Can you draw it?" asked a familiar voice. I turned to see Jack Schitt lurking in the shadows, smoking a small cigarette and overseeing a Goliath technician who was passing a humming sensor over the ground.

"Well, well," I said. "If it isn't Jack Schitt. What's Goliath's interest in my uncle?"

"Can you draw it?" he repeated.

I nodded, and one of the Goliath men gave me a pencil and paper. I sketched out what I had seen, the intricate combination of dials and knobs on the front of the book and the heavy brass straps. Jack Schitt took it from me and studied it with great interest as another Goliath technician walked in from outside.

"Well?" asked Schitt.

The agent saluted neatly and showed Schitt a pair of large and slightly molten G-clamps.

"Professor Next had jury-rigged his own set of cables to the electrical substation just next door. I spoke to the electricity board. They said they had three unexplained power drains of about one point eight megawatts each late last night."

Jack Schitt turned to me.

"You better leave this to us, Next," he said. "Kidnapping and theft are not part of the LiteraTec's responsibility."

"Who did this?" I demanded, but Schitt didn't take crap from anyone—least of all me. He wagged a finger in my direction.

"This investigation is nothing to do with you; we'll keep you informed of any developments. Or not. As I see fit."

He turned and walked away.

"It was Acheron, wasn't it?" I said, slowly and deliberately. Schitt stopped in midstride, and turned to face me.

"Acheron is dead, Next. Burned to a crisp at junction twelve. Don't spread your theories around town, girl. It might make you seem more unstable than you actually are."

He smiled without the least vestige of kindness and walked out of the workshop to his waiting car.

15.

Hello & Goodbye,
Mr. Quaverley

Few people remember Mr. Quaverley anymore. If you had read *Martin Chuzzlewit* prior to 1985 you would have come across a minor character who lived in Mrs. Todger's boarding house. He discoursed freely with the Pecksniffs on the subject of butterflies, of which he knew almost nothing. Sadly, he is no longer there. His hat is hanging on the hat rack at the bottom of page 235, but that is all that remains . . .

MILLON DE FLOSS
—*Thursday Next Casebook*, Volume 6

ASTOUNDING!" SAID Acheron quietly as he surveyed Mycroft's Prose Portal. "*Truly* astounding!"

Mycroft said nothing. He had been too busy wondering whether Polly was still alive and well since the poem closed on her. Against his protestations they had pulled the plug before the portal had reopened; he didn't know if any human could survive in such an environment. They had blindfolded him during the journey and he was now standing in the smoking lounge of what had once been a large and luxurious hotel. Although still grand, the décor was tatty and worn. The pearl-inlaid grand piano didn't look as though it had been tuned for years, and the mirror-backed bar was sadly devoid of any refreshment. Mycroft looked out of the window for a clue as to where he was being held. It wasn't hard to guess. The large quantity of drab-colored Griffin motorcars and the absence of any advertising hoardings told Mycroft all he needed to know; he was in the People's Republic of Wales, somewhere well out of reach of the conventional law enforcement agencies. The possibility of escape was slim, and if he could get away, what then? Even if there was a chance he could make it back across the border, he would never be able to leave without Polly—she was still imprisoned in the poem, itself now little more than printed words on a scrap of paper that Hades had placed in his breast pocket. There seemed to be little chance of regaining the poem without a fearsome struggle, and besides, without the bookworms and the Prose Portal, Polly would stay in her Wordsworthian prison forever. Mycroft bit his lip nervously and turned his attention to the other people in the room. Besides himself and Hades there were four others—and two of them held guns.

"Welcome, Professor Next," said Hades as he grinned broadly, "from one genius to another!"

He gazed fondly at the machine. He ran a finger along the rim of one of the goldfish bowls. The worms were busy reading a copy of *Mansfield Park* and were discussing where Sir Thomas got his money from.

"I can't do this alone, you know," said Hades without looking up. One of the other men shuffled to get more comfortable on one of the few original upholstered armchairs.

"The next step for me is to gain your full support." He looked at Mycroft with a serious expression. "You *will* help me, won't you?"

"I would sooner die!" replied Mycroft coldly.

Acheron looked at him, then broke into another broad grin.

"I don't doubt it for one moment, but I'm being rude! I have abducted you and stolen your life's work and haven't even in-troduced myself!" He walked up to Mycroft and shook him warmly by the hand, a gesture that Mycroft didn't return.

"My name is Hades, Acheron Hades. Perhaps you've heard of me?"

"Acheron the extortionist?" asked Mycroft slowly. "Acheron the kidnapper and the blackmailer?"

Acheron's smile didn't leave his lips.

"Yes, yes and *yes*. But you forgot murderer. Forty-two times a murderer, my friend. The first one is always the hardest. After that it doesn't really matter, they can only hang you once. It's a bit like eating a packet of shortbread; you can never just have one piece." He laughed again. "I had a run-in with your niece, you know. She survived, although," he added, in case Mycroft erroneously believed there was a vestige of goodness in his dark soul, "that wasn't the way I had planned it."

"Why are you doing this?" asked Mycroft.

"Why?" repeated Acheron. "Why? Why, for *fame,* of course!" he boomed. "You see, gentlemen?—" The others nod-ded obediently. "Fame!" he repeated. "And you can share that fame!—"

He ushered Mycroft over to his desk and dug out a file of press clippings.

"Look what the papers say about me!"

He held up a cutting proudly.

HADES 74 WEEKS AT TOP OF
"MOST-WANTED" LIST

"Impressive, eh?" he said proudly. "How about this one?"

TOAD READERS VOTE HADES
"LEAST FAVORITE PERSON"

"*The Owl* said that execution was too good for me and *The Mole* wanted Parliament to reintroduce breaking on the wheel."

He showed the snippet to Mycroft.

"What do you think?"

"I think," began Mycroft, "that you could have used your vast intellect far more usefully by serving mankind instead of stealing from it."

Acheron looked hurt.

"Where's the fun in that? Goodness is weakness, pleasantness is poisonous, serenity is mediocrity and kindness is for losers. The best reason for committing loathsome and detestable acts—and let's face it, I am considered something of an expert in this field—is purely for their own sake. Monetary gain is all very well, but it dilutes the taste of wickedness to a lower level that is obtainable by almost anyone with an overdeveloped sense of avarice. True and baseless evil is as rare as the purest good—"

"I'd like to go home."

"Of course!" said Acheron, smiling. "Hobbes, open the door."

The man nearest the door opened it and stepped aside. The large door led to the lobby of the old hotel.

"I don't speak Welsh," murmured Mycroft.

Hobbes shut the door and rebolted it.

"Bit of a drawback in Merthyr, old boy," said Acheron, smiling. "You'd not get far without it."

Mycroft looked at Hades uneasily.

"But Polly!—"

"Ah, yes!" replied Hades. "Your delightful wife." He pulled out the copy of "I Wandered Lonely as a Cloud" and produced a large gold lighter, which he ignited with a flourish.

"No!—" cried Mycroft, taking several steps forward. Acheron arched an eyebrow, the flame nearly touching the paper.

"I'll stay and help you," said Mycroft wearily.

A broad grin broke out on Hades's features. He put the poem back in his pocket.

"Stout fellow! You won't regret this."

He thought for a moment.

"Actually, you probably will."

Mycroft sat unsteadily on a handy chair.

"By the by," went on Hades, "have I introduced you to all my fiendish compatriots?"

Mycroft shook his head sadly.

"No? Most remiss. The man with the gun over there is Mr. Delamare. His obedience is matched only by his stupidity. He does everything I say and would die for me if necessary. A sort of human red setter, if you will. He has an IQ below that of a Neanderthal and believes only what he reads in *The Gad-fly*. Mr. Delamare, my friend, have you committed your wicked act today?"

"Yes, Mr. Hades. I drove at seventy-three miles per hour."

Hades frowned.

"That doesn't sound very wicked."

Delamare chuckled.

"Through the mall?"

Hades wagged an approving finger and smiled a wicked smile.

"Very good."

"Thank you, Mr. Hades."

"Over there is Mr. Hobbes. He is an actor of some distinction whose talents the English Shakespeare Company foolishly decides to ignore. We will try and rectify that fault; is that not so, Mr. Hobbes?"

"It is, sire," responded Mr. Hobbes, bowing low with a flourish. He was dressed in tights, a leather jerkin and codpiece. He had been passed over for every major part with the ESC for ten years, relegated to walk-ons and understudying. He had become so dangerously unstable that even the other actors noticed. He had joined up with Acheron shortly after his escape from a lengthy prison sentence; pushing thespian interpretation to the limits, he had killed Laertes for real while playing Hamlet.

"The third man over there is Müller, a doctor whom I befriended after he was struck off. The particulars are a bit sordid. We'll talk about it over dinner some time, as long as we're not eating steak tartar. The fourth man is Felix7, who is one of my most trusted companions. He can remember no farther than a week in the past and has no aspirations for the future. He thinks only of the work he has been assigned to carry out. He is without conscience, mercy or pity. A fine man. We should have more like him."

Hades clapped his hands together happily.

"Shall we get to work? I haven't committed a singularly debauched act for almost an hour."

Mycroft reluctantly walked over to the Prose Portal and started to ready it. The bookworms were fed, watered and cleaned, power supplies were laid on and all the details in the child's exercise book neatly followed. As Mycroft worked, Acheron sat down and flicked through an old manuscript filled with spidery writing, replete with scribbled corrections and bound up with faded red ribbon. He skipped through various sections until he found what he was looking for.

"Perfect!" he chortled.

Mycroft finished the testing procedure and stepped back.

"It's ready," he sighed.

"Excellent!" Acheron beamed as he handed over the aged manuscript.

"Open the portal just here."

He tapped the page and smiled. Mycroft slowly took the manuscript and looked at the title.

"*Martin Chuzzlewit!* Fiend!"

"Flattery will get you nowhere, my dear professor."

"But," continued Mycroft, "if you alter anything in the original manuscript!—"

"But that's the *point*, isn't it, my dear Mycroft," said Hades, clasping one of Mycroft's cheeks between finger and thumb and shaking gently. "That's . . . the . . . point. What good is extortion unless you show everyone what massive damage you could do if you wanted? And anyway, where's the fun in robbing banks? Bang, bang, give me the money? Besides, killing civilians is never any *real* fun. It's a bit like shooting rabbits that have been pegged to the ground. Give me a SWAT platoon to deal with any day."

"But the damage!—" continued Mycroft. "Are you mad!?"

Acheron's eyes flashed angrily as he grasped Mycroft tightly by the throat.

"What? What did you say? *Mad*, did you say? Hmm? Eh? What? *What?*"

His fingers tightened on Mycroft's windpipe; the professor could feel himself start to sweat in the cold panic of suffocation. Acheron was waiting for an answer that Mycroft was unable to utter.

"What? What did you say?"

Acheron's pupils started to dilate as Mycroft felt a dark veil fall over his mind.

"Think it's *fun* being christened with a name like mine? Having to live up to what is expected of one? Born with an intellect so vast that all other humans are cretins by comparison?"

Mycroft managed to give out a choke and Acheron slackened his grip. Mycroft fell to the floor, gulping for breath. Acheron stood over him and wagged a reproachful finger.

"Don't *ever* call me mad, Mycroft. I'm not mad, I'm just . . . well, *differently moraled*, that's all."

Hades handed him *Chuzzlewit* again and Mycroft needed no second bidding. He placed the worms with the manuscript inside the heavy old book; within half an hour of feverish activity the device was primed and set.

"It is ready," announced Mycroft miserably. "I have only to press this button and the door will open. It will stay open for ten seconds at most."

He sighed deeply and shook his head.

"May God forgive me!—"

"*I* forgive you," replied Acheron. "It's the closest you'll get!"

Hades walked across to Hobbes, who was now dressed in black combat gear. He wore a webbing harness around his waist upon which hung all sorts of items that might be of use on an unplanned armed robbery—a large torch, bolt cutters, rope, handcuffs and an automatic.

"You know who it is you are after?"

"Mr. Quaverley, sir."

"Splendid. I feel a speech coming on."

He climbed onto a carved oak table.

"My friends!" he began. "This is a very *great* day for science and a very *bad* one for Dickensian literature."

He paused for dramatic effect.

"Comrades, we stand on the very brink of an act of artistic barbarism so monstrous that I am almost ashamed of it myself. All of you have been my faithful servants for many years, and although none of you possesses a soul quite as squalid as mine, and the faces I see before me are both stupid and unappealing, I regard you all with no small measure of fondness."

His four comrades mumbled their thanks.

"Silence! I think it is fair to say that I am the most debased individual on this planet and quite the most brilliant criminal mind this century. The plan that we embark upon now is easily the most diabolical ever devised by man, and will not only take you to the top of everyone's most-wanted list but will also make you wealthy beyond your wildest dreams of avarice." He clapped his hands together. "So let the adventure begin, and here's to the success of our finest criminal endeavor!"

"Sir?"

"What is it, Dr. Müller?"

"All that money. I'm not so sure. I'd settle for a Gainsborough. You know—that one of the kid in the blue suit."

Acheron stared at him for a moment, a smile slowly breaking across his features.

"Why not? Odious *and* art-loving! What a divine dichotomy! You shall have your Gainsborough! And now, let us—What is it, Hobbes?"

"You won't forget to make the ESC put on my improved version of the Scottish play—*Macbeth: No More 'Mr. Nice Guy'*?"

"Of course not."

"A full eight-week run?"

"Yes, yes, and *Midsummer Night's Dream* with chainsaws. Mr. Delamare, is there anything that *you* require?"

"Well," said the man with the brain of a dog, rubbing the back of his head thoughtfully, "could I have a motorway services named after my mum?"

"Insufferably obtuse," remarked Acheron. "I don't think that should be too difficult. Felix7?"

"I require no payment," said Felix7 stoically. "I am merely your willing servant. To serve a good and wise master is the best that can be expected of any sentient being."

"I *love* that man!" said Hades to the others. He chuckled to himself and then turned back to Hobbes, who was waiting to make the jump.

"So you understand what it is you have to do?"

"Perfectly."

"Then, Mycroft, open the portal and my dear Hobbes: Godspeed!"

Mycroft pressed the green "open" button and there was a bright flash and a strong electromagnetic pulse that had every compass for miles around spinning wildly. The portal opened rapidly and Hobbes took a deep breath and stepped through; as he did, Mycroft pressed the red "close" button, the portal slid shut and a hush descended on the room. Acheron looked at Mycroft, who stared at the timer on the large book. Dr. Müller read a paperback of *Martin Chuzzlewit* to check Hobbes's progress, Felix7 kept an eye on Mycroft, and Delamare looked at something sticky he had found inside his ear.

Two minutes later Mycroft pressed the green "open" button once more and Hobbes came back through, dragging a middle-aged man dressed in a badly fitting suit with high collar and necktie. Hobbes was quite out of breath and sat on a nearby chair, panting. The middle-aged man looked around him in mystification.

"My friends," he began, looking at their curious faces, "you find me in a disadvantaged state. Pray explain the meaning of what I can only describe as a bewildering predicament—"

Acheron walked up to him and placed a friendly arm around his shoulders.

"Ah, the sweet, sweet smell of success. Welcome to the twentieth century and reality. My name is Hades."

Acheron extended a hand. The man bowed and shook it gratefully, mistakenly believing he had fallen among friends.

"Your servant, Mr. Hades. My name is Mr. Quaverley, resident of Mrs. Todger's and a proctor by trade. I have to confess that I have no small notion of the large wonder that has been subjected to me, but pray tell me, since I see you are the master of this paradox, what has happened and how I can be of assistance."

Acheron smiled and patted Mr. Quaverley's shoulder affectionately.

"My dear Mr. Quaverley! I could spend many happy hours in discussion with you about the essence of Dickensian narrative, but it would really be a waste of my precious time. Felix7, return to Swindon and leave Mr. Quaverley's body where it will be found in the morning."

Felix7 took Mr. Quaverley firmly by the arm.

"Yes, sir."

"Oh, and Felix7—"

"Yes, sir?"

"While you're out, why don't you quiet down that Sturmey Archer fellow? He's of no earthly use to us anymore."

Felix7 dragged Mr. Quaverley out of the door. Mycroft was weeping.

16.

Sturmey Archer & Felix7

> . . . The finest criminal mind requires the finest accomplices to accompany him. Otherwise, what's the point? I always found that I could never apply my most deranged plans without someone to share and appreciate them. I'm like that. Very *generous* . . .
>
> ACHERON HADES
> —*Degeneracy for Pleasure and Profit*

SO WHO is this guy we're going to see?"

"Fellow named Sturmey Archer," replied Bowden as I pulled my car into the curb. We found ourselves opposite a small factory unit that had a gentle glow of light showing through the windows.

"A few years ago Crometty and myself had the extreme good fortune to arrest several members of a gang which had been attempting to peddle a rather poorly forged sequel to Coleridge's 'The Rime of the Ancient Mariner.' It was entitled 'Rime II—The Mariner Returneth' but no one had been fooled. Sturmey avoided jail by turning state's evidence. I've got some dirt on him about a *Cardenio* scam. I don't want to use it, but I will if I have to."

"What makes you think he has anything to do with Crometty's death?"

"Nothing," said Bowden simply. "He's just next on the list."

We walked across in the gathering dusk. The streetlights were flickering on and the stars were beginning to appear in the twilit sky. In another half hour it would be night.

Bowden thought about knocking but didn't bother. He opened the door noiselessly and we crept in.

Sturmey Archer was a feeble-looking character who had spent too many years in institutions to be able to look after himself properly. Without designated bathtimes he didn't wash and without fixed mealtimes he went hungry. He wore thick glasses and mismatched clothes and his face was a moonscape of healed acne. He made part of his living these days by casting busts of famous writers in plaster of paris, but he had too much bad history to be kept on the straight. Other criminals blackmailed him into helping them and Sturmey, already a weak man, could do little to resist. It wasn't surprising that, out of his forty-six years, only twenty had been spent at liberty.

Inside the workshop we came across a large workbench on which were placed about five hundred foot-high busts of Will Shakespeare, all of them in various states of completion. A large vat of plaster of paris lay empty next to a rack containing twenty rubber casts; it seemed Sturmey had a big order on.

Archer himself was at the back of the shop indulging in his second profession, repairing Will-Speak machines. He had his hand up the back of an Othello as we crept up behind him.

The mannequin's crude voice-box crackled as Sturmey made some trifling adjustments:

It is the cause, it is the cause, (click) *yet I'll not shed a drop of her blood,* (click) *nor scar that whiter skin of hers than snow* . . .

"Hello, Sturmey," said Bowden.

Sturmey jumped and shorted out the Othello's controls. The dummy opened its eyes wide and gave out a terrified cry of *MONUMENTAL ALABASTER!* before falling limp. Sturmey glared at Bowden.

"Creeping around at night, Mr. Cable? Hardly like a Litera-Tec, is it?"

Bowden smiled.

"Let's just say I'm rediscovering the joys of fieldwork. This is my new partner, Thursday Next."

Archer nodded at me suspiciously. Bowden continued:

"You heard about Jim Crometty, Sturmey?"

"I heard," replied Archer with feigned sadness.

"I wondered if you had any information you might want to impart?"

"Me?"

He pointed at the plaster busts of Will Shakespeare.

"Look at those. A fiver each wholesale to a Jap company that wants ten thou. The Japanese have built a seven-eighths-scale replica of Stratford-upon-Avon near Yokohama and love all this crap. Fifty grand, Cable, *that's* literature I can relate to."

"And the *Chuzzlewit* manuscript?" I asked. "How do you relate to that?"

He jumped visibly as I spoke.

"I don't," shrugged Sturmey in an unconvincing manner.

"Listen, Sturmey," said Bowden, who had picked up on Archer's nervousness, "I'd be really, really sorry to have to pull you in for questioning about that *Cardenio* scam."

Archer's lower lip trembled; his eyes darted between the two of us anxiously.

"I don't know *anything*, Mr. Cable," he whined. "Besides, you don't know what he would do."

"*Who* would do *what*, Sturmey?"

Then I heard it. A slight *click* behind us. I pushed Bowden in front of me; he tripped and collapsed on top of Sturmey, who gave a small cry that was drowned out by the loud concussion of a shotgun going off at close quarters. We were lucky; the blast hit the wall where we had been standing. I told Bowden to stay down and dashed low behind the workbench, trying to put some distance between myself and our assailant. When I reached the other side of the room I looked up and saw a man dressed in a black greatcoat holding a pump-action shotgun. He spotted me and I ducked as a blast from the shotgun scattered plaster fragments of Shakespeare all over me. The concussion of the shot had started up a mannequin of Romeo, who intoned pleadingly: *He jests at scars, that never felt a wound. But soft! What light through yonder . . .* until a second shot from the shotgun silenced him. I looked across at Bowden, who shook the plaster out of his hair and drew his revolver. I ran across to the far wall, ducking as our assailant fired again, once more shattering Archer's carefully painted plaster statues. I heard Bowden's revolver crack twice. I stood up and fired at our attacker, who had secreted himself in an office; my shots did nothing except splinter the wood on the door frame. Bowden fired again and his shot ricocheted off a cast-iron spiral staircase and hit a Will-Speak machine of Lord and Lady Macbeth; they started whispering to one another about the wisdom of murdering the king. I caught a glimpse of the man running across the room to outflank us. I had a clear view of him when he stopped, but as he did so Sturmey Archer stood up between us, blocking my shot. I couldn't believe it.

"Felix7!" cried Archer desperately. "You must help me! Dr. Müller said—"

Archer, sadly, had mistaken Felix7's intentions but had little time to regret them as our assailant dispatched him swiftly at close range, then turned to make his escape. Bowden and I must have opened fire at once; Felix7 managed three paces before stumbling under the shots and falling heavily against some packing cases.

"Bowden!" I yelled. "You okay?"

He answered slightly unsteadily but in the affirmative. I advanced slowly on the fallen figure, who was breathing in short gasps, all the time watching me with a disconcertingly calm face. I kicked away the shotgun then ran a hand down his coat while holding my gun a few inches from his head. I found an automatic in a shoulder holster and a Walther PPK in an inside pocket. There was a twelve-inch knife and a baby Derringer in his other pockets. Bowden arrived at my side.

"Archer?" I asked.

"Finished."

"He knew this clown. He called him Felix7. Mentioned something about a Dr. Müller, too."

Felix7 smiled up at me as I took out his wallet.

"James Crometty!" demanded Bowden. "Did you kill him?"

"I kill a lot of people," whispered Felix7. "I don't remember names."

"You shot him six times in the face."

The dying killer smiled.

"*That* I remember."

"Six times! Why?"

Felix7 frowned and started to shiver.

"Six was all I had," he answered simply.

Bowden pulled the trigger of his revolver two inches from Felix7's face. It was lucky for Bowden that the hammer fell harmlessly on the back of a spent cartridge. He threw the gun aside, picked up the dying man by the lapels and shook him.

"WHO ARE YOU?" he demanded.

"I don't even know myself," said Felix7 placidly. "I was married once, I think; and I had a blue car. There was an apple tree in the house where I grew up and I think I had a brother named Tom. The memories are vague and indistinct. I fear nothing because I value nothing. Archer is dead. My job is done. I have served my master; nothing else is of any consequence."

He managed a wan smile.

"Hades was right."

"About what?"

"About *you*, Miss Next. You're a worthy adversary."

"Die easy," I told him. "Where is Hades?"

He smiled for the last time and shook his head slowly. I had been trying to plug his wounds as he lay dying, but it was no good. His breathing became more labored and finally stopped altogether.

"Shit!"

"That's *Mr.* Schitt to you, Next!" said a voice behind us. We turned to see my second-least favorite person and two of his minders. He didn't look in a terribly good mood. I surreptitiously pushed Felix7's wallet under a workbench with my foot and stood up.

"Move to the side."

We did as we were told. One of Schitt's men reached down and felt Felix7's pulse. He looked up at Schitt and shook his head.

"Any ID?"

The minder started to search him.

"You've really screwed things up here, Next," said Schitt with barely concealed fury. "The only lead I've got is flatline. When I've finished with you, you'll be lucky to get a job setting cones on the M4."

I put two and two together.

"You *knew* we were in here, didn't you?"

He glared at me.

"That man could have taken us to the ringleader and *he* has something that we want," asserted Schitt.

"Hades?"

"Hades is dead, Miss Next."

"Horseshit, Schitt. You know as well as I do that Hades is alive and well. What Hades has belongs to my uncle. And if I know my uncle, he would sooner destroy it forever than sell out to Goliath."

"Goliath doesn't buy, Next. They *appropriate*. If your uncle has developed a machine that can help in the defense of his country, then it is his duty to share it."

"Is it worth the life of two officers?"

"Most certainly. SpecOps officers die pointlessly every day. If we can, we should try our best to make those deaths worthwhile."

"If Mycroft dies through your negligence, I swear to God!—"

Jack Schitt was unimpressed.

"You really have no idea who you are talking to, do you, Next?"

"I'm talking to someone whose ambition has throttled his morality."

"Wrong. You're talking to Goliath, a company that has the welfare of England foremost in its heart; everything that you see about you has been given to this country by the benevolence of Goliath. Is it little wonder that the Corporation should expect a small amount of gratitude in return?"

"If Goliath is as selfless as you suggest, Mr. Schitt, then they should expect *nothing* in return."

"Fine words, Miss Next, but cash is always the deciding factor in such matters of moral politics; nothing ever gets done unless motivated by commerce or greed."

I could hear sirens approaching. Schitt and his two minders made a quick exit, leaving us with Felix7 and Archer's bodies. Bowden turned to me.

"I'm glad that he's dead and I'm glad that I'm the one that pulled the trigger. I thought it might be hard but I did not have the slightest hesitation."

He said it as though it were an interesting experience, nothing less; as though he had just been on the roller-coaster at Alton Towers and was describing the experience to a friend.

"Does that sound wrong?" he added.

"No," I assured him. "Not at all. He would have killed until someone stopped him. Don't even think about it."

I reached down and picked up Felix7's wallet. We examined the contents. It contained everything you might expect to find, such as banknotes, stamps, receipts and credit cards—but they were all just plain white paper; the credit cards were simply white plastic with a row of zeros where the numbers usually were.

"Hades has a sense of humor."

"Look at this," said Bowden, pointing at Felix7's fingertips. "Wiped clean by acid. And see here, this scar running down behind the scalp line."

"Yes," I agreed, "it might not even be his face."

There was a screech of tires from downstairs. We put down our weapons and held our badges in the air to avoid any misunderstandings. The officer in charge was a humorless man named Franklin who had heard slightly garbled stories in the canteen about the new LiteraTec.

"You must be Thursday Next. Heard about you. LiteraTec, eh? Kind of a drop from SO-5?"

"At least I made it up there in the first place."

Franklin grunted and looked at the two bodies.

"Dead?"

"Very."

"You lot are becoming quite action-packed. I can't remember the last time a shot was fired in anger by a LiteraTec. Let's not make it a habit, eh? We don't want Swindon turning into a killing field. And if you want a piece of advice, go easy with Jack Schitt. We hear the man's a psychopath."

"Thanks for the tip, Franklin," I said. "I'd never have noticed."

It was after nine when we were finally allowed to leave. Victor had turned up to ask us a few questions out of earshot of the police.

"What the deuce is going on?" he asked. "I've had Braxton yelling on the phone for half an hour; it takes something serious to get him away from his golf club AGM. He wants a full report on the incident on his desk first thing tomorrow morning."

"It was Hades," I said. "Jack Schitt was here with the intention of following one of Acheron's killers after he'd dispatched us both."

Victor looked at me for a moment and was about to comment further when a call came over the wireless from an officer in need of assistance. It was the unmistakable voice of Spike. I went to pick up the microphone but Victor grabbed me by the wrist with a surprising turn of speed. He looked at me grimly.

"No, Thursday. Not with Spike."

"But an officer in need of assistance?—"

"Don't get involved. Spike is on his own and it's best that way."

I looked at Bowden, who nodded agreement and said:

"The powers of darkness are not for everyone, Miss Next. I think Spike understands that. We hear his calls from time to time but I see him in the canteen the following morning, as regular as clockwork. He knows what he's doing."

The wireless was silent; the channel was an open one and perhaps upward of sixty or seventy officers had heard the call. No one had answered.

Spike's voice came over the airwaves again:

"For God's sake, guys!—"

Bowden moved to switch the wireless off but I stopped him. I got into my car and keyed the mike.

"Spike, this is Thursday. Where are you?"

Victor shook his head.

"It was nice knowing you, Miss Next."

I glared at them both and drove off into the night.

Bowden moved across to where Victor was standing.

"Quite a girl," murmured Victor.

"We're going to be married," answered Bowden matter-of-factly.

Victor frowned and looked at him.

"Love is like oxygen, Bowden. When's the happy day?"

"Oh, she doesn't know yet," replied Bowden, sighing. "She is everything a woman should be. Strong and resourceful, loyal and intelligent."

Victor raised an eyebrow.

"When do you suppose you'll ask her?"

Bowden was staring after the taillights of the car.

"I don't know. If Spike is in the sort of trouble that I think he is, perhaps never."

17.

SpecOps-17: Suckers & Biters

. . . I made the assistance calls as a matter of course; had done since Chesney was pulled to the shadows. Never expected anyone to come; was just my way of saying "Ho, guys! I'm still out here!" Nope, never expected it. Never expected it at all . . .

OFFICER "SPIKE" STOKER
—interview in *Van Helsing's Gazette*

WHERE ARE you, Spike?"

There was a pause and then:

"Thursday, think hard before you do this—"

"I have, Spike. Give me your location."

He told me and after a quarter of an hour I pulled up outside the senior school at Haydon.

"I'm here, Spike. What do you need?"

His voice came back on the wireless, but this time slightly strained.

"Lecture room four, and hurry; in the glove box of my black & white you'll find a medical kit—"

There was a yell and he stopped transmitting.

I ran across to where Spike's squad car stood in the dark entrance of the old college. The moon passed behind a cloud and blackness descended; I felt an oppressive hand fall across my heart. I opened the car door and rummaged in the glove box. I found what I was looking for: a small zippered leather case with STOKER embossed on the front in faded gold lettering. I grabbed it and ran up the front steps of the old school. The interior was gloomily lit by emergency lighting; I flicked a panel of switches but the power was out. In the meager light I found a signboard and followed the arrows toward lecture room four. As I ran down the corridor I was aware of a strong odor; it matched the sullen smell of death I had detected in the boot of Spike's car when we had first met. I stopped suddenly, the nape of my neck twitching as a gust of cold wind caught me. I turned around abruptly and froze as I noticed the figure of a man silhouetted against the dim glow of an exit light.

"Spike?" I murmured, my throat dry and my voice cracking.

"I'm afraid not," said the figure, walking softly toward me and playing a torch on my face. "It's Frampton; I'm the janitor. What are you doing here?"

"Thursday Next, SpecOps. There's an officer in need of assistance in lecture room four."

"Really?" said the janitor. "Probably followed some kids in. Well, you'd better come with me."

I looked at him carefully; a glint from one of the exit lights caught the metallic gold of a crucifix around his throat. I breathed a sigh of relief.

He walked swiftly down the corridor; I followed closely.

"This place is so old it's embarrassing," muttered Frampton, leading me down a second corridor off the first. "Who did you say you were looking for?"

"An officer named Stoker."

"What does he do?"

"He looks for vampires."

"Really? Last infestation we had was in '78. Student by the name of Parkes. Went backpacking in the Forest of Dean and came back a changed man."

"Backpacking in the Forest of Dean?" I repeated incredulously, "Whatever possessed him to do that?"

The janitor laughed. "Good choice of words. Symonds Yat wasn't as secure then as it is now; we've taken precautions too. The whole college was consecrated as a church."

He flashed his torch at a large crucifix on the wall.

"We won't have *that* sort of problem here again. This is it, lecture room four."

He pushed open the door and we entered the large room. Frampton's torch flicked across the oak-paneled walls but a quick search revealed nothing of Spike.

"Are you sure he said number four?"

"Certain," I replied. "He—"

There was a sound of breaking glass and a muffled curse a small way distant.

"What was that?"

"Probably rats," said Frampton.

"And the swearing?"

"*Uncultured* rats. Come, let's—"

But I had moved off to a doorway beyond the lecture room, taking Frampton's torch with me. I pushed the door open wide and an appalling stench of formaldehyde greeted me. The room was an anatomy lab, dark except for the moonlight coming in through the window. Against the wall were rack upon rack of pickled specimens: mostly animal parts, but a few human parts too, things for the boys to frighten the girls with during sixth-form biology lessons. There was the sound of a jar smashing, and I flicked the torch across to the other side of the room. My heart froze. Spike, his self-control having apparently abandoned him, had just thrown a specimen jar to the floor and was now scrabbling in the mess. Around his feet were the smashed remnants of many jars; it had obviously been quite a feast.

"What are you doing?" I asked, the revulsion rising in my throat.

Spike turned to me, his eyes gaping, his mouth cut from the glass, a look of horror and fear in his eyes.

"I was hungry!" he howled. "And I couldn't find any mice!—"

He closed his eyes for a moment, gathered his thoughts with a Herculean effort, then stammered:

"My medication!—"

I forced down a foul gagging sensation and opened the medical kit to reveal a retractable penlike syringe. I unclipped the pen and moved toward Spike, who had collapsed in a heap and was sobbing silently. There was a hand on my shoulder, and I whirled round. It was Frampton, and he had an unpleasant smile on his lips.

"Let him carry on. He's happier this way, believe me."

I pushed his hand off my shoulder and for an instant my flesh touched his. It was icy cold and I felt a shiver run through me. I backed away hastily and tripped over a stool, falling heavily and dropping Spike's injector. I drew my gun and pointed it at Frampton, who seemed to be gliding toward me without walking. I didn't shout a warning; I just pulled the trigger and a bright flash illuminated the lab. Frampton was catapulted across the floor toward the blackboard and fell in a heap. I scrabbled around for the injector, found it and ran toward Spike, who had picked up a particularly large jar with a very recognizable and unspeakably unpleasant specimen in it. I flashed the torch into his frightened eyes and he mumbled:

"Help me!"

I pulled the cap off the injector and jabbed it in his leg, giving him two clicks. I took the jar from him and he sat down looking confused.

"Spike? Say something."

"That *really* hurt."

But it wasn't Spike talking. It was Frampton. He had picked himself up from the floor and was tying what looked like a lobster bib around his neck.

"Time for dinner, Miss Next. I won't trouble you with the menu because . . . well, *you're it!*"

The door of the biology lab slammed shut and I looked at my gun; it was now about as much use as a water pistol.

I got up and backed away from Frampton, who once more seemed to glide toward me. I fired again but Frampton was ready for it; he simply winced and continued.

"But the crucifix!—" I shouted, backing toward the wall. "And this college—it's a church!"

"Little fool!" replied Frampton. "Do you really suppose that Christianity has a monopoly on people like me?"

I looked around desperately for some kind of weapon, but apart from a chair—which drew out of my grasp as I reached for it—there was nothing.

"*Thoon* be over." Frampton grinned. He had sprouted an inordinately long single front tooth which grew over his bottom lip and gave him a lisp.

"Thoon you will be joining Thpike for a little thnack. *After* I have finithed!"

He smiled and opened his mouth wider; impossibly so—it seemed almost to fill the room. Quite suddenly Frampton stopped, looked confused and rolled his eyes up into his sockets. He grew gray, then black, then seemed to slough away like burned pages in a book. There was a musty smell of decay that almost blotted out the reek of formaldehyde, and soon there was nothing at all except Spike, who was still holding the sharpened stake that had so quickly destroyed the abomination that had been Frampton.

"You okay?" he asked with a triumphant look on his face.

"I'm good," I replied shakily. "Yuh, I feel okay. Well, now I do, anyway."

He lowered the stake and drew me up a chair as the lights flickered back on.

"Thanks for that," I murmured. "My blood is my own and I aim to keep it that way. I guess I owe you."

"No way, Thursday. *I owe you.* No one's ever answered a call of mine before. The symptoms came on as I was sniffing out Fang here. Couldn't get to my injector in time . . ."

His voice trailed off as he looked forlornly at the broken glass and spilled formaldehyde.

"They'll not believe this report," I murmured.

"They don't even *read* my reports, Thursday. Last person who did is now in therapy. So they just file 'em and forget 'em. Like me, I guess. It's a lonely life."

I hugged him on an impulse. It seemed the right thing to do. He returned it gratefully; I didn't expect that he had touched another human for a while. He had a musty smell about him—but it wasn't unpleasant; it was like damp earth after a spring rain shower. He was muscular and at least a foot taller than me, and as we stood in each other's arms I suddenly felt as though I really wouldn't mind if he made a move on me. Perhaps it was the closeness of the experience that we had just shared; I don't know—I don't usually act in this manner. I moved my hand up his back and onto his neck, but I had misjudged the man and the occasion. He slowly let me go and smiled, shaking his head softly. The moment had passed.

I paused for a second and then holstered my automatic carefully.

"What about Frampton?"

"He was good," admitted Spike, "*real* good. Didn't feed on his own turf and was never greedy; just enough to sate his thirst."

We walked out of the lab and back down the corridor.

"So how did you get onto him?" I asked.

"Luck. He was behind me in his motor at the lights. Looked in the rearview mirror—empty car. Followed him and *pow*; I knew he was a sucker soon as he spoke. I would have staked him earlier 'cept for my trouble."

We stopped at his squad car.

"And what about you? Any chance of a cure?"

"Top virologists are doing their stuff but for the moment I just keep my injector handy and stay out of the sunlight."

He stopped, took out his automatic and pulled the slide back, ejecting a single shiny bullet.

"Silver," he explained as he gave it to me. "I never use anything else." He looked up at the clouds. They were colored orange by the street lamps and moved rapidly across the sky. "There's weird shit about; take it for luck."

"I'm beginning to think there's no such thing."

"My point precisely. God keep you, Thursday, and thanks once again."

I took the shiny bullet and started to say something but he was gone already, rummaging in the boot of his squad car for a vacuum cleaner and a bin-liner. For him, the night was far from over.

18.

Landen Again

When I first heard that Thursday was back in Swindon I was delighted. I never fully believed that she had gone for good. I had heard of her problems in London and I also knew how she reacted to stress. All of us who returned from the peninsula were to become experts on the subject whether we liked it or not . . .

LANDEN PARKE-LAINE
—*Memoirs of a Crimean Veteran*

I TOLD Mr. Parke-Laine that you had hemorrhagic fever but he didn't believe me," said Liz on reception at the Finis.

"The flu would have been more believable."

Liz was unrepentant.

"He sent you this."

She passed across an envelope. I was tempted just to throw it in the bin, but I felt slightly guilty about giving him a hard time when we had met the previous night. The envelope contained a numbered ticket for *Richard III* which played every Friday evening at the Ritz Theater. We used to attend almost every week when we were going out together. It was a good show; the audience made it even better.

"When did you last go out with him?" asked Liz, sensing my indecision.

I looked up.

"Ten years ago."

"*Ten years?* Go, darling. Most of my boyfriends would have trouble even remembering that long."

I looked at the ticket again. The show began in an hour.

"Is that why you left Swindon?" asked Liz, keen to be of some help.

I nodded.

"And did you keep a photo of him all those years?"

I nodded again.

"I see," replied Liz thoughtfully. "I'll call a cab while you go and change."

It was good advice, and I trotted off to my room, had a quick shower and tried on almost everything in my wardrobe. I put my hair up, then down again, then up once more, muttered "Too boyish" at a pair of trousers and slipped into a dress. I selected some earrings that Landen had given me and locked my automatic in the room safe. I just had time to put on a small amount of eyeliner before I was whisked through the streets of Swindon by a taxi driver, an ex-Marine involved in the retaking of Balaclava in '61. We chatted about the Crimea. He didn't know where Colonel Phelps was going to talk either, but when he found out, he said, he would heckle for all his worth.

The Ritz looked a good deal shabbier. I doubted whether it had been repainted at all since we were last here. The gold-painted plaster moldings around the stage were dusty and unwashed, the curtain stained with the rainwater that had leaked in. No other play but *Richard III* had been performed here for over fifteen years, and the theater itself had no company to speak of, just a backstage crew and a prompter. All the actors were pulled from an audience who had been to the play so many times they knew it back to front. Casting was usually done only half an hour before curtain-up.

Occasionally seasoned actors and actresses would make guest appearances, although never by advance booking. If they were at a loose end late Friday night, perhaps after their performance at one of Swindon's three other theaters, they might come along and be selected by the manager as an impromptu treat for audience and cast. Just the week before, a local Richard III had found himself playing opposite Lola Vavoom, currently starring in the musical stage version of *Fancy-free in Ludlow* at the Swindon Crucible. It had been something of a treat for him; he didn't need to buy dinner for a month.

Landen was waiting for me outside the theater. It was five minutes to curtain-up and the actors had already been chosen by the manager, plus one in reserve in case anybody had a bad attack of the nerves and started chucking up in the bathroom.

"Thanks for coming," said Landen.

"Yeah," I replied, kissing him on the cheek and taking a deep breath of his aftershave. It was Bodmin; I recognized the earthy scent.

"How was your first day?" he asked.

"Kidnappings, vampires, shot dead a suspect, lost a witness to a gunman, Goliath tried to have me killed, puncture on the car. Usual shit."

"A puncture? Really?"

"Not really. I made that bit up. Listen, I'm sorry about yesterday. I think I'm taking my work a bit too seriously."

"If you weren't," agreed Landen with an understanding smile, "I'd really start worrying. Come on, it's nearly curtain-up."

He took my arm in a familiar gesture that I liked and led me inside. The theatergoers were chattering noisily, the brightly colored costumes of the unchosen actors in the audience giving a gala flavor to the occasion. I felt the electricity in the air and realized how much I had missed it. We found our seats.

"When was the last time you were here?" I asked when we were comfortable.

"With you," replied Landen, standing up and applauding wildly as the curtain opened to a wheezing alarum. I did the same.

A compère in a black cloak with red lining swept onto the stage.

"Welcome, all you Will-loving R3 fans, to the Ritz at Swindon, where tonight (drum roll), for your DELECTATION, for your GRATIFICATION, for your EDIFICATION, for your JOLLIFICATION, for your SHAKESPEARIFICATION, we will perform Will's *Richard III*, for the audience, to the audience, BY THE AUDIENCE!"

The crowd cheered and he held up his hands to quieten them.

"But before we start!—Let's give a big hand to Ralph and Thea Swanavon who are attending for their two hundredth time!!"

The crowd applauded wildly as Ralph and Thea walked on. They were dressed as Richard and Lady Anne and bowed and curtsied to the audience, who threw flowers onto the stage.

"Ralph has played Dick the shit twenty-seven times and Creepy Clarence twelve times; Thea has been Lady Anne thirty-one times and Margaret eight times!"

The audience stamped their feet and whistled.

"So to commemorate their bicentennial, they will be playing opposite each other for the first time!"

They respectively bowed and curtsied once more as the audience applauded and the curtains closed, jammed, opened slightly and closed again.

There was a moment's pause and then the curtains re-opened, revealing Richard at the side of the stage. He limped up and down the boards, eyeing the audience malevolently past a particularly ugly prosthetic nose.

"Ham!" yelled someone at the back.

Richard opened his mouth to speak and the whole audience erupted in unison:

"*When* is the winter of our discontent?"

"Now," replied Richard with a cruel smile, "is the winter of our discontent . . ."

A cheer went up to the chandeliers high in the ceiling. The play had begun. Landen and I cheered with them. *Richard III* was one of those plays that could repeal the law of diminishing returns; it could be enjoyed over and over again.

". . . made glorious summer by this son of York," continued Richard, limping to the side of the stage. On the word "summer" six hundred people placed sunglasses on and looked up at an imaginary sun.

". . . and all the clouds that lower'd upon our house in the deep bosom of the ocean, buried . . ."

"*When* were our brows bound?" yelled the audience.

"Now are our brows bound with victorious wreaths," continued Richard, ignoring them completely. We must have been to this show thirty times and even now I could feel myself mouthing the words with the actor on the stage.

". . . to the lascivious pleasing of a lute . . ." continued Richard, saying "lute" loudly as several other members of the audience gave alternative suggestions.

"Piano!" shouted out one person near us. "Bagpipes!" said another. Someone at the back, missing the cue entirely, shouted in a high voice "Euphonium!" halfway through the next line and was drowned out when the audience yelled: "Pick a card!" as Richard told them that he "was not shaped for sportive tricks . . ."

Landen looked across at me and smiled. I returned the smile instinctively; I was enjoying myself.

"I that am rudely stamp'd . . ." muttered Richard, as the audience took its cue and stamped the ground with a crash that reverberated around the auditorium.

Landen and I had never wanted to tread the boards ourselves and had never troubled to dress up. The production was the only show at the Ritz; it was empty the rest of the week. Keen amateur thespians and Shakespeare fans would drive from all over the country to participate, and it was never anything but a full house. A few years back a French troupe performed the play in French to rapturous applause; a troupe went to Sauvignon a few months later to repay the gesture.

". . . and that so lamely and unfashionable, that dogs bark at me . . ."

The audience barked loudly, making a noise like feeding time at the dogs' home. Outside in the alley several cats new to the vicinity momentarily flinched, while more seasoned moggies looked at each other with a knowing smile.

The play went on, the actors doing sterling work and the audience parrying with quips that ranged from the intelligent to the obscure to the downright vulgar. When Clarence explained that the king was convinced that ". . . by the letter 'G' his issue disinherited shall be . . ." the audience yelled out:

"Gloucester begins with G, dummy!"

And when the Lady Anne had Richard on his knees in front of her with his sword at his throat, the audience encouraged her to run him through; and just before one of Richard's nephews, the young Duke of York, alluded to Richard's hump: "Uncle, my brother mocks both you and me; because that I am little, like an ape, he thinks that you should bear me on your shoulders—!!!" the audience yelled out: "Don't mention the hump, kid!," and after he did: "The Tower! The Tower!"

The play was the Garrick cut and lasted only about two and a half hours; at Bosworth field most of the audience ended up on the stage as they helped reenact the battle. Richard, Catesby and Richmond had to finish the play in the aisle as the battle raged about them. A pink pantomime horse appeared on cue when Richard offered to swap his kingdom for just such a beast, and the battle finally ended in the foyer. Richmond then took one of the girls from behind the ice-cream counter as his Elizabeth and continued his final speech from the balcony with the audience below hailing him as the new king of England, the soldiers who had fought on Richard's side proclaiming their new allegiance. The play ended with Richmond saying: "God say Amen!"

"Amen!" said the crowd, amid happy applause. It had been a good show. The cast had done a fine job and fortunately this time no one had been seriously injured during Bosworth. Landen and I filed out quickly and found a table in a café across the road. Landen ordered two coffees and we looked at one another.

"You're looking good, Thursday. You've aged better than me."

"Nonsense," I replied. "Look at these lines!—"

"Laughter lines," asserted Landen.

"Nothing's *that* funny."

"Are you here for good?" he asked suddenly.

"I don't know," I answered. I dropped my gaze. I had promised myself I wouldn't feel guilty about leaving, but—

"It depends."

"On?—"

I looked at him and raised an eyebrow.

"—on SpecOps."

The coffee arrived at that point and I smiled brightly.

"So, how have you been?"

"I've been good," he said, then added in a lower tone, "I've been lonely too. Very lonely. I'm not getting any younger, either. How have *you* been?"

I wanted to tell him that I'd been lonely too, but some

things can't easily be said. I wanted him to know that I still wasn't happy with what he had done. Forgive and forget is all very well, but no one was going to forgive and forget my brother. Anton's dead name was mud and that was solely down to Landen.

"I've been fine." I thought about it. "I haven't, actually."

"I'm listening."

"I'm having a shitty time right now. I lost two colleagues in London. I'm chasing after a lunatic who most people think is dead, Mycroft and Polly have been kidnapped, Goliath is breathing down my neck and the regional commander at SpecOps might just have my badge. As you can see, things are just peachy."

"Compared to the Crimea, this is small beer, Thursday. You're stronger than all this crap."

Landen stirred three sugars into his coffee and I looked at him again.

"Are you hoping for us to get back together?"

He was taken aback by the directness of my question. He shrugged.

"I don't think we were ever truly apart."

I knew exactly what he meant. Spiritually, we never were.

"I can't apologize anymore, Thursday. You lost a brother, I lost some good friends, my whole platoon and a leg. I know what Anton means to you but I saw him pointing up the wrong valley to Colonel Frobisher just before the armored column moved off. It was a crazy day and crazy circumstances, but it happened and I had to say what I saw!—"

I looked him squarely in the eye.

"Before going to the Crimea I thought that death was the worst thing that could happen to anyone. I soon realized it was only for starters. Anton died; I can accept that. People get killed in war; it's inevitable. Okay, so it was a military debacle of staggering proportions. They also happen from time to time. It's happened many times before in the Crimea."

"Thursday!" implored Landen. "What I said. It was the truth!"

I rounded on him angrily.

"Who can say what the truth was? The truth is whatever we are most comfortable with. The dust, the heat, the noise! Whatever happened that day, the truth is now what everyone reads in the history books. What *you* told the military inquiry! Anton may have made a mistake, but he wasn't the only one that day."

"I saw him point down the wrong valley, Thursday."

"He would never have made that mistake!"

I felt an anger I hadn't felt for ten years. Anton had been blamed for the charge, it was as simple as that. The military leaders managed to squirm out of their responsibilities once again and my brother's name had entered the national memory and the history books as that of the man who lost the Light Armored Brigade. The commanding officer and Anton had both died in the charge. It had been up to Landen to tell the story.

I got up.

"Walking out again, Thursday?" said Landen sardonically. "Is this how it will always be? I was hoping you would have mellowed, that we could have made something out of this mess, that there was still enough love in us to make it work."

I shot a furious look at him.

"What about loyalty, Landen? He was your greatest friend!"

"And I *still* said what I said," sighed Landen. "One day you'll have to come to terms with the fact that Anton fucked up. It happens, Thursday. It happens."

I stared at him and he stared back.

"Can we *ever* get over this, Thursday? I need to know as a matter of some urgency."

"Urgency? What urgency? No," I replied, "no, no, we can't. I'm sorry to have wasted your fucking precious time!"

I ran out of the café, eyes streaming and angry with myself, angry with Landen and angry with Anton. I thought about Snood and Tamworth. We should all have waited for backup; Tamworth and I fucked up by going in and Snood fucked up by taking on an enemy which he knew he was not physically or mentally prepared to face. We had all been flushed with excitement by the chase; it was the sort of impetuous action that Anton would have taken. I had felt it once before in the Crimea and I had hated myself for it then too.

I got back to the Finis at about one in the morning. The John Milton weekend was ending with a disco. I took the lift up to my room, the distorted beat of the music softening to a dull thud as I was transported upward. I leaned against the mirror in the lift and took solace in the coolness of the glass. I should never have come back to Swindon, that much was obvious. I would speak to Victor in the morning and transfer out as soon as possible.

I opened my room door and kicked off my shoes, lay on the bed and stared at the polystyrene ceiling tiles, trying to come to terms with what I had always suspected but never wanted to face. My brother had fucked up. Nobody had bothered to put it so simply before; the military tribunal spoke of "tactical errors in the heat of the battle" and "gross incompetence." Somehow "fucked up" made it seem more believable; we all make mistakes at some time in our lives, some more than others. It is only when the cost is counted in human lives that people really take notice. If Anton had been a baker and forgotten the yeast, nothing would have been made of it, but he would have fucked up just the same.

As I lay there thinking I slowly drifted into sleep and with sleep came troubled dreams. I was back at Styx's apartment block, only this time I was standing outside the back entrance with the upturned car, Commander Flanker and the rest of the SO-1 interview panel. Snood was there too. He had an ugly hole in his wrinkled forehead and was standing, arms crossed and looking at me as if I had taken his football and he had sought out Flanker for some kind of redress.

"Are you *sure* you didn't tell Snood to go and cover the back?" asked Flanker.

"Positive," I said, looking at them both in turn.

"She did, you know," said Acheron as he walked past. "I heard her."

Flanker stopped him.

"Did you? What *exactly* did she say?"

Acheron smiled at me and then nodded at Snood, who returned his greeting.

"*Wait!*" I interrupted. "How can you believe what he says? The man's a liar!"

Acheron looked offended and Flanker turned to me with a steely gaze.

"We only have *your* word for that, Next."

I could feel myself boil with inner rage at the unfairness of it all. I was just about to cry out and wake up when I felt a tap on my arm. It was a man dressed in a dark coat. He had heavy black hair that fell over his dour, strong features. I knew immediately who he was.

"Mr. Rochester?"

He nodded in return. But now we were no longer outside the warehouses in the East End; we were in a well-furnished hall, lit by the dim glow of oil lamps and the flickering light from a fire in the large hearth.

"Is your arm well, Miss Next?" he asked.

"Very well, thanks," I said, moving my hand and wrist to demonstrate.

"I should not trouble yourself with them," he added, indicating Flanker, Acheron and Snood, who had started to argue in the corner of the room near the bookcase. "They are merely in your dream and thus, being illusory, are of no consequence."

"And what about you?"

Rochester smiled, a forced, gruff smile. He was leaning on the mantelpiece and looked into his glass, swirling his Madeira delicately.

"I was never real to begin with."

He placed the glass on the marble mantel and flipped out a large silver hunter, popped it open, read the time and returned it to his waistcoat pocket in one smooth easy movement.

"Things are becoming more urgent, I can feel it. I trust I can count on your fortitude when the time comes?"

"What do you mean?"

"I can't explain. I don't know how I managed to get here or even how you managed to get to me. You remember when you were a little girl? When you chanced upon us both that chill winter's evening?"

I thought about the incident at Haworth all those years ago when I entered the book of *Jane Eyre* and caused Rochester's horse to slip.

"It was a long time ago."

"Not to me. You remember?"

"I remember."

"Your intervention *improved* the narrative."

"I don't understand."

"Before, I simply bumped into my Jane and we spoke briefly.

If you had read the book prior to your visit you would have noticed. When the horse slipped to avoid you it made the meeting more dramatic, wouldn't you agree?"

"But hadn't that happened already?"

Rochester smiled.

"Not at all. But you weren't the first visitor we have had. And you won't be the last, if I'm correct."

"What do you mean?"

He picked up his drink again.

"You are about to rouse from your sleep, Miss Next, so I shall bid you adieu. Again: I can trust in your fortitude when the time comes?"

I didn't have time to answer or question him further. I was woken by my early morning call. I was in my clothes from the previous evening, the light and the television still on.

19.

The Very Irrev. Joffy Next

Dearest Mum,

Life here in the **DELETED BY CENSORS** *camp is great fun. The weather is good, the food average, the company AOK. Colonel* **DELETED BY CENSORS** *is our CO; he is a cracking fellow. I see Thurs quite often & although you told me to look after her I think she can look after herself. She won the battalion ladies' boxing tournament. We move up to* **DELETED BY CENSORS** *next week, I will write again when I have more news.*

Your son, Anton
Letter from Anton Next sent two weeks before he died

APART FROM one other person I had the breakfast room all to myself. As fate would have it, that one other person was Colonel Phelps.

"Good morning, Corporal!" he said cheerfully as he spotted me trying to hide behind a copy of *The Owl*.

"Colonel."

He sat down opposite me without asking.

"Good response to my presence here so far, y'know," he said genially, taking some toast and waving a spoon at the waiter. "You there, sir, more coffee. We're having the talk next Sunday; you *are* still coming, I trust?"

"I just *might* be there," I responded, quite truthfully.

"Splendid!" he gushed. "I must confess I thought you'd stumbled off the path when we spoke on the gasbag."

"Where is it being held?"

"A bit hush-hush, old girl. Walls have ears, careless talk, all that rot. I'll send a car for you. Seen this?"

He showed me the front page of *The Mole*. It was, like all the papers, almost exclusively devoted to the upcoming offensive that everyone thought was so likely there didn't seem even the slightest hope that it wouldn't happen. The last major battle had been in '75 and the memories and lessons of that particular mistake didn't seem to have sunk in.

"More *coffee* I said, sir!" roared Phelps to the waiter, who had given him tea by mistake. "This new plasma rifle is going to clinch it, y'know. I've even thought of modifying my talk to include a request for anyone wanting a new life on the peninsula to start filing claims now. I understand from the foreign secretary's office that we will need settlers to move in as soon as the Russians are evicted for good."

"Don't you understand?" I asked in an exasperated tone. "There won't be an end. Not while we have troops on Russian soil."

"What's that?" murmured Phelps. "Mmm? Eh?"

He fiddled with his hearing aid and cocked his head to one side like a parakeet. I made a noncommittal noise and left as soon as I could.

It was early; the sun had risen but it was still cold. It had rained during the night and the air was heavy with water. I put the roof of the car down in an attempt to blow away the memories of the night before, the anger that had erupted when I realized that I couldn't forgive Landen. It was the dismay that I would always feel the same rather than the dismay over the unpleasant ending to the evening which upset me most. I was thirty-six, and apart from ten months with Filbert I had been alone for the past decade, give or take a drunken tussle or two. Another five years of this and I knew that I would be destined not to share my life with anyone.

The wind tugged at my hair as I drove rapidly along the sweeping roads. There was no traffic to speak of and the car was humming sweetly. Small pockets of fog had formed as the sun rose, and I drove through them as an airship flies through cloud. My foot rolled off the throttle as I entered the small parcels of gloom, then gently pressed down again as I burst free into the morning sun once more.

The village of Wanborough was not more than ten minutes' drive from the Finis Hotel. I parked outside the GSD temple—once a C of E church—and turned off the engine, the silence of the country a welcome break. In the distance I could hear some farm machinery but it was barely a rhythmical hum; I had never appreciated the peace of the country until I had moved to the city. I opened the gate and entered the well-kept graveyard. I paused for a moment, then ambled at a slow respectful pace past the rows of well-tended graves. I hadn't visited Anton's memorial since the day I left for London, but I knew that he wouldn't have minded. Much that we had appreciated about one another had been left unsaid. In humor, in life and in love, we had understood. When I arrived in Sebastopol to join the 3rd Wessex Tank Light Armored Brigade, Landen and Anton were already good friends. Anton was attached to the brigade as signals captain; Landen was a lieutenant. Anton had introduced us; against strict orders we had fallen in love. I had felt like a schoolgirl, sneaking around the camp for forbidden trysts. In the beginning the Crimea just seemed like a whole barrel of fun.

None of the bodies came home. It was a policy decision. But many had private memorials. Anton's was near the end of the row, underneath the protective bough of an old yew and sand-wiched between two other Crimean memorials. It was well kept up, obviously weeded regularly, and fresh flowers had recently been placed there. I stood by the unsophisticated gray limestone tablet and read the inscription. Simple and neat. His name, rank and the date of the charge. There was another stone not unlike this one sixteen hundred miles away marking his grave on the peninsula. Others hadn't fared so well. Fourteen of my colleagues on the charge that day were still "unaccounted for." It was military jargon for "not enough bits to identify."

Quite suddenly I felt someone slap me on the back of my head. It wasn't hard but enough to make me jump. I turned to find the GSD priest looking at me with a silly grin on his face.

"Wotcha, Doofus!" he bellowed.

"Hello, Joffy," I replied, only slightly bemused. "Want me to break your nose again?"

"I'm cloth now, Sis!" he exclaimed. "You can't go around bashing the clergy!"

I stared at him for a moment.

"Well, if I can't bash you," I told him, "what can I do?"

"We at the GSD are very big on hugs, Sis."

So we hugged, there in front of Anton's memorial, me and my loopy brother Joffy, whom I had never hugged in my life.

"Any news on Brainbox and the Fatarse?" he asked.

"If you mean Mycroft and Polly, no."

"Loosen up, Sis. Mycroft *is* a Brainbox and Polly, well, she *does* have a fat arse."

"The answer's still no. Mind you, she and Mum have put on a bit of weight, haven't they?"

"A *bit*? I should say. Tesco's should open a superstore just for the pair of them."

"Does the GSD encourage such blatant personal attacks?" I asked.

Joffy shrugged.

"Sometimes it does and sometimes it doesn't," he answered. "That's the beauty of the Global Standard Deity—it's whatever you want it to be. And besides, you're family so it doesn't count."

I looked around at the well-kept building and graveyard.

"How's it all going?"

"Pretty well, thanks. Good cross section of religions and even a few Neanderthals, which is quite a coup. Mind you, attendances have almost tripled since I converted the vestry into a casino and introduced naked greasy-pole dancing on Tuesdays."

"You're joking!"

"Yes, of course I am, *Doofus*."

"You little shit!" I laughed. "I *am* going to break your nose again!"

"Before you do, do you want a cup of tea?"

I thanked him and we walked toward the vicarage.

"How's your arm?" he asked.

"It's okay," I replied. Then, since I was eager to try to keep up with his irreverence, I added: "I played this joke on the doctor in London. I said to him when he rebuilt the muscles in my arm, 'Do you think I'll be able to play the violin?' and he said: 'Of course!' and then I said: 'That's good, I couldn't before!'"

Joffy stared at me blank-faced.

"SpecOps Christmas parties must be a riot, Sis. You should get out more. That's probably the worst joke I've ever heard."

Joffy could be infuriating at times, but he probably had a point—although I wasn't going to let him know it. So I said instead:

"Bollocks to you, then."

That *did* make him laugh.

"You were always *so* serious, Sis. Ever since you were a little girl. I remember you sitting in the living room staring at the

News at Ten, soaking in every fact and asking Dad and the Brainbox a million questions—Hello, Mrs. Higgins!"

We had just met an old lady coming through the lichgate carrying a bunch of flowers.

"Hello, Irreverend!" she replied jovially, then looked at me and said in a hoarse whisper: "Is this your girlfriend?"

"No, Gladys—this is my sister, Thursday. She's SpecOps and consequently doesn't have a sense of humor, a boyfriend or a life."

"That's nice, dear," said Mrs. Higgins, who was clearly quite deaf, despite her large ears.

"Hello, Gladys," I said, shaking her by the hand. "Joffy here used to bash the bishop so much when he was a boy we all thought he would go blind."

"Good, good," she muttered.

Joffy, not to be outdone, added: "And little Thursday here made so much noise during sex that we had to put her in the garden shed whenever her boyfriends stayed the night."

I elbowed him in the ribs but Mrs. Higgins didn't notice; she smiled benignly, wished us both a pleasant day, and teetered off into the churchyard. We watched her go.

"A hundred and four next March," murmured Joffy. "Amazing, isn't she? When she goes I'm thinking of having her stuffed and placed in the porch as a hat stand."

"Now I know you're joking."

He smiled.

"I don't have a serious bone in my body, Sis. Come on, I'll make you that tea."

The vicarage was huge. Legend had it that the church's spire would have been ten feet taller had the incumbent vicar not taken a liking to the stone and diverted it to his own residence. An unholy row broke out with the bishop and the vicar was relieved of his duties. The larger-than-usual vicarage, however, remained.

Joffy poured some strong tea out of a Clarice Cliff teapot into a matching cup and saucer. He wasn't trying to impress; the GSD had almost no money and he couldn't afford to use anything other than what came with the vicarage.

"So," said Joffy, placing a teacup in front of me and sitting down on the sofa, "do you think Dad's boffing Emma Hamilton?"

"He never mentioned it. Mind you, if you were having an affair with someone who died over a hundred years ago, would you tell your wife?"

"How about me?"

"How about you what?"

"Does he ever mention me?"

I shook my head and Joffy was silent in thought for a moment, which is unusual for him.

"I think he wanted me to be in that charge in Ant's place, Sis. Ant was always the favored son."

"That's stupid, Joffy. And even if it were true—which it isn't—there's nothing anyone can do about it. Ant is gone, finished, dead. Even if you *had* stayed out there, let's face it, army chaplains don't exactly dictate military policy."

"Then why doesn't Dad ever come and see me?"

I shrugged.

"I don't know. Perhaps it's a ChronoGuard thing. He rarely visits me unless on business—and never for more than a couple of minutes."

Joffy nodded then asked:

"Have you been attending church in London, Sis?"

"I don't really have the time, Joff."

"We *make* time, Sis."

I sighed. He was right.

"After the charge I kind of lost my faith. SpecOps have chaplains of their own but I just never felt the same about anything."

"The Crimea took a lot away from all of us," said Joffy quietly. "Perhaps that is why we have to work twice as hard to hang onto what we have left. Even I was not immune to the passion of the battle. When I first went to the peninsula I was excited by the war—I could feel the insidious hand of nationalism holding me upright and smothering my reason. When I was out there I *wanted* us to win, to kill the foe. I reveled in the glory of battle and the camaraderie that only conflict can create. No bond is stronger than that welded in conflict; no greater friend is there than the one who stood next to you as you fought."

Joffy suddenly seemed that much more human; I presumed this was the side of him his parishioners saw.

"It was only afterward that I realized the error of what we were doing. Pretty soon I could see no difference between Russian and English, French or Turk. I spoke out and was banned from the frontline in case I sowed disharmony. My bishop told me that it was not my place to judge the errors of the conflict, but to look after the spiritual well-being of the men and women."

"So that's why you returned to England?"

"That's why I returned to England."

"You're wrong, you know," I told him.

"About what?"

"About not having a serious bone in your body. Did you know Colonel Phelps was in town?"

"I did. What an arse. Someone should poison him. I'm speaking opposite him as 'the voice of moderation.' Will you join me at the podium?"

"I don't know, Joff, really I don't."

I stared at my tea and refused a chocolate biscuit that he offered me.

"Mum keeps the memorial well, doesn't she?" I said, desperate to change the subject.

"Oh, it's not her, Doofus. She couldn't bear to even walk past the stone—even if she did slim down enough to get through the lich-gate."

"Who, then?"

"Why, *Landen,* of course. Did he not tell you?"

I sat up.

"No. No, he didn't."

"He might write crap books and be a bit of a dork, but he was a good friend to Anton."

"But his testimony damned him forever!—"

Joffy put his tea down and leaned forward, lowered his voice to a whisper and placed his hand on mine.

"Sister dearest, I know this is an old cliché but it's true: *The first casualty of war is always truth.* Landen was trying to redress that. Don't think that he didn't agonize long and hard over it—it would have been easier to lie and clear Ant's name. But a small lie always breeds a bigger one. The military can ill afford more than it has already. Landen knew that and so too, I think, did our Anton."

I looked up at him thoughtfully. I wasn't sure what I was going to say to Landen but I hoped I would think of something. He had asked me to marry him ten years ago, just before his evidence at the tribunal. I had accused him of attempting to gain my hand by stealth, knowing what my reaction would be following the hearing. I had left for London within the week.

"I think I'd better call him."

Joffy smiled.

"Yes, perhaps you'd better—*Doofus.*"

20.

Dr. Runcible Spoon

. . . Several people have asked me where I find the large quantity of prepositions that I need to keep my Bookworms fit and well. The answer is, of course, that I use *omitted* prepositions, of which, when mixed with dropped definite articles, make a nourishing food. There are a superabundance of these in the English language. *Journey's end,* for instance, has one omitted preposition and two definite articles: **the** *end* **of the** *journey.* There are many other examples, too, such as *bedside* (**the** *side* **of the** *bed*) and *streetcorner* (**the** *corner* **of the** *street),* and so forth. If I run short I head to my local newspapers, where omitted prepositions can be found in *The Toad's* headlines every day. As for the worm's waste products, these are chiefly composed of apostrophes—something that is becoming a problem—I saw a notice yesterday that read: *Cauliflower's, three shilling's each* . . .

MYCROFT NEXT,
writing in the "Any Questions?"
page of *New Splicer* magazine

BOWDEN AND Victor were out when I arrived at the office; I poured myself some coffee and sat down at my desk. I called Landen's number but it was engaged; I tried a few minutes later but without any luck. Sergeant Ross called from the front desk and said that he was sending someone up who wanted to see a

LiteraTec. I twiddled my thumbs for a bit, and had failed to reach Landen a third time when a small, academic-looking man with an overpowering aura of untidiness shambled into the office. He wore a small bowler hat and a herringbone-pattern shooting jacket pulled hastily over what looked like his pajama top. His briefcase had papers protruding from where he had caught them in the lid and the laces of both his shoes were tied in reef knots. He stared up at me. It was a two-minute walk from the front desk and he was still fumbling with his visitor's pass.

"Allow me," I said.

The academic stood impassively as I clipped his pass on and then thanked me absently, looking around as he tried to determine where he was.

"You're looking for me and you're on the right floor," I said, glad that I had had plenty of experience of academics in the past.

"I am?" he said with great surprise, as though he had long ago accepted that he would always end up in the wrong place.

"Special Operative Thursday Next," I said, holding out a hand for him to shake. He shook it weakly and tried to raise his hat with the hand that was holding the briefcase. He gave up and tipped his head instead.

"Er . . . thank you, Miss Next. My name is Dr. Runcible Spoon, Professor of English Literature at Swindon University. I expect you've heard of me?"

"I'm sure it was only a matter of time, Dr. Spoon. Would you care to sit down?"

Dr. Spoon thanked me and followed me across to my desk, pausing every now and then as a rare book caught his eye. I had to stop and wait a number of times before I had him safely ensconced in Bowden's chair. I fetched him a cup of coffee.

"So, how can I be of assistance, Dr. Spoon?"

"Perhaps I should show you, Miss Next."

Spoon rummaged through his case for a minute, taking out

some unmarked students' work and a paisley-patterned sock before finally finding and handing me a heavy blue-bound volume.

"*Martin Chuzzlewit,*" explained Dr. Spoon, pushing all the papers back into his case and wondering why they had expanded since he took them out.

"Chapter nine, page one eighty-seven. It is marked."

I turned to where Spoon had left his bus pass and scanned the page.

"See what I mean?"

"I'm sorry, Dr. Spoon. I haven't read *Chuzzlewit* since I was in my teens. You're going to have to enlighten me."

Spoon looked at me suspiciously, wondering if I was, perhaps, an impostor.

"A student pointed it out to me early this morning. I came out as quickly as I could. On the bottom of page one eighty-seven there was a short paragraph outlining one of the curious characters who frequent Todger's, the boarding house. A certain Mr. Quaverley by name. He is an amusing character who only converses on subjects that he knows nothing about. If you scan the lines I think you will agree with me that he has vanished."

I read the page with growing consternation. The name of Quaverley did ring a bell, but of his short paragraph there appeared to be no sign.

"He doesn't appear later?"

"No, Officer. My student and I have been through it several times. There is no doubt about it. Mr. Quaverley has inexplicably been excised from the book. It is as if he had never been written."

"Could it be a printing error?" I asked with a growing sense of unease.

"On the contrary. I have checked seven different copies and they all read exactly the same. *Mr. Quaverley is no longer with us.*"

"It doesn't seem possible," I murmured.

"I agree."

I felt uneasy about the whole thing, and several links between Hades, Jack Schitt and the *Chuzzlewit* manuscript started to form in unpleasant ways in my mind.

The phone rang. It was Victor. He was at the morgue and requested me to come over straight away; they had discovered a body.

"What's this to do with me?" I asked him.

As Victor spoke I looked over at Dr. Spoon, who was staring at a food stain he had discovered on his tie.

"No, on the contrary," I replied slowly, "considering what has just happened here I don't think that sounds odd at all."

The morgue was an old Victorian building that was badly in need of refurbishment. The interior was musty and smelled of formaldehyde and damp. The employees looked unhealthy and shuffled around the confines of the small building in a funereal manner. The standard joke about Swindon's morgue was that the corpses were the ones with all the charisma. This rule was especially correct when it came to Mr. Rumplunkett, the head pathologist. He was a lugubrious-looking man with heavy jowls and eyebrows like thatch. I found him and Victor in the pathology lab.

Mr. Rumplunkett didn't acknowledge my entrance, but just continued to speak into a microphone hanging from the ceiling, his monotonous voice sounding like a low hum in the tiled room. He had been known to send his transcribers to sleep on quite a few occasions; he even had difficulty staying awake himself when practicing speeches to the forensic pathologists' annual dinner dance.

"I have in front of me a male European aged about forty with gray hair and poor dentition. He is approximately five foot eight inches tall and dressed in an outfit that I would describe as Victorian . . ."

As well as Bowden and Victor there were two homicide detectives present, the ones who had interviewed us the night before. They looked surly and bored and glared at the LiteraTec contingent suspiciously.

"Morning, Thursday," said Victor cheerfully. "Remember the Studebaker belonging to Archer's killer?"

I nodded.

"Well, our friends in Homicide found this body in the trunk."

"Do we have an ID?"

"Not so far. Have a look at this."

He pointed to a stainless-steel tray containing the corpse's possessions. I sorted through the small collection. There was half a pencil, an unpaid bill for starching collars and a letter from his mother dated June 5, 1843.

"Can we speak in private?" I said.

Victor led me into the corridor.

"It's Mr. Quaverley," I explained.

"Who?"

I repeated what Dr. Spoon had told me. Victor did not seem surprised in the least.

"I thought he looked like a book person," he said at length.

"You mean this has happened before?"

"Did you ever read *The Taming of the Shrew?*"

"Of course."

"Well, you know the drunken tinker in the introduction who is made to think he is a lord, and whom they put the play on for?"

"Sure," I replied. "His name was Christopher Sly. He has a few lines at the end of act one and that is the last we hear of him . . ."

My voice trailed off.

"Exactly," said Victor. "Six years ago an uneducated drunk who spoke only Elizabethan English was found wandering in a confused state just outside Warwick. He said that his name was Christopher Sly, demanded a drink and was very keen to see how the play turned out. I managed to question him for half an hour, and in that time he convinced me that he was the genuine article—yet he never came to the realization that he was no longer in his own play."

"Where is he now?"

"Nobody knows. He was taken for questioning by two un-specified SpecOps agents soon after I spoke to him. I tried to find out what happened but you know how secretive SpecOps can be."

I thought about my time up at Haworth when I was a small girl.

"What about the other way?"

Victor looked at me sharply.

"What do you mean?"

"Have you ever heard of anyone jumping in the other direction?"

Victor looked at the floor and rubbed his nose. "That's pretty radical, Thursday."

"But do you think it's possible?"

"Keep this under your hat, Thursday, but I'm beginning to think that it is. The barriers between reality and fiction are softer than we think; a bit like a frozen lake. Hundreds of people can walk across it, but then one evening a thin spot develops and someone falls through; the hole is frozen over by the following morning. Have you read Dickens's *Dombey and Son*?"

"Sure."

"Remember Mr. Glubb?"

"The Brighton fisherman?"

"Correct. *Dombey* was finished in 1848 and was reviewed extensively with a list of characters in 1851. In that review Mr. Glubb was *not* mentioned."

"An oversight?"

"Perhaps. In 1926 a collector of antiquarian books named Redmond Bulge vanished while reading *Dombey and Son*. The incident was widely reported in the press owing to the fact that his assistant had been convinced he saw Bulge 'melt into smoke.' "

"And Bulge fits Glubb's description?"

"Almost exactly. Bulge specialized in collecting stories about the sea and Glubb specializes in telling tales of precisely that. Even Bulge's name spelled backward reads " 'Eglub,' a close enough approximation to Glubb to make us think he made it up himself." He sighed. "I suppose you think that's incredible?"

"Not at all," I replied, thinking of my own experiences with Rochester, "but are you absolutely sure he *fell* into *Dombey and Son*?"

"What do you mean?"

"He could have made the jump by choice. He might have preferred it—and stayed."

Victor looked at me strangely. He hadn't dared tell anyone about his theories for fear of being ostracized, but here was a re-spected London LiteraTec nearly half his age going farther than even he had imagined. A thought crossed his mind.

"You've done it, haven't you?"

I looked him straight in the eye. For this we could both be pensioned off.

"Once," I whispered. "When I was a very young girl. I don't think I could do it again. For many years I thought even that was a hallucination."

I was going to go farther and tell him about Rochester jump-ing back after the shooting at Styx's apartment, but at that moment Bowden put his head into the corridor and asked us to come in.

Mr. Rumplunkett had finished his initial examination.

"One shot through the heart, very clean, very professional. Everything about the body otherwise normal except evidence of rickets in childhood. It's quite rare these days so it shouldn't be difficult to trace, unless of course he spent his youth in another country. Very poor dental work and lice. It's probable he hasn't had a bath for at least a month. There is not a lot I can tell you except his last meal was suet, mutton and ale. There'll be more when the tissue samples come back from the lab."

Victor and I exchanged looks. I was correct. The corpse had to be Mr. Quaverley's. We all left hurriedly; I explained to Bowden who Quaverley was and where he came from.

"I don't get it," said Bowden as we walked toward the car. "How did Hades take Mr. Quaverley out of *every* copy of *Chuzzlewit?*"

"Because he went for the original manuscript," I answered, "for the maximum disruption. All copies anywhere on the planet, in whatever form, originate from that first act of creation. When the original changes, all the others have to change too. If you could go back a hundred million years and change the genetic code of the first mammal, every one of us would be completely different. It amounts to the same thing."

"Okay," said Bowden slowly, "but why is Hades doing this? If it was extortion, why kill Quaverley?"

I shrugged.

"Perhaps it was a warning. Perhaps he has other plans. There are far bigger fish than Mr. Quaverley in *Martin Chuzzlewit.*"

"Then why isn't he telling us?"

21.

Hades & Goliath

All my life I have felt destiny tugging at my sleeve. Few of
us have any real idea what it is we are here to do and when
it is that we are to do it. Every small act has a knock-on
consequence that goes onto affect those about us in unseen ways. I was lucky that I had so clear a purpose.

THURSDAY NEXT
—*A Life in SpecOps*

BUT HE was. When we got back a letter was waiting for me
at the station. I had hoped it was from Landen but it wasn't. It
bore no stamp and had been left on the desk that morning. No
one had seen who delivered it.

I called Victor over as soon as I had read it, laying the sheet
of paper on my desk to avoid touching it any more than I had
to. Victor put his spectacles on and read the note aloud.

Dear Thursday,

*When I heard you had joined the LiteraTec staff I almost believed
in divine intervention. It seems that we will at last be able to sort out
our differences. Mr. Quaverley was just for starters. Martin Chuzzlewit himself is next for the ax unless I get the following: £10 million in
used notes, a Gainsborough, preferably the one with the boy in blue,
an eight-week run of* Macbeth *for my friend Thomas Hobbes at the
Old Vic, and I want you to rename a motorway services "Leigh Dela-*

mare" after the mother of an associate. *Signal your readiness by a small ad in the Wednesday edition of the* Swindon Globe *announcing Angora rabbits for sale and I will give you further instructions.*

Victor sat down.

"It's signed Acheron. Imagine *Martin Chuzzlewit* without Chuzzlewit!" he exclaimed earnestly, running through all the possibilities. "The book would end within a chapter. Can you imagine the other characters sitting around, waiting for a lead character who never appears? It would be like trying to stage *Hamlet* without the prince!"

"So what do we do?" asked Bowden.

"Unless you have a Gainsborough you don't want and ten million in loose change, we take this to Braxton."

Jack Schitt was in Braxton Hicks's office when we entered. He didn't offer to leave when we told Hicks it was important and Hicks didn't ask him to.

"So what's up?" asked Braxton, glancing at Schitt, who was practicing his putting on the carpet.

"Hades is alive," I told him, staring at Jack Schitt, who raised an eyebrow.

"Goodness!" muttered Schitt in an unconvincing tone. "That *is* a surprise."

We ignored him.

"Read this," said Victor, handing across Acheron's note in a cellophane wrapper. Braxton read it before passing it to Schitt.

"Place the ad, Officer Next," said Braxton loftily. "You seem to have impressed Acheron enough for him to trust you. I'll speak to my superiors about his demands and you can inform me when he contacts you again."

He stood up to let us know that the interview had ended but I stayed seated.

"What's going on, sir?"

"Classified, Next. We'd like you to make the drop for us but that's the only way you can be involved in the operation. Mr. Schitt has an extremely well-trained squad behind him who will take care of Hades's capture. Good-day."

Still I didn't rise.

"You're going to have to tell me more, sir. My uncle is involved, and if you want me to play ball I'm going to have to know what's happening."

Braxton Hicks looked at me and narrowed his eyes.

"I'm afraid—"

"What the hell," interjected Schitt. "Tell 'em."

Braxton looked at Schitt, who continued to practice his putting.

"*You* may have the honor, Schitt," said Braxton angrily. "It's *your* show after all."

Schitt shrugged and finished the putt. The ball hit its mark and he smiled.

"Over the last hundred years there has been an inexplicable cross-fertilization between works of fiction and reality. We know that Mr. Analogy has been investigating the phenomenon for some time, and we know about Mr. Glubb and several other characters who have crossed into books. We knew of no one to have returned so we considered it a one-way journey. Christopher Sly changed all that for us."

"You have him?" asked Victor.

"No; he went back. Quite of his own accord, although unfortunately because he was so drunk he went back not to Will's version of *The Taming of the Shrew,* but to an uneven rendition in one of the Bad Quartos. Melted into thin air one day while under observation."

He paused for effect and polished his putter with a large red-spotted handkerchief.

"For some time now, the Goliath Advanced Weapons Division has been working on a device that will open a door into a work of fiction. After thirty years of research and untold expenditure, all we have managed to do is synthesize a poor-quality cheddar from volumes one to eight of *The World of Cheese*. We knew that Hades was interested, and there was talk of clandestine experiments here in England. When the *Chuzzlewit* manuscript was stolen and we found that Hades had it, I knew we were on the right track. Your uncle's kidnapping suggested that he had perfected the machine and the Quaverley extraction proved it. We'll get Hades, although it's the machine that we really want."

"You forget," I said slowly, "that the machine does not belong to you; knowing my uncle he'd destroy the idea forever rather than sell out to the military."

"We know all about Mycroft, Miss Next. He will learn that such a quantum leap in scientific thought should not be the property of a man who is incapable of understanding the true potential of his device. The technology belongs to the nation."

"You're wrong," I said obstinately, getting up to leave. "About as wrong as you can possibly be. Mycroft destroys any machine that he believes might have devastating military potential; if only scientists stopped to think about the possible effects of their discoveries, the planet would be a much safer place for all of us."

Schitt clapped his hands slowly.

"Brave speech but spare me the moralizing, Next. If you want your fridge-freezer and your car and a nice house and asphalt on the roads and a health service, then thank the weapons business. Thank the war economy that drives us to this and thank Goliath. The Crimea is good, Thursday—good for England and especially good for the economy. You deride the weapons business but without it we'd be a tenth-rate country struggling to maintain a standard of living anywhere near that of our European neighbors. Would you prefer that?"

"At least our conscience would be clear."

"Naive, Next, very naive."

Schitt returned to his golf and Braxton took up the explanation:

"Officer Next, we are extending all possible support to the Goliath Corporation in these matters. We want you to help us capture Hades. You know him from your college days and he addressed this to you. We'll agree to his demands and arrange a drop. Then we tail him and arrest him. Simple. Goliath gets the Prose Portal, we get the manuscript, your uncle and aunt are freed, and SpecOps-5 gets Hades. Everyone gets something so everyone is happy. So for now, we sit tight and wait for news of the drop."

"I know the rules on giving in to extortionists as well as you do, sir. Hades is not one to try and fool."

"It won't come to that," replied Hicks. "We'll give him the money and nab him long before he gets away. I have complete confidence in Schitt's operatives."

"With every respect, sir, Acheron is smarter and tougher than you can possibly imagine. We should do this on our own. We don't need Schitt's hired guns blasting off in all directions."

"Permission denied, Next. You'll do as I tell you, or you'll do nothing. I think that's all."

I should have been more angry but I wasn't. There had been no surprises—Goliath *never* compromised. And when there are no surprises, it's harder to get riled. We would have to work with what we were given.

When we got back to the office I called Landen again. This time a woman answered; I asked to speak to him.

"He's asleep," she said shortly.

"Can you wake him?" I asked. "It's kind of important."

"No, I can't. Who are you?"

"It's Thursday Next."

The woman gave a small snigger that I didn't like.

"He told me all about you, Thursday."

She said it disdainfully; I took an instant dislike to her.

"Who *is* this?"

"This is Daisy Mutlar, darling, Landy's *fiancée*."

I leaned back in my chair slowly and closed my eyes. This couldn't be happening. No wonder Landen asked me as a matter of some urgency if I was going to forgive him.

"Changed your mind, have you, sweetheart?" asked Daisy in a mocking tone. "Landen's a good man. He waited nearly ten years for you but I'm afraid now he's in love with me. Perhaps if you're lucky we'll send you some cake, and if you want to send a present, the wedding list is down at Camp Hopson."

I forced down a lump in my throat.

"When's the happy day?"

"For you or for me?" Daisy laughed. "For you, who knows? As for me, darling Landy and I are going to be Mr. and Mrs. Parke-Laine two weeks on Saturday."

"Let me speak to him," I demanded, my voice rising.

"I *might* tell him you called when he wakes up."

"Do you want me to come around and bang on the door?" I asked, my voice rising further. Bowden looked at me from the other side of the desk with an arched eyebrow.

"Listen here, you stupid bitch," said Daisy in a hushed tone in case Landen heard, "you could have married Landen and you blew it. It's all over. Go and find some geeky LiteraTec or something—from what I've seen all you SpecOps clowns are a bunch of weirdos."

"Now just you listen to—"

"No," snapped Daisy. "*You* listen. If you try anything at all to interfere with my happiness I'll wring your stupid little neck!"

The phone went dead. I quietly returned the receiver to its cradle and took my coat from the back of the chair.

"Where are you going?" asked Bowden.

"The shooting range," I replied, "and I may be some time."

22.

The Waiting Game

To Hades, the loss of every Felix brought back the sadness of the first Felix's death. On that occasion it had been a terrible blow; not only the loss of a trusted friend and colleague in crime, but also the terrible realization that the alien emotions of loss he had felt betrayed his half-human ancestry, something he abhorred. It was little wonder that he and the first Felix had got on so well. Like Hades, Felix was truly debased and amoral. Sadly for Felix, he did not share any of Hades' more demonic attributes and had stopped a bullet in the stomach the day that he and Hades attempted to rob the Goliath Bank at Hartlepool in 1975. Felix accepted his death stoically, urging his friend to "carry on the good work" before Hades quietly put him out of his pain. Out of respect for his friend's memory he removed Felix's face and carried it with him away from the crime scene. Every servant *expropriated* from the public since then had been given the dubious honor not only of being named after Acheron's one true friend, but also of wearing his features.

MILLON DE FLOSS
—*Life after Death for Felix Tabularasa*

BOWDEN PLACED the ad in the *Swindon Globe*. It was two days before we all sat down in Victor's office to compare notes.

"We've had seventy-two calls," announced Victor. "Sadly, all inquiries about rabbits."

"You did price them kind of low, Bowden," I put in playfully.

"I am not very conversant in matters concerning rabbits," asserted Bowden loftily. "It seemed a fair price to me."

Victor placed a file on the table. "The police finally got an ID on that guy you shot over at Sturmey Archer's. He had no fingerprints and you were right about his face, Thursday—it wasn't his own."

"So who was he?"

Victor opened the file.

"He was an accountant from Newbury named Adrian Smarts. Went missing two years ago. No criminal record; not so much as a speeding fine. He was a good person. Family man, churchgoer and enthusiastic charity worker."

"Hades stole his will," I muttered. "The cleanest souls are the easiest to soil. There wasn't much left of Smarts by the time we shot him. What about the face?"

"They're still working on that. It might be harder to identify. According to forensic reports Smarts wasn't the only person to wear that face."

I started.

"So who's to say he'll be the last?"

Victor guessed my concern, picked up the phone and called Hicks. Within twenty minutes an SO-14 squad had surrounded the funeral parlor where Smarts's body had been released to his family. They were too late. The face that Smarts had been wearing for the past two years had been stolen. Security cameras, unsurprisingly, had seen nothing.

The news of Landen's upcoming wedding had hit me pretty badly. I found out later that Daisy Mutlar was someone he met at a book signing over a year earlier. She was pretty and beguiling, apparently, but a bit overweight, I thought. She had no great mind either, or at least, that's what I told myself. Landen had said he wanted a family and I guessed he deserved one. In coming to terms with this I had even begun reacting positively to Bowden's sorry attempts to ask me out to dinner. We didn't have much in common, except for an interest in who *really* wrote Shakespeare's plays. I stared across the desk at him as he studied a small scrap of paper with a disputed signature scrawled upon it. The paper was original and so was the ink. The writing, sadly, was not.

"Go on, then," I said, recalling our last conversation when we were having lunch together, "tell me about Edward De Vere, the Earl of Oxford."

Bowden looked thoughtful for a moment.

"The Earl of Oxford was a writer, we can be sure of that. Meres, a critic of the time, mentioned as much in his *Palladis Tamia* of 1598."

"Could he have written the plays?" I asked.

"He *could* have," replied Bowden. "The trouble is, Meres also goes onto list many of Shakespeare's plays and credits Shakespeare with them. Sadly that places Oxford, like Derby and Bacon, into the front-man theory, according to which we have to believe that Will was just the beard for greater geniuses now hidden from history."

"Is that hard to believe?"

"Perhaps not. The White Queen used to believe six impossible things before breakfast and it didn't seem to do her any harm. The front-man theory is *possible*, but there're a few more things in favor of Oxford as Shakespeare."

There was a pause. The authorship of the plays was something that a lot of people took very seriously, and many fine minds had spent lifetimes on the subject.

"The theory goes that Oxford and a group of courtiers were employed by the court of Queen Elizabeth to produce plays in support of the government. In this there seems some truth."

He opened a book and read from an underlined passage.

" 'A crew of courtly makers, noblemen and Gentlemen, who have written excellently well, as it would appear if their doings could be found out and made public with the rest, of which number is first that noble Gentleman, the Earl of Oxford.' "

He snapped the book shut.

"Puttenham in 1598. Oxford was given an annual grant of a thousand pounds for just such a purpose, although whether this was for writing the plays or another quite different project it is impossible to tell. There is no *positive* evidence that it was he who actually penned the plays. A few lines of poetry similar to Shakespeare's do survive, but it's not conclusive; neither is the lion shaking a spear on Oxford's coat of arms."

"And he died in 1604," I said.

"Yes, there is that. Front-man theories just don't seem to work. If you think Shakespeare might have been a nobleman anxious to remain anonymous, I should forget it. If someone else *did* write the plays I should be looking at another Elizabethan commoner, a man of quite staggering intellect, daring and charisma."

"Kit Marlowe?" I asked.

"The same."

There was a commotion on the other side of the office. Victor slammed down the phone and beckoned us over.

"That was Schitt; Hades has been in touch. He wants us in Hicks's office in half an hour."

23.

The Drop

I was to make the drop. I'd never held a case containing
£10 million before. In fact, I wasn't then and never have.
Jack Schitt, in his arrogance, had assumed he would capture Hades long before he got to look at the money. What
a sap. The Gainsborough's paint was barely dry and the
English Shakespeare Company weren't playing ball. The
only part of Acheron's deal that had been honored was
the changing of the motorway services' name. Kington
St. Michael was now Leigh Delamare.

THURSDAY NEXT
—*A Life in SpecOps*

BRAXTON HICKS outlined the plan to us soon after—there
was an hour to go until the drop. This was Jack Schitt's way of
ensuring that none of us tried to make our own plans. In every
way this was a Goliath operation—myself, Bowden and Victor
were only there to add credibility in case Hades was watching.
The drop was at a redundant railway bridge; the only ways in
were by two roads and the disused railway line, which was only
passable in a four-by-four. Goliath men were to cover both roads
and the railway track. They were ordered to let him in, but not
out. It all seemed pretty straightforward—on paper.

* * *

The ride out to the disused railway line was uneventful, although the phony Gainsborough took up more room in the Speedster than I had imagined. Schitt's men were well hidden; Bowden and I didn't see a single soul as we drove to the deserted spot.

The bridge was still in good condition, even though it had long since ceased to function. I parked the car a little way off and walked alone to the bridge. The day was fine, and there was barely a sound in the air. I looked over the parapet but couldn't see anything remiss, just the large aggregate bed, slightly undulated where the sleepers had been pulled up all those years ago. Small shrubs grew among the stones, and next to the track was a deserted signal box from where I could just see the top half of a periscope watching me. I assumed it to be one of Schitt's men and looked at my watch. It was time.

The muffled sound of a wireless beeping caught my attention. I cocked my head and tried to figure out where it was coming from.

"I can hear a wireless beeping," I said into my walkie-talkie.

"It's not one of ours," responded Schitt from the control base in a deserted farmhouse a quarter of a mile away. "I suggest you find it."

The wireless was wrapped in plastic and stashed in the branches of a tree on the other side of the road. It was Hades and it was a bad line—it sounded as though he was in a car somewhere.

"Thursday?"

"Here."

"Alone?"

"Yes."

"How are you? I'm sorry I had to do what I did but you know how desperate we psychopaths get."

"Is my uncle okay?"

"In the pink, dear girl. Enjoying himself tremendously; such an intellect, you know, but so *very* vague. With his mind and my drive I could rule the globe instead of resorting to all this banal extortion."

"You can finish it now," I told him. Hades ignored me and carried on:

"Don't try anything heroic, Thursday. As you must have guessed, I have the *Chuzzlewit* manuscript and I'm not afraid to disrupt it."

"Where are you?"

"Tut, tut, Thursday, who do you think you're talking to? We'll discuss terms for your uncle's release just as soon as I have my money. You'll see on the parapet a karabiner attached to a length of wire. Place the money and the Gainsborough on the parapet and clip them on. Once that's done I'll come and pick them up. Until we meet again, Miss Thursday Next!"

I repeated to the others what he had said. They told me to do as I was told.

I placed the Gladstone with the money on the parapet and attached it to the Gainsborough. I walked back to the car, sat on the bonnet and watched Hades' booty intently. Ten minutes went by, then half an hour. I asked Victor for advice but he just told me to stay where I was.

The sun became hotter and the flies buzzed merrily around the hedgerows. I could smell the faint odor of freshly turned hay and hear far off the gentle thrum of traffic. It looked as though Hades was just testing us, a not unusual occurrence in the delicate task of paying ransoms. When the poet writer general was kidnapped five years previously it had taken nine attempts before the ransom was successfully delivered. In the event the PWG was returned unharmed; it turned out that he had engineered the whole thing himself to boost flagging sales of his decidedly lame autobiography.

I got bored and walked up to the parapet again, ignoring Schitt's request to back off. I toyed with the karabiner and absently followed the thin high-tensile cable that had been hidden in the brickwork. I traced its course to the loose soil at the base of the parapet, where it led off the bridge. I pulled it up slowly and found it attached to a bungee cord, coiled like a snake beneath some dried grass. Intrigued, I traced the bungee back to another length of high-tensile braided cable. This was taped carefully to a telegraph pole and then stretched ten feet above my head in a large double loop to another pole at the far end of the bridge. I frowned as the low growl of an engine made me turn. I couldn't see anything but the engine was definitely coming toward me, and quite quickly. I looked along the gravel bed of the old railway, expecting to see a four-wheel-drive, but there was nothing. The noise of the approaching engine increased dramatically as a light aircraft appeared from behind an embankment, where it had obviously flown in low to avoid detection.

"Plane!" I shouted into my walkie-talkie. "They've got a plane!"

Then the firing began. It was impossible to say who started it, or even where it came from, but in an instant the quiet countryside was filled with the sharp, directionless crackle of small-arms fire. I ducked instinctively as several rounds hit the parapet, throwing up a shower of red brick dust. I pulled out my automatic and released the safety as the plane passed overhead. I recognized it as the sort of high-wing observation plane they used in the Crimea for artillery spotting; the side door had been removed and sitting half out of the plane with one foot on the wing strut was Acheron. He was holding a light machine-gun and was blazing away quite happily at everything he could see. He peppered the dilapidated signal box and the Goliath men returned fire with equal enthusiasm; I could already see several holes open up in the plane's fabric. Behind the plane, swinging in the slipstream, trailed a grapnel hook. As it passed over, the hook caught the wire strung between the telegraph poles and whisked off the Gladstone bag and the painting, the bungee cord taking the initial strain out of the pickup. I jumped up and started to fire at the retreating plane, but it banked steeply away and dived behind the embankment, the bag and the Gainsborough flapping dangerously on the end of the rope. To delay now would definitely mean losing them and maybe the last real chance to catch Hades, so I sprinted to the car and reversed out in a shower of earth and small stones. Bowden clung on grimly and reached for his seat belt.

But the airplane had not quite finished with us. The small craft went into a shallow dive to gain more airspeed then pulled up into a near vertical left bank, the port wingtip scraping through the top of a large beech as the pilot turned back toward us. A Studebaker full of Goliath men had set off after the aircraft but braked violently as the airplane came skidding toward them, the pilot booting full left rudder to allow Acheron a better view of his target. The black car was soon a mass of small bullet holes and it swung into a ditch. I stamped on the brakes as another Studebaker pulled in front of me. It too was peppered by Acheron and careered into a low wall approaching the bridge. The aircraft flew on over me, the Gainsborough now so low that it banged on the bonnet of my car, the rattle of gunfire now only weakly returned by Schitt's men.

I pressed hard on the accelerator and drove off in pursuit of the aircraft, past the two shattered cars and over the bridge. There was a straight road ahead of us and Hades' plane was laboring against a slight headwind; with a bit of luck we might catch them. At the end of the straight there was a fork and a gated entry to a field straight on. The plane carried straight on. Bowden looked at me nervously.

"Which way?" he yelled.

In answer I pulled out my automatic, aimed it at the gate and fired. The first two shots missed but the next three hit their mark; the hinges shattered and the gate collapsed as I bounced into the field, which happened to be populated by a herd of bemused cows. The plane droned on, and while not exactly gaining on it we did at least seem to be keeping up.

"In pursuit of suspects in airplane heading, er, east, I think," yelled Bowden into the police wireless. An aircraft was the one thing none of us had thought of. Although a police airship was in the area it would be too slow to be able to cut off the plane's escape.

We carried on down a shallow slope, dodging heifers and making for the far end of the field, where a farmer in his Land Rover was just closing the gate. He looked perplexed as he saw the mud-spattered sports car fast approaching him but opened the gate anyway. I yanked the wheel hard over, turned right and slewed broadside down the road with one rear wheel in the ditch before I recovered and accelerated rapidly, now at right angles to where we wanted to go. The next turning on the left was into a farm, so in we went, scattering frightened chickens in all directions as we searched for a way out into the fields beyond. The aircraft was still visible, but detours like this only increased the distance between us.

"Hollycroft farm!" Bowden shouted into the wireless as he tried to keep anyone who might be interested informed of our progress. I found my way past the farmyard and out through the orchard by way of a barbed-wire fence that put five deep horizontal scratches along the paintwork of the car. We drove faster across the grass, bumping heavily over hardened ruts made the previous winter. Twice the car bottomed out, but at last we were making headway. As we pulled up beneath the plane, it abruptly banked left. I did likewise and entered a forest on a logging track. We could just see the aircraft above us through the foliage that flicked and rushed above our heads.

"Thursday!—"shouted Bowden against the rasp of the engine.

"What?"

"Road."

"Road?"

"Road."

We hit the road at full speed and were lifted off the ground by the camber. The car flew through the air, landed slightly askew and skidded sideways into a bramble thicket. The engine stalled but I quickly restarted it and headed off in the direction taken by the airplane. I accelerated up the road and emerged clear of the forest; the aircraft was ahead of us by only a hundred yards. I pressed the accelerator again and the car surged forward. We turned right into another field and tore across the grass, gaining on the plane, which was still flying into the headwind.

"Thursday!"

"What is it now?"

"We're coming to a river!"

It was true. To left and right of us and not more than half a mile distant, the broad expanse of the Severn blocked our route. Acheron was heading off to Wales and the Marches and there didn't seem to be anything we could do about it.

"Hold the wheel!" I yelled as we drew closer behind and beneath the aircraft. Bowden eyed the approaching riverbank nervously. We were doing almost seventy across the flat grassland, and it wouldn't be long before we passed the point of no return. I took careful aim with both hands and fired into the airplane. It jinked and banked violently. For a moment I thought I had hit the pilot but the plane quickly changed direction; it had merely gone into a dive to gain speed.

I swore, stamped on the brake and pulled the wheel around. The car skittered on the grass and drifted sideways through another fence before sliding down a bank and coming to rest at the water's edge with a front wheel in the river. I jumped out and fired at the retreating aircraft in a futile gesture until my gun was empty, half expecting Acheron to turn about and make a low pass, but he never did. The aircraft, with Hades, a forged Gainsborough and ten million pounds in dud notes, droned away into the distance.

We got out and looked at the damaged car.

"A write-off," murmured Bowden after making a last position report over the wireless. "It won't be long before Hades realizes that the money we have given him is *not* of the highest quality."

I stared at the aircraft, which was now a small dot on the horizon.

"Heading into the Republic?" suggested Bowden.

"Could be," I replied, wondering how we should ever get to him if he took refuge in Wales. Extradition agreements did exist but Anglo-Welsh relations were not good and the Politburo tended to regard any enemy of the English as a friend.

"What now?" asked Bowden.

"I'm not sure," I replied slowly, "but I think that if you've never read *Martin Chuzzlewit* you should do so as soon as possible. I've a feeling that as soon as Acheron finds he's been hoodwinked Martin will be the first for the chop."

Hades' plane vanished into the distance. All was quiet except for the gentle lap of the river. I lay down on the grass and closed my eyes, attempting to get a few moments of peace before we were thrown back into the maelstrom of Goliath, Hades, *Chuzzlewit* and all the rest. It was a calm moment—the eye of the hurricane. But I wasn't thinking about any of them. I was still thinking about Daisy Mutlar. The news about her and Landen was both expected and unexpected at the same time; he might have mentioned it, of course, but then, after a ten-year absence, he was under no obligation to do so. I found myself wondering what it would be like to have children and then wondering what it would be like never to know.

Bowden joined me on the grass. He took a shoe off and emptied out some gravel.

"That post I was talking about in Ohio, you remember?"

"Yes?"

"They confirmed the appointment this morning."

"Terrific! When do you start?"

Bowden looked down.

"I haven't agreed to it yet."

"Why not?"

"Have you ever . . . um . . . been to Ohio?" he asked in an innocent tone of voice.

"No; I've been to New York several times, though."

"It's very beautiful, I am told."

"A lot of America is."

"They are offering me twice Victor's pay."

"Good deal."

"And they said I could bring someone with me."

"Who do you have in mind?"

"You."

I looked at him, and his urgent and hopeful expression said

it all. I hadn't thought of him as a permanent boss or partner. I supposed that working with him might be like working under Boswell again. A workaholic who expected much the same from his charges.

"That's a very generous offer, Bowden."

"Then you'll consider it?"

I shrugged.

"I can't think of anything beyond Hades. After living with him all day I had hoped that I would be spared his presence at night, but he is there too, leering at me in my dreams."

Bowden had had no such dreams, but then he hadn't seen as much of Hades as I had. We both lapsed into silence and stayed that way for an hour, watching the river flow languidly past until the tow truck arrived.

I stretched out in my mother's huge iron bathtub and took a swig from the large G&T I had smuggled in with me. The garage had said they would have been happier to scrap the Speedster, but I told them to get it back on the road *no matter what,* as it still had important work to do. As I was drifting off to sleep in the warm pine-smelling waters there was a knock at the door. It was Landen.

"Holy shit, Landen! Can't a girl have a bath in peace?"

"Sorry, Thurs."

"How did you get into the house?"

"Your mother let me in."

"Did she now. What do you want?"

"Can I come in?"

"No."

"You spoke to Daisy."

"Yes I did. Are you really going to marry that cow?"

"I understand you're angry, Thursday. I didn't want you to

find out this way. I was going to tell you myself but you kind of dashed off the last time we were together."

There was an awkward silence. I stared at the taps.

"I'm getting on," said Landen finally. "I'll be forty-one next June and I want a family."

"And Daisy will give you that?"

"Sure; she's a great girl, Thursday. She's not you, of course, but she's a great girl; very . . ."

"Dependable?"

"Solid, perhaps. Not exciting, but *reliable*."

"Do you love her?"

"Of course."

"Then there seems little to talk about. What do you want from me?"

Landen hesitated.

"I just wanted to know that I was making the right decision."

"You said you loved her."

"I do."

"And she will give you the children you want."

"That too."

"Then I think you should marry her."

Landen hesitated slightly.

"So that's okay with you?"

"You don't need my permission."

"That's not what I meant. I just wanted to ask if you think this could all have had some other outcome?"

I placed a flannel over my face and groaned silently. It wasn't something I wanted to deal with right now.

"No. Landen, you *must* marry her. You promised her and besides—" I thought quickly. "—I have a job in Ohio."

"Ohio?"

"As a LiteraTec. One of my colleagues at work offered it to me."

"Who?"

"A guy named Cable. Great fellow he is too."

Landen gave up, sighed, thanked me and promised to send me an invitation. He left the house quietly—when I came downstairs ten minutes later, my mother was still wearing a forlorn "I wish he were my son-in-law" sort of look.

24.

Martin Chuzzlewit
Is Reprieved

My chief interest in all the work that I have conducted over the past forty or so years has been concerned with the elasticity of bodies. One tends to think only of substances such as rubber in this category but almost everything one can think of can be bent and stretched. I include, of course, space, time, distance and reality . . .

PROFESSOR MYCROFT NEXT

"CROFTY!—"

"Polly!—"

They met at the shores of the lake, next to the swath of daffodils that rocked gently in the warm breeze. The sun shone brightly, throwing a dappled light upon the grassy bank on which they found themselves. All about them the fresh smell of spring lay upon the land, bringing with it a feeling of calm and serenity that hushed the senses and relaxed the soul. A little way down the water's edge an old man in a black cape was seated upon a stone, idly throwing pebbles into the crystal water. It might have been almost perfect, in fact, apart from the presence of Felix8, his face not yet healed, standing on the daffodils and keeping a careful eye on his charges. Worried about Mycroft's commitment to his plan, Acheron had allowed him back into "I Wandered Lonely as a Cloud" to see his wife.

"Have you been well, my love?" asked Mycroft.

She pointed surreptitiously in the direction of the caped figure.

"I've been fine, although Mr. W over there seems to think that he's God's gift to women. He invited me to join him in a few unpublished works. A few flowery phrases and he thinks I'm his."

"The cad!" exclaimed Mycroft, getting up. "I think I might just punch him on the nose!"

Polly pulled his sleeve and made him sit down. She was flushed and excited at the idea of her septuagenarian husband and Wordsworth getting into a fight over her—it would have been quite a boast at the Women's Federation meeting.

"Well, really!—" said Mycroft. "These poets are terrible philanderers." He paused. "You said no, of course?"

"Well, yes, naturally."

She looked at Mycroft with her sweetest smile, but he had moved on.

"Don't leave 'Daffodils' otherwise I won't know where to find you."

He held her hand and together they looked out across the lake. There was no opposite shore, and the pebbles that Wordsworth flicked into the water popped back out after a moment or two and landed back on the foreshore. Aside from that, the countryside was indistinguishable from reality.

"I did something a bit silly," announced Mycroft quite suddenly, looking down and smoothing the soft grass with his palm.

"How silly?" asked Polly, mindful of the precariousness of the situation.

"I burned the *Chuzzlewit* manuscript."

"You did *what*?"

"I said—"

233

"I heard. Such an original manuscript is almost beyond value. Whatever made you do a thing like that?"

Mycroft sighed. It was not an action he had taken upon himself lightly.

"Without the original manuscript," he explained, "major disruption of the work is impossible. I told you that maniac removed Mr. Quaverley and had him killed. I didn't think he'd stop there. Who would be next? Mrs. Gamp? Mr. Pecksniff? Martin Chuzzlewit himself? I rather think I might have been doing the world a favor."

"And destroying the manuscript stops this, does it?"

"Of course; no original manuscript, no mass disruption."

She held his hand tightly as a shadow fell across them both.

"Time's up," said Felix8.

I had been right *and* wrong over my predictions regarding Acheron's actions. As Mycroft told me later, Hades had been furious when he discovered that no one had taken him seriously, but Mycroft's action in destroying *Chuzzlewit* simply made him laugh. For a man unused to being hoodwinked, he enjoyed the experience. Instead of tearing him limb from limb as Mycroft had suspected, he merely shook him by the hand.

"Congratulations, Mr. Next." He smiled. "Your act was brave and ingenious. Brave, ingenious but sadly self-defeating. I didn't choose *Chuzzlewit* by chance, you know."

"No?" retorted Mycroft.

"No. I was made to study the book at O-level and really got to hate the smug little shit. All that moralizing and endless harking on about the theme of selfishness. I find *Chuzzlewit* only marginally less tedious than *Our Mutual Friend*. Even if they had paid the ransom I would have killed him anyway and enjoyed the experience tremendously."

He stopped talking, smiled at Mycroft and continued:

"Your intervention has allowed Martin Chuzzlewit to continue his adventures. Todger's boarding house will not be torched and they can continue their unamusing little lives unperturbed."

"I am glad of that," replied Mycroft.

"Save your sentiments, Mr. Next, I haven't finished. In view of your actions I will have to find an alternative. A book that unlike *Chuzzlewit* has genuine literary merits."

"Not *Great Expectations?*"

Acheron looked at him sadly.

"We're beyond Dickens now, Mr. Next. I would have liked to have gone into *Hamlet* and throttled that insufferably gloomy Dane, or even skipped into *Romeo and Juliet* and snuffed out that little twerp Romeo." He sighed before continuing. "Sadly, none of the Bard's original manuscripts survive." He thought for a moment. "Perhaps the Bennett family could do with some thinning . . ."

"*Pride and Prejudice!?*" yelled Mycroft. "You heartless monster!"

"Flattery will not help you now, Mycroft. *Pride and Prejudice* without Elizabeth or Darcy would be a trifle lame, don't you think? But perhaps not Austen. Why not Trollope? A well-placed nail-bomb in Barchester might be an amusing distraction. I'm sure the loss of Mr. Crawley would cause a few feathers to fly. So you see, my dear Mycroft, saving Mr. Chuzzlewit might have been a very foolish act indeed."

He smiled again and spoke to Felix8.

"My friend, why don't you make some enquiries and find out the extent of original manuscripts and their whereabouts?"

Felix8 looked at Acheron coldly.

"I'm not a clerk, sir. I think Mr. Hobbes would be eminently more suitable for that task."

Acheron frowned. Of all the Felixes only Felix3 had ever

contradicted a direct order. The hapless Felix3 was liquidated following a very disappointing performance when he hesitated during a robbery. It had been Acheron's own fault, of course; he had tried to endow Felix3 with slightly more personality at the expense of allowing him a pinch of morality. Ever since then he had given up on the Felixes as anything but loyal servants; Hobbes and Dr. Müller had to be his company these days.

"Hobbes!" shouted Hades at the top of his voice. The unemployed actor scuttled in from the direction of the kitchens holding a large wooden spoon.

"Yes, sire?"

Acheron repeated the order to Hobbes, who bowed and withdrew.

"Felix8!"

"Sir?"

"If it's not too much trouble, lock Mycroft in his room. I dare say we will have no need of him for a couple of weeks. Give him no water for two days and no food for five. That should be punishment enough for disposing of the manuscript."

Felix8 nodded and removed Mycroft from the hotel's old lounge. He took him out into the lobby and up the broad marble staircase. They were the only ones in the moldering hotel; the large front door was locked and bolted.

Mycroft stopped by the window and looked out. He had once visited the Welsh capital as a guest of the Republic to give a talk on synthesizing oil from coal. He had been put up in this very hotel, met anyone who was anyone and even had a rare audience with the highly revered Brawd Ulyanov, octogenarian leader of the modern Welsh Republic. It would have been nearly thirty years ago, and the low-lying city had not changed much. The signs of heavy industry still dominated the landscape and the odor of ironworks hung in the air. Although many of the mines had closed in recent years, the winding gears had not been removed; they punctuated the landscape like sentinels, rising darkly above the squat slate-roofed houses. Above the city on Morlais Hill the massive limestone statue of John Frost looked down upon the Republic he had founded; there had been talk of moving the capital away from the industrialized South but Merthyr was as much a spiritual center as anything else.

They walked on and presently came to Mycroft's cell, a windowless room with only the barest furniture. As he was locked in and left alone, Mycroft's thoughts turned to that which troubled him most: Polly. He had always thought she was a bit of a flirt but nothing more; and Mr. Wordsworth's continued interest in her caused him no small amount of jealous anxiety.

25.

Time Enough for Contemplation

I hadn't thought that *Chuzzlewit* was a popular book, but
I was wrong. Not one of us expected the public outcry
and media attention that his murder provoked. Mr. Quaverley's autopsy was a matter of public record; his burial
was attended by 150,000 Dickens fans from around the
globe. Braxton Hicks told us to say nothing about the LiteraTec involvement, but news soon leaked out.

BOWDEN CABLE,
speaking to *The Owl* newspaper

COMMANDER BRAXTON HICKS threw the newspaper on the
desk in front of us. He paced around for a bit before collapsing
heavily into his chair.

"I want to know who told the press," he announced. Jack
Schitt was leaning on the window frame and watching us all
while smoking a rather small and foul-smelling Turkish cigarette. The headline was unequivocal:

CHUZZLEWIT DEATH: SPECOPS BLAMED

It went onto outline specifically how "unnamed sources"
within Swindon SpecOps had intimated that a botched ransom
payment had been the cause of Quaverley's death. It was arse

about face but the basic facts were correct. It had placed Hicks under a lot of pressure and caused him to overspend his precious budget by a phenomenal amount to try to discover Hades' whereabouts. The spotter plane that Bowden and I had pursued had been found a burned-out wreck in a field on the English side of Hay-on-Wye. The Gladstone full of the counterfeit money was close by along with the ersatz Gainsborough. It hadn't fooled Acheron for one second. We were all convinced that Hades was in Wales but even political intervention at the highest level had drawn a blank—the Welsh Home Secretary himself had sworn that they would not knowingly stoop to harbor such a notorious criminal. With no jurisdiction on the Welsh side of the border, our searches had centered around the marches—to no avail.

"If the press found out, it wasn't from us," said Victor. "We have nothing to gain from press coverage and everything to lose." He glanced over at Jack Schitt, who shrugged.

"Don't look at me," said Schitt noncommittally, "I'm just an observer, here at the behest of Goliath."

Braxton got up and paced the room. Bowden, Victor and I watched him in silence. We felt sorry for him; he wasn't a bad man, just weak. The whole affair was a poisoned chalice, and if he wasn't removed by the regional SpecOps commander, Goliath would as likely as not do the job themselves.

"Does anyone have any ideas?"

We all looked at him. We had a few ideas, but nothing that could be said in front of Schitt; since he was so willing to let us be killed that evening at Archer's place, not one of us would have given Goliath so much as the time of day.

"Has Mrs. Delamare been traced?"

"We found her okay," I replied. "She was delighted to discover that she had a motorway services named after her. She hasn't seen her son for five years but is under surveillance in case he tries to make contact."

"Good," murmured Braxton. "What else?"

Victor spoke.

"We understand Felix7 has been replaced. A young man named Danny Chance went missing from Reading; his face was found in a waste basket on the third floor of the multistory. We've distributed the morgue photos of Felix7; they should match the new Felix."

"Are you sure Archer didn't say anything but 'Felix7' before you killed him?" asked Hicks.

"Positive," assured Bowden in his best lying voice.

We returned to the LiteraTec office in a glum mood. Braxton's removal might provoke a dangerous shake-up in the department, and I had Mycroft and Polly to think of. Victor hung up his coat and called across to Finisterre, asking him if there had been any change. Finisterre looked up from a much-thumbed copy of *Chuzzlewit*. He, Bailey and Herr Bight had been rereading it on a twenty-four-hour relay basis since Acheron's escape. Nothing seemed to have changed. It was slightly perplexing. The Forty brothers had been working on the only piece of information we had that SO-5 or Goliath didn't. Sturmey Archer had made a reference to a Dr. Müller before expiring and that had been the subject of a rigorous search on SpecOps and police databases. A rigorous yet *secretive* search; that was what had taken the time.

"Anything, Jeff?" asked Victor, rolling up his shirtsleeves.

Jeff coughed.

"There are no Dr. Müllers registered in England or on the continent, either in medicine or philosophy—"

"So it's a false name."

"—who are *alive*." Jeff smiled. "However, there *was* a Dr. Müller in attendance at Parkhurst prison in 1972."

"I'm listening."

"It was at the same time that Delamare was banged up for fraud."

"This is getting better."

"And Delamare had a cellmate named Felix Tabularasa."

"There's a face that fits," murmured Bowden.

"Right. Dr. Müller was already under investigation for selling donor kidneys. He committed suicide in '74 shortly before the hearing. Swam into the sea after leaving a note. His body was never recovered."

Victor rubbed his hands together happily.

"Sounds like a faked death. How do we go about hunting down a dead man?"

Jeff held up a fax.

"I've had to use up a lot of favors at the English Medical Council; they don't like giving out personal files whether the subject is alive or dead, but here it is."

Victor took the fax and read out the pertinent points.

"Theodore Müller. Majored in physics before pursuing a career in medicine. Struck off in '74 for gross professional misconduct. He was a fine tenor, a good Hamlet at Cambridge, Brother of the Most Worshipful Order of the Wombat, keen train-spotter and a founding member of the Earthcrossers."

"Hmm," I murmured. "It's a good bet that he might continue to indulge himself in old hobbies even if he was living under an assumed name."

"What do you suggest?" asked Victor. "Wait until the next steam train extravaganza? I understand the *Mallard* is defending her speed record next month."

"Not soon enough."

"The Wombats *never* disclose membership," observed Bowden.

Victor nodded. "Well, that's that, then."

"Not exactly," I said slowly.

"Go on."

"I was thinking more about someone infiltrating the next Earthcrossers meeting."

"Earthcrossers?" said Victor with more than his fair share of incredulity. "You've got no chance, Thursday. Weird lunatics doing strange things privately on deserted hillsides? Do you know what you have to go through to be admitted to their exclusive club?"

I smiled.

"It's mostly distinguished and respected professional people of mature years."

Victor looked at Bowden and me in turn.

"I don't like that look you're giving me."

Bowden quickly scoured a copy of the current *Astronomer's Almanac*.

"Bingo. It says here that they meet on Liddington Hill at two P.M. the day after tomorrow. That gives us fifty-five hours to prepare."

"No way," said Victor indignantly. "There is no way, I repeat, no way on God's own earth that you are going to get me to pose as an Earthcrosser."

26.

The Earthcrossers

An asteroid can be any size from a man's fist to a mountain. They are the detritus of the solar system, the rubbish left over after the workmen have been and gone. Most of the asteroids around today occupy a space between Mars and Jupiter. There are millions of them, yet their combined mass is a fraction of the Earth's. Every now and then an asteroid's orbit coincides with that of Earth. An *Earthcrosser.* To the Earthcrossers Society the arrival of an asteroid at a planet is the return of a lost orphan, a prodigal son. It is a matter of some consequence.

MR. S. A. ORBITER
—*The Earthcrossers*

LIDDINGTON HILL overlooks the RAF and later Luftwaffe airfield of Wroughton. The low hill is also home to an Iron Age fort, one of several that ring the Marlborough and Lambourn downs. The antiquity of the site, however, was not what attracted the Earthcrossers. They had gathered in almost every country of the globe, following the peculiar predictions of their calling in an apparently random fashion. They always observed the same routine: name the site, do a very good deal with the owners for exclusivity, then move in the month before using either local security or more junior members of the group to ensure that no infiltrators find their way in. It was perhaps due to this extreme secrecy that the militant astronomical group managed to keep what they did absolutely quiet. It seemed an almost perfect hiding place for Dr. Müller, who co-devised the society in the early fifties with Samuel Orbiter, a notable television astronomer of the time.

Victor parked his car and walked nonchalantly up to two huge gorilla-sized men who were standing next to a Land Rover. Victor looked to the left and right. Every three hundred yards was a group of armed security men with walkie-talkies and dogs, keeping an eye out for trespassers. There was no way on earth that anyone could slip by unseen. The best means of entering anywhere you aren't allowed to go is to walk in the front door as though you own the place.

"Afternoon," said Victor, attempting to walk past. One of the gorillas stepped into his way and put a huge hand on his shoulder.

"Good afternoon, sir. Fine day. May I see your pass?"

"Of course," said Victor, fumbling in his pocket. He produced the pass inserted behind the worn plastic window of his wallet. If the gorillas took it out and saw that it was a photocopy, then all would be lost.

"I haven't seen you around before, sir," said one of the men suspiciously.

"No," replied Victor evenly, "you'll see from my card that I belong to the Berwick-upon-Tweed spiral arm."

The first man passed the wallet to his comrade.

"We've been having problems with infiltrators, isn't that so, Mr. Europa?"

The second man grunted and passed the wallet back to Victor.

"Name?" asked the first, holding up a clipboard.

"I probably won't be on the list," said Victor slowly. "I'm a latecomer. I called Dr. Müller last night."

"I don't know of any Dr. Müller," said the first, sucking in air through his teeth as he looked at Victor with narrowed eyes, "but if you *are* an Earthcrosser you will have no problem telling me which of the planets has the highest density."

Victor looked from one to the other and laughed. They laughed with him.

"Of course not."

He took a step forward but the smile on the men's faces dropped. One of them put out another massive hand to stop him.

"Well?"

"This is preposterous," said Victor indignantly. "I've been an Earthcrosser for thirty years and I've never had this sort of treatment before."

"We don't like infiltrators," said the first man again. "They try to give us a bad name. Do you want to know what we do to bogus members? Now. Again. Which of the planets has the highest density?"

Victor looked at the two men, who looked back at him menacingly.

"It's Earth. The lowest is Pluto, okay?"

The two security men were not yet convinced.

"Kindergarten stuff, mister. How long is a weekend on Saturn?"

Two miles away in Bowden's car, Bowden and I were frantically calculating the answer and transmitting it down the line to the earpiece that Victor was wearing. The car was stuffed with all sorts of reference books on astronomy; all that we could hope was that none of the questions would be too obscure.

"Twenty hours," said Bowden down the line to Victor.

"About twenty hours," said Victor to the two men.

"Orbital velocity of Mercury?"

"Would that be aphelion or perihelion?"

"Don't get smart, pal. Average will do."

"Let me see now. Add the two together and—ah, good Lord, is that a ringed chaffinch?"

The two men didn't turn to look.

"Well?"

"It's, um, one hundred and six thousand miles per hour."

"Uranus' moons?"

"Uranus?" replied Victor, stalling for time. "Don't you think it's amusing that they changed the pronunciation?"

"The moons, sir."

"Of course. Oberon, Titania, Umb—"

"Hold it! A *real* Earthcrosser would have logged the closest first!"

Victor sighed as Bowden reversed the order over the airwaves.

"Cordelia, Ophelia, Bianca, Cressida, Desdemona, Juliet, Portia, Rosalind, Belinda, Puck, Miranda, Ariel, Umbriel, Titania and Oberon."

The two men looked at Victor, nodded and then stepped back to let him pass, their manner changed abruptly to acute politeness.

"Thank you, sir. Sorry about that but, as I'm sure you realize, there are very many people who would like to see us stopped. I'm sure you understand."

"Of course, and may I congratulate you on your thoroughness, gentlemen. Good-day."

As Victor walked by they stopped him again.

"Aren't you forgetting something, sir?"

Victor turned. I had wondered about some sort of password, and if that was what they wanted now we were sunk. He decided to let them lead the situation.

"Leave it in the car, sir?" asked the first man after a pause. "Here, borrow mine."

The security man reached inside his jacket and pulled out, not a gun as Victor expected, but a baseball catcher's glove. He smiled and handed it over.

"I dare say I won't make it up there today."

Victor slapped his own forehead with the ball of his hand.

"Mind like a string bag. I must have left it at home. Imagine, coming to an Earthcrossers meet and forgetting my catcher's glove!"

They all laughed with him dutifully; the first guard said:

"Have a good time, sir. Earthstrike is at 14:32."

He thanked them both and hopped into the waiting Land Rover before they changed their minds. He looked at the catcher's glove uneasily. What on earth were they up to?

The Land Rover dropped him at the east entrance to the hill-fort. He could see about fifty people milling around, all wearing steel helmets. A large tent had been set up in the center of the fort and it bristled with aerials and a large satellite dish. Farther up the hill was a radar scanner that revolved slowly. He had expected to see a large telescope or something, but no such apparatus seemed to have been set up.

"Name?"

Victor turned to see a small man staring up at him. He was holding a clipboard and wearing a steel helmet and seemed to be taking full advantage of his limited authority.

Victor attempted a bluff.

"That's me there," he said, pointing at a name at the bottom of the list.

"Mr. Continued Overleaf, are you?"

"Above that," Victor countered hurriedly.

"Mrs. Trotswell?"

"Oh, er, no. Ceres. Augustus Ceres."

The small man consulted his list carefully, running a steel ballpoint pen down the row of names.

"No one of that name here," he said slowly, looking at Victor suspiciously.

"I'm from Berwick-upon-Tweed," explained Victor. "Late entry. I don't suppose the news filtered through. Dr. Müller said I could drop in any time."

The small man jumped.

"Müller? There's no one here of that name. You must mean Dr. Cassiopeia." He winked and smiled broadly. "Okay. Now," he added, consulting his list and looking around the fort, "we're a bit thin on the outer perimeter. You can take station B3. Do you have a glove? Good. What about a helmet? Never mind. Here, take mine; I'll get another from stores. Earthstrike at 14:32. Good-day."

Victor took the helmet and wandered off in the direction that the small man had indicated.

"Hear that, Thursday?" he hissed. "Dr. Cassiopeia."

"I heard it," I replied. "We're seeing what we've got on him."

Bowden was already contacting Finisterre, who was waiting back at the LiteraTec office for just such a call.

Victor filled his briar pipe and was walking toward station B3 when a man in a Barbour jacket nearly marched straight into him. He recognized Dr. Müller's face from the mugshot immediately. Victor raised his hat, apologized and walked on.

"Wait!" yelled Müller. Victor turned. Müller raised an eyebrow and stared at him.

"Haven't I seen your face somewhere else?"

"No, it's always been right here on the front of my head," replied Victor, attempting to make light of the situation. Müller simply stared at him with a blank expression as Victor carried on filling his pipe.

"I've seen you somewhere before," continued Müller, but Victor was not so easily shaken.

"I don't think so," he announced, offering his hand. "Ceres," he added. "Berwick-upon-Tweed spiral arm."

"Berwick-upon-Tweed, eh?" said Müller. "Then you know my good friend and colleague Professor Barnes?"

"Never heard of him," announced Victor, guessing that Müller was suspicious. Müller smiled and looked at his watch. "Earthstrike in seven minutes, Mr. Ceres. Perhaps you'd better take your station."

Victor lit his pipe, smiled and walked off in the direction he had been given earlier. There was a stake in the ground marked B3, and he stood around feeling slightly stupid. All the other Earthcrossers had donned their helmets and were scanning the sky to the west. Victor looked around and caught the eye of an attractive woman of about his own age a half-dozen paces away at B2.

"Hello!" he said cheerfully, tipping his helmet.

The woman fluttered her eyelashes demurely.

"All well?" she asked.

"Top hole!" returned Victor elegantly, then added quickly: "Actually, not. This is my first time."

The lady smiled at him and waved her catcher's glove.

"Nothing to it. Catch away from the body and keep your eyes sharp. We may get a lot or none at all, and if you *do* catch one, be sure to put it down on the grass straight away. After deaccelerating through the Earth's atmosphere, they tend to be a trifle hot."

Victor stared at her.

"You mean, we aim to *catch* meteors?"

The lady laughed a delicious laugh.

"No, no, silly!—They're called *meteorites*. Meteors are things that burn up in the Earth's atmosphere. I've been to seventeen of these suspected Earthstrikes since '64. I once nearly caught one in Tierra del Fuego in '71. Of course," she added more slowly, "that was when dear George was still alive . . ."

She caught his eye and smiled. Victor smiled back. She carried on:

"If we witness an Earthstrike today, it will be the first predicted strike in Europe to be successful. Imagine catching a meteorite! The rubble made during the creation of the universe over four and a half billion years ago! It's like an orphan finally coming home!"

"Very . . . poetic," responded Victor slowly as I started talking in his ear by way of the wire.

"There's no one listed anywhere by the name of Dr. Cassiopeia," I told him. "For goodness' sake don't let him out of your sight!"

"I won't," replied Victor, looking around for Müller.

"Pardon?" asked the lady at B2, who had being eyeing him up and not staring at the sky at all.

"I won't, er, drop one if I catch one," he replied hurriedly.

The Tannoy announced the Earthstrike in two minutes. There was a murmur from the expectant crowd.

"Good luck!" said the lady, giving him a broad wink and staring up into the cloudless sky.

There was a voice from close behind Victor.

"I *do* remember you."

He turned to see the very unwelcome face of Dr. Müller staring at him. A little farther on stood a burly security guard, hand at the ready in his breast pocket.

"You're SpecOps. LiteraTec. Victor Analogy, isn't it?"

"No, the name's Dr. Augustus Ceres, Berwick-upon-Tweed." Victor laughed nervously and added: "What sort of a name is Victor Analogy?"

Müller beckoned to the henchman, who advanced on Victor

drawing his automatic. He looked like the sort of person who was itching to use it.

"I'm sorry, my friend," said Müller kindly, "but that's not really good enough. If you *are* Analogy, you're clearly meddling. If, however, you turn out to be Dr. Ceres from Berwick-upon-Tweed, then you have my sincerest apologies."

"Now wait a moment—" began Victor, but Müller interrupted.

"I'll let your family know where to find the body," he said magnanimously.

Victor glanced around for possible help but all the other Earthcrossers were staring at the sky.

"Shoot him."

The henchman smiled, his finger tightening on the trigger. Victor winced as a high-pitched scream filled the air and a fortuitous incoming meteorite shattered on the henchman's helmet. He collapsed like a sack of potatoes. The gun went off and put a neat hole in Victor's baseball glove. Suddenly, the air was full of red-hot meteorites screaming to earth in a localized shower. The assembled Earthcrossers were thrown into confusion by the sudden violence and couldn't quite make up their minds whether to avoid the meteorites or try to catch them. Müller fumbled in his jacket pocket for his own pistol as someone yelled "*Yours!*" close at hand. They both turned, but it was Victor who caught the small meteorite. It was about the size of a cricket ball and was still glowing red hot; he tossed it to Müller, who instinctively caught it. Sadly, he did not have a catcher's glove. There was a hiss and a yelp as he dropped it, then a cry of pain as Victor took the opportunity to thump him on the jaw with a speed that belied his seventy-five years. Müller went down like a ninepin and Victor leaped on the dropped gun. He thrust it against Müller's neck, dragged him to his feet and started to march him out of the hill-fort. The meteorite shower was easing up as he backed out, my voice in his earpiece telling him to go easy.

"It is Analogy, isn't it?" said Müller.

"It is. SpecOps-27 and you're under arrest."

Victor, Bowden and I had got Müller as far as interview room 3 before Braxton and Schitt realized who we had captured. Victor had barely asked Müller to confirm his name before the interview room door burst open. It was Schitt flanked by two SO-9 operatives. None of them looked like they had a sense of humor.

"My prisoner, Analogy."

"*My* prisoner, Mr. Schitt, I think," replied Victor firmly. "*My* collar, *my* jurisdiction; I am interviewing Dr. Müller about the *Chuzzlewit* theft."

Jack Schitt looked at Commander Hicks, who was standing behind him. The commander sighed and cleared his throat.

"I'm sorry to say this, Victor, but the Goliath Corporation and their representative have been granted jurisdiction over SO-27 and SO-9 in Swindon. Withholding material from Acting SpecOps Commander Schitt may result in criminal proceedings for concealment of vital information pertinent to an ongoing inquiry. Do you understand what this means?"

"It means Schitt does what he pleases," returned Victor.

"Relinquish your prisoner, Victor. The Goliath Corporation takes precedence."

Victor stared at him hotly, then pushed his way out of the interview room.

"I'd like to stay," I requested.

"No chance," said Schitt. "An SO-27 security clearance is *not* permissible."

"It's as well, then," I replied, "that I still hold an SO-5 badge."

Jack Schitt cursed but said nothing more. Bowden was ordered out and the two SO-9 operatives stood either side of the door; Schitt and Hicks sat down at the table behind which Müller nonchalantly smoked a cigarette. I leaned against the wall and impassively watched the proceedings.

"He'll get me out, you know," Müller said slowly as he smiled a rare smile.

"I don't think so," remarked Schitt. "Swindon SpecOps is currently surrounded by more SO-9 operatives and SWAT men than you can count in a month. Not even that madman Hades would try and get in here."

The smile dropped from Müller's lips.

"SO-9 is the finest antiterrorist squad on the planet," continued Schitt. "We'll get him, you know. It's only a question of when. And if you help us, things might not look so bad in court for you."

Müller wasn't impressed.

"If your SO-9 operatives are the best on the planet, how come it takes a seventy-five-year-old LiteraTec to arrest me?"

Jack Schitt couldn't think of an answer to this. Müller turned to me.

"And if SO-9 are so shit hot, why does this young lady have the best luck cornering Hades?"

"I got lucky," I replied, adding: "Why hasn't Martin Chuzzlewit been killed? It's not like Acheron to make idle threats."

"No indeed," replied Müller. "No indeed."

"Answer the question, Müller," said Schitt pointedly. "I can make things *very* uncomfortable for you."

Müller smiled at him.

"Not half as uncomfortable as Acheron could. He lists slow murder, torture and flower arranging as his hobbies in *Which Criminal*."

"So you want to do some serious time?" asked Hicks, who

wasn't going to be left out of the interview. "The way I see it you're looking at quintuple life. Or you could walk free in a couple of minutes. What's it to be?"

"Do as you will, officers. You'll get nothing out of me. No matter what, Hades *will* get me out."

Müller folded his arms and leaned back in the chair. There was a pause. Schitt bent forward and switched off the tape recorder. He pulled a handkerchief out of his pocket and draped it across the video camera in the corner of the interview room. Hicks and I looked at one another nervously. Müller watched the proceedings but didn't seem unduly alarmed.

"Let's try it again," said Schitt, pulling out his automatic and pointing it at Müller's shoulder. "Where is Hades?"

Müller looked at him.

"You can kill me now or Hades kills me later when he finds I've talked. I'm dead either way and your death is probably a great deal less painful than Acheron's. I've seen him at work. You wouldn't believe what he is capable of."

"I would," I said slowly.

Schitt released the safety on his automatic. "I'll count to three."

"I can't tell you!—"

"One."

"He'd kill me."

"Two."

I took my cue. "We can offer you protective custody."

"From him?" demanded Müller. "Are you *completely* nuts?"

"Three!"

Müller closed his eyes and started to shake. Schitt put the gun down. This wasn't going to work. Suddenly, I had a thought.

"He doesn't have the manuscript anymore, does he?"

Müller opened an eye and looked at me. It was the sign I'd been looking for.

"Mycroft destroyed it, didn't he?" I continued, reasoning as my uncle might have—and did.

"Is that what happened?" asked Jack Schitt. Müller said nothing.

"He'll be wanting to find an alternative," observed Hicks.

"There must be thousands of original manuscripts out there," murmured Schitt. "We can't cover them all. Which one is he after?"

"I can't tell you," stuttered Müller, his resolve beginning to leave him. "He'd kill me."

"He'll kill you when he finds out you told us that Mycroft destroyed the *Chuzzlewit* manuscript," I responded evenly.

"But I didn't!—"

"He's not to know. We can protect you, Müller, but we need to capture Hades. Where is he?"

Müller looked at us one by one.

"Protective custody?" he stammered. "It'll need a small army."

"I can supply that," asserted Schitt, using the truth with an economy for which he had become famous. "The Goliath Corporation is prepared to be generous in this matter."

"Okay . . . I'll tell you."

He looked at us all and wiped his brow, which had suddenly started to glisten.

"Isn't it a bit hot in here?" he asked.

"No," replied Schitt. "Where's Hades?"

"Well, he's at . . . the—"

He suddenly stopped talking. His face contorted with fear as a violent spasm of pain hit his lower back and he cried out in agony.

"Tell us quick!" shouted Schitt, leaping to his feet and grabbing the stricken man's lapels.

"Pen-deryn!—" he screamed. "He's at!—"

"Tell us more!" roared Schitt. "There must be a thousand Penderyns!"

"Guess!" screamed Müller. "G-weuess . . . *ahhh!*"

"I'll not play your games!" yelled Schitt, shaking the man vigorously. "Tell me or I'll kill you with my bare hands right now!"

But Müller was now beyond rational thought or Schitt's threats. He squirmed and fell to the floor, writhing in agony.

"Medic!" I screamed, dropping to the floor next to the convulsing Müller, whose open mouth screamed a silent scream as his eyes rolled up into his head. The smell of scorched clothes reached my nostrils. I leaped back as a bright orange flame shot out of Müller's back. It ignited the rest of him and we all had to beat a hasty retreat as the intense heat reduced Müller to ash in under ten minutes.

"Damn!" muttered Schitt when the acrid smoke had cleared. Müller was a heap of cinders on the floor. There wouldn't even be enough to identify him.

"Hades," I murmured. "Some sort of built-in safety device. As soon as Müller starts to blab . . . up he goes. Very neat."

"You sound as if you almost respect him, Miss Next," observed Schitt.

"I can't help it." I shrugged. "Like the shark, Acheron has evolved into the almost perfect predator. I've never hunted big game and never would, but I can understand the appeal. The first thing," I went on, ignoring the smoking pile of ash that had recently been Müller, "is to treble the guards on any places where original manuscripts are held. After that we want to start looking at *anywhere* called Penderyn."

"I'll get onto it," said Hicks, who had been looking for a reason to go for some time.

Schitt and I were left looking at one another.

"Looks like we're on the same side, Miss Next."

"Sadly," I replied disdainfully. "You want the Prose Portal. I want my uncle back. Acheron has to be destroyed before either of us gets what we want. Until then we'll work together."

"A useful and happy union," replied Schitt with anything but happiness on his mind.

I pressed a finger to his tie.

"Understand this, Mr. Schitt. You may have might in your back pocket but I have right in mine. Believe me when I say I will do *anything* to protect my family. Do you understand?"

Schitt looked at me coldly.

"Don't try to threaten me, Miss Next. I could have you posted to the Lerwick LiteraTec office quicker than you can say 'Swift.' Remember that. You're here because you're good at what you do. Same reason as me. We are more alike than you think. Good-day, Miss Next."

A quick search revealed eighty-four towns and villages in Wales named Penderyn. There were twice as many streets and the same number again of pubs, clubs and associations. It wasn't surprising there were so many; Dic Penderyn had been executed in 1831 for wounding a soldier during the Merthyr riots—he was innocent and so became the first martyr of the Welsh rising and something of a figurehead for the republican struggle. Even if Goliath *could* infiltrate Wales, they wouldn't know which Penderyn to start with. Clearly, this was going to take some time.

Tired, I left to go home. I picked up my car from the garage, where they had managed to replace the front axle, shoehorn in a new engine and repair the bullet holes, some of which had come perilously close. I rolled up at the Finis Hotel as a clipper-class airship droned slowly overhead. Dusk was just settling and the navigation lights on either side of the huge airship blinked languidly in the evening sky. It was an elegant sight, the ten propellers beating the air with a rhythmic hum; during the day an airship could eclipse the sun. I stepped inside the hotel. The Milton conference was over and Liz welcomed me now as a friend rather than as a guest.

"Good evening, Miss Next. All well?"

"Not really." I smiled. "But thanks for asking."

"Your dodo arrived this evening," announced Liz. "He's in kennel five. News travels fast; the Swindon Dodo Fanciers have been up already. They said he was a very rare Version one or something—they want you to call them."

"He's a 1.2," I murmured absently. Dodos weren't high on my list of priorities right now. I paused for a moment. Liz sensed my indecision.

"Can I get you anything?"

"Has, er, Mr. Parke-Laine called?"

"No. Were you expecting him to?"

"No—not really. If he calls, I'm in the Cheshire Cat if not my room. If you can't find me, can you ask him to call again in half an hour?"

"Why don't I just send a car to fetch him?"

"Oh God, is it that obvious?"

Liz nodded her head.

"He's getting married."

"But not to you?"

"No."

"I'm sorry to hear that."

"Me too. Has anyone ever asked you to marry them?"

"Sure."

"What did you say?"

"I said: 'Ask me again when you get out.' "

"Did he?"

"No."

*   *   *

I checked in with Pickwick, who seemed to have settled in well. He made excited *plock plock* noises when he saw me. Contradicting the theories of experts, dodos had turned out to be surprisingly intelligent and quite agile—the ungainly bird of common legend was quite wrong. I gave him some peanuts and smuggled him up to my room under a coat. It wasn't that the kennels were dirty or anything; I just didn't want him to be alone. I put his favorite rug in the bath to give him somewhere to roost and laid out some paper. I told him I'd move him to my mother's the following day, then left him staring out of the window at the cars in the car park.

"Good evening, miss," said the barman in the Cheshire Cat. "Why is a raven like a writing desk?"

"Because there is a 'B' in 'both'?"

"Very good. Half of Vorpal's special, was it?"

"You must be kidding. Gin and tonic. A double."

He smiled and turned to the optics.

"Police?"

"SpecOps."

"LiteraTec?"

"Yup."

I took my drink.

"I trained to be a LiteraTec," he said wistfully. "Made it to cadetship."

"What happened?"

"My girlfriend was a militant Marlovian. She converted some Will-Speak machines to quote from *Tamburlaine* and I was implicated when she was nabbed. And that was that. Not even the military would take me."

"What's your name?"

"Chris."

"Thursday."

We shook hands.

"I can only speak from experience, Chris, but I've been in the military *and* SpecOps and you should be thanking your girlfriend."

"I do," hastened Chris. "Every day. We're married now and have two kids. I do this bar job in the evenings and run the Swindon branch of the Kit Marlowe Society during the day. We have almost four thousand members. Not bad for an Elizabethan forger, murderer, gambler and atheist."

"There are some who say he might have written the plays usually attributed to Shakespeare."

Chris was taken aback. He was suspicious too.

"I'm not sure I should be discussing this with a LiteraTec."

"There's no law against discussion, Chris. Who do you think we are, the thought police?"

"No, that's SO-2 isn't it?"

"But about Marlowe—?"

Chris lowered his voice.

"Okay. I think Marlowe *might* have written the plays. He was undoubtedly a brilliant playwright, as *Faust, Tamburlaine* and *Edward II* would attest. He was the only person of his age who could have actually done it. Forget Bacon and Oxford; Marlowe has to be the odds-on favorite."

"But Marlowe was murdered in 1593," I replied slowly. "Most of the plays were written *after* that."

Chris looked at me and lowered his voice.

"Sure. *If* he died in the bar fight that day."

"What are you saying?"

"It's possible his death was faked."

"Why?"

Chris took a deep breath. This was a subject he knew something about.

"Remember that Elizabeth was a Protestant queen. Anything like atheism or papism would deny the authority of the Protestant Church and the queen as the head."

"Treason," I murmured. "A capital offense."

"Exactly. In April 1593 the Privy Council arrested one Thomas Kyd in connection with some antigovernment pamphleteering. When his rooms were searched they revealed some atheistic writings."

"So?"

"Kyd fingered Marlowe. Said Marlowe had written them two years ago when they were rooming together. Marlowe was arrested and questioned on May 18, 1593; he was freed on bail so presumably there wasn't enough evidence to commit him for trial."

"What about his friendship with Walsingham?" I asked.

"I was coming to that. Walsingham had an influential position within the secret service; they had known each other for a number of years. With more evidence arriving daily against Marlowe, his arrest seemed inevitable. But on the morning of May 30, Marlowe is killed in a bar brawl, apparently over an unpaid bill."

"Very convenient."

"Very. It's my belief that Walsingham faked his friend's death. The three men in the tavern were all in his pay. He bribed the coroner and Marlowe set up Shakespeare as the front man. Will, an impoverished actor who knew Marlowe from his days at the Shoreditch Theater, probably leaped at the chance to make some money; his career seems to have taken off as Marlowe's ended."

"It's an interesting theory. But wasn't *Venus and Adonis* published a couple of months before Marlowe's death? Earlier even than Kyd's arrest?"

Chris coughed.

"Good point. All I can say is that the plot must have been hatched somewhat ahead of time, or that records have been muddled."

He paused for a moment, looked about and lowered his voice further.

"Don't tell the other Marlovians, but there is something else that points away from a faked death."

"I'm all ears."

"Marlowe was killed within the jurisdiction of the queen's coroner. There were sixteen jurors to view the *supposedly* switched body, and it is unlikely that the coroner could have been bribed. If I had been Walsingham I would have had Marlowe's death faked in the boonies where coroners were more easily bought. He could have gone farther and had the body disfigured in some way to make identification impossible."

"What are you saying?"

"That an equally probable theory is that Walsingham *himself* had Marlowe killed to stop him talking. Men say anything when tortured, and it's likely that Marlowe had all kinds of dirt on Walsingham."

"What then?" I asked. "How would you account for the lack of any firm evidence regarding Shakespeare's life, his curious double existence, the fact that no one seemed to know about his literary work in Stratford?"

Chris shrugged.

"I don't know, Thursday. Without Marlowe there is no one else in Elizabethan London even *able* to write the plays."

"Any theories?"

"None at all. But the Elizabethans were a funny bunch. Court intrigue, the secret service . . ."

"The more things change—"

"My point entirely. Cheers."

We clinked glasses and Chris wandered off to serve another customer. I played the piano for half an hour before retiring to bed. I checked with Liz but Landen hadn't called.

27.

Hades Finds Another Manuscript

I had hoped that I would find a manuscript by Austen or Trollope, Thackeray, Fielding or Swift. Maybe Johnson, Wells or Conan Doyle. Defoe would have been fun. Imagine my delight when I discovered that Charlotte Brontë's masterpiece *Jane Eyre* was on show at her old home. How can fate be more fortuitous? . . .

ACHERON HADES
—*Degeneracy for Pleasure and Profit*

OUR SAFETY recommendations had been passed to the Brontë museum and there were five armed security guards on duty that night. They were all burly Yorkshiremen, specially chosen for this most august of duties because of their strong sense of literary pride. One stayed in the room with the manuscript, another was on guard within the building, two patrolled outside, and the fifth was in a little room with six TV screens. The guard in front of the monitors ate an egg-and-onion sandwich and kept a diligent eye on the screens. He didn't see anything remiss on the monitors, but then Acheron's curious powers had never been declassified below SO-9.

It was easy for Hades to gain entry; he just slipped in through the kitchen door after forcing the lock with a crowbar. The guard patrolling inside didn't hear Acheron approach. His lifeless body was later found wedged beneath the Belfast sink. Acheron carefully mounted the stairs, trying not to make any noise. In reality he could have made as much noise as he liked. He knew the guards' .38s couldn't harm him, but what was the fun of just walking in and helping himself? He padded slowly up the corridor to the room where the manuscript was displayed and peered in. The room was empty. For some reason the guard was not in attendance. He walked up to the armored glass case and placed his hand just above the book. The glass beneath his flattened palm started to ripple and soften; pretty soon it was pliable enough for Hades to push his fingers through and grasp the manuscript. The destabilized glass twisted and stretched like rubber as the book was pulled clear and then rapidly reformed itself back into solid glass; the only evidence that its molecules had been rearranged was a slight mottling on the surface. Hades smiled triumphantly as he read the front page:

Jane Eyre
An autobiography by CURRER BELL
October 1847

Acheron meant to take the book straight away, but he had always liked the story. Succumbing to temptation, he started to read.

It was open at the section where Jane Eyre is in bed and hears a low cackle of demonic laughter outside her room. Glad that the laughter is not coming from *within* her room, she arises and throws the bolt on the door, crying out:

"Who is there?"

By way of an answer there is only a low gurgle and a moan, the sound of steps retreating and then the shutting of a door. Jane wraps a shawl around her shoulders and slowly pulls back the bolt, opening the door a crack and peering cautiously outside. Upon the matting she espies a single candle and also notices that the corridor is full of smoke. The creak of Rochester's half-open door catches her attention, and then she notices the dim flicker of a fire within. Jane springs into action, forsaking all thoughts as she runs into Rochester's burning chamber and attempts to rouse the sleeping figure with the words:

"Wake! Wake!"

Rochester does not stir and Jane notices with growing alarm that the sheets of the bed are starting to turn brown and catch fire. She grasps the basin and ewer and throws water over him, running to her bedroom to fetch more to douse the curtains. After a struggle she extinguishes the fire and Rochester, cursing at finding himself waking in a pool of water, says to Jane:

"Is there a flood?"

"No, sir," she replies, "but there has been a fire. Get up, do; you are quenched now. I will fetch you a candle."

Rochester is not fully aware of what has happened.

"In the name of all the elves in Christendom, is that Jane Eyre?" he demands. "What have you done with me, witch, sorceress? Who is in the room besides you? Have you plotted to drown me?"

"Turn around *really* slowly."

The last line belonged to the guard, whose own demand broke into Acheron's reading.

"I *hate* it when that happens!" he lamented, turning to face the officer, who had his gun trained on him. "*Just* when you get to a good bit!"

"Don't move and put the manuscript down."

Acheron did as he was told. The guard unclipped his walkie-talkie and brought it up to his mouth.

"I shouldn't do that," said Acheron softly.

"Oh yes?" retorted the guard confidently. "And why the hell not?"

"Because," said Acheron slowly, catching the guard's eye and looking deep inside him, "you will never find out why your wife left you."

The guard lowered his walkie-talkie.

"What do you know about Denise?"

I was dreaming fitfully. It was the Crimea again; the *crump-crump-crump* of the guns and the metallic scream that an armored personnel carrier makes when hit. I could even taste the dust, the cordite and the amatol in the air, the muffled cries of my comrades, the directionless sound of the gunfire. The eighty-eight-caliber guns were so close they didn't need a trajectory. You never heard the one that hit you. I was back in the APC, returning to the fray despite orders to the contrary. I was driving across the grassland, past wreckage from previous battles. I felt something large pluck at my vehicle and the roof opened up, revealing a shaft of sunlight in the dust that was curiously beautiful. The same unseen hand picked up the carrier and threw it in the air. It ran along on one track for a few yards and then fell back upright. The engine was still functioning, the controls still felt right; I carried on, oblivious to the damage. It was only when I reached up for the wireless switch that I realized the roof had been blown off. It was a sobering discovery, but I had little time to muse. Ahead of me was the smoking wreckage of the pride of the Wessex Tank: the Light Armored Brigade. The Russian eighty-eights had fallen silent; the sound was now of small arms as the Russians and my comrades exchanged fire. I drove to the closest group of walking wounded and released the rear door. It was jammed but it didn't matter; the side door had vanished with the roof and I rapidly packed twenty-two wounded and dying soldiers into an APC designed to carry eight. Punctuating all this was the incessant ringing of a telephone. My brother, minus his helmet and with his face bloodied, was dealing with the wounded. He told me to come back for him. As I drove off the *spang* of rifle fire ricocheted off the armor; the Russian infantry were approaching. The phone was still ringing. I fumbled in the darkness for the handset, dropped it and scrabbled on the floor, swearing as I did so. It was Bowden.

"Are you okay?" he asked, sensing something was not quite right.

"I'm fine," I replied, by now well used to making everything appear normal. "What's the problem?" I looked across at my clock. It was 3 A.M. I groaned.

"Another manuscript has been stolen. I just got it over the wire. Same MO as *Chuzzlewit*. They just walked in and took it. Two guards dead. One by his own gun."

"*Jane Eyre?*"

"How the dickens did you know that?"

"Rochester told me."

"What?—"

"Never mind. Haworth House?"

"An hour ago."

"I'll pick you up in twenty minutes."

Within the hour we were driving north to join the M1 at Rugby. The night was clear and cool, the roads almost deserted. The roof was up and the heating full on, but even so it was drafty as the gale outside tried to find a toehold in the hood. I shuddered to think what it might be like driving the car in winter. By 5 A.M. we would make Rugby and it would be easier from there.

"I hope I shan't regret this," murmured Bowden. "Braxton won't be terribly happy when he finds out."

"Whenever people say: 'I hope I won't regret this,' they do. So if you want me to let you out, I will. Stuff Braxton. Stuff Goliath and stuff Jack Schitt. Some things are more important than rules and regulations. Governments and fashions come and go but *Jane Eyre* is for all time. I would give everything to ensure the novel's survival."

Bowden said nothing. Working with me, I suspected, was the first time he had really started to enjoy being in SpecOps. I shifted down a gear to overtake a slow-moving lorry and then accelerated away.

"How did you know it was *Jane Eyre* when I rang?"

I thought for a minute. If I couldn't tell Bowden, I couldn't tell anyone. I pulled Rochester's handkerchief out of my pocket.

"Look at the monogram."

"EFR?"

"It belongs to Edward Fairfax Rochester."

Bowden looked at me doubtfully.

"Careful, Thursday. While I fully admit that I might not be the best Brontë scholar, even I know that these people aren't actually *real*."

"Real or not, I've met him several times. I have his coat too."

"Wait—I understand about Quaverley's extraction but what are you saying? That characters can jump spontaneously from the pages of novels?"

"I heartily agree that something odd is going on; something I can't possibly explain. The barrier between myself and Rochester has softened. It's not just him making the jump either; I once entered the book myself when I was a little girl. I arrived at the moment they met. Do you remember it?"

Bowden looked sheepish and stared out of the sidescreen at a passing petrol station.

"That's very cheap for unleaded."

I guessed the reason.

"You've never read it, have you?"

"Well—" he stammered. "It's just that, er—"

I laughed.

"Well, well, a LiteraTec who hasn't read *Jane Eyre*?"

"Okay, okay, don't rub it in. I studied *Wuthering Heights* and *Villette* instead. I meant to give it my fullest attention but like many things it must have slipped my mind."

"I had better run it by you."

"Perhaps you should," agreed Bowden grumpily.

I told him the story of *Jane Eyre* over the next hour, starting with the young orphan Jane, her childhood with Mrs. Reed and her cousins, her time at Lowood, a frightful charity school run by a cruel and hypocritical evangelist; then the outbreak of typhus and the death of her good friend Helen Burns; after that of how Jane rises to become a model pupil and eventually student teacher under the principal, Miss Temple.

"Jane leaves Lowood and moves to Thornfield, where she has one charge, Rochester's ward, Adele."

"Ward?" asked Bowden. "What's that?"

"Well," I replied, "I guess it's a polite way of saying that she is the product of a previous liaison. If Rochester lived today Adele would be splashed all over the front page of *The Toad* as a 'love child.' "

"But he did the decent thing?"

"Oh, yes. Anyhow, Thornfield is a pleasant place to live, if not slightly strange—Jane has the idea that there is something going on that no one is talking about. Rochester returns home after an absence of three months and turns out to be a sullen, dominating personality, but he is impressed by Jane's fortitude when she saves him from being burned by a mysterious fire in his bedroom. Jane falls in love with Rochester but has to witness his courtship of Blanche Ingram, a sort of nineteenth-century bimbo. Jane leaves to attend to Mrs. Reed, who is dying and when she returns, Rochester asks her to marry him; he has realized in her absence that the qualities of Jane's character far outweigh those of Miss Ingram, despite the difference in their social status."

"So far so good."

"Don't count your chickens. A month later the wedding ceremony is interrupted by a lawyer who claims that Rochester is already married and his first wife—Bertha—is still living. He accuses Rochester of bigamy, which is found to be true. The mad Bertha Rochester lives in a room on the upper floor of Thornfield, attended to by the strange Grace Poole. It was she who had attempted to set fire to Rochester in his bed all those months ago. Jane is deeply shocked—as you can imagine—and Rochester tries to excuse his conduct, claiming that his love for her was real. He asks her to go away with him as his mistress, but she refuses. Still in love with him, Jane runs away and finds herself in the home of the Rivers, two sisters and a brother who turn out to be her first cousins."

"Isn't that a bit unlikely?"

"Shh. Jane's uncle, who is also *their* uncle, has just died and leaves her all his money. She divides it among them all and settles down to an independent existence. The brother, St. John Rivers, decides to go to India as a missionary and wants Jane to marry him and serve the church. Jane is quite happy to serve him, but not to marry him. She believes that marriage is a union of love and mutual respect, not something that should be a duty. There is a long battle of wills and finally she agrees to go with him to India as his assistant. It is in India, with Jane building a new life, that the book ends."

"And that's it?" asked Bowden in surprise.

"How do you mean?"

"Well, the ending does sound a bit of an anticlimax. We try to make art perfect because we never manage it in real life and here is Charlotte Brontë concluding her novel—presumably something which has a sense of autobiographical wishful thinking about it—in a manner that reflects her own disappointed love life. If I had been Charlotte I would have made certain that Rochester and Jane were reunited—married, if possible."

"Don't ask me," I said, "I didn't write it." I paused. "You're right, of course," I murmured. "It is a crap ending. Why, when all was going so well, does the ending just cop out on the reader? Even the *Jane Eyre* purists agree that it would have been far better for them to have tied the knot."

"How, with Bertha still around?"

"I don't know; she could die or something. It is a problem, isn't it?"

"How do you know it so well?" asked Bowden.

"It's always been a favorite of mine. I had a copy of it in my jacket pocket when I was shot. It stopped the bullet. Rochester appeared soon after and kept pressure on my arm wound until the medics arrived. He and the book saved my life."

Bowden looked at his watch.

"Yorkshire is still many miles away. We shan't get their until— Hello, what's this?"

There appeared to be an accident on the motorway ahead. Two dozen or so cars had stopped in front of us and when nothing moved for a couple of minutes I pulled onto the hard shoulder and drove slowly to the front of the queue. A traffic cop hailed us to stop, looked doubtfully at the bullet holes in the paintwork of my car and then said:

"Sorry, ma'am. Can't let you through—"

I held up my old SpecOps-5 badge and his manner changed.

"Sorry, ma'am. There's something *unusual* ahead."

Bowden and I exchanged looks and got out of the car. Behind us a crowd of curious onlookers was being held back by a POLICE LINE DO NOT CROSS tape. They stood in silence to watch the spectacle unfold in front of their eyes. Three squad cars and an ambulance were on the scene already; two paramedics were attending to a newborn infant who was wrapped up in a blanket and howling plaintively. The officers were all relieved that I had arrived—the highest rank there was sergeant and they were glad to be able to foist the responsibility onto someone else, and someone from SO-5 was as high an operative as any of them had even *seen*.

I borrowed a pair of binoculars and looked up the empty motorway. About five hundred yards away the road and starry night sky had spiraled into the shape of a whirlpool, a funnel that was crushing and distorting the light that managed to penetrate the vortex. I sighed. My father had told me about temporal distortions but I had never seen one. In the center of the whirlpool, where the refracted light had been whipped up into a jumbled pattern, there was an inky black hole, which seemed to have neither depth nor color, just shape: a perfect circle the size of a grapefruit. Traffic on the opposite motorway had also been stopped by the police, the flashing blue lights slowing to red as they shone through the fringes of the black mass, distorting the image of the road beyond like the refraction on the edge of a jam jar. In front of the vortex was a blue Datsun, the bonnet already starting to stretch as it approached the distortion. Behind that was a motorcycle, and behind this and closest to us was a green family sedan. I watched for a minute or so, but all the vehicles appeared motionless on the tarmac. The rider, his motorcycle and all the occupants of the cars seemed to be frozen like statues.

"Blast!" I muttered under my breath as I glanced at my watch. "How long since it opened up?"

"About an hour," answered the sergeant. "There was some kind of accident involving an ExcoMat containment vehicle. Couldn't have happened at a worse time; I was about to come off shift."

He jerked a thumb in the direction of the baby on the stretcher, who had put his fingers in his mouth and stopped yelling. "That was the driver. Before the accident he was thirty-one. By the time we got here he was eight—in a few minutes he'll be nothing more than a damp patch on the blanket."

"Have you called the ChronoGuard?"

"I called 'em," he answered resignedly. "But a patch of bad time opened up near Tesco's in Wareham. They can't be here for at least four hours."

I thought quickly.

"How many people have been lost so far?"

"Sir," said an officer, pointing up the road, "I think you had better see this!"

We all watched as the blue Datsun started to contort and stretch, fold and shrink as it was sucked through the hole. Within a few seconds it had disappeared completely, compressed to a billionth of its size and catapulted to Elsewhere.

The sergeant pushed his cap to the back of his head and sighed. There was nothing he could do.

I repeated my question.

"How many?"

"Oh, the truck has gone, an entire mobile library, twelve cars and a motorcycle. Maybe twenty people."

"That's a lot of matter," I said grimly. "The distortion could grow to the size of a football field by the time the ChronoGuard get here."

The sergeant shrugged. He had never been briefed on what to do with temporal instabilities. I turned to Bowden.

"Come on."

"What?"

"We've a little job to do."

"You're crazy!"

"Perhaps."

"Can't we wait for the ChronoGuard?"

"They'd never get here in time. It's easy. A lobotomized monkey could do it."

"And where are we going to find a lobotomized monkey at this time of night?"

"You're being windy, Bowden."

"True. Do you know what will happen if we fail?"

"We won't. It's a doddle. Dad was in the ChronoGuard; he told me all about this sort of thing. The secret is in the spheres. In four hours we could be seeing a major global disaster occurring right in front of our eyes. A rent in time so large we won't know for sure that the here-and-now isn't the there-and-then. The rout of civilization, panic in the streets, the end of the world as we know it. Hey, kid!—"

I had seen a young lad bouncing a basketball on the road. The boy reluctantly gave it to me and I returned to Bowden, who was waiting uneasily by the car. We put the hood down and Bowden sat in the passenger seat, clutching the basketball grimly.

"A basketball?"

"It's a sphere, isn't it?" I replied, remembering Dad's advice all those years ago. "Are you ready?"

"Ready," replied Bowden in a slightly shaky voice.

I started the car and rolled slowly up to where the traffic police stood in shocked amazement.

"Are you sure you know what you're doing?" asked the young officer.

"Sort of," I replied, truthfully enough. "Does anyone have a watch with a second hand?"

The youngest traffic cop took his watch off and handed it over. I noted the *real* time—5:30 A.M.—and then reset the hands to twelve o'clock. I strapped the watch onto the rear-view mirror.

The sergeant wished us good luck as we drove off, yet his thoughts were more along the lines of "sooner you than me."

Around us the sky was lightening into dawn, yet the area around the vehicles was still night. Time for the trapped cars had stood still, but only to observers from the outside. To the occupants, everything was happening as normal, except that if they looked behind them they would witness the dawn breaking rapidly.

The first fifty yards seemed plain enough to Bowden and me, but as we drove closer the car and bike seemed to speed up and by the time we had drawn level with the green car we were both moving at about sixty miles per hour. I glanced at the watch on the rear-view mirror and noted that precisely three minutes had elapsed.

Bowden had been watching what was going on behind us. As he and I drove toward the instability the officers' movements seemed to accelerate until they were just a blur. The cars that had been blocking the carriageway were turned around and directed swiftly back down the hard shoulder at a furious rate. Bowden also noticed the sun rising rapidly behind us and wondered quite what he had let himself in for.

The green sedan had two occupants; a man and a woman. The woman was asleep and the driver was looking at the dark hole that had opened up in front of them. I shouted to him to stop. He wound down his window and I repeated myself, added "SpecOps!" and waved my ID. He dutifully applied his brakes and his stoplights came on, puncturing the darkness. Three minutes and twenty-six seconds had elapsed since we had begun our journey.

From where the ChronoGuard were standing, they could just see the brake lights on the green sedan come languidly on in the funnel of darkness that was the event's influence. They watched the progress of the green sedan over the next ten minutes as it made an almost imperceptible turn toward the hard shoulder. It was nearly 10 A.M. and an advance ChronoGuard outfit had arrived direct from Wareham. Their equipment and operatives were being airlifted in an SO-12 Chinook helicopter, and Colonel Rutter had flown ahead to see what needed to be done. He had been surprised that two ordinary officers had volunteered for this hazardous duty, especially as nobody could tell him who we were. Even a check of my car registration didn't help, as it was still listed as belonging to the garage I had bought it from. The only positive thing about the whole damn mess, he noted, was the fact that the passenger seemed to be holding a sphere of some sort. If the hole grew any bigger and time slowed down even more it might take them several months to reach us, even in the fastest vehicle they had. He lowered the binoculars and sighed. It was a stinking, lousy, lonely job. He had been working in the ChronoGuard for almost forty years, Standard Earth Time. In logged work time he was 209. In his own personal physiological time he was barely 28. His children were older than him and his wife was in a nursing home. He had thought the higher rates of pay would compensate him for any problems, but they didn't.

As the green sedan fell quickly away behind us, Bowden again looked back and saw the sun rising faster and higher. A helicopter arrived in a flash with the distinctive "CG" motif of the ChronoGuard. Ahead of us now there was only the motorcyclist, who seemed to be perilously close to the dark, swirling hole. He wore red leathers and was driving a top-of-the-range Triumph motorcycle, ironically enough about the only bike capable of escape from the vortex if he had known what the problem was. We had taken another six minutes to catch up with him and as we approached a roaring sound started to rise above the wind noise; the sort of scream a typhoon might make as it passed over the top of you. We were still about twelve feet behind and finding it difficult to keep up. The speedometer needle on the Porsche touched ninety as we roared along together. I blew my horn but the screaming drowned it out.

"Get ready!" I shouted to Bowden as the wind whipped our hair and the air tugged at our clothes. I flashed my lights at the bike again and at last he saw us. He turned around and waved, mistook our intent for a desire to initiate a race, kicked down a gear and accelerated away. The vortex caught him in an instant and he seemed to stretch out and around and inside out as he flowed rapidly into the instability; within what appeared to be a second he had gone. As soon as I thought we could get no closer I stamped on the brakes and yelled:

"Now!"

Smoke poured off the tires as we careened across the tarmac; Bowden threw the basketball, which seemed to swell in size with the hole, the ball flattening to a disc and the hole stretching out to a line. We saw the basketball hit the hole, bounce once and let us through. I glanced at the watch as we tipped through into the abyss, the basketball shutting out the last glimpse of the world we had left behind as we dropped through to Elsewhere. Up until the point we passed the event, twelve minutes and forty-one seconds had elapsed. Outside it had been closer to seven hours.

"Motorcycle's gone," remarked Colonel Rutter. His second-in-command grunted in reply. He didn't approve of non-Chronos attempting his work. They had managed to maintain the job's mysticism for over five decades with the wages to suit; have-a-go heroes could only serve to weaken people's undying trust in what they did. It wasn't a difficult job; it just took a long time. He had mended a similar rent in spacetime that had opened up in Weybridge's municipal park just between the floral clock and the bandstand. The job itself had taken ten minutes; he had simply walked in and stuck a tennis ball across the hole while outside seven months flashed by—seven months on double pay plus privileges, thank you very much.

The ChronoGuard operatives set up a large clock facing inward so any operatives within the field's influence would know what was happening. A similar clock on the back of the helicopter gave the officers outside a good idea of how slow time was running within.

After the motorcycle disappeared they waited another half-an-hour to see what would happen. They watched Bowden slowly rise and throw what appeared to be a basketball.

"Too late," murmured Rutter, having seen this sort of thing before. He ordered his men into action, and they were just starting to crank up the rotors of the helicopter when the darkness around the hole evaporated. The night slid back and a clear road confronted them. They could see the people in the green sedan get out and look around in amazement at the sudden day. A hundred yards farther on, the basketball had neatly blocked the tear and now stood trembling slightly in midair as the vortex behind the rip sucked at the ball. Within a minute the tear healed and the basketball dropped harmlessly to the asphalt, bouncing a few times before rolling to the side of the road. The sky was clear and there was no evidence that time wasn't the same as it had always been. But of the Datsun, the motorcyclist and the brightly painted sports car, there was no trace at all.

My car slid on and on. The motorway had been replaced by a swirling mass of light and color that had no meaning to either of us. Occasionally a coherent image would emerge from the murk and on several occasions we thought we had arrived back in a stable time, but were soon whisked back into the vortex, the typhoon raging in our ears. The first occasion was on a road somewhere in the Home Counties. It looked like winter, and ahead of us a lime-green Austin Allegro estate pulled out from a slip road. I swerved and drove past at great speed, sounding my horn angrily. That image collapsed abruptly and fragmented itself into the dirty hold of a ship. The car was wedged between two packing cases, the closest of which was bound for Shanghai. The howl of the vortex had diminished, but we could hear a new roar, the roar of a storm at sea. The ship wallowed and Bowden and I looked at one another, unsure as to whether this was the end of the journey or not. The roaring sound grew as the dank hold folded back into itself and vanished, only to be replaced by a white hospital ward. The tempest subsided, the car's engine ticking over happily. In the only occupied bed there was a drowsy and confused woman with her arm in a sling. I knew what I had to say.

"Thursday—!" I shouted excitedly.

The woman in the bed frowned. She looked across at Bowden, who waved back cheerily.

"He didn't die!" I continued, saying now what I knew to be the truth. I could hear the tempest starting to howl again. It wouldn't be long before we were taken away.

"The car crash was a blind! Men like Acheron don't die that easily! Take the LiteraTec job in Swindon!"

The woman in the bed just had time to repeat my last word before the ceiling and floor opened up and we plummeted back into the maelstrom. After a dazzling display of colorful noise and loud light, the vortex slid back to be replaced by the parking lot of a motorway services somewhere. The tempest slowed and stopped.

"Is this it?" asked Bowden.

"I don't know."

It was night and the streetlamps cast an orange glow over the parking lot, the roadway shiny from recent rain. A car pulled in next to us; it was a large Pontiac containing a family. The wife was berating her husband for falling asleep at the wheel and the children were crying. It looked like it had been a near-miss.

"Excuse me!" I yelled. The man wound down his window.

"Yes?"

"What's the date?"

"The date?"

"It's July 8," replied the man's wife, shooting him and me an annoyed glance.

I thanked her and turned back to Bowden.

"We're three weeks in the past?" he queried.

"Or fifty-six weeks into the future."

"Or one hundred and eight."

"I'm going to find out where we are."

I turned off the ignition and got out. Bowden joined me as we walked toward the cafeteria. Beyond the building we could see the motorway, and beyond that the connecting bridge to the services on the opposite motorway.

Several tow trucks drove past us with empty cars hitched to the back of them.

"Something's not right."

"I agree," replied Bowden. "But what?"

Suddenly, the doors to the cafeteria burst open and a woman pushed her way out. She was carrying a gun and pushing a man in front of her, who stumbled as they hurried out. Bowden pulled me behind a parked van. We peered cautiously out and saw that the woman had unwelcome company; several men had appeared seemingly from nowhere and all of them were armed.

"What the?—" I whispered, suddenly realizing what was happening. "That's me!"

And so it was. I looked slightly older but it was definitely me. Bowden had noticed too.

"I'm not sure I like what you've done with your hair."

"You prefer it long?"

"Of course."

We watched as one of the three men told the other me to drop her gun. I-me-she said something we couldn't hear and then put her gun down, releasing her hold on the man, who was then grabbed roughly by one of the other men.

"What's going on?" I asked, thoroughly confused.

"We've got to go!" replied Bowden.

"And leave me like this?"

"Look."

He pointed at the car. It was shaking slightly as a localized gust of wind seemed to batter it.

"I can't leave her—me—in this predicament!"

But Bowden was pulling me toward the car, which was rocking more violently and starting to fade.

"Wait!"

I struggled free, pulled out my automatic and hid it behind one of the wheels of the nearest car, then ran after Bowden and leaped into the back of the Speedster. I was just in time. There was a bright flash and a peal of thunder and then silence. I opened an eye. It was daylight. I looked at Bowden, who had made it into the driver's seat. The motorway services car park had vanished and in its place was a quiet country lane. The journey was over.

"You all right?" I asked.

Bowden felt the three-day stubble that had inexplicably grown on his chin.

"I think so. How about you?"

"As well as can be expected."

I checked my shoulder holster. It was empty.

"I'm bursting for a pee, though. I feel like I haven't gone for a week."

Bowden made a pained expression and nodded.

"I think I could say the same."

I nipped behind a wall. Bowden walked stiffly across to the other side of the road and relieved himself in the hedge.

"Where do you suppose we are?" I shouted to Bowden from behind the wall. "Or more to the point, when?"

"Car twenty-eight," crackled the wireless, "come in please."

"Who knows?" called out Bowden over his shoulder. "But if you want to try that again you can do it with someone else."

Much relieved, we reconvened at the car. It was a beautiful day, dry and quite warm. The smell of haymaking was in the air, and in the distance we could hear a tractor lumbering across a field.

"What was all that motorway services thing about?" asked Bowden. "Last Thursday or next Thursday?"

I shrugged.

"Don't ask me to explain. I just hope I got out of that jam. Those guys didn't look as though they were out collecting for the church fund."

"You'll find out."

"I guess. I wonder who that man was I was trying to protect?"

"Search me."

I sat on the hood and donned a pair of dark glasses. Bowden walked to a gate and looked over. In a dip in the valley was a village built of gray stone, and in the field a herd of cows was grazing peacefully.

Bowden pointed to a milestone he had found.

"That's a spot of luck."

The milestone told him we were six miles from Haworth.

I wasn't listening to him. I was now puzzling over seeing

myself in the hospital bed. If I hadn't seen myself I wouldn't have gone to Swindon and if I hadn't gone to Swindon I wouldn't have been able to warn myself to go there. Doubtless it would make complete sense to my father, but I might well go nuts trying to figure it out.

"Car twenty-eight," said the wireless, "come in please."

I stopped thinking about it and checked the position of the sun.

"It's about midday, I'd say."

Bowden nodded agreement.

"Aren't *we* car twenty-eight?" he asked, frowning slightly. I picked up the mike.

"Car twenty-eight, go ahead."

"At last!" sounded a relieved voice over the speaker. "I have Colonel Rutter of the ChronoGuard who wants to speak to you."

Bowden walked over so he could hear better. We looked at each other, unsure of what was going to happen next; a chastisement or a heap of congratulations, or, as it turned out, both.

"Officers Next and Cable. Can you hear me?" said a deep voice over the wireless.

"Yes, sir."

"Good. Where are you?"

"About six miles from Haworth."

"All the way up there, eh?" he guffawed. "Jolly good." He cleared his throat. We could sense it coming.

"Unofficially, that was one of the bravest acts I've ever seen. You saved a great number of lives and stopped the event from becoming a matter of some consequence. You can both be very proud of your actions and I would be honored to have two fine officers like you serving under me."

"Thank you, sir, I—"

"I'm still talking!" he snapped, causing us both to jump. "*Officially*, though, you broke every rule in the book. And I should have both your butts nailed to the wall for not following procedure. If you ever try anything like this again, I most certainly will. Understand?"

"Understood, sir."

I looked at Bowden. There was only one question we wanted to ask.

"How long have we been gone?"

"The year is now 2016," said Rutter. *"You've been gone thirty-one years!!"*

28.

Haworth House

Some would say the ChronoGuard have a terrific sense of humor. I would say they were just plain annoying. I had heard that they used to bundle up new recruits in gravity suits and pop them a week into the future just for fun. The game was banned when one recruit vanished outside the cone. Theoretically he is still there, just outside our time, unable to return and unable to communicate. It is calculated we will catch up with him about fourteen thousand years from now—sadly, he will have aged only twelve minutes. Some joke.

THURSDAY NEXT
—*A Life in SpecOps*

WE WERE both victims of the ChronoGuard's bizarre sense of humor. It was just past noon the following day. We had been gone only seven hours. We both reset our watches and drove slowly into Haworth, each sobered by the experience.

At Haworth House a full media circus was in progress. I had hoped to arrive before this sort of thing really gained a toehold, but the hole in the M1 had put paid to that. Lydia Startright from the Toad News Network had arrived and was recording for the lunchtime bulletin. She stood outside the steps of Haworth

House with a microphone and composed herself before beginning. She signaled to her cameraman to roll, adopted one of her most serious expressions, and began.

". . . As the sun rose over Haworth House this morning the police began to investigate a bold theft and double murder. Some time last night a security guard was shot dead by an unknown assailant as he attempted to stop him stealing the original manuscript of *Jane Eyre*. Police have been at the crime scene since early morning and have as yet given no comment. It is fairly certain that parallels must be drawn with the theft of the *Martin Chuzzlewit* manuscript, which, despite continued police and SpecOps efforts, has so far not come to light. Following Mr. Quaverley's extraction and murder, it can only be surmised that a similar fate is in store for Rochester or Jane. The Goliath Corporation, whose presence this morning was an unusual development, have no comment to make—as usual."

"And—*cut*! That was *very* good, darling," declared Lydia's producer. "Can we do it once more without the reference to Goliath? You know they'll only cut it out!"

"Then let them."

"Lyds, baby—! Who pays the bills? I like free speech as much as the next man, but on someone else's airtime, hmm?"

She ignored him and looked around as a car arrived. Her face lit up and she walked briskly across, gesturing for her cameraman to follow.

A lean officer of about forty with silver hair and bags under his eyes looked to heaven as she approached, cracking his unfriendly face into a smile. He waited patiently for her to make a brief introduction.

"I have with me Detective Inspector Oswald Mandias, Yorkshire CID. Tell me, Inspector, do you think this crime is in any way connected to the *Chuzzlewit* theft?"

He smiled benignly, fully aware that he would be on thirty million television screens by the evening.

"It's far too early to say anything; a full press release will be issued in due course."

"Isn't this a case for the Yorkshire LiteraTecs, sir? *Jane Eyre* is one of this county's most valued treasures."

Mandias stopped to face her.

"Unlike other SpecOps departments, the Yorkshire Litera-Tecs rely on evidence supplied by the regular police. LiteraTecs are *not* police and have no place in a police environment."

"Why do you suppose the Goliath Corporation made an appearance this morning?"

"No more questions!" called out Mandias's deputy as a throng of other news crews started to converge. Goliath had been and gone but no one was going to learn anymore about it. The police pushed their way past and Lydia stopped to have a snack; she had been reporting live since before breakfast. A few minutes later Bowden and I drove up in the Speedster.

"Well, well," I muttered as I got out of the car, "Startright keeps herself busy. Morning, Lyds!"

Lydia almost choked on her SmileyBurger and quickly threw it aside. She picked up her microphone and chased after me.

"Although the Yorkshire LiteraTecs and Goliath are claimed not to be present," muttered Lydia as she tried to keep up, "events have taken an interesting turn with the arrival of Thursday Next of SO-27. In a departure from normal procedure, the LiteraTecs have come out from behind their desks and are visiting the crime scene in person."

I stopped to have some fun. Lydia composed herself and started the interview.

"Miss Next, tell me, what are you doing so far out of your jurisdiction?"

"Hi, Lydia. You have mayonnaise on your upper lip from that SmileyBurger. It has a lot of salt in it and you really shouldn't eat them. As for the case, I'm afraid it's the same old shit: 'You will understand that anything we may discover will have to remain a blah-de-blah-de-blah.' How's that?"

Lydia hid a smile.

"Do you think the two thefts are linked?"

"My brother Joffy is a big fan of yours, Lyds; can you let me have a signed picture? 'Joffy' with two Fs. Excuse me."

"Thanks for nothing, Thursday!" called out Startright. "I'll be seeing you!"

We walked up to the police line and showed our IDs to the constable on duty. He looked at the badges, then at the two of us. We could see he was not impressed. He spoke to Mandias.

"Sir, these two Wessex LiteraTecs want to get at the crime scene."

Mandias ambled over painfully slowly. He looked us both up and down and chose his words with care.

"Here in Yorkshire LiteraTecs don't leave their desks."

"I've read the arrest reports. It shows," I replied coldly.

Mandias sighed. Keeping what he described as eggheads in check, especially those from another SpecOps region, was obviously not something he was keen to do.

"I have two murders on my hands here and I don't want the crime scene disturbed. Why don't you wait until you get the report and then take your investigation from there?"

"The murders are tragic, obviously," I replied, "but *Jane Eyre* is the thing here. It is imperative that we get to see the crime scene. *Jane Eyre* is bigger than me and bigger than you. If you refuse I'll send a report to your superior officer complaining of your conduct."

But Mandias was not a man to listen to threats, idle or otherwise. This was Yorkshire, after all. He stared at me and said softly:

"Do your worst, pen-pusher."

I took a step forward and he bridled slightly; he wasn't going to give way. A nearby officer moved in behind him to give assistance if needed.

I was about to lose my temper when Bowden spoke up.

"Sir," he began, "if we could *move slowly* toward a goal we might be able to *burrow* our way out of the predicament we find ourselves *shuffling* into."

Mandias's attitude abruptly changed and he smiled solemnly.

"If *that* is the case, I am sure we could manage a quick look for you—as long as you promise not to touch anything."

"On my word," replied Bowden pointedly, patting his stomach. The two of them shook hands and winked and we were soon escorted into the museum.

"How the hell did you do that?" I hissed.

"Look at his ring."

I looked. He had a large ring on his middle finger with a curious and distinctive pattern on it.

"What of it?"

"The Most Worshipful Brotherhood of the Wombat."

I smiled.

"So what have we got?" I asked. "A double murder and a missing script? They just took the manuscript, right? Nothing else?"

"Right," replied Mandias.

"And the guard was shot with his own gun?"

Mandias stopped and looked sternly at me.

"How did you know that?"

"A lucky guess," I replied evenly. "What about the video-tapes?"

"We're studying them at the moment."

"There's no one on them, is there?"

Mandias looked at me curiously.

"Do you know who did this?"

I followed him into the room that once held the manuscript. The untouched glass case was sitting forlornly in the middle of the floor. I ran my fingertips across a mottled and uneven patch on the glass.

"Thanks, Mandias, you're a star," I said, walking back out. Bowden and Mandias looked at one another and hastened after me.

"That's it?" said Mandias. "That's your investigation?"

"I've seen all I need to see."

"Can you give me anything?" asked Mandias, trotting to keep up. He looked at Bowden. "Brother, *you* can tell me."

"We should tell the DI what we know, Thursday. We owe him for allowing us in."

I stopped so suddenly Mandias almost bumped into me.

"Ever hear of a man named Hades?"

Mandias went visibly pale and looked around nervously.

"Don't worry; he's long gone."

"They say he died in Venezuela."

"They say he can walk through walls," I countered. "They also say he gives off colors when he moves. Hades is alive and well and I have to find him before he starts to make use of the manuscript."

Mandias seemed to have undergone a humbling change as soon as he realized who was behind it all.

"Anything I can do?"

I paused for a moment.

"Pray you never meet him."

The drive back to Swindon was uneventful, the area on the M1 where all the trouble had been now back to normal. Victor was waiting for us in the office; he seemed slightly agitated.

"I've had Braxton on the phone all morning bleating on about insurance cover being inoperative if his officers act outside their jurisdiction."

"Same old shit."

"That's what I told him. I've got most of the office reading *Jane Eyre* at the moment in case anything unusual happens—all quiet so far."

"It's only a matter of time."

"Hmm."

"Müller mentioned Hades being at Penderyn somewhere," I said to Victor. "Anything come of that?"

"Nothing that I know of. Schitt said he had looked into it and drawn a blank—there are over three hundred possible Penderyns that Müller might have meant. More worrying, have you seen this morning's paper?"

I hadn't. He showed me the inside front page of *The Mole*. It read:

TROOP MOVEMENTS
NEAR WELSH BORDER

I read on with some alarm. Apparently there had been troop movements near Hereford, Chepstow and the disputed border town of Oswestry. A military spokesman had dismissed the maneuvers as simple "exercises," but it didn't sound good at all. Not at all. I turned to Victor.

"Jack Schitt? Do you think he wants the Prose Portal badly enough to go to war with Wales?"

"Who knows what power the Goliath Corporation wields. He might not be behind this at all. It could be coincidence or just saber-rattling; but in any event I don't think we can ignore it."

"Then we need to steal a march. Any ideas?"

"What did Müller say again?" asked Finisterre.

I sat down.

"He screamed: 'He's at Penderyn'; nothing else."

"Nothing else?" asked Bowden.

"No; when Schitt asked him *which* Penderyn he meant, as there must be hundreds, Müller told him to guess."

Bowden spoke up.

"What were his *precise* words?"

"He said 'Guess,' then repeated it but it turned into a yell—he was in grave pain at the time. The conversation was recorded but there is about as much chance as getting hold of that as—"

"Maybe he meant something else."

"Like what, Bowden?"

"I really only speak tourist Welsh but 'Gwesty' means hotel."

"Oh my God," said Victor.

"Victor?" I queried, but he was busy rummaging in a large pile of maps we had accumulated; each of them had a Penderyn of some sort marked on it. He spread a large street plan of Merthyr Tydfil out on the table and pointed at a place just between the Palace of justice and Government House. We craned to see where his finger was pointing but the location was unmarked.

"The Penderyn Hotel," announced Victor grimly. "I spent my honeymoon there. Once the equal of the Adelphi or Raffles, it's been empty since the sixties. If *I* wanted a safe haven—"

"He's there," I announced, looking at the map of the Welsh capital city uneasily. "That's where we'll find him."

"And how do you suppose we'll manage to enter Wales undetected, make our way into a heavily guarded area, snatch Mycroft and the manuscript and get out in one piece?" asked Bowden. "It takes a month to even get a visa!"

"We'll find a way in," I said slowly.

"You're crazy!" said Victor. "Braxton would never allow it!"

"That's where you come in."

"Me? Braxton doesn't listen to *me*."

"I think he's about to start."

29.

Jane Eyre

Jane Eyre was published in 1847 under the pseudonym Currer Bell, a suitably neuter name that disguised Charlotte Brontë's sex. It was a great success; William Thackeray described the novel as "The master work of a great genius." Not that the book was without its critics: G. H. Lewes suggested that Charlotte should study Austen's work and "correct her shortcomings in the light of that great artist's practice." Charlotte replied that Miss Austen's work was barely—in the light of what she wanted to do—a novel at all. She referred to it as "a highly cultivated garden with no open country." The jury is still out.

W. H . H . F . RENOUF
—*The Brontës*

HOBBES SHOOK his head in the relative unfamiliarity of the corridors of Rochester's home, Thornfield Hall. It was night and a deathly hush had descended on the house. The corridor was dark and he fumbled for his torch. A glimmer of orange light stabbed the darkness as he walked slowly along the upstairs hall. Ahead of him he could see a door which was slightly ajar, through which showed a thin glimmer of candlelight. He paused by the door and peered around the corner. Within he could see a woman dressed in tatters and with wild unkempt hair pouring oil from a lantern onto the covers under which Rochester lay asleep. Hobbes got his bearings; he knew that Jane would soon be in to put out the fire, but from which door he had no way of knowing. He turned back into the corridor and nearly leaped out of his skin as he came face to face with a large, florid-looking woman. She smelled strongly of drink, had an aggressive countenance and glared at him with thinly disguised contempt. They stood staring at each other for some moments, Hobbes wondering what to do and the woman wavering slightly, her eyes never leaving his. Hobbes panicked and went for his gun, but with wholly unlikely speed the woman caught his arm and held it pinched so tightly that it was all he could do to stop yelling out in pain.

"What are you doing here?" she hissed, one eyebrow twitching.

"Who in Christ's name are you?" asked Hobbes.

She smacked him hard across the face; he staggered before recovering.

"My name is Grace Poole," said Grace Poole. "In service I might be, but you have no right to utter the Lord's name in vain. I can see by your attire that you do not belong here. What do you want?"

"I'm, um, with Mr. Mason," he stammered.

"Rubbish," she replied, staring at him dangerously.

"I want Jane Eyre," he stammered.

"So does Mr. Rochester," she replied in a matter-of-fact tone. "But he doesn't even kiss her until page one hundred and eighty-one."

Hobbes glanced inside the room. The madwoman was now dancing around, smiling and cackling as the flames grew higher on Rochester's bed.

"If she doesn't arrive soon, there won't be a page one hundred and eighty-one."

Grace Poole caught his eye again and fixed him with a baleful glare.

"She will save him as she has before thousands of times, as she will again thousands of times. It is the way of things here."

"Yeah?" replied Hobbes. "Well, things just might change."

At that moment the madwoman rushed out of the room and into Hobbes with her fingernails outstretched. With a maniacal laugh that made his ears pop she lunged at him and pressed her uncut and ragged nails into both his cheeks. He yelled out in pain as Grace Poole wrestled Mrs. Rochester into a half nelson and frogmarched her to the attic. As Grace got to the door she turned to Hobbes and spoke again.

"Just remember: It is the way of things here."

"Aren't you going to try and stop me?" asked Hobbes in a puzzled tone.

"I take poor Mrs. Rochester upstairs now," she replied. "It is written."

The door closed behind her as a voice shouting "Wake, wake!" brought Hobbes's attention back to the blazing room. Within he could see the night-robed Jane throwing a jug of water over the recumbent form of Rochester. Hobbes waited until the fire was out before stepping into the room, drawing his gun as he did so. They both looked up, the "elves of Christendom" line dying on Rochester's lips.

"Who are you?" they asked, together.

"Believe me, you couldn't possibly begin to understand."

Hobbes took Jane by the arm and dragged her back toward the corridor.

"Edward! My Edward!" implored Jane, her arms outstretched to Rochester. "I won't leave you, my love!"

"Wait a minute," said Hobbes, still backing away, "you guys haven't fallen in love yet!"

"In that you would be mistaken," murmured Rochester, pulling out a percussion pistol from beneath his pillow. "I have suspected something like this might happen for some time." He aimed at Hobbes and fired in a single quick movement. He missed, the large lead ball burying itself in the door frame. Hobbes fired back a warning shot; Hades had expressly forbidden anyone in the novel to be hurt. Rochester pulled a second pistol after the first and cocked it.

"Let her go," he announced, his jaw set, his dark hair falling into his eyes.

Hobbes pulled Jane in front of him.

"Don't be a fool, Rochester! If all goes well Jane will be returned to you forthwith; you won't even know she has gone!"

Hobbes backed down the hall toward where the portal was due to open as he spoke. Rochester followed, gun outstretched, his heart heavy as his one and only true love was dragged un-ceremoniously from the novel to that place, that *other* place, where he and Jane could never enjoy the life they enjoyed at Thornfield. Hobbes and Jane vanished back through the portal, which closed abruptly after them. Rochester put up his gun and glowered.

A few moments later Hobbes and a very confused Jane Eyre had fallen back through the Prose Portal and into the dilapidated smoking lounge of the old Penderyn Hotel.

Acheron stepped forward and helped Jane up. He offered her his coat to warm herself. After Thornfield Hall the hotel was decidedly drafty.

"Miss Eyre!—" announced Hades kindly. "My name is Hades, Acheron Hades. You are my respected guest; please take a seat and compose yourself."

"Edward?—"

"Quite well, my young friend. Come, let me take you to a warmer part of the hotel."

"Will I see my Edward again?"

Hades smiled.

"It rather depends on how valuable people think you are."

30.

A Groundswell of
Popular Feeling

> Until Jane Eyre was kidnapped I don't think anyone—
> least of all Hades—realized quite how popular she was.
> It was as if a living national embodiment of England's lit-
> erary heritage had been torn from the masses. It was the
> best piece of news we could have hoped for.
>
> BOWDEN CABLE
—Journal of a LiteraTec

WITHIN TWENTY seconds of Jane's kidnapping, the first worried member of the public had noticed strange goings-on around the area of page 107 of their deluxe hidebound edition of *Jane Eyre*. Within thirty minutes all the lines into the English Museum library were jammed. Within two hours every Litera-Tec department was besieged by calls from worried Brontë readers. Within four hours the president of the Brontë Federation had seen the prime minister. By suppertime the prime minister's personal secretary had called the head of SpecOps. By nine o'-clock the head of SpecOps had batted it down the line to a miserable Braxton Hicks. By ten he had been called personally by the prime minister, who asked him what the hell he was going to do about it. He stammered down the line and said something wholly unhelpful. Meanwhile, the news was leaked to the press that Swindon was the center of the *Jane Eyre* investigation, and by midnight the SpecOps building was encircled by concerned readers, journalists and news network trucks.

Braxton was not in a good mood. He had started to chain-smoke and locked himself in his office for hours at a time. Not even putting practice managed to soothe his ruffled nerves, and shortly after the prime minister's call he summoned Victor and me for a meeting on the roof, away from the prying eyes of the press, the Goliath representatives and especially from Jack Schitt.

"Sir?" said Victor as we approached Braxton, who was leaning against a smokestack that squeaked as it turned. Hicks was staring out at the lights of Swindon with a detachment that made me worried. The parapet was barely two yards away, and for an awful moment I thought perhaps he was going to end it all.

"Look at them," he murmured.

We both relaxed as we realized that Braxton was on the roof so he could see the public that his department had pledged to help. There were thousands of them, encircling the station behind crowd barriers, silently holding candles and clutching their copies of *Jane Eyre,* now seriously disrupted, the narrative stopping abruptly halfway down page 107 after a mysterious "Agent in black" enters Rochester's room following the fire.

Braxton waved his own copy of *Jane Eyre* at us.

"You've read it, of course?"

"There isn't much to read," Victor replied. "*Eyre* was written in the first person; as soon as the protagonist has gone, it's anyone's guess as to what happens next. My theory is that Rochester becomes even more broody, packs Adele off to boarding school, and shuts up the house."

Braxton looked at him pointedly.

"That's conjecture, Analogy."

"It's what we're best at."

Braxton sighed.

"They want me to bring her back and I don't even know where she is! Before all this happened, did you have any idea how popular *Jane Eyre* was?"

We looked at the crowd below.

"To be truthful, no."

Braxton's reserve was all gone. He wiped his brow; his hand was visibly shaking.

"What am I going to do? This is off the record but Jack Schitt takes over in a week if this whole stinking matter hasn't made any favorable headway."

"Schitt isn't interested in Jane," I said, following Braxton's gaze over the mass of Brontë fans. "All he wants is the Prose Portal."

"Tell me about it, Next. I've got seven days to obscurity and historical and literary damnation. I know we've all had our differences in the past, but I want to give you the freedom to do what you need to do. And," he added magnanimously, "this is irrespective of cost." He checked himself and added: "But having said that, of course, don't just spend money like water, okay?"

He looked at the lights of Swindon again.

"I'm as big a fan of the Brontës as the next man, Victor. What will you have me do?"

"Agree to his terms whatever they are; keep our movements completely and utterly secret from Goliath; and I need a manuscript."

Braxton narrowed his eyes.

"What sort of manuscript?"

Victor handed him a scrap of paper. Braxton read it and raised his eyebrows.

"I'll get it," he said slowly, "even if I have to steal it myself!"

31.

The People's Republic
of Wales

Ironically, without the efficient and violent crushing of
the simultaneous Pontypool, Cardiff and Newport ris-
ings in 1839, Wales might never have been a republic at
all. Under pressure from landowners and a public outcry
at the killing of 236 unarmed Welsh men and women,
the Chartists managed to push the government to early
reform of the parliamentary system. Buoyed by success
and well represented in the house, they succeeded in securing Welsh home rule following the eight-month
"Great Strike" of 1847. In 1854, under the leadership of
John Frost, Wales declared its independence. England,
weighed down with troubles in the Crimea and Ireland,
saw no good reason to argue with a belligerent and committed Welsh assembly. Trade links were good and devo-
lution, coupled with an Anglo-Welsh nonaggression
treaty, was passed the following year.

FROM ZEPHANIA JONES'S
Wales—Birth of a Republic

WHEN THE Anglo-Welsh border was closed in 1965, the A4
from Chepstow to Abertawe became an access corridor through
which only businessmen or truck drivers were allowed to pass,
either to conduct trade in the city or to pick up goods from the
docks. On either side of the Welsh A4 there were razor-wire

fences to remind visitors that straying from the designated route was not permitted.

Abertawe was considered an open city—a "free trade zone." Tax was low and trade tariffs almost nonexistent. Bowden and I drove slowly into the city, the glassy towers and global banking institutions that lined the coast obvious testament to a free trade philosophy that, while profitable, was *not* enthusiastically promoted by all the Welsh people. The rest of the Republic was much more reserved and traditional; in places the small nation had hardly changed at all over the past hundred years.

"What now?" asked Bowden as we parked in front of the Goliath First National Bank. I patted the briefcase Braxton had given me the night before. He had told me to use the contents wisely; the way things were going this was about the last chance we had before Goliath stepped in.

"We get a lift into Merthyr."

"You wouldn't suggest it unless you had a plan."

"I wasn't wasting my time when I was in London, Bowden. I've got a few favors up my sleeve. This way."

We walked up the road, past the bank and into a side street that was lined with shops dealing in banknotes, medals, coins, gold—and books. We squeezed past the traders, who conversed mostly in Welsh, and stopped outside a small antiquarian bookshop whose window was piled high with ancient volumes of forgotten lore. Bowden and I shared an anxious look and, taking a deep breath, I opened the door and we entered.

A small bell tinkled at the back of the shop and a tall man with a stoop came out to greet us. He looked at us suspiciously from between a shock of gray hair and a pair of half-moon spectacles, but the suspicion turned to a smile when he recognized me.

"Thursday, *bach*!" he murmured, hugging me affectionately.

"What brings you out this way? Not all the way to Abertawe to see an old man, surely?"

"I need your help, Dai," I said softly. "Help like I've never needed before."

He must have been following the news broadcasts because he fell silent. He gently took an early volume of R. S. Thomas out of the hands of a prospective customer, told him it was closing time and ushered him out of the bookshop before he had time to complain.

"This is Bowden Cable," I explained as the bookseller bolted the door. "He's my partner; if you can trust me you can trust him. Bowden, this is Jones the Manuscript, my Welsh contact."

"Ah!" said the bookseller, shaking Bowden's hand warmly. "Any friend of Thursday's is a friend of mine. This is Haelwyn the Book," he added, introducing us to his assistant, who smiled shyly. "Now, young Thursday, what can I do for you?"

I paused.

"We need to get to Merthyr Tydfil—"

The bookseller laughed explosively.

"—*tonight*," I added.

He stopped laughing and walked behind the counter, tidying absently as he went.

"Your reputation precedes you, Thursday. They tell me you seek *Jane Eyre*. They say you have a good heart—and have faced wickedness and lived."

"What else do people say?"

"That Darkness walks in the valleys," interrupted Haelwyn with a good deal of doom in her voice.

"Thank you, Haelwyn," said Jones. "The man you seek—"

"—and the Rhondda has lain in shadow these past few weeks," continued Haelwyn, who obviously hadn't finished yet.

"That's enough, Haelwyn," said Jones more sternly. "There

are some new copies of *Cold Comfort Farm* that need to be dispatched to Llan-dod, hmm?"

Haelwyn walked off with a pained expression.

"What about—" I began.

"—and the milk is delivered sour from the cows' udders!" called Haelwyn from behind a bookshelf. "*And* the compasses in Merthyr have all gone mad these past few days!"

"Take no heed of her," explained Jones apologetically. "She reads a lot of books. But how can I help you? Me, an old bookseller with no connections?"

"An old bookseller with Welsh citizenship and free access across the border doesn't need connections to get to where he wants to go."

"Wait a moment, Thursday, bach; you want *me* to take *you* to Merthyr?"

I nodded. Jones was the best and last chance I had, all rolled into one. But he wasn't as happy with the plan as I thought he might be.

"And why would I want to do that?" he asked sharply. "You know the punishment for smuggling? Want to see an old man like me end my days in a cell on Skokholm? You ask too much. I'm a crazy old man—not a stupid one."

I had thought he might say this.

"If you'll help us," I began, reaching into my briefcase, "I can let you have . . . *this*."

I placed the single sheet of paper on the counter in front of him; Jones gave a sharp intake of breath and sat heavily on a chair. He knew what it was without close examination.

"How . . . how did you get this?" he asked me suspiciously.

"The English government rates the return of *Jane Eyre* very highly—high enough to wish to trade."

He leaned forward and picked up the sheet. There, in all its glory, was an early handwritten draft of "I See the Boys of Summer," the opening poem in the anthology that would later become *18 Poems,* the first published work of Dylan Thomas; Wales had been demanding its return for some time.

"This belongs not to one man but to the Republic," announced the bookseller slowly. "It is the heritage."

"Agreed," I replied. "You can do with the manuscript what you will."

But Jones the Manuscript was not going to be swayed. I could have brought him *Under Milk Wood* and Richard Burton to read it and he *still* wouldn't have taken us to Merthyr.

"Thursday, you ask too much!" he wailed. "The laws here are *very* strict! The HeddluCyfrinach have eyes and ears everywhere!—"

My heart sank.

"I understand, Jones—and thanks."

"I'll take you to Merthyr, Miss Next," interrupted Haelwyn, fixing me with a half-smile.

"It is too dangerous," muttered Jones. "I forbid it!"

"Hush!" replied Haelwyn. "Enough of that talk from you. I read adventures every day—now I can be in one. Besides—the streetlights dimmed last night; *it was a sign!*"

We sat in Jones's parlor until it was dark, then spent a noisy and uncomfortable hour in the trunk of Haelwyn the Book's Griffin-12 motorcar. We heard the murmur of Welsh voices as she took us across the border and we were pummeled mercilessly by the potholed road on the trip into Merthyr. There was a second checkpoint just outside the capital, which was unusual; it seemed that English troop movements had made the military edgy. A few minutes later the car stopped and the trunk creaked open. Haelwyn bade us jump out and we stretched painfully after the cramped journey. She pointed the way to the Penderyn Hotel and I told her that if we weren't back by daybreak we wouldn't be coming. She smiled and shook our hands, wished us good luck and headed off to visit her aunt.

Hades was in the Penderyn Hotel's abandoned bar at that time, smoking a pipe and contemplating the view from the large windows. Beyond the beautifully lit Palace of Justice the full moon had risen and cast a cool glow upon the old city, which was alive with lights and movement. Beyond the buildings were the mountains, their summits hidden in cloud. Jane was on the other side of the room, sitting on the edge of her seat, angrily glaring at Hades.

"Pleasant view, wouldn't you say, Miss Eyre?"

"It pales when compared to my window at Thornfield, Mr. Hades," replied Jane in a restrained tone. "While not the finest view I had learned to love it as an old friend, dependable and unchanging. I demand that you return me there forthwith."

"All in good time, dear girl, all in good time. I mean you no harm. I just want to make a lot of money, then you can return to your Edward."

"Greed will get the better of you, I think, sir," responded Jane evenly. "You may think it will bring you happiness, but it will not. Happiness is fed by the food of love, not by the stodgy diet of money. The love of money is the root of all evil!"

Acheron smiled.

"You are so dull, you know, Jane, with that puritanical streak. You should have gone with Rochester when you had the chance instead of wasting yourself with that drip St. John Rivers."

"Rivers is a fine man!" declared Jane angrily. "He has more goodness than you will ever know!"

The telephone rang and Acheron interrupted her with a wave of his hand. It was Delamare, speaking from a phone box in Swindon. He was reading from *The Mole*'s classified section.

"Lop-eared rabbits will be available soon to good homes," he quoted down the line. Hades smiled and replaced the receiver. The authorities, he thought, were playing ball after all. He motioned to Felix8, who followed him out of the room, dragging a recalcitrant Jane with him.

Bowden and I had forced a window in the dark bowels of the hotel and found ourselves in the old kitchen: a damp and dilapidated room packed with large food preparation equipment.

"Where now?" hissed Bowden.

"Upstairs—I would expect them to be in a ballroom or something."

I snapped on a flashlight and looked at the hastily sketched plans. Searching for the real blueprints would have been too risky with Goliath watching our every move, so Victor had drawn the basic layout of the building from memory. I pushed open a swing door and we found ourselves on the lower ground floor. Above us was the entrance lobby. By the glimmer of the streetlights that shone through the dirty windows we made our way carefully up the water-stained marble staircase. We were close; I could sense it. I pulled out my automatic and Bowden did the same. I looked up into the lobby. A brass bust of Y Brawd Ulyanov sat in pride of place in the large entrance hall opposite the sealed main doors. To the left was the entrance to the bar and restaurant, and to the right was the old reception desk; above us the grand staircase swept upstairs to the two ballrooms. Bowden tapped me on the shoulder and pointed. The doors to the main lounge were ajar, and a thin sliver of orange light shone from within. We were about to make a move when we heard footsteps from above. We pushed ourselves into the shadows and waited, breath bated. From the upstairs floor a small procession of people walked down the broad marble staircase. Leading the way was a man I recognized as Felix8; he held a candelabra aloft with one hand and clasped a small woman by the wrist with the other. She was dressed in Victorian night-clothes and had a greatcoat draped across her shoulders. Her face, although resolute, also spoke of despair and hopelessness. Behind her was a man who cast no shadows in the flickering light of the candles—Hades.

We watched as they entered the smoking lounge. We quickly tiptoed across the hall floor and found ourselves at the ornate door. I counted to three and we burst in.

"Thursday! My dear girl, how *predictable*!"

I stared. Hades was sitting in a large armchair, smiling at us. Mycroft and Jane were looking dejected on a chaise longue with Felix8 behind them holding two machine pistols trained on Bowden and me. In front of them all was the Prose Portal. I cursed myself for being so stupid. I could sense Hades was here; did I suppose he could not do the same with me?

"Drop your weapons, please," said Felix8. He was too close to Mycroft and Jane to risk a shot; the last time we met he had died as I watched. I said the first thing that popped into my head.

"Haven't I seen your face somewhere before?"

He ignored me.

"Your guns, please."

"And let you shoot us like dodos? No way. We're keeping them."

Felix8 didn't move. Our weapons were by our side and his were pointing straight at us. It wouldn't be much of a contest.

"You seem surprised that I was expecting you," said Hades with a slight smile.

"You could say that."

"The stakes have changed, Miss Next. I thought my ten million ransom was a lot of money but I was approached by someone who would give me ten times that for your uncle's machine alone."

Mycroft shuffled unhappily. He had long ago ceased to complain, knowing it to be useless. He now looked forward only to the short visits he was permitted to Polly.

"If that is the case," I said slowly, "then you can return Jane to the book."

Hades thought for a minute.

"Why not? But first, I want you to meet someone."

A door opened to the left of us and Jack Schitt walked in. He was flanked by three of his men and they were all carrying plasma rifles. The situation, I noted, was on the whole less than favorable. I muttered an apology to Bowden then said:

"Goliath? Here, in Wales?"

"No doors are closed to the Corporation, Miss Next. We come and go as we please."

Schitt sat down on a faded red upholstered chair and pulled out a cigar.

"Siding with criminals, Mr. Schitt? Is that what Goliath does these days?"

"It's a relativist argument, Miss Next—desperate situations require desperate measures. I wouldn't expect you to understand. But listen, we have a great deal of money at our disposal and Acheron is willing to be generous in the use of Mr. Next's notable invention."

"And that is?"

"Ever seen one of these?" asked Schitt, waving the stubby weapon he held at us both.

"It's a plasma rifle."

"Correct. A one-man portable piece of field artillery, firing supercharged quanta of pure energy. It will cut through a foot of armor plate at a hundred yards; I think you will agree it is the high ground for land forces anywhere."

"*If* Goliath can deliver—" put in Bowden.

"It's a mite more complicated than that, Officer Cable," replied Schitt. "You see—*it doesn't work*. Almost a billion dollars of funding and the bloody thing doesn't work. Worse than that, it has recently been proved that it will *never* work; this sort of technology is *quite* impossible."

"But the Crimea is on the brink of war!" I exclaimed angrily. "What happens when the Russians realize that the new technology is all bluff?"

"But they won't," replied Schitt. "The technology might be impossible out here but it isn't impossible in *there*."

He patted the large book that was the Prose Portal and looked at Mycroft's genetically engineered bookworms. They were on rest & recuperation at present in their goldfish bowl; they had just digested a recent meal of prepositions and were happily farting out apostrophes and ampersands; the air was heav'y with th'em&. Schitt held up a book whose title was clearly visible. It read: *The Plasma Rifle in War.* I looked at Mycroft, who nodded miserably.

"That's right, Mis's Next."

Schitt smiled & tapped the cover with the back of his hand.

"In he're the Pla'sma Rifle work's perf&ectly. All we ha've to do is open' the book with the Pros'e Portal, bring out the we'apons & is'sue them. It' "s the ultimate weapon, Mis's' Next."

But he wasn't referring to the plasma rifle. He was pointing to the Prose Portal. The bookworms responded by belching out large quantities of unnecessary capitalizations.

"Any'thing That The Hu'man Imag'ination Can Think Up, We Can Reproduce. I Look At The Port'al as Les's Of A Gateway To A Million World's, But More Like A Three Dim'ensional

P'hotocopier. With It We Can Ma'ke Anything We Want; Even Another Portal—a H&held Version. Chri'stmas Every Day, Miss Next."

"More Death In The Cr'imea; I Ho'pe You Can Sleep W'ell At Night, Schitt."

"On The Co'ntrary, Miss' Next. Russia Will Roll Over & Piss' Over Itself When It Witnesse's The Power Of Stonk. The Czar Will Permanently Cede The Peninsula To England; a New Riviera, Won't That be nice?"

"*Nice?* Sun Lounger's & High-Rise Hotel's? Built On L& That Will Be Dem&ed Back Half a Century From Now? You're Not S'olving Anything, Schitt, Merely Delaying It. When The Russian's Have a Plasma Rifle Of Their Own, Then What?"

Jack Schitt was unrepentant.

"Oh, Don't Worry About That, Miss Next, I'll Charge The'm *Twice* What I'll Charge The Eng'lish Gov'ernment!"

"Hear, Hear!" put in Hades, who was deeply impressed by Schitt's total absence of scruples so far.

"A Hundred Million' Dollars Fo'r The Portal, Thursday," added Hades excitedly, "& a 50% Cut On Every'thing That' Comes Out Of It!"

"A Lackey For The Goliath Corpor'ation, Acheron? That Doesn't Sound Like You At All."

Hades' cheek quivered but he fought it, answering:

"Out Of Small Acorn's, Thur'sday . . ."

Schitt looked at him suspiciously. He nodded to one of his men, who levelled a small anti-tank gun at Hades.

"Hade's, The Instructio'n Manual."

"Please!" pleaded Mycroft. "You're Upsetting The Wor'ms! They're Starting to hy-phe-nate!"

"Shut-up, My-croft," snapped Schitt. "Ha-de's, please, The In-Struc-tion Man-ual."

"Man-ual, My De'ar Chap?"

"Yes, Mr. Hade's. Ev-en You Will Not be Im-Pervious To My Associate's Small Artill-ery Piece. You Have My-croft's Manual For The Por-tal & The Po-em In Which You Have Im-pris-oned Mrs. Next. Give-Them-To-Me."

"No, Mr. Schitt. Give *Me* The Gun—"

But Schitt didn't flicker; the power that had stolen Snood and countless other people's reason had no effect on Schitt's dark soul. Hades' face fell. He had not come across someone like Schitt before; not since the first Felix, anyhow. He laughed.

"You Dare To Dou-ble—Cross-*Me*?"

"Sure I Do. If I Did-n't You'd Have No Res'-pect From Me & That's No Basis' For A Work-able Part-ner-ship."

Hades dodged in front of the Prose Portal.

"& To Think We Were All Get-ti'ng A-long So Well, Too—!" he exclaimed, placing the original manuscript of *Jane Eyre* back into the machine and adding the bookworms, who settled down, stopped farting, belching and hyphenating and got to work.

"Really!" continued Hades. "I expected better from you, I must say. I almost thought I had found someone who could be a partner."

"But you'd want it all, Hades," replied Schitt. "Sooner or later and most probably sooner."

"True, very true."

Hades nodded to Felix8 who immediately started shooting. Bowden and I were directly in his line of fire; there was no way he could miss. My heart leaped but strangely the first bullet slowed and stopped in midair three inches from my chest. It was the initial volley of a deadly procession that snaked lazily all the way back to Felix8's weapon, its muzzle now a frozen chrysanthemum of fire. I looked across at Bowden, who was also in line for a slug; the shiny bullet had stopped a foot from his head. But he was not stirring. Indeed, the whole room was not stirring. My father, for once, had arrived at precisely the *right* moment.

"Have I come at a bad time?" asked Dad, looking up from where he was sitting at the dusty grand piano. "I can go away again if you want."

"N-no, Dad, this is good, *real* good," I muttered.

I looked around the room. My father never stayed for longer than five minutes, and when he left the bullets would almost certainly carry onto their intended victim. My eyes alighted on a heavy table and I upended it, sending dust, debris and empty Leek-U-Like containers to the floor.

"Have you ever heard of someone named Winston Churchill?" asked my father.

"No; who's he?" I gasped as I heaved the heavy oak table in front of Bowden.

"Ah!" said my father, making a note in a small book. "Well, he was meant to lead England in the last war but I think he was killed in a fall as a teenager. It's *most* awkward."

"Another victim of the French revisionists?"

My father didn't answer. His attention had switched to the middle of the room, where Hades was working on the Prose Portal. Time, for men like Hades, rarely stood still.

"Oh, don't mind me!" said Hades as a shaft of light opened up in the gloom. "I'm just going to step inside until all this unpleasantness is over. I have the instruction manual and Polly, so we can still bargain."

"Who's that?" asked my father.

"Acheron Hades."

"Is it? I expected someone shorter."

But Hades had gone; the Prose Portal buzzed slightly and then closed after him.

"I've got some repairs to do," announced my father, getting up and closing his notebook. "Time waits for no man, as we say."

I just had time to duck behind a large bureau as the world started up again. The hail of lead from Felix8 struck the heavy oak table I had maneuvered in front of Bowden, and the bullets that had been destined for me thudded into the wooden door behind where I had been standing. Within the space of two seconds the room was full of gunfire as the Goliath operatives joined in, covering Jack Schitt, who, perplexed that Hades had vanished in mid-sentence, was now beating a retreat to the door leading to the old Atlantic Grill. Mycroft threw himself to the floor followed closely by Jane as dust and debris were scattered about the room. I bellowed into Jane's ear to stay where she was as a shot came perilously close to our heads, knocking some molding off the furniture and showering us with dust. I crawled around to where I could see Bowden exchanging shots with Felix8, who was now trapped behind an upended mock-Georgian table next to the entrance of the Palm Court Tea Rooms. I had just loosed off a few shots at Goliath's men, who had rapidly dragged Schitt from the room, when the firing stopped as quickly as it had begun. I reloaded.

"Felix8!" I shouted. "You can still surrender! Your real name is Danny Chance. I promise you we will do all we can to—"

There was a strange gurgling noise and I peeked around the back of the sofa. I thought Felix8 had been wounded but he hadn't. He was laughing. His usually expressionless face was convulsed with mirth. Bowden and I exchanged quizzical looks—but we stayed hidden.

"What's so funny?" I yelled.

"Haven't I seen your face somewhere before!" he giggled. "I get it now!"

He raised his gun and fired repeatedly at us as he backed

out of the lounge doors and into the darkness of the lobby outside. He had sensed his master's escape and had no more work
to do here.

"Where's Hades?" said Bowden.

"In *Jane Eyre*," I replied, standing up. "Cover the portal—
and if he returns, use this."

I handed him the anti-tank weapon as Schitt, alerted to the
end of the gunfire, returned. He appeared at the door to the bar.

"Hades?"

"In *Jane Eyre* with the instruction manual."

Schitt told me to surrender the Prose Portal to him.

"Without the instruction manual you've got nothing," I
said. "Once I have Hades out of Thornfield and have returned
my aunt to Mycroft you can have the manual. There is no other
deal; that's it. I'm taking Jane back with me now."

I turned to my uncle.

"Mycroft, send us back to just *before* Jane comes out of her
room to put out the fire in Rochester's bedroom. It will be as if
she had never left. When I want to come back I'll send a signal.
Can you do that?"

Schitt threw up his arms. "What sweet madness is this?" he
cried.

"That's the signal," I said, "the words 'sweet madness.' As
soon as you hear them, open the door immediately."

"Are you sure you know what you're doing?" asked Bowden
as I helped Jane to her feet.

"Never been more certain. Just don't turn the machine off;
much as I enjoy the book I've no desire to stay there forever."

Schitt bit his lip. He had been outmaneuvered. His hand,
such as it was, would have to be played upon my return.

I checked that my gun was still loaded, took a deep breath
and nodded to Jane, who smiled back eagerly. We grasped each
other's hands tightly and stepped through the doorway.

32.

Thornfield Hall

It wasn't how I imagined it. I thought Thornfield Hall would be bigger and more luxuriously furnished. There was a strong smell of polish and the air was chill in the upstairs corridor. There was barely any light in the house and the corridors seemed to stretch away into inky blackness. It was dour and unappealing. I noticed all this but most of all I noticed the quiet; the quiet of a world free from flying machines, traffic and large cities. The industrial age had only just begun; the planet had reached its Best Before date.

THURSDAY NEXT
—*A Life in SpecOps*

I STAGGERED slightly as we made the jump; there had been a bright flash of light and a short blast of static. I found myself in the master bedroom corridor, a few lines above where Hobbes had taken Jane out. The fire was ablaze and Jane took her cue instinctively, opening the door and leaping into Rochester's room to pour a ewer full of water over the burning covers. I looked quickly around the dark corridor but of Hades there was no sign; at the far end I could just see Grace Poole escorting Bertha to her attic room. The madwoman looked back over her shoulder and smiled crazily. Grace Poole followed her gaze and glared disapprovingly at me. I suddenly felt very alien; this world was not mine and I didn't belong here. I stepped back as Jane rushed out of Rochester's room to fetch some more water; upon her face, I noted, was a look of great relief. I smiled and permitted myself a peek inside the bedroom. Jane had managed to extinguish the fire and Rochester was swearing at finding himself in a pool of water.

"Is there a flood?" he asked.

"No, sir," she replied, "but there has been a fire. Get up, do; you are quenched now. I will fetch you a candle."

Rochester caught sight of me at the door and winked before rapidly returning his features to a look of consternation.

"In the name of all the elves in Christendom," he asked, his eyes glistening at her return, "is that Jane Eyre? What have you done with me . . ."

I stepped outside the door, confident in the knowledge that back home the book would be starting to rewrite itself across the page. The reference to the "agent in black" would be overwritten and with luck, and Hades willing, things could get back to normal. I picked up the candle that had been left on the mat and relit it as Jane came out, smiled her thanks, took it from me and returned to the bedroom. I walked down the corridor, looked at a particularly fine Landseer painting and sat down upon a Regency chair, one of a pair. Although the house was not big, it afforded all sorts of hiding places for Acheron. I spoke his name to let him know I was about and heard a door slam somewhere in the house. I pulled open a shutter and saw the unmistakable figure of Hades walking rapidly across the lawn by the light of the moon. I watched his form fade into the shadows. He would be as good as safe in the countryside but I still had the upper hand. I knew how to reopen the door and he didn't; I thought it unlikely he would harm me. I sat down again and was just thinking about Daisy Mutlar and Landen when I drifted off to sleep. I was jolted awake as the door to

Rochester's bedroom opened and the figure of Edward emerged. He was holding a candle and spoke to Jane at the door.

". . . I must pay a visit to the third story. Don't move, remember, or call anyone."

He padded softly down the corridor and hissed: "Miss Next, are you there?"

I stood up.

"Here, sir."

Rochester took me by the arm and led me along the gallery and onto the landing above the stairs. He stopped, placed the candle on a low table and clasped both my hands in his.

"I thank you, Miss Next, from the bottom of my heart! It has been a living hell of torment; not knowing when or even if my beloved Jane would return!"

He spoke with keen and very real passion; I wondered if Landen had ever loved me as much as Rochester loved Jane.

"It was the least I could do, Mr. Rochester," I responded happily, "after your kind attention to my wounds that night outside the warehouse."

He dismissed my words with a wave of his hand.

"You are returning straight away?"

I looked down.

"It's not quite as easy as that, sir. There is another interloper in this book aside from me."

Rochester strode to the balustrade. He spoke without turning around.

"It's *him*, isn't it?"

"You have met him?" I asked, surprised.

"He has several names. You have a plan?"

I explained the use of a signal and made it clear that it would be safer for me to remain at Thornfield until the book had run its course. Then I would take Hades with me—somehow.

"The end of the book," murmured Rochester unhappily.

"How I *hate* the ending. The thought of my sweet Jane traveling to India with that poltroon St. John Rivers makes my blood turn to ice." He bolstered himself. "But I have at least a few months of real happiness before that time. Come, you must be hungry." He walked off down the corridor and beckoned me to follow, talking as he went.

"I suggest we try and trap *him* when Jane has left after—" he shivered slightly at the thought of it. "—the wedding. We will be quite alone as Jane takes the narrative with her to Moor House and those fatuous cousins. I am not featured again in the book, so we may do as we please, and I am best disposed to be of assistance. However, as you have guessed, you must do nothing that might disturb Jane; this novel is written in the first person. I can get away to speak with you when I am, to all intents and purposes, out of the story. But you must promise me that you will stay out of Jane's way. I will speak to Mrs. Fairfax and Adele privately; they will understand. The servants Mary and John will do whatever I tell them."

We had arrived at a door and Rochester knocked impatiently. There was a groaning and a thump and presently a very disheveled character appeared at the door.

"Mrs. Fairfax," said Rochester, "this is Miss Next. She will be staying with us for a month or two. I want you to fetch her some food and have a bed made ready; she has traveled far to be here and I think she needs sustenance and rest. It would please me if you were not to discuss her presence with anyone, and I would be grateful if you could engineer that Miss Next and Miss Eyre do not meet. I hardly need to stress the importance of this to you."

Mrs. Fairfax looked me up and down, was particularly intrigued and shocked at the same time by my ponytail and jeans, and then nodded and led me off toward the dining room.

"We will speak again tomorrow, Miss Next," said Rochester,

a smile breaking out on his troubled face. "And I thank you once again."

He turned and left me to Mrs. Fairfax, who bustled downstairs. The housekeeper told me to wait in the dining room while she brought me something to eat. She returned shortly with some cold cuts of meat and some bread. I ate hungrily as Pilot—who I thought had been let in when Hades went out—sniffed at my trouser leg and wagged his tail excitedly.

"He remembers you," remarked Mrs. Fairfax slowly, "yet I have been working here for many years and I do not recall having laid eyes upon you before."

I tickled Pilot's ear.

"I threw a stick for him once. When he was out with his master."

"I see," replied Mrs. Fairfax, suspiciously. "And how do you know Mr. Rochester?"

"I, ah, met the Rochesters in Madeira. I knew his brother."

"I see. *Very* tragic." Her eyes narrowed. "Then you know the Masons?"

"Not well."

She had been eyeing my jeans again.

"Women wear breeches where you come from?"

"Often, Mrs. Fairfax."

"And where is it that you come from? London?"

"Farther than that."

"Ah!" said Mrs. Fairfax with a knowing smile. "Osaka!"

She bustled out, leaving me alone with Pilot, having made me promise that I would not feed him from the table. She returned ten minutes later with a tray of tea things, then left me for another half hour to make up a room. She led me up to a second-story chamber with a fine view out of the front of the house. I had insisted that Pilot stay with me, and he slept against the locked door, somehow sensing the possible danger that his new mistress might be in. I slept fitfully and dreamed of Hades laughing at me.

As I slept, Victor and the others back at the Swindon LiteraTec office had been celebrating the return of the narrative to the novel. Apart from a brief mention of Mrs. Fairfax making noises on the night of the bedroom fire, it was all pretty much as anyone remembered it. A member of the Brontë Federation had been called in to examine the text as it wrote itself across the last two hundred pages, which up until this moment had been blank. The Brontë scholar knew the book by heart and his pleased expression gave them no cause for complaint.

I woke to the sound of Pilot scratching on the door to be let out. I quietly unlocked it and peeped out. I could see Jane bustling down the corridor and quickly shut the door and looked at my watch. It was barely 6 A.M. and only a few of the domestic staff were awake. I waited a couple of minutes, let Pilot out and then followed, cautious lest I bumped into Jane. The morning was spent with almost everyone in the house setting Rochester's room to rights, so after breakfast I was about to make my way out of the house when Mrs. Fairfax stopped me.

"Miss Next," announced the housekeeper, "Mr. Rochester has explained to me about the events of the past week and I wanted to add my thanks to his."

She said it without emotion but I was in no doubt that she meant it. She added:

"He has instructed me to have the house guarded against agents who would wish Miss Eyre harm."

I looked out of the window; from where we stood I could see an estate worker standing on sentry duty with a large pickax handle. As we watched he glanced into the house and scurried out of sight. A few moments later Jane herself walked out of the door, looked about her, took a deep breath in the crisp morning air, and then went back inside. After a few moments the estate worker reappeared and took up his post once more.

"Miss Eyre must never know we are watching and guarding her," said Mrs. Fairfax severely.

"I understand."

Mrs. Fairfax nodded and looked at me critically.

"Do women go about with their heads uncovered where you come from?"

"Frequently."

"It isn't the accepted thing *here*," she said reproachfully. "Come with me and I shall make you presentable."

Mrs. Fairfax took me to her own room and gave me a bonnet to wear along with a thick black cloak that covered me to my feet. I thanked her and Mrs. Fairfax bobbed courteously.

"Is Mr. Rochester at home today?" I asked.

"He has gone to make arrangements. I understand he went to Mr. Eshton's place; there is quite a party going on. Colonel Dent will be there as well as Lord Ingram. I don't expect him back for a week."

"With all that is going on here, do you think it is wise?"

Mrs. Fairfax looked at me as though I were an infant.

"You don't understand, do you? After the fire Mr. Rochester goes away for a week. That's how it happens."

I wanted to ask more but the housekeeper excused herself and I was left alone. I collected my thoughts, smoothed the cloak and went outside to walk around the house, checking that everything was secure. All the estate workers nodded to me respectfully as I passed, each of them armed with a weapon of some sort. Hoping that none of them would have to face him, I walked across the lawn in the direction that Hades had taken the previous night. I was just passing the large beeches near the ha-ha when a familiar voice made me turn.

"Do we stand a chance against him?"

It was Rochester. He was standing behind one of the large tree trunks, looking at me with grave concern etched upon his face.

"Every chance, sir," I responded. "Without me he is trapped here; if he wants to return he *has* to negotiate."

"And where is he?"

"I was going to try the town. Aren't you meant to be at Mr. Eshton's?"

"I wanted to speak to you before I left. You will do all you can, won't you?"

I assured him that I would do everything in my power and then set off for the town.

Millcote was a good-sized town. I made my way to the center, where I found a church, a stagecoach stop, three inns, a bank, two draper's, a bagged-goods merchant and assorted other trades. It was market day and the town was busy. No one gave me a second glance as I walked through the stalls, which were piled high with winter produce and game. Apart from the faint odor of ink that pervaded the scene, it might have been real. The first hostelry I chanced across was The George. Since it was actually named in the book I supposed it might offer the best chance.

I entered and asked the innkeeper whether a man of large stature had taken a room at the inn that morning. The landlord proclaimed that he had not but added that his was not the only inn in the town. I thanked him and walked to the door, but was arrested by the incongruous sound of a camera shutter. I slowly turned around. Behind me was a Japanese couple, dressed in period costume but with one of them holding a large Nikon camera. The woman hastily tried to conceal the blatant anachronism and started to drag the man out of the door.

"Wait!"

They stopped and looked nervously at one other.

"What are you doing here?" I asked incredulously.

"Visiting from Osaka," affirmed the woman, at which the man—he seemed not to speak English—nodded his head vigorously and started to consult a Brontë guidebook written in Japanese.

"How?—"

"My name is Mrs. Nakajima," announced the woman, "and this is Mr. Suzuki."

The man grinned at me and shook my hand excitedly.

"This is crazy!" I said angrily. "Are you trying to tell me that you two are *tourists*?"

"Indeed," admitted Mrs. Nakajima, "I make the jump once a year and bring a visitor with me. We touch nothing and never speak to Miss Eyre. As you can see, we are dressed fittingly."

"Japanese? In mid-nineteenth-century England?"

"Why not?"

Why not indeed.

"How do you manage it?"

The woman shrugged.

"I just *can*," she answered simply. "I think hard, speak the lines and, well, here I am."

I didn't have time for this at all.

"Listen to me. My name is Thursday Next. I work with Victor Analogy at the LiteraTec office in Swindon. You heard about the theft of the manuscript?"

She nodded her head.

"There is a dark presence in this book but my plan to extract him is dependent on there being only one way in and one way out. He will stop at nothing to use you to get out if he can. I implore you to jump back home while you still can."

Mrs. Nakajima consulted for some time with her client. She

explained that Mr. Suzuki was hoping to see Jane if possible, but that if he were taken back now he would want a refund. I reiterated my position on the matter and they eventually agreed. I followed them to their room upstairs and waited while they packed. Mrs. Nakajima and Mr. Suzuki both shook me by the hand, held onto each other and evaporated. I shook my head sadly. It seemed there were very few places that the tourist business hadn't touched.

I left the warmth of the inn for the chill exterior and made my way past a stall selling late root vegetables and onto The Millcote, where I inquired about any new guests.

"And who would be wanting to see Mr. Hedge?" inquired the innkeeper, spitting into and then polishing a crude beer mug.

"Tell him Miss Next is here to see him."

The innkeeper vanished upstairs and returned presently.

"Room seven," he replied shortly, and returned to his duties.

Acheron was sitting by the window, his back to the door. He didn't move when I entered.

"Hello, Thursday."

"Mr. Hedge?"

"Locals in mid-nineteenth-century England are a superstitious lot. I thought Hades might seem a little strong for them."

He turned to face me, his piercing blue eyes seeming to look straight into me. But his power over me had waned; he could not read me as he had others. He sensed this immediately, gave a half-smile and resumed staring out of the window.

"You grow strong, Miss Next."

"I thrive on adversity."

He gave a short laugh.

"I should have made quite sure of you back at Styx's apartment."

"And spoiled all the fun? Your life would be considerably more dull without me and the rest of SpecOps to louse it up."

He ignored me and changed the subject.

"Someone as resourceful as you would never have come in here without a way out. What is it, Thursday? A prearranged code to let Mycroft know when to open the door?"

"Something like that. If you give me the instruction manual and Polly I promise you shall have a fair trial."

Hades laughed.

"I think I am way beyond a fair trial, Thursday. I could kill you now and I feel a strong urge to do precisely that, but the prospect of being trapped in this narrative for all time bars me from that action. I tried to get to London but it's impossible; the only towns that exist in this world are the places that Charlotte Brontë wrote about and which feature in the narrative. Gateshead, Lowood—I'm surprised that there is even as much of *this* town. Give me the code word to get out and you can have the manual and Polly."

"No. You give me the manual and my aunt first."

"You see? Impasse. You'll want to wait until the book is written again, though, won't you?"

"Of course."

"Then you will expect no trouble from me until such time as Jane leaves Thornfield for good. After that, we negotiate."

"I won't negotiate, Hades."

Hades shook his head slowly.

"You'll negotiate, Miss Next. You may be disgustingly right-eous but even you will balk at spending the rest of your life in here. You're an intelligent woman; I'm sure you'll think of something."

I sighed and walked back outside, where the bustle of the shoppers and traders was a welcome break from the dark soul of Hades.

33.

The Book Is Written

From our position in the lounge of the Penderyn Hotel
we could see Thursday's good work. The narrative continued rapidly; weeks passed in the space of a few lines.
As the words wrote themselves back across the page they
were read aloud by Mycroft or myself. We were all waiting for the phrase "sweet madness" to appear in the text,
but it didn't. We prepared ourselves to assume the worst;
that Hades was not caught and might never be. That
Thursday might stay in the book as some sort of permanent caretaker.

From Bowden Cable's journal

THE WEEKS passed rapidly at Thornfield and I busied myself
with the task of making Jane secure without her ever knowing it.
I had a young lad positioned at the Millcote to warn of Hades'
movements, but he seemed quite happy just to go out walking
every morning, borrow books from the local doctor, and spend
his time at the inn. His inaction was a cause of some worry, but I
was glad it was merely that for the time being.

Rochester had sent a note advising of his return and a party
was arranged for local friends of his. Jane seemed to be severely
agitated by the arrival of the airhead Blanche Ingram, but I gave
it little heed. I was busy trying to arrange security with John,
the cook's husband, who was a resourceful and intelligent man.

I had taught him to shoot with Rochester's pistols and he was, I was delighted to find out, an excellent shot. I had thought that Hades might make an appearance with one of the guests but, apart from the arrival of Mr. Mason from the West Indies, nothing out of the ordinary occurred.

The weeks turned into months and I saw little of Jane—on purpose, of course—but kept in contact with the household and Mr. Rochester to make sure that all was going well. And it appeared that all *was* going well. As usual, Mr. Mason was bitten by his mad sister in the upper room; I was standing outside the locked door when Rochester went for the doctor and Jane tended to Mason's wounds. When the doctor arrived I kept watch in the arbor outside, where I knew Jane and Rochester would meet. And so it went on until a brief respite when Jane went away to visit her dying aunt in Gateshead. Rochester had decided to marry Blanche Ingram by this time and things had been slightly tense between him and Jane. I felt some relief that she was away; I could relax and talk to Rochester quite easily without Jane suspecting anything.

"You aren't sleeping," observed Rochester as we walked together on the front lawn. "Look how your eyes are dark-rimmed and languorous."

"I don't sleep well here, not while Hades is barely five miles distant."

"Your spies, surely, would alert you to any movement of his?"

It was true; the network worked well, although not without some considerable expenditure on Rochester's part. If Hades set off anywhere I knew about it within two minutes from a rider who stood by for just such an occasion. It was in this manner that I was able to find him when he was out, either walking or reading or beating peasants with his stick. He had never come within a mile of the house, and I was happy to keep it that way.

"My spies afford me peace of mind, but I still can't believe that Hades could be so passive. It chills and worries me."

We walked on for a while, Rochester pointing out places of interest to me around the grounds. But I was not listening.

"How did you come to me, that night outside the warehouse, when I was shot?"

Rochester stopped and looked at me.

"It just *happened*, Miss Next. I can't explain it anymore than you can explain arriving here when you were a little girl. Apart from Mrs. Nakajima and a traveler named Foyle, I don't know of anyone else who has done it."

I was surprised at this.

"You have met Mrs. Nakajima, then?"

"Of course. I usually do tours of Thornfield for her guests when Jane is up at Gateshead. It carries no risk and is extremely lucrative. Country houses are not cheap to run, Miss Next, even in this century."

I allowed myself a smile. I thought that Mrs. Nakajima must be making a very sizeable profit; it was, after all, the ultimate trip for a Brontë fan, and there were plenty of those in Japan.

"What will you do after this?" asked Rochester, pointing out a rabbit to Pilot, who barked and ran off.

"Back to SpecOps work, I guess," I replied. "What about you?"

Rochester looked at me broodingly, his eyebrows furrowed and a look of anger rising across his features.

"There is nothing for me after Jane leaves with that slimy and pathetic excuse for a vertebrate, St. John Rivers."

"So what will you do?"

"Do? I won't *do* anything. Existence pretty much ceases for me about then."

"Death?"

"Not as such," replied Rochester, choosing his words carefully. "Where you come from you are born, you live and then you die. Am I correct?"

"More or less."

"A pretty poor way of living, I should imagine!" laughed Rochester. "And you rely upon that inward eye we call a memory to sustain yourself in times of depression, I suppose?"

"Most of the time," I replied, "although memory is but one hundredth of the strength of currently felt emotions."

"I concur. Here, I neither am born, nor die. I come into being at the age of thirty-eight and wink out again soon after, having fallen in love for the first time in my life and then lost the object of my adoration, my being! . . ."

He stopped and picked up the stick that Pilot had considerately brought him in place of the rabbit he couldn't catch.

"You see, I can move myself to anywhere in the book I wish at a moment's notice and back again at will; the greatest parts of my life lie between the time I profess my true love to that fine, impish girl and the moment the lawyer and that fool Mason turn up to spoil my wedding and reveal the madwoman in the attic. Those are the weeks to which I return most often, but I go to the bad times too—for without a yardstick sometimes the high points can be taken for granted. Sometimes I muse that I might have John stop them at the church gate and stall them until the wedding is over, but it is against the way of things."

"So while I am talking to you here—"

"—I am also meeting Jane for the first time, wooing her, then losing her forever. I can even see you now, as a small child, your expression of fear under the hooves of my horse—"

He felt his elbow.

"And feel the pain of the fall, too. So you see, my existence, although limited, is not without benefits."

I sighed. If only life were that simple; if one could jump to the good parts and flick through the bad—

"You have a man you love?" asked Rochester suddenly.

"Yes; but there is much bad air between us. He accused my brother of a crime that I thought unfair to lay upon the shoulders of a dead man; my brother never had a chance to defend himself and the evidence was not strong. I find it hard to forgive."

"What is there to forgive?" demanded Rochester. "Ignore forgive and concentrate on *living*. Life for you is short; far too short to allow small jealousies to infringe on the happiness which can be yours only for the briefest of times."

"Alas!" I countered. "He is engaged to be married!"

"And what of that?" scoffed Rochester. "Probably to someone as unsuitable for him as Blanche Ingram is for me!"

I thought about Daisy Mutlar and there did, indeed, seem to be a strong similarity.

We walked along together in silence until Rochester pulled out a pocket watch and consulted it.

"My Jane is returning from Gateshead as we speak. Where is my pencil and notebook?"

He rummaged within his jacket and produced a bound drawing-book and a pencil.

"I am to meet her as if by accident; she walks across the fields shortly in this direction. How do I look?"

I straightened his necktie and nodded my satisfaction.

"Do you think me handsome, Miss Next?" he asked quite suddenly.

"No," I answered truthfully.

"Bah!" exclaimed Rochester. "Pixies both! Begone with you; we will talk later!"

I left them to it and walked back to the house by way of the lake, deep in thought.

And so the weeks wore on, the air becoming warmer and the buds starting to shoot on the trees. I hardly saw anything of Rochester or Jane, as they had eyes only for each other. Mrs. Fairfax was not highly impressed by the union but I told her not to be so unreasonable. She flustered like an old hen at this remark and went about her business. The routine of Thornfield didn't waver from normalcy for the next few months; the season moved into summer and I was there on the day of the wedding, invited specifically by Rochester and hidden in the vestry. I saw the clergyman, a large man named Mr. Wood, ask whether anyone knew of an impediment that might prevent the wedding being lawful or joined by God. I heard the solicitor call out his terrible secret. Rochester, I could see, was beside himself with rage as Briggs read out the affidavit from Mason to declare that the madwoman was Bertha Rochester, Mason's sister and Rochester's legal wife. I remained in hiding as the argument ensued, emerging only when the small group was led over to the house by Rochester to meet his mad wife. I didn't follow; I went for a walk, breathing in the fresh air and avoiding the sadness and anguish in the house as Rochester and Jane realized they could not marry.

By the following day Jane was gone. I followed at a safe distance to see her take the road to Whitcross, looking like a small stray searching for a better life elsewhere. I watched her until she was out of sight and then walked into Millcote for lunch. Once I had finished my meal at The George I played cards with three traveling gamblers; by suppertime I had taken six guineas off them. As I played, a small boy appeared at our table.

"Hello, William!" I said. "What news?"

I bent down to the height of the waif, who was dressed in adult-sized hand-me-downs that had been sewn up to fit.

"Begging your pardon, Miss Next, but Mr. Hedge has vanished."

I leaped up in some alarm, broke into a run and didn't stop until I arrived at The Millcote. I flew upstairs to the landing, where one of my most trusted spies was tugging at his flat cap nervously. Hades' room was empty.

"I'm sorry, miss. I was in the bar downstairs, not drinking, mind; I swear to it. He must have slipped past me—"

"Did anyone else come down the stairs, Daniel? Tell me quick!"

"No one. No one save the old lady . . ."

I took the horse from one of my riders and was at Thornfield in double-quick time. Neither of the guards at the doors had seen anything of Hades. I entered and found Edward in the morning room, toasting himself from a bottle of brandy. He raised his glass as I entered.

"She's gone, hasn't she?" he asked.

"She has."

"Damnation! Curse the circumstances that allowed me to be trapped into the wedding with that half-wit and curse my brother and father for entreating such a union!"

He fell into a chair and stared at the floor.

"Your work is done here?" he asked me resignedly.

"I think so, yes. I have only to find Hades and I can be off."

"Is he not at The Millcote?"

"Not any longer."

"But you expect to capture him?"

"I do; he seems weakened here."

"Then you had better tell me your password. Time may not be on our side when the moment comes. Forewarned is forearmed."

"True," I conceded. "To open the portal, you have to say—"

But at that moment the front door slammed, a gust of wind disturbed some papers, and a familiar footfall rang out on the tiles in the hall. I froze and looked across at Rochester who was staring into his glass.

"The code word?—"

I heard a voice calling to Pilot. It had the deep bass resonance of the master of the house.

"Blast!" murmured Hades as he melted from his disguise as Rochester and leaped at the wall in a flash, bursting through the lath and plaster as though it were rice paper. By the time I had made my way to the hallway outside he had gone; vanished somewhere deep into the house. Rochester joined me as I listened intently up the stairs, but no sound reached us. Edward guessed what had happened and quickly mustered his estate workers. Within twenty minutes he had them guarding the outside of the house, under strict orders to fire upon anyone who tried to escape without giving a prearranged password. This done, we returned to the library and Rochester drew out a set of pistols and loaded each carefully. He looked uneasily at my Browning automatic as he placed two percussion caps atop the nipples of the pistols and replaced the hammers.

"Bullets just make him mad," I told him.

"You have a better idea?"

I said nothing.

"Then you had better follow me. The sooner this menace is out of my book the better!"

All except Grace Poole and the madwoman had been removed from the house, and Mrs. Poole had been entreated not to open the door to anyone until the morning on any account, not even to Mr. Rochester. Rochester and I started at the library and moved through to the dining room and then the afternoon reception room. After this we searched the morning reception room and then the ballroom. All were empty. We returned to the staircase where we had placed John and Mathew, who both swore no one had passed them. Night had descended by this time; the men who stood guard had been given torches and their meager light flickered in the hall. The stairs and paneling of the house were of a dark wood which reflected light poorly; the belly of a whale would have been brighter. We reached the top of the stairs and looked left and right, but the house was dark and I cursed myself for not bringing a good flashlight. As if in answer to my thoughts a gust of wind blew out the candles and somewhere ahead a door banged. My heart missed a beat and Rochester muttered an oath as he stumbled into an oak chest. I quickly relit the candelabrum. In the warm glow we could see each other's timorous faces, and Rochester, realizing that my face was a reflection of his own, steeled himself to the task ahead and shouted:

"Coward! Show yourself!"

There was a loud concussion and a bright orange flash as Rochester fired off a shot in the direction of the staircase leading to the upper rooms.

"There! There he goes, like a rabbit; I fancy I winged him too!"

We hurried to the spot but there was no blood; merely the heavy lead ball embedded in the banister rail.

"We have him!" exclaimed Rochester. "There is no escape from up here except the roof and no way down without risking his neck on the guttering!"

We climbed the stairs and found ourselves in the upper corridor. The windows were larger up here but even so the interior was still insufferably gloomy. We stopped abruptly. Halfway down the corridor, standing in the shadows and with his face lit by the light of a single candle, was Hades. Running and hiding were not his style at all. He was holding the lighted candle close to a rolled-up piece of paper that I knew could only be the Wordsworth poem in which my aunt was imprisoned.

"The code word, if you will, Miss Next!"

"Never!"

He placed the candle closer to the paper and smiled at me.

"The code word, *please*!"

But his smile became an expression of agony; he let out a wild cry and the candle and poem fell to the ground. He turned slowly to reveal the cause of his pain. There, on his back and clinging on with grim determination, was Mrs. Rochester, the madwoman from Jamaica. She cackled maniacally and twisted a pair of scissors that she had buried between Hades' shoulder blades. He cried out once again and fell to his knees as the flame from the lit candle set fire to the layers of wax polish that had built up on a bureau. The flames greedily enveloped the piece of furniture and Rochester pulled some curtains down in order to smother them. But Hades was up again, his strength renewed: The scissors had been withdrawn. He swiped at Rochester and caught him on the chin; Edward reeled and fell heavily to the floor. A manic glee seemed to overcome Acheron as he took a spirit lamp from the sideboard and hurled it to the end of the corridor; it burst into flames and ignited some wall hangings. He turned on the madwoman, who went for him in a blur of flailing limbs. She deftly whipped Mycroft's battered instruction booklet from Hades' pocket, gave a demonic and triumphant cry and then ran off.

"Yield, Hades!" I yelled, firing off two shots. Acheron staggered with the force of the slugs but recovered quickly and ran after Bertha and the book. I picked up the precious poem and coughed in the thick smoke that had started to fill the corridor.

The drapes were now well alight. I dragged Rochester to his feet. We ran after Hades, noticing as we did so that other fires had been started by Acheron in his pursuit of the instruction manual and the insane Creole. We caught up with them in a large back bedroom. It seemed as good a moment as any to open the portal; already the bed was ablaze and Hades and Bertha were playing a bizarre game of cat-and-mouse with her holding the booklet and brandishing the scissors at him, something he seemed to be genuinely fearful of.

"Say the words!" I said to Rochester.

"And they are?"

"Sweet madness!"

Rochester yelled them. Nothing. He yelled them even louder. Still nothing. I had made a mistake. *Jane Eyre* was written in the first-person narrative. Whatever was being read by Bowden and Mycroft back home was what Jane was experiencing—anything that happened to us didn't appear in the book and never would. I hadn't thought of this.

"Now what?" asked Rochester.

"I don't know. *Look out!!*"

Bertha made a wild lunge at us both and ran out of the door, swiftly followed by Hades, who was so intent on regaining the instruction manual that the two of us seemed of secondary importance. We followed them down the corridor, but the stairwell was now a wall of flame and the heat and smoke pushed us back. Coughing and with eyes streaming, Bertha escaped onto the roof with Hades, myself and Rochester not far behind. The cool air was welcome after the smoky interior of Thornfield. Bertha led us all down onto the lead roof of the ballroom. We could see that the fire had spread downstairs, the heavily polished furniture and floors giving the hungry flames plenty of nourishment; within a few minutes the large and tinder-dry house would be an inferno.

The madwoman was dancing a languid dance in her night-clothes; a dim memory, perhaps, from the time when she was a lady, and a far cry from the sad and pathetic existence she now endured. She growled like a caged animal and threatened Hades with the scissors as he cursed and entreated the return of the booklet, which she waved at him in a mocking fashion. Rochester and I watched, the shattering of windows and the crackle of the fire punctuating the silence of the night.

Rochester, annoyed at having nothing to do and tiring of watching his wife and Hades dance the danse macabre, loosed off the second pistol and hit Hades in the small of the back. Hades turned, unhurt but enraged. He drew his own gun and fired several shots in return as Rochester and I leaped behind a chimney stack. Bertha took full advantage of the opportunity and plunged the scissors deep into Hades' arm. He yelled in pain and terror and dropped his gun. Bertha danced happily around him, cackling wildly, as Hades fell to his knees.

A groan made me turn. One of Acheron's shots had passed straight through Rochester's palm. He pulled out his handker-chief and I helped him wrap it around his shattered hand.

I looked up again as Hades knocked the scissors from his arm; they flew through the air and landed close by. Powerful again and as angry as a lion, he leaped upon Bertha, held her tightly by the throat and retrieved the booklet. He then picked her up and held her high above his head, she all the while utter-ing a demented yell that managed to drown out the sound of the fire. For a moment they were silhouetted against the flames that even now licked up against the night sky, then Hades took two quick steps to the parapet and threw Bertha over, her yell only silenced by the dull thud as she hit the ground three sto-ries below. He stepped back from the parapet and turned to us with eyes blazing.

"Sweet madness, eh?" He laughed. "Jane is with her cousins; the narrative is with her. And I have the manual!"

He waved it at me, deposited it in his pocket and picked up his gun.

"Who's first?"

I fired but Hades clapped his open hand on the approaching bullet. He opened his fist; the slug was flattened into a small lead disc. He smiled and a shower of sparks flew up behind him. I fired again and he caught the slug once more. The slide on my automatic parked itself in the rearward position, empty and ready for the next clip. I had one but I didn't think it would make much difference. The inevitable presented itself: I'd had a good run, survived him more than any other living person and done all that was humanly possible. But luck doesn't always walk in your favor—mine had just run out.

Hades smiled at me.

"Timing is everything, Miss Next. I have the password, the manual, and the upper hand. The waiting game, as you can see, paid off."

He looked at me with a triumphant expression.

"It may come as some consolation that I planned to bestow upon you the honor of being Felix9. I will remember you always as my greatest adversary; I salute you for it. And you were right—you never did negotiate."

I wasn't listening. I was thinking about Tamworth, Snood and the rest of Hades' victims. I looked across at Rochester, who was cradling his blood-soaked hand; the fight had gone out of him.

"The Crimea will make us a fortune," went on Hades. "How much profit can we make on each plasma rifle? Five hundred pounds? A thousand? Ten thousand?"

I thought of my brother in the Crimea. He had called for me

to come back for him, but I never did. My APC was hit by an artillery shell as I returned. I had to be forcibly restrained from taking another vehicle and returning to the battlefield. I never saw him again. I had never forgiven myself for leaving him.

Hades was still rambling, and I found myself almost wishing that he'd get on with it. Death, after all I had been through, suddenly seemed like a very comfortable option. At the height of any battle some say that there is a quietness where one can think calmly and easily, the trauma of the surroundings screened off by the heavy curtain of shock. I was about to die, and only one seemingly banal question came to mind: Why on earth did Bertha's scissors have such a detrimental effect on Hades? I looked up at Acheron, who was mouthing words that I could not hear. I stood up and he fired. He was merely playing with me and the bullet flew wide—I didn't even blink. The scissors were the key; they had been made of *silver.* I reached into my trouser pocket for the silver bullet that Spike had given me. Acheron, vain and arrogant, was wasting time with pompous self-congratulation. He would pay dearly for the error. I slipped the shiny slug into my automatic and released the slide. It chambered the around smoothly, I aimed, pulled the trigger and saw something pluck at his chest. For a moment nothing happened. Then Acheron stopped talking and put his hand to where the round had hit home. He brought his fingers up to his face and looked at them with shocked surprise; he was used to having blood on his hands—but never his own. He turned to me, started to say something but then staggered for a moment before pitching heavily forward onto his face and moving no more. Acheron Hades, third-most evil man on the planet, was finally dead, killed on the roof of Thornfield Hall and mourned by no one.

* * *

342

There was little time to ponder Hades' demise; the flames were growing higher. I took Mycroft's manual and then pulled Rochester to his feet. We made our way to the parapet; the roof had grown hot and we could feel the beams beneath our feet starting to flex and buckle, causing the lead roof to ripple as though it were alive. We looked over but there was no way down. Rochester grasped my hand and ran along the roof to another window. He smashed it open and a blast of hot air made us duck.

"Servants' staircase!" he coughed. "This way!"

Rochester knew the way through the dark and smoky corridor by feel, and I followed him obediently, clutching his jacket tails to stop myself getting lost. We arrived at the top of the servants' staircase; the fire didn't seem to be as strong here and Rochester led me down the steps. We were halfway down when a fireball flared up in the kitchen and sent a mass of fire and hot gases through the corridor and up the staircase. I saw a huge red glow erupt in front of me as the stairway gave way beneath us. After that, blackness.

34.

Nearly the End of
Their Book

> We waited for Thursday's call, the code word, but it
> didn't come. I read the narrative carefully, looking for
> some clue as to what had happened to her. I had sus-
> pected that Thursday might decide to stay if it was im-
> possible to capture Hades. The denouement was drawing
> near; Jane would go to India and the book would end.
> Once that had happened we could switch the machine
> off. Thursday and Polly would be lost forever.
>
> From Bowden Cable's journal

I OPENED my eyes, frowned, and looked around. I was in a
small yet well-furnished room quite close to a half-open window. Across the lawn some tall poplars swayed in the breeze, but
I didn't recognize the view; this was not Thornfield. The door
opened and Mary walked in.

"Miss Next!" she said kindly. "What a fright you gave us!"

"Have I been unconscious long?"

"Three days. A very bad concussion, Dr. Carter said."

"Where?—"

"You're at Ferndean, Miss Next," replied Mary soothingly,
"one of Mr. Rochester's other properties. You will be weak; I'll
bring some broth."

I grabbed her arm.

"And Mr. Rochester?"

She paused and smiled at me, patted my hand and said she would fetch the broth.

I lay back, thinking about the night Thornfield burned. Poor Bertha Rochester. Had she realized that she had saved our lives by her fortuitous choice of weapons? Perhaps, somewhere in her addled mind, she was in tune with the abomination that had been Hades. I would never know, but I thanked her anyway.

Within a week I was able to get up and move about, although I still suffered badly from headaches and dizziness. I learned that after the servants' staircase had collapsed I had been knocked unconscious. Rochester, in great pain himself, had wrapped me in a curtain and dashed with me from the burning house. He had been hit by a falling beam in the attempt and was blinded; the hand shattered by Acheron's bullet had been amputated the morning following the fire. I met with him in the darkness of the dining room.

"Are you in much pain, sir?" I asked, looking at the bedraggled figure; he still had bandaged eyes.

"Luckily, no," he lied, wincing as he moved.

"Thank you; you have saved my life for a second time."

He gave a wan smile.

"You returned my Jane to me. For those few months of happiness, I would suffer twice these wounds. But let us not speak of my wretched state. You are well?"

"Thanks to you."

"Yes, yes, but how will you return? I expect Jane is already in India by now with that gutless pantaloon Rivers; and with her goes the narrative. I don't see your friends being able to rescue you."

"I will think of something," I said, patting him on the sleeve. "You never know what the future will bring."

It was the morning of the following day; my months in the book had passed in as much time as it takes to read them. The

Welsh Politburo, alerted to the wrongdoings on their doorstep, had given Victor, Finisterre and a member of the Brontë Federation a safe conduct to the moldering Penderyn Hotel, where they now stood with Bowden, Mycroft and an increasingly nervous Jack Schitt. The representative of the Brontë Federation was reading the words as they appeared on the yellowed manuscript in front of him. Aside from a few minor changes, the book was traveling the same course it always did; it had been word perfect for the past two hours. Jane was being proposed to by St. John Rivers, who wanted her to go with him to India as his wife, and she was about to make up her mind.

Mycroft drummed his fingers on the desk and glanced at the rows of flicking dials on his contraption; all he needed was somewhere to open the door. Trouble was, they were fast running out of pages.

Then, the miraculous happened. The Brontë Federation expert, a small, usually unexcitable man named Plink, was suddenly ignited by shock.

"Wait a minute; this is new! This didn't happen!"

"What?" cried Victor, rapidly flicking to his own copy. Indeed, Mr. Plink was correct. There, as the words etched themselves across the paper, was a new development in the narrative. After Jane promised St. John Rivers that if it was God's will that they should be married, then they would, there was a voice—a *new* voice, Rochester's voice, calling to her across the ether. But from where? It was a question that was being asked simultaneously by nearly eighty million people worldwide, all following the new story unfolding in front of their eyes.

"What does it mean?" asked Victor.

"I don't know," replied Plink. "It's pure Charlotte Brontë but it *definitely* wasn't there before!"

"Thursday," murmured Victor. "It has to be. Mycroft, stay on your toes!"

They read delightedly as Jane changed her mind about India and St. John Rivers and decided to return to Thornfield.

I made it back to Ferndean and Rochester just before Jane did. I met Rochester in the dining room and told him the news; how I had found her at the Riverses' house, gone to her window and barked: "Jane, Jane, Jane!" in a hoarse whisper the way that Rochester did. It wasn't a good impersonation but it did the trick. I saw Jane start to fluster and pack almost immediately. Rochester seemed less than excited about the news.

"I don't know whether I should thank you or curse you, Miss Next. To think that I should be seen like this, a blind man with one good arm. And Thornfield a ruin! She shall hate me, I know it!"

"You are wrong, Mr. Rochester. And if you know Jane as well as I think you do, you would not even begin to entertain such thoughts!"

There was a rap at the door. It was Mary. She announced that Rochester had a visitor but that they would not give their name.

"Oh Lord!" exclaimed Rochester. "It's her! Tell me, Miss Next, could she love me? Like this, I mean?"

I leaned across and kissed his forehead.

"Of course she could. Anyone could. Mary, refuse her entry; if I know her she will enter anyway. Goodbye, Mr. Rochester. I can think of no way to thank you, so I shall just say that you and Jane will be in my thoughts always."

Rochester moved his head, trying to gauge where I was by sound alone. He put out his hand and held mine tightly. He was warm to the touch, yet soft. Thoughts of Landen entered my mind.

"Farewell, Miss Next! You have a great heart; do not let it go to waste. You have one who loves you and whom you love yourself. Choose happiness!"

I slipped quickly out into the adjoining room as Jane entered. I quietly latched the door as Rochester did a fine job of pretending that he didn't know who she was.

"Give me the water, Mary," I heard him say. There was a rustle and then I heard Pilot padding about.

"What is the matter?" asked Rochester in his most annoyed and gruff expression. I stifled a giggle.

"Down, Pilot!" said Jane. The dog was quiet and there was a pause.

"This is you, Mary, is it not?" asked Rochester.

"Mary is in the kitchen," replied Jane.

I pulled the now battered manual out of my pocket with the slightly charred poem. I still had Jack Schitt to contend with, but that would have to wait. I sat down on a chair as an exclamation from Rochester made its way through the door:

"*Who* is it? *What* is it? Who speaks?"

I strained to hear the conversation.

"Pilot knows me," returned Jane happily, "and John and Mary know I am here. I came only this afternoon!"

"Great God!" exclaimed Rochester. "What delusion has come over me? What sweet madness has seized me?"

I whispered: "Thank you, Edward," as the portal opened in the corner of the room. I took one last look around at a place to which I would never return, and stepped through.

There was a flash and a blast of static, Ferndean Manor was gone, and in its place I saw the familiar surroundings of the shabby lounge of the Penderyn Hotel. Bowden, Mycroft and Victor all rushed forward to greet me. I handed the manual and poem to Mycroft, who swiftly set about opening the door to "I Wandered Lonely as a Cloud."

"Hades?" asked Victor.

"Dead."

"Completely?"

"*Utterly.*"

In a few moments the Prose Portal reopened and Mycroft rushed inside, returning shortly afterward clutching Polly by the hand; she was holding a bunch of daffodils and trying to explain something.

"We were just *talking,* Crofty, my love! You don't think I would be interested in a dead poet, do you?"

"*My* turn," said Jack Schitt excitedly, waving his copy of *The Plasma Rifle in War.* He placed it with the bookworms and signaled to Mycroft to open the portal. As soon as the worms had done their work Mycroft did as he was bid. Schitt grinned and reached through the shimmering white doorway, feeling around for one of the plasma rifles that had been so well described in the book. Bowden had other ideas. He gave him a small shove and Jack Schitt disappeared through the doorway with a yell. Bowden nodded at Mycroft, who pulled the plug; the machine fell silent, the gateway to the book severed. It was bad timing on Jack Schitt's part. In his eagerness to get his hands on the rifle he had not made sure his Goliath officers were with him. By the time the two guards had returned, Bowden was assisting Mycroft in smashing the Prose Portal after carefully transferring the bookworms and returning the original manuscript of *Jane Eyre*—the ending now slightly altered— to the Brontë Federation.

"Where's Colonel Schitt?" asked the first officer.

Victor shrugged.

"He went away. Something to do with plasma rifles."

The Goliath officers would have asked more questions but the Welsh foreign secretary himself had arrived and announced that since the matter was now resolved we would be escorted from the Republic. The Goliath operatives started to argue but were soon ushered from the room by several members of the Welsh Republican Army, who were definitely *not* impressed by their threats.

We were driven in the presidential limousine out of Merthyr and dropped in Abertawe. The Brontë Federation representative was icily quiet during the entire trip—I sensed he wasn't that happy about the new ending. When we got to the town I gave them the slip, ran to my car and hastily drove back to Swindon, Rochester's words ringing in my ears. Landen's marriage to Daisy was happening at three that afternoon and I was sure as hell going to be there.

35.

Nearly the End of
Our Book

> I had disrupted *Jane Eyre* quite considerably; my cry of
> "Jane, Jane, Jane!" at her window had altered the book
> for good. It was against my training, against everything
> that I had sworn to uphold. I didn't see it as anything
> more than a simple act of contrition for what I felt was
> my responsibility over Rochester's wounds and the burn-
> ing of Thornfield. I had acted out of compassion, not
> duty, and sometimes that is no bad thing.
>
> THURSDAY NEXT
> —private diaries

AT FIVE past three I screeched to a halt outside the Church
of Our Blessed Lady of the Lobsters, much to the surprise of the
photographer and the driver of a large Hispano-Suiza that was
parked in readiness for the happy couple. I took a deep breath,
paused to gather my thoughts and, shaking slightly, walked up
the steps to the main doors. The organ music was playing loudly
and my pace, which up to that point had been a run, suddenly
slowed as my nerve abandoned me. What the hell was I playing
at? Did I think I had any real chance of appearing from nowhere
after a ten-year absence and then expecting the man I was once
in love with just to drop everything and marry me?

"Oh yes," said a woman to her companion as they walked
past me, "Landen and Daisy are *so* much in love!"

My walk slowed to a snail's pace as I found myself hoping to be too late and have the burden of decision taken from me. The church was full, and I slid unnoticed into the back, just next to the lobster shaped font. I could see Landen and Daisy at the front, attended to by a small bevy of pages and bridesmaids. There were many uniformed guests in the small church, friends of Landen's from the Crimea. I could see someone whom I took to be Daisy's mother sniveling into her handkerchief and her father looking impatiently at his watch. On Landen's side his mother was on her own.

"I require and charge you both," the clergyman was saying, "that if either of you know any impediment why ye may not be lawfully joined together in matrimony, ye do now confess it."

He paused, and several guests shuffled. Mr. Mutlar, whose lack of chin had been amply compensated by increased girth in his neck, seemed ill at ease and looked about the church nervously. The clergyman turned to Landen and opened his mouth to speak, but as he did so there came a loud, clear voice from the back of the church:

"The marriage cannot go on: I declare the existence of an impediment!"

One hundred and fifty heads turned to see who the speaker was. One of Landen's friends laughed out loud; he obviously thought it was a joke. The speaker's countenance did not, however, look as though any humor was intended. Daisy's father was having none of it. Landen was a good catch for his daughter and a small and tasteless joke was not going to delay her wedding.

"Proceed!" he said, his face like thunder.

The clergyman looked at the speaker, then at Daisy and Landen, and finally at Mr. Mutlar.

"I cannot proceed without some investigation into what has been asserted and evidence of its truth or falsehood," he said with a pained expression; nothing like this had ever happened to him before.

Mr. Mutlar had turned an unhealthy shade of crimson and might have struck the speaker had he been close enough.

"What is this nonsense?" he shouted instead, setting the room buzzing.

"Not nonsense, sir," replied the speaker in a clear voice. "Bigamy is hardly nonsense, I think, sir."

I stared at Landen, who looked confused at the turn of events. Was he married already? I couldn't believe it. I looked back at the speaker and my heart missed a beat. It was Mr. Briggs, the solicitor I had last seen in the church at Thornfield! There was a rustle close by and I turned to find Mrs. Nakajima standing next to me. She smiled and raised a finger to her lips. I frowned, and the clergyman spoke again.

"What is the nature of this impediment? Perhaps it may be got over—explained away?"

"Hardly," was the answer. "I have called it insuperable and I speak advisedly. It consists simply of a previous marriage."

Landen and Daisy looked at one another sharply.

"Who the hell are you?" asked Mr. Mutlar, who seemed to be the only person galvanized into action.

"My name is Briggs, a solicitor of Dash Street, London."

"Well, Mr. Briggs, perhaps you would be good enough to explain the previous marriage of Mr. Parke-Laine so we may all know the extent of this man's cowardly action."

Briggs looked at Mr. Mutlar and then at the couple at the altar.

"My information does not concern Mr. Parke-Laine; I am speaking of Miss Mutlar, or, to give her her married name, Mrs. Daisy Posh!"

There was a gasp from the congregation. Landen looked at Daisy, who threw her garland on the floor. One of the bridesmaids started to cry, and Mr. Mutlar strode forward and took Daisy's arm.

"Miss Mutlar married Mr. Murray Posh on October 20, 1981," yelled Mr. Briggs above the uproar. "The service was held at Southwark. There was no divorce petition filed."

It was enough for everyone. A clamor started up as the Mutlar family beat a hasty retreat. The vicar offered an unheard-of prayer to no one in particular as Landen took a much needed seat on the pew that the Mutlar family had just vacated. Someone yelled "gold digger!" from the back, and the Mutlar family quickened their pace at the abuse that followed, much of which shouldn't have been heard in church. One of the pages tried to kiss a bridesmaid in the confusion and was slapped for his trouble. I leaned against the cool stone of the church and wiped the tears from my eyes. I know it was wrong of me, but I was laughing. Briggs stepped through the arguing guests and joined us, tipping his hat respectfully.

"Good afternoon, Miss Next."

"A *very* good afternoon, Mr. Briggs! What on earth are you doing here?"

"The Rochesters sent me."

"But I only left the book three hours ago!"

Mrs. Nakajima interrupted.

"You left it barely twelve pages from the end. In that time over ten years have elapsed at Thornfield; time enough for *much* planning!"

"Thornfield?"

"Rebuilt, yes. My husband retired and he and I manage the house these days. None of us is mentioned in the book and Mrs. Rochester aims to keep it that way; much more pleasant than Osaka and certainly more rewarding than the tourist business."

There didn't seem much I could say.

"Mrs. Jane Rochester asked Mrs. Nakajima to bring me here to assist," said Mr. Briggs simply. "She and Mr. Rochester were eager to help you as you helped them. They wish you all happiness and health for the future and thank you for your timely intervention."

I smiled.

"How are they?"

"Oh, they're fine, miss," replied Briggs happily. "Their first-born is now five; a fine healthy boy, the image of his father. Jane produced a beautiful daughter this spring gone past. They have named her Helen Thursday Rochester."

I looked across at Landen, who was standing at the entrance to the church and trying to explain to his Aunt Ethel what was going on.

"I must speak to him."

But I was talking to myself. Mrs. Nakajima and the solicitor had gone; melted back to Thornfield to report to Jane and Edward on a job well done.

As I approached, Landen sat on the church steps, took out his carnation and sniffed at it absently.

"Hello, Landen."

Landen looked up and blinked.

"Ah," he said, "Thursday. I might have known."

"May I join you?"

"Be my guest."

I sat down next to him on the warm limestone steps. He stared straight ahead.

"Was this your doing?" he asked at last.

"No, indeed," I replied. "I confess I came here to interrupt the wedding but my nerve failed me."

He looked at me.

"Why?"

"Why? Well, because . . . because I thought I'd make a better Mrs. Parke-Laine than Daisy, I suppose."

"I know *that*," exclaimed Landen, "and agree wholeheartedly. What I wanted to know is why your nerve failed you. After all, you chase after master criminals, indulge in high-risk SpecOps work, will quite happily go against orders to rescue comrades under an intense artillery barrage, yet—"

"I get the point. I don't know. Maybe those sorts of yes-or-no life-and-death decisions are easier to make because they are so black and white. I can cope with them because it's easier. Human emotions, well . . . they're just a fathomless collection of grays and I don't do so well on the midtones."

"Midtones is where I've lived for the past ten years, Thursday."

"I know and I'm sorry. I had a lot of trouble reconciling what I felt for you and what I saw as your betrayal of Anton. It was an emotional tug-of-war and I was the little pocket handkerchief in the middle, tied to the rope, not moving."

"I loved him too, Thursday. He was the closest thing to a brother that I ever had. But I couldn't hang onto my end of the rope forever."

"I left something behind in the Crimea," I murmured, "but I think I've found it again. Is there time to try and make it all work?"

"Bit eleventh-hour, isn't it?" he said with a grin.

"No," I replied, "more like three seconds to midnight!"

He kissed me gently on the lips. It felt warm and satisfying, like coming home to a roaring log fire after a long walk in the rain. My eyes welled up and I sobbed quietly into his collar as he held me tightly.

"Excuse me," said the vicar, who had been lurking close by. "I'm sorry to have to interrupt, but I have another wedding to perform at three-thirty."

We muttered our apologies and stood up. The wedding guests were still waiting for some sort of decision. Nearly all of them knew about Landen and me and few, if any, thought Daisy a better match.

"Will you?" asked Landen in my ear.

"Will I what?" I asked, stifling a giggle.

"*Fool!* Will you marry me?"

"Hmm," I replied, heart thumping like the artillery in the Crimea. "I'll have to think about it!—"

Landen raised a quizzical eyebrow.

"Yes! Yes, *yes!* I will, I will, with all my heart!"

"At last!" said Landen with a sigh. "The lengths I have to go to to get the woman I love! . . ."

We kissed again but for longer this time; so long in fact that the vicar, still staring at his watch, had to tap Landen on the shoulder.

"Thank you for the rehearsal," said Landen, shaking the vicar vigorously by the hand. "We'll be back in a month's time for the real thing!"

The vicar shrugged. This was fast becoming the most ludicrous wedding of his career.

"Friends," announced Landen to the remaining guests, "I would like to announce the engagement of myself to this lovely SpecOps agent named Thursday Next. As you know, she and I have had our differences in the past but they are now *quite* forgotten. There is a marquee at my house stuffed with food and drink and I understand Holroyd Wilson will be playing from six o'clock onward. It would be a crime to waste it all so I suggest we just change the reason!"

There was an excited yell from the guests as they started to organize transport for themselves. Landen and I went in my car but we drove the long way round. We had plenty to talk about and the party . . . well, it could continue without us for a while.

The celebrations didn't finish until 4 A.M. I drank too much and took a cab back to the hotel. Landen was all for me staying the night, but I told him slightly coquettishly that he could wait until after the wedding. I vaguely remember getting back to my hotel room but nothing else; it was blackness until the phone rang at nine the following morning. I was half dressed, Pickwick was watching breakfast TV, and my head ached like it was fit to burst.

It was Victor. He didn't sound in a terribly good mood but politeness was one of his stronger points. He asked me how I was.

I looked at the alarm clock as a hammer banged inside my head.

"I've been better. How are things at work?"

"Not brilliant," replied Victor with a certain reserve in his voice. "The Goliath Corporation want to speak to you about Jack Schitt and the Brontë Federation are hopping mad over the damage to the book. Was it *absolutely* necessary to burn Thornfield to the ground?"

"That was Hades—"

"And Rochester? Blinded and with a shattered hand? I suppose that was Hades too?"

"Well, yes."

"This is the mother of all balls-ups, Thursday. You'd better come in and explain yourself to these Brontë people. I've got their Special Executive Committee with me and they are not here to pin a medal on your chest."

There was a knock at the door. I told Victor I would be in directly and got unsteadily to my feet.

"Hello?" I called out.

"Room service!" replied a voice outside the door. "A Mr. Parke-Laine rang in some coffee for you!"

"Hang on!" I said as I tried to shoo Pickwick back into the bathroom; the hotel had strict rules about pets. Unusually for him he seemed slightly aggressive; if he had possessed any wings he would probably have flapped them angrily.

"This . . . is . . . no . . . time . . . to . . . be . . . a . . . pest!" I grunted as I pushed the recalcitrant bird into the bathroom and locked the door.

I held my head for a moment as it thumped painfully, wrapped myself in a dressing gown and opened the door. *Big mistake.* There was a waiter there but he wasn't alone. As soon as the door was fully open two other men in dark suits entered and pressed me against the wall with a gun to my head.

"You're going to need another two cups if you want to join me for coffee," I groaned.

"Very funny," said the man dressed as the waiter.

"Goliath?"

"In one."

He pulled back the hammer on the revolver.

"Gloves are off, Next. Schitt is an important man and we need to know where he is. National security and the Crimea depend upon it and one lousy officer's life isn't worth diddly shit when you look at the big picture."

"I'll take you to him," I gasped, trying to give myself some breathing space. "It's a little way out of town."

The Goliath agent relaxed his grip and told me to get dressed. A few minutes later we were walking out of the hotel. My head was still sore and a dull pain thumped in my temples, but at least I was thinking more clearly. There was a small crowd ahead of me, and I was delighted to see it was the Mutlar family preparing to return to London. Daisy was arguing with her father and Mrs. Mutlar was shaking her head wearily.

"Gold digger!" I yelled.

Daisy and her father stopped arguing and looked at me as the Goliath men tried to steer me past.

"What did you say!?"

"You heard. I can't think who the bigger tart is, your daughter or your wife."

It had the desired effect. Mr. Mutlar turned an odd shade of crimson and threw a fist in my direction. I ducked and the blow struck one of the Goliath men fairly and squarely on the jaw. I bolted for the car park. A shot whistled over my shoulder; I jinked and stepped into the road as a big black military-style Ford motor car screeched to a halt.

"Get in!" shouted the driver. I didn't need to be asked twice. I jumped in and the Ford sped off as two bullet holes appeared in the rear windshield. The car screeched around the corner and was soon out of range.

"Thanks," I murmured. "Any later and I might have been worm food. Can you drop me at SpecOps HQ?"

The driver didn't say anything; there was a glass partition between me and him and all of a sudden I had that out-of-the-frying-pan-and-into-the-fire feeling.

"You can drop me anywhere," I said. He didn't answer. I tried the door handles but they were locked. I thumped on the glass but he ignored me; we drove past the SpecOps building and headed off to the old town. He was driving fast too. Twice he went through a red light and once he cut up a bus; I was thrown against the door as he flew around a corner, just missing a brewer's dray.

"Here, stop this car!" I shouted, banging again on the glass partition. The driver simply accelerated, clipping another car as he took a corner a little too fast.

I pulled hard at the door handles and was about to use my heels against the window when the car abruptly screeched to a halt; I slid off the seat and collapsed in a heap in the footwell. The driver got out, opened the door for me and said:

"There you go, missy, didn't want you to be late. Colonel Phelps's orders."

"Colonel Phelps?" I stammered. The driver smiled and saluted briskly as the penny dropped. Phelps had said he would send a car for me to appear at his talk, and he had.

I looked out of the door. We had pulled up outside Swindon Town Hall, and a vast crowd of people were staring at me.

"Hello, Thursday!" said a familiar voice.

"Lydia?" I asked, caught off guard by the sudden change of events.

And so it was. But she wasn't the only TV news reporter; there were six or seven of them with their cameras trained on me as I sat sprawled inelegantly in the footwell. I struggled to get out of the car.

"This is Lydia Startright of the Toad News Network," said Lydia in her best reporter's voice, "here with Thursday Next, the SpecOps agent responsible for saving *Jane Eyre*. First let me congratulate you, Miss Next, on your successful reconstruction of the novel!"

"What do you mean?" I responded. "I loused it all up! I burned Thornfield to the ground and half-maimed poor Mr. Rochester!"

Miss Startright laughed.

"In a recent survey ninety-nine out of a hundred readers who expressed a preference said they were delighted with the new ending. Jane and Rochester married! Isn't that *wonderful*?"

"But the Brontë Federation—?"

"Charlotte didn't leave the book to them, Miss Next," said a man dressed in a linen suit who had a large blue Charlotte Brontë rosette stuck incongruously to his lapel.

"The federation are a bunch of stuffed shirts. Allow me to introduce myself. Walter Branwell, chairman of the federation splinter group 'Brontë for the People.'"

He thrust out a hand for me to shake and grinned wildly as several people near by applauded. A battery of flashguns went off as a small girl handed me a bunch of flowers and another journalist asked me what sort of a person Rochester *really* was. The driver took my arm and guided me into the building.

"Colonel Phelps is waiting for you, Miss Next," murmured the man in an affable tone. The crowds parted as I was led into a large hall that was filled to capacity. I blinked stupidly and looked around. There was an excited buzz, and as I walked down the main aisle I could hear people whispering my name. There was an improvised press box in the old orchestra pit in which a sea of pressmen from all the major networks were seated. The meeting at Swindon had become the focus of the grassroots feeling about the war; what was said here would be highly significant. I made my way to the stage, where two tables had been set up. The two sides to the argument were clearly delineated. Colonel Phelps was sitting beneath a large English flag; his table was heavily festooned with bunting and several pot plants, flip-over pads and stacks of leaflets for ready distribution. With him were mostly uniformed members of the armed forces who had seen service on the peninsula. All of them were willing to speak vociferously about the importance of the Crimea. One of the soldiers was even carrying the new plasma rifle.

At the other end of the stage was the "anti" table. This too was liberally populated by veterans, but none of them wore uniforms. I recognized the two students from the airship park and my brother Joffy, who smiled and mouthed "Wotcha, Doofus!" at me. The crowd hushed; they had heard I was going to attend and had been awaiting my arrival.

The cameras followed me as I approached the steps to the stage and walked calmly up. Phelps rose to meet me, but I walked on and sat down at the "anti" table, taking the seat that one of the students had given up for me. Phelps was appalled; he went bright red, but checked himself when he saw that the cameras were watching his every move.

Lydia Startright had followed me onto the stage. She was there to adjudicate the meeting; it was she and Colonel Phelps who had insisted on waiting for me. Startright was glad they had; Phelps was not.

"Ladies and gentlemen," announced Lydia grandly, "the negotiating table is empty at Budapest and the offensive lies waiting to happen. As a million troops face each other across no-man's-land, we ask the question: What price the Crimea?"

Phelps got up to speak but I beat him to it.

"I know it's an old joke," I began, "but a simple anagram of 'Crimea' is 'A Crime.' " I paused. "That's the way I see it and I would defy anyone to say that it isn't. Even Colonel Phelps over there would agree with me that it's high time the Crimea was put to bed permanently."

Colonel Phelps nodded.

"Where the Colonel and I differ is my belief that Russia has the better claim to the territory."

It was a controversial remark; Phelps's supporters were well primed, and it took ten minutes to restore order. Startright quieted them all down and finally managed to get me to finish my point.

"There was a good chance for all this nonsense to end barely two months ago. England and Russia were around the table, discussing terms for a complete withdrawal of all English troops."

There was a hush. Phelps had leaned back in his chair and was watching me carefully.

"But then along came the plasma rifle. Code name: Stonk."

I looked down for a moment.

"This Stonk was the key, the secret to a new offensive and the possible restart of the war that has—thank God—been relatively free of actual fighting these past eight years. But there's a problem. The offensive has been built on air; despite all that has been said and done, the plasma rifle is a phony—*Stonk does not work!*"

There was an excited murmuring in the chamber. Phelps

stared at me sullenly, eyebrow twitching. He whispered something to a brigadier who was sitting next to him.

"The English troops are waiting for a new weapon that will *not* turn up. The Goliath Corporation have been playing the English government for a bunch of fools; despite a billion-pound investment, the plasma rifle is about as much use in the Crimea as a broom handle."

I sat down. The significance of this was not lost on anyone either there or watching the program live; the English minister for war was at that moment reaching for his phone. He wanted to speak to the Russians before they did anything rash—like attack.

Back at the hall in Swindon, Colonel Phelps had stood up.

"Large claims from someone who is tragically ill informed," he intoned patronizingly. "We have all seen the destructive power of Stonk and its effectiveness is hardly the reason for this talk."

"Prove it," I responded. "I see you have a plasma rifle with you. Lead us outside to the park and show us. You can try it on me, if you so wish."

Phelps paused, and in that pause he lost the argument—and the war. He looked at the soldier carrying the weapon, who looked back at him nervously.

Phelps and his people left the stage to barracking from the crowd. He had been hoping to give his carefully rehearsed hour-long lecture over the memory of the lost brethren and the value of comradeship; he never spoke in public again.

Within four hours a ceasefire had been called for the first time in 131 years. Within four weeks the politicians were around the table in Budapest. Within four months every single English soldier was out of the peninsula. As for the Goliath Corporation, they were soon called to account over their deceit. They expressed wholly unconvincing ignorance of the whole affair and laid the blame entirely on Jack Schitt. I had hoped the Corporation would be chastized further, but at least it got Goliath off my back.

36.

Married

Landen and I were married the same day as peace was declared in the Crimea. Landen told me it was to save on the fee for bell-ringers. I looked around nervously when the vicar got to the bit about "Speak now or forever hold their peace" but there was no one there. I met with the Brontë Federation and they soon got used to the idea of the new ending, especially when they realized that they were the only people who objected. I was sorry about Rochester's wounds and the burning down of his house, but I was very glad that he and Jane, after over a hundred years of dissatisfaction, finally found the true peace and happiness that they both so richly deserved.

THURSDAY NEXT
—*A Life in SpecOps*

T HE RECEPTION turned out to be bigger than we thought and by ten o'clock it had spilled out into Landen's garden. Boswell had got a little drunk so I popped him in a cab and sent him to the Finis. Paige Turner had been getting along well with the saxophonist—no one had seen either of them for at least an hour. Landen and I were enjoying a quiet moment to ourselves. I squeezed his hand, and asked:

"Would you *really* have married Daisy if Briggs hadn't intervened?"

"I've got those answers you wanted, Sweetpea!"

"Dad?"

He was attired in the full dress uniform of a colonel in the ChronoGuard.

"I've been thinking about what you said and I made a few enquiries."

"I'm sorry, Dad, I've got no idea what you're talking about."

"You remember, we spoke about two minutes ago?"

"No."

He frowned and looked at us both in turn, then at his watch.

"Great Scott!" he exclaimed. "I must be early. Damn these chronographs!"

He tapped the dial and left quickly without saying another word.

"Your father?" asked Landen. "I thought you said he was on the run?"

"He was. He is. He will be. You know."

"Sweetpea!" said my father again. "Surprised to see me?"

"In a manner of speaking."

"Congratulations to the two of you!"

I glanced around at the party still in full swing. Time was *not* standing still. It wouldn't be long before the ChronoGuard tracked him down.

"To hell with SO-12, Thursday!" said he, divining my thoughts and taking a glass from a passing waiter. "I wanted to meet my son-in-law."

He turned to Landen, grasped his hand and sized him up carefully.

"How are you, my boy? Have you had a vasectomy?"

"Well, no," replied Landen, vaguely embarrassed.

"How about a heavy tackle playing rugby?"

"No."

"Kick from a horse in the nether regions?"

"No."

"What about a cricket ball in the goolies?"

"*No!*"

"Good. Then we might get some grandchildren out of this fiasco. It's high time little Thursday here was popping out some sprogs instead of dashing around like some wild mountain piglet—" He paused. "You're both looking at me very oddly."

"You were here not a minute ago."

He frowned, raised an eyebrow and looked about furtively.

"If it *was* me, and if I *know* me, I'd be hiding somewhere close by. Oh yes, look! Look there!"

He pointed to a corner of the garden where a figure was hiding in the shadows behind the potting shed. He narrowed his eyes and thought through the most logical train of events.

"Let's see. I must have offered to do you a favor, done it and come back but a little out of time; not uncommon in my line of work."

"What favor would I have asked you to do?" I ventured, still confused but more than willing to play along.

"I don't know," said my father. "A burning question that has been much discussed over the years but has, so far, remained unanswered."

I thought for a moment.

"How about the authorship of the Shakespeare plays?"

He smiled. "Good point. I'll see what I can do."

He finished his drink.

"Well, congratulations again to the two of you; I must be off. Time waits for no man, as we say."

He smiled, wished us every happiness for the future, and departed.

"Can you explain just *what* is going on?" asked Landen,

thoroughly confused, not so much by the events themselves as by the order in which they were happening.

"Not really."

"Have I gone, Sweetpea?" asked my father, who had returned from his hiding place behind the shed.

"Yes."

"Good. Well, I found out what you wanted to know. I went to London in 1610 and found that Shakespeare was only an actor with a potentially embarrassing sideline as a purveyor of bagged commodities in Stratford. No wonder he kept it quiet—wouldn't you?"

This was interesting indeed.

"So who wrote them? Marlowe? Bacon?"

"No; there was a bit of a problem. You see, no one had even *heard* of the plays, much less written them."

I didn't understand.

"What are you saying? There aren't any?"

"That's exactly what I'm saying. They don't exist. They were never written. Not by him, not by anyone."

"I'm sorry," said Landen, unwilling to take much more of this, "but we saw *Richard III* only six weeks ago."

"Of course," said my father. "Time is out of joint *big time*. Obviously something had to be done. I took a copy of the complete works back with me and gave them to the actor Shakespeare in 1592 to distribute on a given timetable. Does that answer your question?"

I was still confused.

"So it *wasn't* Shakespeare who wrote the plays."

"Decidedly not!" he agreed. "Nor Marlowe, Oxford, De Vere, Bacon or any of the others."

"But that's not possible!" exclaimed Landen.

"On the contrary," replied my father. "Given the huge

timescale of the cosmos, impossible things are commonplace. When you've lived as long as I have you'll know that absolutely *anything* is possible. Time is out of joint; O cursed spite, that ever I was born to set it right!"

"*You* put that in?" I asked, always assuming he was quoting from *Hamlet* and not the other way round.

He smiled.

"A small personal vanity that I'm sure will be forgiven, Thursday. Besides: Who's to know?"

My father stared at his empty glass, looked around in vain for a waiter, then said:

"Lavoisier will have locked onto me by now. He swore he'd catch me and he's good. He should be; we were partners for almost seven centuries. Just one more thing: how did the Duke of Wellington die?"

I remembered he had asked me this once before.

"As I said, Dad, he died in his bed in 1852."

Father smiled and rubbed his hands.

"That's *excellent* news indeed! How about Nelson?"

"Shot by a French sniper at Trafalgar."

"Really? Well, some you win. Listen: good luck, the pair of you. A boy or a girl would be fine; one of each would be better."

He leaned closer and lowered his voice.

"I don't know when I am going to be back, so listen carefully. Never buy a blue car or a paddling pool, stay away from oysters and circular saws, and don't be near Oxford in June 2016. Got it?"

"Yes, but!—"

"Well, pip pip, time waits for no man!"

He hugged me again, shook Landen's hand and then disappeared into the crowd before we could ask him anything more.

"Don't even *try* to figure it out," I said to Landen, placing a finger to his lips. "This is one area of SpecOps that it's really better not to think about."

"But if!—"

"Landen!—" I said more severely. "No!—"

Bowden and Victor were at the party too. Bowden was happy for me and had come easily to the realization that I wouldn't be joining him in Ohio, as either wife or assistant. He had been offered the job officially but had turned it down; he said there was too much fun to be had at the Swindon LiteraTecs and he would reconsider it in the spring; Finisterre had taken his place. But at present, something else was preying on his mind. Helping himself to a stiff drink, he approached Victor, who was talking animatedly to an elderly woman he had befriended.

"What ho, Cable!" Victor murmured, introducing his newfound friend before agreeing to have a quiet word with him.

"Good result, eh? Balls to the Brontë Federation; I'm with Thursday. I think the new ending is a wiz!" He paused and looked at Bowden. "You've got a face longer than a Dickens novel. What's the problem? Worried about Felix8?"

"No, sir; I know they'll find him eventually. It's just that I *accidentally* mixed up the dust covers on the book that Jack Schitt went into."

"You mean he's not with his beloved rifles?"

"No, sir. I took the liberty of slipping *this* book into the dust cover of *The Plasma Rifle in War.*"

He handed over the book that had made its way into the Prose Portal. Victor looked at the spine and laughed. It was a copy of *The Poems of Edgar Allan Poe.*

"Have a look at page twenty-six," said Bowden. "There's something funny going on in 'The Raven.' "

Victor opened the book and scanned the page. He read the first verse out loud:

Once upon a midnight dreary, while I pondered weak and weary,
o'er a plan to venge myself upon that cursed Thursday Next—
This Eyre affair, so surprising, gives my soul such loath despising,
Here I plot my temper rising, rising from my jail of text.
"Get me out!" I said, advising, "Pluck me from this jail of text—
                                   or I swear I'll wring your neck!"

Victor shut the book with a snap.

"The last line doesn't rhyme very well, does it?"

"What do you expect?" replied Bowden. "He's Goliath, not a poet."

"But I read 'The Raven' only yesterday," added Victor in a confused tone. "It wasn't like this then!"

"No, no," explained Bowden. "Jack Schitt is only in *this* copy—if we had put him in an original manuscript then who knows what he might have done."

"Con-g'rat-ula'tions!" exclaimed Mycroft as he walked up to us. Polly was with him and looked radiant in a new hat.

"We're Bo'th *Very* Hap-py For You!" added Polly.

"Have you been working on the bookworms again?" I asked.

"Doe's It Sh'ow?" asked Mycroft. "Mu'st Dash!"

And they were off.

"Bookworms?" asked Landen.

"It's not what you think."

"Mademoiselle Next?"

There were two of them. They were dressed in sharp suits and displayed SpecOps-12 badges that I hadn't seen before.

"Yes?"

"Préfet Lavoisier, ChronoGendarmerie. *Où est votre père?*"

"You've just missed him."

He cursed out loud.

"Colonel Next est un homme très dangereux, mademoiselle. Il est important de lui parler concernant ses activités de trafic de temps."

"He's my father, Lavoisier."

Lavoisier stared at me, trying to figure out whether anything he could say or do would make me help him. He sighed and gave up.

"Si vous changez votre avis, contactez-moi par les petites an-nonces du Grenouille. Je lis toujours les archives."

"I shouldn't count on it, Lavoisier."

He mulled this over for a moment, thought of something to say, decided against it and smiled instead. He saluted briskly, told me in perfect English to enjoy my day, and walked away. But his younger partner also had something to say:

"A piece of advice to you," he muttered slightly self-consciously. "If you ever have a son who wants to be in the ChronoGuard, try and dissuade him."

He smiled and followed his partner in their quest for my father.

"What was that son thing about?" asked Landen.

"I don't know. He looked kind of familiar, though, didn't he?"

"Kinda."

"Where were we?"

"Mrs. Parke-Laine?" asked a very stocky individual, who stared at me earnestly from two deep-set brown eyes.

"SO-12?" I asked, wondering quite where the little beetle-browed man had sprung from.

"No, ma'am," he replied, seizing a plum from a passing waiter and sniffing at it carefully before eating it, stone and all. "My name Bartholomew Stiggins; with SO-13."

"What do *they* do?"

"Not at liberty to discuss," he replied shortly, "but we may have need your skills and talents."

"What kind of—"

But Mr. Stiggins was no longer listening to me. Instead, he was staring at a small beetle he had found on a flowerpot. With great care and a dexterity that belied his large and clumsy-looking hands, he picked the small bug up and popped it in his mouth. I looked at Landen, who winced.

"Sorry," said Stiggins, as though he had just been caught picking his nose in public. "What the expression? Old habits die hard?"

"There's more in the compost heap," said Landen helpfully.

The little man grinned very softly through his eyes; I didn't suppose he showed much emotion.

"If interested, I'll be in touch."

"Be in touch," I told him.

He grunted, replaced his hat, bid us both a happy day, inquired about the whereabouts of the compost heap and was gone.

"I've never seen a Neanderthal in a suit before," observed Landen.

"Never mind about Mr. Stiggins," I said, reaching up to kiss him.

"I thought you'd finished with SpecOps?"

"No," I replied with a smile. "In fact, I think I'm only just beginning! . . ."

Jasper Fforde's seventh Thursday Next novel
is available from Viking.

Read on for the first chapter of . . .

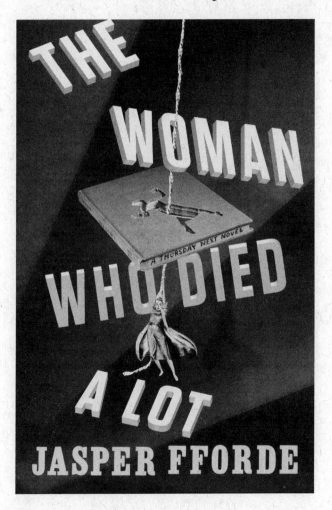

ISBN 978-0-670-02502-2

1.

Monday: Swindon

The Special Operations Network was formed in 1928 to handle policing duties considered too specialized to be tackled by the regular force. Despite considerable success in the many varied areas of expertise in which SpecOps operated, all but six of the thirty-six divisions were disbanded in the winter of 1991–92, allegedly due to budgetary cutbacks. By 2004 it was realized that this had been a bad move, and plans were drawn up to re-form the service.

Millon de Floss, *A Short History of SpecOps*

*E*verything comes to an end. A good bottle of wine, a summer's day, a long-running sitcom, one's life, and eventually our species. The question for many of us is not that everything *will* come to an end but *when*. And can we do anything vaguely useful until it does?

In the case of a good bottle of wine, probably not much— although the very act of consumption might make one believe otherwise. A well-lazed summer's day should not expect too much of itself either, and sitcoms never die. They simply move to a zombielike existence in rerun heaven. Of the remaining two—the end of one's life and that of our species—regular subscribers to my exploits will recall that I had seen myself die a few years back, and, given my past record, it was probable that much useful work would be done between then and now. As to the end of our species, the possibility of annihilation was quite real, well documented, and went by the unimaginative title of Asteroid HR-6984. Whether the human race managed to figure out a worthwhile function for itself in the thirty-seven years until possible collision was dependent upon one's level of optimism.

But it wasn't all bad news. In fact, due to a foible of human nature that denies us the ability to focus on more than one threat at a time, the asteroid was barely news at all. HR-6984's convenient lack of urgency and its current likelihood of hitting the earth at only around 34 percent had relegated it well past such front-page news as the stupidity surplus and the current round of fiery cleansings by an angry deity. Instead the hurtling lump of space debris was consigned to pop-culture damnation on page twelve: sandwiched somewhere between guinea-pig accessorizing and the apparently relevant eating habits of non-celebrities.

My take on it was this: A 34 percent chance that something might happen was also a 66 percent chance it *wouldn't* happen, and, given the rocky road our species had traveled to get here in the first place, these were considerably better odds than we'd seen so far. As for finding a collective purpose for ourselves in what might potentially be the last thirty-seven years of our existence, I was always struck by the paradox that while *collective* purpose might be at best unknowable and at worst irrelevant, *individual* purpose was of considerable importance.

But I'm getting ahead of myself. The events described here occurred during a busier-than-usual week in the late summer of 2004. A week that began with a trip into Swindon in order to find myself a job and ended with a pillar of cleansing fire descending from the heavens, a rethink on the Wessex Library Service operating budget, and my son shooting Gavin Watkins dead. The last one was a serious downer—especially for Gavin. It's a long story, and with a few twists and turns that take a bit of figuring. What the hell. We'll just run the story in real time as it happened and worry about the logic afterward. My name is

Thursday Next. You'll probably have heard of me as "the one who improved the ending of Jane Eyre," but even if you haven't, it doesn't matter. You'll know me well enough soon enough.

So there we were—my husband, Landen, and I, sitting in the comfort of a Skyrail car, gliding effortlessly above the North Wessex countryside on the Newbury-Hungerford-Swindon monorail. We'd boarded at Aldbourne, where we now lived, and the car was almost empty. We weren't talking about Asteroid HR-6984, or about the stupidity surplus or Landen's latest book, *Dogs Who Wonder Why Their Owners Think They Know When They Are Coming Home Because We Dogs Don't Really but Agree It Might Appear as If We Do*. We weren't even talking about other issues of the day, such as pissed-off deities, Phoebe Smalls, the movie of *Bonzo the Wonder Hound*, Synthetic Thursdays or the ongoing "brains kept alive in jars" ethical debate in *New Splicer* magazine. No, we were talking about our daughter Jenny and why I needed a tattoo to remind me she was somewhat less than I imagined, or indeed every bit as I imagined.

"I never thought I'd get a second," I said, staring at the scarlet rawness on the back of my hand.

"I'm amazed you even got the first," said Landen.

"It was on a drunken night in Sevastopol," I replied wistfully, "a week off the troopship and still without an ounce of combat experience or sense."

"Happy days," said Landen, "to have experienced the camaraderie before the loss."

He gave me a half smile, and I knew precisely what he meant. Before the *ziiip* of a round heralded a near miss, the Crimea had seemed like nothing more than a bit of a lark.

"The brigade tattoo was one of those bonding moments," I said, "like agreeing to box Corporal Dwight for a kilo of best beluga caviar."

He chuckled.

"You were mad. Dwight was a *serious* bruiser."

"I know that *now*," I replied, "but give me credit for the attempt."

Lance Corporal Betty "Basher" Dwight remained unbeaten in twenty-seven kickboxing bouts, thirteen of them against men. She was to become a loyal companion and friend, but not beyond my eighteen months of active service. Basher stayed in the Crimea, and I don't mean to open a bar or something.

That first tattoo had been inked the night of my fight with Dwight and had actually been quite useful. Clearly not *that* drunk, I'd asked the tattooist to add my blood and tissue grouping to the brigade motif, a simple act that had saved my life at least twice. The boxing bout was not so successful. I hit the canvas ten seconds into the third after a punishing couple of rounds—my nose is still a bit bent—and the unit had to go without caviar on their blinis for a month.

My second tattoo was done only two weeks ago, just after I'd turned fifty-four. It was of a purely practical nature and, unlike the first, which was etched unobtrusively on my upper arm, was on the back of my hand for all to see, *especially* me. It was at my family's request, too—an attempt to remind myself that my second daughter, Jenny, wasn't real at all but a troublesome mindworm foisted on me by a vengeful adversary.

"Did it have to go on my hand?" I said to Landen as the Sky-rail car docked at Clary-Lamarr Travelport, Swindon's main hub.

"It has to be somewhere you'll have a chance of seeing it. The constant reminding might help you get over her."

I stared at it again in order to keep the thoughts in my head as long as possible. Now that we were talking about Jenny's non-existence, everything seemed fine, but I knew also that these moments were fleeting. In a few minutes, all knowledge of the mindworm would be gone and I'd be fretting over Jenny again. Where she was, how she was, and why the teachers called Landen when I came to school to pick her up.

"Do you think it will?"

"I'm hoping yes but thinking no," replied Landen in a typically stoical manner. "The only person who can fix your Jenny problem is the person who infected you with the mindworm: Aornis."

This might seem strange until you realize that Aornis is a mnemonomorph—someone who can manipulate memories. She could rob a bank and no one would remember she'd been there. Besides, trying to capture someone who can manipulate memories is like trying to sweep a partial vacuum into a bell jar using only a yard broom. But we could make inquiries about her, and that was another reason we were in Swindon.

I grunted resignedly and then, after a short and oddly treacly pause, wondered what I was grunting resignedly *about*.

We drifted down the escalators from the south entrance of Clary-Lamarr and stepped onto the large concourse outside, which was dominated by the thirty-foot-high bronze statue of Lola Vavoom. We had missed the rush hour, and only latecomers and shoppers were walking out of the travelport.

"What were we just talking about?" I asked.

"Stuff," replied Landen vaguely, taking a deep breath. "You know, I'm not sure I'm going to get used to living out of town. To me, grass is simply a transitional phase for turning sunlight into milk."

"You're changing the subject," I replied suspiciously.

"I do that sometimes."

"You do, don't you?"

But Landen was right. He wasn't really a country dweller.

"After a few months, you'll be wondering how you lived anywhere else."

"Perhaps."

We'd moved out of Swindon four months before, not long after I'd been discharged from the hospital. The main reason was that our daughter Tuesday needed more room to experiment, but an equally good reason was security. I had more enemies than was considered healthy for the peaceful family life I had half promised myself, and a country home was more easily defended—from enemies on either side of the printed page.

"I think the city council is taking the threat of a smiting a bit lightly, don't you?" I asked, as aside from a few billboards outlining the possibility that the Almighty would lay the center of Swindon to waste in an all-consuming fire next Friday, little seemed to be going on.

"Joffy said the cathedral received a leaflet slipped under the west door," murmured Landen. "It was called *Vengeful Cleansing by a Wrathful Deity and You.*"

"Helpful?

"Not really. A few tips for a safe evacuation when the order is given—covering the windows with brown paper, hiding under tables, mumbling—that sort of thing. I'm not sure they're taking the threat seriously, either."

"It was serious enough for Oswestry," I replied, recalling the first of the nine random smitings that had been undertaken around the globe by a clearly disgruntled deity, eager to show His wayward creations the error of their ways.

"Perhaps so, but that was the first time, and no one believed that it would happen. If they'd evacuated the town, all would have been fine and only the buildings destroyed."

"I suppose so. Did they ever decide whether it was ethical for those turned to pillars of salt to be ground up for use as winter road grit?"

"I don't know. Probably not." He looked at his watch. "What time are you meeting with Braxton?"

"As soon as I've had the psychological evaluation."

"I thought you'd have to be a bit nuts to want to run SO-27," mused Landen.

"Undoubtedly," I replied, "but it's not so much a question of how mad applications for the job might be as the *style* of madness.

Obsessive drive is probably good, speaking in tongues and shouting at the walls less so."

"Do you think Phoebe Smalls has the requisite loopiness to get the job?"

Commander Smalls, it should be noted, was the only other person who could realistically lead the re-formed Literary Detectives division. She was good, but then so was I.

I thought for a moment. "Perhaps. She applied for the job, after all—no one would do that unless they were a little bit odd."

"She hasn't got your experience," said Landen. "Running SO-27 isn't for tenderfoots."

"But she's got the *youth*," I replied, "and her health."

"Phoebe Smalls might look a sound bet on paper," he replied, "but when weird comes knocking, gray hairs count. Braxton knows this. Besides, the boss need never leave the office. Consign the running around to the young pups."

He smiled at me, but he knew I wasn't happy. I had yet to walk without a stick, or pain. My broken femur had knit badly in the two weeks before I was found following my accident, and it had to be broken and reset with pins, which is never satisfactory. I wasn't particularly worried; running is overrated anyway, and sport only makes you sweaty and smug and wears out the knees. Besides, Landen had been missing his leg for longer than he hadn't, and *he* was fine. In fact, since he had a left limp and I had a right one, if we walked side by side, it apparently looked quite comical. I told Tuesday we were her "cute cripple parents," and she retorted that "cripple" wasn't *really* a polite term, and I told her that since my leg got mashed, I could define myself in any way I chose. In answer to *that*, she huffed, glared and then pouted, as teenagers are wont to do.

"She's right," Landen had remarked when I told him. He'd lost his leg to a land mine in the Crimea almost three decades before and referred to himself as either a "deconstructed bipedalist" or, more simply, "a man unjustly overcharged for socks."

"Will you be okay?" he asked.

"I'm fine," I told him, "with a stick to lean on and four Dizu-peradol patches."

"Four?" said Landen. "Are you sure that's wise?"

"It's the only thing that seems to have any lasting effect. Slow and constant release—double thickness, too."

I'd recently moved to the more effective stick-on patches rather than Dizuperadol taken orally. The patches seemed to work for longer, and I'd been prescribed the double-strength ones. Sometimes it felt like I had a waffle stuck to my bum. They were effective, but there were side effects.

"How's the vision?" asked Landen.

"In focus more often than it's not. And that's good, right?"

"A Zen dog dreams of a medium-size bone."

"Actually, there is one thing you could do. Can you put my cell phone in my right pocket so I can get it out?"

Landen did as I asked. I'd been working on the grip of my left hand, but it was slow going. The damage to my hand had been caused by the taxi's indicator stalk as it passed through my fore-arm during the vehicle's sudden stop in the swamp, and it had caused all sorts of mayhem on the way. The stalk broke off when it hit my jaw. These days I used it as a tea stirrer. The stalk, that is, not my jaw.

"I'll meet you in TJ-Maxx around two," said Landen, giving me an affectionate nuzzle. "And don't be too mean with the shrink, will you? They've got feelings, too."

"I'll play nice. What's the password this time?"

For a few years now, Goliath had been sending Synthetic Thursdays out into the world to try to get information from peo-ple who would speak only to me—Landen being an obvious ex-ample. They had also tried to gain access to my house, to the SpecOps records department, and they'd even tried to scam a free membership at a health farm. The copies were initially crude but had made steady and sustained advances in sophistication since first appearing eighteen months before. The Mark IVs and Vs wouldn't have fooled anyone, but the Mark VIs were impressive and had been able to crack single code words, which was why we used the more cloak-and-daggerish sentences and responses.

"What about if I say, 'No cookies at the hunt, sir!' and then you reply with, 'It's not a cookie, it's a Newton'?"

"Sounds random enough."

So with the passwords committed to memory, we limped off in opposite directions. I turned once to take a look at him, and he turned as well, and we smiled a simple smile of understanding. Parting for us was generally sweet sorrow, as past experience had taught us there was a fair possibility we might not see each other for a while, if at all—a state of affairs for which I took full responsibility. Sadly, a lifetime in law enforcement tends not to create a bunch of grateful villains happy that you have shown them the error of their ways, but rather a lot of disgruntled ne'er-do-wells eager for payback.

I hobbled across the pedestrian walkway and passed beneath the shadow of Swindon's centrally located anti-smite tower, the primary defense against God's planned cleansings of the sinful. I stopped to stare for a moment at the sixty-foot tower. It looked like an electricity pylon topped with a domed metallic mushroom. The burnished copper sheathing glowed in the sun, and even though the many towers dotted about the country were *mechanically* complete, there were still several hurdles to overcome. The software regulating the 8.2 million independently controlled lasers inside the dome had yet to be fine-tuned, and until it was, the defense shield remained nonoperational.

Perhaps the members of the city council weren't so bothered about Swindon's smiting because they'd convinced themselves the tower would be running in good time to deflect the wrath of the Almighty four days from now. I didn't think it would, and with good reason: I knew the genius behind the technology, and despite much midnight oil, the Anti-Smite Defense Shield remained firmly on the theoretical side of reality.

I hurried on, past the Thistle Hotel to my right, and presently found myself outside the front entrance of the Wessex Special Operations headquarters.

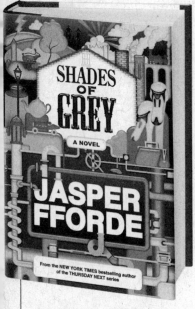